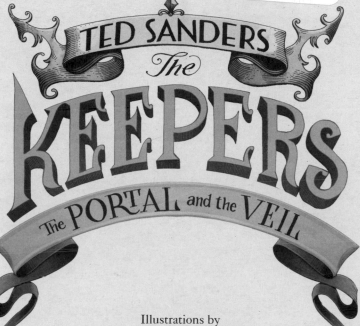

TED SANDERS
The
KEEPERS
The PORTAL and the VEIL

Illustrations by
IACOPO BRUNO

WITHDRAWN

HARPER
An Imprint of HarperCollinsPublishers

ISBN 978-0-06-227589-9

Typography by Carla Weise

18 19 20 21 22 CG/BRR 10 9 8 7 6 5 4 3 2 1

❖

First paperback edition, 2018

For Rowan,
whose mind I often envy.

For Bridget,
who I am proud to call my daughter.

And for Milo,
who I hope will discover these books some day.

————ᕁᕁᕁ————

Through our eyes, the universe is perceiving itself. Through
our ears, the universe is listening to its harmonies. We
are the witnesses through which the universe becomes
conscious of its glory, of its magnificence.
— ALAN WILSON WATTS

CONTENTS

Into the Havens

PART ONE

As the Rabbit Runs

CHAPTER ONE

Joshua

JOSHUA KNEW ABOUT SECRETS.

A secret was something you kept. A secret was a promise, and a promise—the way Isabel explained it—was like a burning light in the dark. A light that showed you where to go. If you kept your eyes on that light, kept walking toward it, you would never get lost, and your friends wouldn't either.

But as Joshua lay here alone, thinking hard in the cool quiet of the Warren, he wondered how you were supposed to know who your friends were. April was his friend, and her raven, Arthur, too. He felt pretty sure of that. They were far away now, in danger, and he was very worried about them. Worried in a way that you only worried for friends. Horace and Chloe and the other Wardens were far away too, out there trying to rescue April, and he liked them for that. He was also worried about them a little bit—maybe they were sort of friends. And now he was alone in the Warren with Brian and Mrs. Hapstead. They were very nice to him, especially Mrs. Hapstead. She was old, but was she a friend?

Because if she was a friend, Joshua had maybe done a terrible thing.

He hadn't meant to. Not really. He had made a promise to Isabel, even though he wasn't exactly sure what the promise meant. He wasn't even sure "promise" was the right word. What he had said he would do—what he had done, what he was *doing right now*—it didn't feel like a light in the dark. It felt like something heavy and cloudy. Doubt instead of hope.

He opened his hand. Isabel's wooden ring lay in his palm, warm with his worry.

"Take it," she'd told him. *"Take it into the Warren, and then I can fix everything. Tell no one. Take it, and I can make us both the way we were meant to be. You'll see."*

A promise. And Joshua had nodded back at her. Was that a promise too? He thought maybe it was.

But was Isabel a friend?

She was his protector, that was for sure. She'd taken him away from his last foster home, where no one seemed to care whether he stayed or went, a place he wasn't sorry to leave. She'd protected him from the Riven, right from the start, and had kept him safe more times than he could count. She'd promised she would help him, and she had—finally—brought him here to the Wardens.

But was she a *friend*?

4

Joshua sighed. Whether Isabel was a friend or not, he had done what she had told him to. He had brought the ring down the scary elevator and across the waters of Vithra's Eye and into the Warren, right into this round stone room Mr. Meister and Mrs. Hapsteade were letting him stay in. The Warden's sanctuary was cozy for a cave, maybe the coziest place he'd stayed in all his time traveling with Isabel.

Isabel, meanwhile, was far above somewhere, in her room in the Mazzoleni Academy, the boarding school that sat atop the Warren. She wasn't allowed to come into the Warren. The Wardens had taken her harp, Miradel, and were guarding it here. They didn't trust Isabel. And Isabel couldn't find the Warren even if she tried, not ever—Mr. Meister had fixed it that way, using something called a spitestone. But thanks to Joshua, Isabel's ring was inside the Warren now. He hadn't figured out yet what that meant. He was afraid to even wonder.

He got out of bed. He paced back and forth slowly, his bare feet curling on the cold stone floor, the ring warm and smooth between his fingers. He should tell Mrs. Hapsteade about the ring. He really should. He should have told her already.

"But I don't want to get in trouble," he explained to himself out loud—not too loud, because Mrs. Hapsteade was in the next doba over. Her stone house was simple and tidy and somehow cold and warm at the same time, just like Mrs. Hapsteade herself. But even as Joshua murmured the words, he felt—he knew—that they weren't quite right. Getting in trouble wasn't the reason he hadn't told Mrs. Hapsteade about the ring. The real reason, a reason that scared him and thrilled him, was this: the nod he'd given to Isabel when she handed him the ring *was* a promise. A promise he'd *wanted* to make.

"Take it, and I can make us both the way we were meant to be."

Joshua knew what that meant. He knew, and the knowing was almost more than he could bear. The whole reason he'd been traveling with Isabel in the first place—the whole reason for everything in his life that he could remember at all—was that he, Joshua, would one day become a Keeper.

Isabel had told him so, over and over again. She told him so the first day they met, before she took him away. She said she could see it in him. And even if Isabel was lying, Mrs. Hapsteade said she could see it too. She and Mr. Meister both had told him he had potential. But they hadn't actually helped him yet. No one had told him what kind of Keeper he might be, or what his instrument was. Maybe a compass, or a sextant. Something to do with maps, he hoped.

The Wardens were all Keepers, of course, dedicated to protecting the Tanu from the Riven. They all had their own Tan'ji, instruments that gave them their amazing powers. April had her Ravenvine, and Horace his box. Chloe had her dragonfly, and Gabriel his staff. Lately, Joshua had spent a lot more time than he wanted to admit thinking about what his own instrument might look like, and what powers it might have.

And now at last, just like she'd been promising all along, it

6

seemed like Isabel might be going to help him find out.

But there was a problem. Isabel was a thief and a liar. She had told him that she too was a Keeper—that she was Tan'ji. But she wasn't, it turned out. She wasn't Tan'ji and neither was Miradel, her harp. Those were lies. And when she and April and Joshua finally found the Wardens, it turned out Isabel had known all along who the Wardens were, and that she'd only been using April and Joshua to find them for her own reasons. *That* was a lie. And she'd done other things, too, things worse than lies. Things that had put his friends—his real friends—in danger.

Joshua squeezed the ring. He should destroy it. Or no—it could be a trap. Isabel was good at setting traps. He would tell Mrs. Hapsteade what he had done. He would show her Isabel's ring and try to explain. She didn't trust Isabel. She was guarding Miradel even now. Maybe the ring was nothing. Or maybe it was something, but Mrs. Hapsteade would be so busy dealing with it she'd forget to be mad.

Before he could change his mind, he started down the ladder to the first floor of his doba. He was so nervous he almost slipped and fell. Although Mrs. Hapsteade had been kind to him so far, he got the feeling that she could be cruel, too. But that was okay. Maybe he deserved it. He'd been a bad friend.

Joshua stepped out of the doba and into the Great Burrow, the uppermost level of the Warren. The Great Burrow was as wide as a football field and five times as long, lit by dozens of golden lights from which swirling clouds of soft sparks drifted. Joshua had noticed the lights got a bit darker at night, and now the whole chamber was lit like a forest at sunset. And it *was* like a forest, except here the trees were huge stone columns as wide as houses, and the columns really *were* little houses. Almost all of the dobas were empty now. All but one.

He moved slowly through the golden gloom to Mrs. Hapsteade's doba. He was in no hurry. In fact, he had to make himself move forward, the ring still clenched in his fist. Mrs. Hapsteade's front door was a thick black curtain, which meant there was no good way to knock.

"Mrs. Hapsteade?" he called.

No answer. Cautiously, he peeked inside. "Mrs. Hapsteade? It's Joshua. From next door." He squeezed the ring again, searching for words. "I have something to tell you."

Mrs. Hapsteade's Tan'ji, a long white writing quill called the Vora, sat in its usual place atop a squat bookcase across the room. Three calm candles threw three feathered shadows up the wall. If the Vora was here, so was Mrs. Hapsteade.

He took a step in. "Hello? Mrs. Hap—"

And then she spoke from the shadows off to his right, her usually firm voice thin with strain. "I am Mrs. Hapsteade," she croaked. "I am Dorothy Hapsteade."

The words pulled Joshua inside, heart racing. Just beyond a tipped-over chair, Mrs. Hapsteade lay on the floor curled into a crescent, chin against her chest. The hem of her dress had ridden up over her knees and her hands were in her hair, pulling strands loose from the tight bun.

"I'm going," she breathed through clenched teeth. "Going gone. Lost and found and lost."

She was in pain, he could see that. Her eyes were cloudy and frightened. It had to be the ring, Isabel's terrible ring. It had done something to her . . . poison or a trap or something. He'd made a stupid promise and waited too long and now—

Mrs. Hapsteade groaned. Joshua dropped to his knee in a blind rush of fear, scarcely thinking. With the ring cupped awkwardly in his hand, he smashed his palm flat against the stone floor. Isabel's ring snapped like a crisp twig, a broken edge stabbing him sharply. On his palm, a bloody speck. On the floor, the ring shattered into three brown moonshapes. But still Mrs. Hapsteade writhed and muttered. What was wrong with her?

"The harp," Mrs. Hapsteade moaned. "My fault."

"Miradel?" said Joshua. "Where is it?"

"Here," said a new voice.

Joshua lurched up and staggered back, swallowing all his breath.

From a dark nook across the room, a small scribbled cloud of green light swelled into existence, pulsing like a heart, coming closer. "Don't be angry, Joshua. Don't be afraid." Isabel stepped forward, her red hair like curls of copper in the emerald light. Miradel, her harp, hung from her neck. The tangled ball of wicker throbbed slowly, glowing green from within.

"No one is being harmed," Isabel said. "No one is doing anything wrong. I only came to set things right."

Joshua took a step sideways, toward Mrs. Hapsteade curled on the floor, head in her hands. He understood now, should have understood right away. Isabel had found the Warren. She had found Miradel here, and had severed Mrs. Hapsteade.

"I promise she is okay," said Isabel, watching. "She'll be fine."

With her harp, Joshua knew, Isabel could control the Medium, the energy that flowed between Keepers and their instruments. She had severed Mrs. Hapsteade, cutting her off from her Tan'ji. Joshua had seen Isabel sever people before, including April. It only lasted a little while, but according to April it was awful. For a Keeper, being unable to feel your Tan'ji was like being dead alive.

"Let her go," he said.

"The knots will come undone later," said Isabel. "I didn't want to do it, but I had to. She had Miradel here. She was expecting me." Isabel came right up to him, bending to pick up the broken pieces of her ring. She crossed to Mrs. Hapsteade and knelt, holding out the shards. "This is how I found my way in," she said. "I'm telling you so you can trust me, later. I'm telling you my secrets."

"The ring," Joshua whispered, his stomach twisting. It wasn't poison, no. But something just as bad.

"A trap," said Mrs. Hapsteade.

"A signal," Isabel said. "A lighthouse. You know the spite-stone casts a cloud around this place, a cloud made just for me. But I wove a tiny thread of inversion inside the ring before I gave it to Joshua. Once he brought it into your precious Warren, into the cloud of the spitestone, the ring gave out a tiny light inside the dark—also made just for me. The ring called to me, the same way your Tan'ji calls to you." She waggled a finger at the white quill across the room and smiled sadly. "The way it *usually* calls to you, I mean." She sighed almost giddily. "I followed the ring's call down from the Academy, and across Vithra's Eye. The spitestone couldn't stop me." She dumped the broken pieces of the ring onto the floor and stood up. "And you had Miradel. Thank you for keeping her safe. Now Joshua and I can begin."

"I don't want to begin," said Joshua, only half hearing her. "You tricked me."

Isabel raised her eyebrows, smiling. "Did I truly?"

Joshua squeezed his eyes shut, shame crawling over his skin like worms.

"Don't look backward now, Joshua," said Isabel. "We've been searching for so long, you and I. Can't you feel it?"

"Feel what?"

"Your instrument—your Tan'ji. It's here in the Warren. I know it is. But the spitestone is still clouding me."

Joshua opened his eyes. His heart felt like it would burst. *His instrument.* It was here in the Warren after all, a thought he had barely allowed himself to have. But he had to shake his head. "I can't feel anything." And it was true, he couldn't. Did he even want to? *I wouldn't even know* what *to feel*, he almost said.

Isabel ignored him, instead bending over Mrs. Hapsteade. "Where is the Laithe?" she asked the older woman sweetly.

The word was new to Joshua, but it pushed a soft tremor of warmth through his chest. *Laithe.* It sounded like "blade," a dangerous word, but this word sang with comfort and confidence. With promise. He almost hated the sound of it, but thought he might die if he never heard it again. What was it?

Mrs. Hapsteade's angry eyes found Isabel's. "No," she muttered, "No, you can't. Can't this way."

"It's the only way," Isabel replied.

"Forbidden."

"I never liked all your rules," Isabel said lightly. "Not when I was young, and certainly not now. But it doesn't matter. We'll find it, wherever you've hidden it." She stood and turned away, Miradel swinging at her chest, a forest of faint green shadows tumbling over them all. Abruptly she stopped. "Oh," she said, as if she'd forgotten something. "One more thing." She crouched over Mrs. Hapsteade again, her smile growing as wide and sweet as a snake's. "I believe there's a young man here named Brian. I'll be needing his help."

Mrs. Hapsteade grimaced. "Can't . . . help you. There is no help."

"That's what you always said. I'm not Tan'ji. Only a Tuner. Never mind that you were the ones who made me that way."

She cupped Miradel in her hand and lifted it, still pulsing. "If Brian fixed April's Tan'ji, then he can fix me too. All I'm asking for is a little loan. Just to borrow Brian's powers for a while. So he can fix what you made wrong."

Mrs. Hapsteade turned her face into the stone floor, muttering. "All wrong."

Isabel straightened, frowning down at Mrs. Hapsteade, and strode to the door. "We'll fend for ourselves," she said, seemingly to no one in particular. "We always do." She jerked her chin at Joshua. "Come, Joshua," she said, and swept out.

Joshua looked back at Mrs. Hapsteade, still severed on the floor and tangled in the invisible threads Isabel had woven around her. "I'm sorry," he said.

"Sorry," Mrs. Hapsteade slurred. "Sorry so sorry."

"I don't know what to do."

Somehow Mrs. Hapsteade's eyes managed to find his. They were so empty—so full of lost things—that he almost had to look away.

"Don't let her fix," she said through gritted teeth, "your mistakes."

Joshua stared for a second, and then stumbled out of the room. He squinted in the golden gloom of the Great Burrow, blinking back a sudden wetness.

Isabel took his hand. She smiled down at him. Miradel sparkled darkly. "And now we begin," she said.

13

CHAPTER TWO

Puzzling the Pieces

HORACE WOKE UP.

Overhead, a sprinkling of stars gleamed. Vega and Deneb shone brightly, and briefly Horace thought he was in his bedroom. But after a groggy moment he understood that these stars were real—distant suns in a distant past instead of glowing stickers on a painted ceiling. And there were trees here too, dark boughs heavy with fluttering fan-shaped leaves. Ginkgoes, yes. A nebulous memory came to him: eating hot ginkgo-leaf soup in the House of Answers with Chloe. But this was not the House of Answers. He looked around and saw a curving brick wall, ten feet high, that surrounded this quiet garden. No, not a garden either. A cloister—a safe haven of the Wardens.

Horace rolled over. His back ached. Beside him on the ground, Chloe lay snoozing, her fists in balls and her brow puckered into a scowl. The huge crucible scar on her forearm, wide as a hand and twice as long, pointed at her face like a dark dagger. Her dragonfly pendant, the Alvalaithen, seemed to glow in the dark.

A few feet away, Neptune slept flat on her back atop her cloak, her long legs still crossed and her hands loose in her lap. One of her pinkies was dislocated, jutting sideways from her hand like the pinky of a disfigured doll. Horace flinched, grimacing, and then remembered: Neptune had fallen during the night's battle, when an Auditor had taken over her Tan'ji. Powerless, and suddenly exposed to the forces of gravity, Neptune had fallen to the ground.

The battle. Snippets of the night's events came to Horace slowly, piecemeal, in no particular order. The Riven surrounding April's house. The charging Mordin in the woods. The phalanx. The tense standoff with Dr. Jericho, and Horace's narrow escape.

Slowly he strung the images into the full story. It wasn't easy, because traveling by falkrete stone had fogged his memory. There was a circle of falkretes here, of course—every cloister had one. He examined the wide ring of motley stones now and recognized the bear-shaped stone that had transported him and the other Wardens to the ruined cloister near April's house in the countryside. He recognized another that would lead them back toward the Warren, the secret sanctuary hidden under the busy downtown streets of Chicago. But the evening had begun long before any of that.

15

So much had happened, so many paths taken. Horace had made seven leaps by falkrete stone tonight, each leap leaving him feeling split in two. The Horace who teleported forward to the next circle was haunted by the feeling that an entirely separate Horace had chosen to stay behind. But gradually this Horace here—himself, the only Horace—remembered dinner earlier that night, in his own home in the city. Not a normal dinner, by any stretch of the imagination.

Horace and Chloe had arranged for their mothers to meet, for the first time in decades. How strange that Horace and Chloe had met each other only recently—both of them powerful Keepers with powerful Tan'ji—only to find out that their mothers had not only known each other as children, but had actually known the Wardens. They even seemed to have known Mr. Meister and Mrs. Hapsteade well, if such a thing was even possible. This whole time, Horace's mom had been aware all of it: the Tan'ji, the Keepers, the Warren, the Riven, and even what it meant for a Keeper to join the Wardens, as Horace and Chloe had.

Not that Horace's mom nor Chloe's—Isabel—had actually *been* Keepers. To be a Keeper, and become Tan'ji, you had to bond to an instrument. Chloe's instrument was the Alvalaithen, the dragonfly pendant that allowed her to move through solid matter. Horace's Tan'ji was the Fel'Daera, the small box at his side that allowed him to look into the near future. And Neptune's was her gravity-defying tourminda.

No, Isabel and Horace's mom weren't Keepers, but they

had powers nonetheless. Potentially dangerous powers. They were Tuners, and they used instruments called harps to manipulate the Medium, twisting that energy, braiding it, and even severing or cleaving it. Horace shuddered at the thought and placed his hand on the Fel'Daera.

When they were younger, Isabel and Horace's mom, Jessica, had worked for the Wardens, tuning unclaimed instruments that were in search of new Keepers. Isabel had been particularly talented. Isabel alone was strong enough to use the powerful harp she called Miradel, even if she couldn't control it completely. In fact, Isabel had used Miradel to tune the Fel'Daera years before Horace was even born, a revelation that made Horace squirm. Isabel, in a way, had helped to make him. And yet she had also betrayed them all.

Horace sat cross-legged and watched Chloe sleep. This was a common occurrence, what with all their late-night adventures and Chloe's prodigious napping abilities. He plucked at cluster of weeds, wondering what stormy dreams she was wrestling with now. Except for her black hair—and her many scars—Chloe looked almost exactly like her mother. Tiny and fierce. Pretty like a prowling cat. Chloe surely saw the resemblance, but she would hate to hear Horace say it.

Chloe had never really known her mother, and showed no interest now. Horace couldn't blame her. Isabel was difficult to trust, to put it mildly. As a girl, after stealing Miradel from the Warren, Isabel had run away from the Wardens, and had been banished for good. As an adult, she had run away from

17

her family not long after Chloe became Tan'ji, seven years ago.

Chloe had never forgiven her. Isabel had returned suddenly only a few days ago, unsettling everyone. The way Horace saw it, people who ran away usually had selfish reasons for running—good or bad—and nothing he'd learned about Isabel so far gave him much confidence that her reasons were good.

Still, they'd tried the dinner. It had been Chloe's idea, thinking that Horace's mom could help her figure out the real reason Isabel had returned. For family, Isabel claimed. To set things right. Horace wanted to believe her, but he still wasn't sure, especially after what had happened with the expired raven's eye.

A raven's eye was a weak kind of leestone, a Tanu that protected Keepers from the Riven. But an expired raven's eye, blackened and depleted, was useless—or so Chloe had thought when she let Isabel take one from her room.

After dinner at Horace's, Isabel had sneaked upstairs and found the harp belonging to Horace's mom. With the harp, Isabel had toyed with the weaving inside the old raven's eye. They'd caught her in the act, and suspected—even though Horace's mom couldn't prove it—that she'd been up to no good. Only later, after Chloe and her family left, with Joshua along for the ride, did they realize what Isabel had truly done.

She had reversed the weaving inside the raven's eye, turning it from what had once been a shield against the Riven into a beacon. She claimed it was an accident, but accident or not, the new weaving she'd made had led the Riven straight to Chloe's family as they drove back to the Academy, nearly getting them all captured, or worse.

The only reason they escaped was because Isabel had struck a deal with the Riven. If they left Chloe alone, they could have April, Keeper of the Ravenvine, an empath who had left the safety of the Warren and had returned to her home outside the city, with only Gabriel as an escort. But Isabel's efforts only put them all in more danger, forcing the Wardens to come to April and Gabriel's rescue. It was that rescue, and the desperate battle it sparked, from which Horace and the others had only narrowly escaped.

But all that was over now. They were all safe. Back here in this cloister with its protective leestone—always a bird, this one orange with a gray head. The Riven could never find them here. Still, now that he'd slept the edge off his exhaustion, Horace found it hard to relax. They still had to jump five more times to return to the Warren, and Chloe and Neptune had already made a problematic number of jumps tonight. They'd leapt all the way back to the Warren before returning to search for Horace, when his final encounter with Dr. Jericho had kept him from following them right away. That was six jumps home and five jumps back.

He was worried about the other Wardens, too. Would those traveling by car be back at the Warren by now? Horace looked up at the stars again and tried to clear his head, to let the time come to him. He'd always been able to do this—to simply know the time without looking. It was a talent suitable for the Keeper of the Box of Promises. Abruptly he knew that it was 11:58, give or take a minute. He'd escaped the battle just over a half hour ago, and had slept for fifteen minutes after that. The other Wardens probably wouldn't get back to the Warren for another fifteen minutes more.

Horace waited for the girls to wake. He'd give them ten minutes and then rouse them for the journey home. As he waited, he tried not to think about what Dr. Jericho had said just before Horace fled the meadow next to April's home—his warning about the Mothergates, the remote and mysterious artifacts from which the Medium flowed. Dr. Jericho was one of the Riven, bent on taking all Tan'ji and ridding the world of human Keepers like Horace. He was a trickster and a beast. Nothing he said could be trusted.

And yet.

Neptune had sort of confirmed the Mordin's warning just before falling asleep. Loopy and careless from the falkrete jumps, she had mentioned the Mothergates too, suggesting that there was something wrong with them. When pressed, she wouldn't explain, but did eventually drop a bomb of a hint that clung to Horace still, a teasing echo of what Dr. Jericho had said outright: *Nothing lasts forever.*

Horace had tried to interpret this hint any other way, but he couldn't.

The Mothergates were dying.

According to Dr. Jericho. But also, apparently, according

to Neptune. Meanwhile Mr. Meister, the leader of their little pack of Wardens, had yet to utter a single word about it. As for Horace, he struggled to let himself believe a thing he so *hated* to believe. But it was impossible to ignore.

Horace took the Fel'Daera from its pouch. The striped wood shimmered; on its front, the silver sun with its twenty-four rays was almost entirely dark, an indication that the breach was very small right now. The box felt perfect in his hands. Perfect. How could he live without this? Logically speaking, if the Mothergates were dying, and every Tan'ji depended on the Mothergates for power, then the Fel'Daera was dying too. The thought was so agonizing and frightening that Horace could hardly find a place for it. He was a Keeper. The Fel'Daera was as much a part of him as his hands, his brain, his heart. Without the Fel'Daera . . . would he even exist?

He thought for a moment, orienting himself, and then opened the box. The lid split in two, its wings unfolding smoothly to the sides. Inside, the blue glass bottom rippled in the starlight. Through that glass lay the future—the future four minutes and thirty-four seconds from now, to be precise. That's how wide the breach was at the moment, the gap between the present and the future the box opened into. He raised the box and looked through it at future Chloe—*still sleeping; fists still clenched*.

He briefly considered putting a handful of grass into the box and closing it above Chloe's head. The grass would disappear, only to reappear four minutes and thirty-four seconds

21

later, to fall onto his friend's sleeping face. He snorted a soft laugh at the thought, but almost immediately felt childish. Would it be funny? He decided it would, but it would not be mature. It was the sort of thing his dad would do. And a part of Horace suspected that the real reason he wanted to send the grass had nothing to do with jokes. He wanted to reassure himself that the Fel'Daera was working fine, that nothing bad was coming, that the Mothergates—whatever and wherever they were—would last forever.

Despite his worry, the box *was* working just as it always had. He swung it toward Neptune.

"Whoa!" said Horace. Through the glass, a surprise—*Neptune awake and very close, sitting up, eyes and mouth open; shaking her head and gesturing with her disfigured hand.* She was looking up at something, or someone, and when Horace swung the box to see, he saw—*himself, tall and shaggy haired, standing and talking animatedly.*

It was always unsettling, seeing his future self. What were he and Neptune talking about? He watched his lips move, crisp and clear through the rippling glass. He couldn't hear, of course, but he was getting better at reading lips. As he watched, he saw his future self say, quite plainly—*But what if she can?*

Horace snapped the box closed, frowning. What if who can? He slipped the Fel'Daera back into its pouch and told himself not to analyze it. The future came as it would. It was better not to overthink it.

But Horace had never been an underthinker. Through

22

the box, his future self had looked upset. And the scene had been crisp and clear, which usually meant that the Fel'Daera was seeing truly. What would possibly upset him in the next four minutes? He and Neptune seemed to be arguing. Was it something about the Mothergates again? Horace glanced over at Neptune, who was still sound asleep, but he resisted the urge to wake her.

He watched the stars instead, naming the ones he knew by heart. Altair, Polaris, Kochab. He picked out one of his favorites, Eltanin, which was headed in earth's direction and which—in a couple of million years—would become the brightest star in the sky. But tonight, as always, Vega was far brighter. Vega lay in a tiny constellation that was hard to pick out, but he knew it was there. He let his mind paint its shape on the night sky. Lyra, the harp.

"But what if she can?"

She was Isabel. He was sure of that. Isabel the Tuner and her strange wicker harp.

What if Isabel can . . . what?

As far as Horace knew, Isabel was still back at the Mazzoleni Academy. She was powerless, too, because Mr. Meister had confiscated Miradel. And yes, she had given up her harp willingly, which was comforting, but Horace also remembered what Chloe had once said about her mother. Isabel would never truly surrender Miradel. Isabel *believed* she was Tan'ji; she believed she was meant to be a Keeper. Isabel thought the Wardens could somehow *make* her a Keeper, and in fact Horace and Chloe had talked about whether Brian, with his incredible powers, could possibly—

"Oh, no no no," Horace said, realization dawning over him. He stood up, reasoning it through quickly as he could. "No no no," he said again.

Abruptly, Neptune sat up, groaning and rising from the ground like a reanimated corpse. "Gahhh," she moaned. "Oh man, I hurt."

"Isabel wants Brian," Horace blurted out, not even waiting for her to fully wake.

"I'm sorry, what?" Neptune said, her voice thick with skepticism. She swept tangled strands of long brown hair out of her face, gazing at him with her sad, flat eyes.

"This whole night, all of it, Isabel planned it," Horace said.

Neptune hummed doubtfully and frowned down at her jagged pinky. "Even my pinky?" she asked, pouting. "That's just mean."

"I'm serious. The raven's eye she altered—it wasn't an accident. She did it on purpose. She lured the Riven and then, to save Chloe, she sent them after April. She knew we'd have to mount a rescue. She wanted to get us out of the Warren."

"Why?"

"I told you. Brian. She thinks Brian can make her Tan'ji." Brian, the most elusive member of the Wardens, was the Keeper of Tunraden, a Loomdaughter, an ancient instrument that gave him the power to create new Tan'ji—and other kinds of Tanu as well. Horace found it hard to believe that

24

Brian, even with his immense powers, actually *could* make Isabel a Keeper somehow. But he definitely believed that Isabel believed it.

Neptune hugged her knees to her chest, watching him intently. "You didn't see this through the box."

"No. How could I?"

"You're just guessing."

"It's more than a guess. It's the only way the whole night makes sense. Isabel wants Brian."

"Isabel doesn't even know Brian exists! No one does."

Horace couldn't reply. He wondered if Neptune could see the blush of shame that burned across his cheeks. He glanced at Chloe, still sleeping.

Neptune eyes widened. "Oh, god, Horace."

"It was an accident. Me and Chloe were talking at dinner tonight. Isabel was there. We were talking about Brian fixing April's Tan'ji, and half an hour later Isabel was messing with the raven's eye."

"So, basically, you were monumentally stupid," Neptune said.

"We didn't know she was listening," Horace protested, but Neptune was right. It was stupid to be so careless. Brian's powers were so valuable and rare that he wasn't allowed to leave the Warren. His instrument, Tunraden, was a prize the Riven would have dearly loved to get their horrible hands on, along with Brian himself. Brian, to put it simply, was a Maker. His existence had to remain utterly secret.

But thanks to Horace and Chloe, Isabel knew.

"Monumental or not, it doesn't matter," Neptune said. "Isabel can't get into the Warren. She can't even find it. The spitestone is there."

The spitestone, yes. Horace had seen it himself in Mr. Meister's office, an owl figurine with a single glowing eye. Attuned to Isabel personally, the spitestone was designed to cloud her memories and her senses regarding the Warren. The Wardens had created the spitestone to banish Isabel all those years ago. As long as it existed, she could neither remember nor discover the location of the Warren, try as she might.

But what if things had changed?

"I don't really know how spitestones work," said Horace. "But what about Joshua? He's inside the Warren right now."

"Joshua?" Neptune said, laughing. "You don't trust Joshua?"

But no, that wasn't it. Horace was only grasping at straws. Yes, Joshua had been traveling with Isabel, and yes, he was a little weird, but he was just a boy, only eight or nine years old. Mr. Meister had welcomed him into the Warren, something the old man never would have done if he suspected him in any way. Plus, it was clear that Mr. Meister and Mrs. Hapstead believed Joshua would become a Keeper, and maybe Horace was being a little unfair now because he had reason to believe that Joshua's talents were somehow just like his own. He felt a tiny—very tiny, but embarrassing—bit of jealousy over the fact.

Neptune leaned forward. "Joshua's in the Warren, yeah,"

she prodded. "But so is Mrs. Hapsteade. You think he's going to overpower her and bring Isabel down to Brian's workshop?"

"No, I don't think that," Horace admitted, but the mention of Mrs. Hapsteade brought a memory back to him. His dread instantly doubled. "I'm not crazy, though—Mrs. Hapsteade stayed back at the Warren tonight because she was worried about Isabel."

"No she didn't. She just stayed. She didn't say why."

"Mr. Meister told me that was why," Horace said, remembering. "She stayed because of Isabel, even after he reminded her that the spitestone would keep the Warren safe."

Neptune shook her head, waving her hands. "I didn't hear him say that. And anyway, he's right. The spitestone has kept the Warren hidden from Isabel for twenty years. Why would it stop now?"

"What if she figured out a way around it?" Horace insisted.

"Nobody can get past a spitestone."

"But what if she can?"

"She can't."

Horace paused, a queasy kind of déjà vu rolling over him. The future he'd witnessed through the box had just come to pass.

"But what if she can?"

He'd just spoken the words he'd seen himself say four minutes and thirty-four seconds ago. And here was a weirdness that only the Keeper of the Fel'Daera could truly understand: Horace had only begun to suspect Isabel like this because he had seen his future self say those words, and yet . . . he only

27

said those words *because he started suspecting her.* It was the chicken and the egg, impossible to say which came first.

He shook off the dizzying notion. The truth was this: through the box, Horace had seen what Horace would do. And as the Keeper of the Fel'Daera, he had to remember that the seeing and the doing were a single act, two sides of the same coin. If you were true to the box, the box would be true to you. So instead of resisting, he embraced the moment. Isabel couldn't be trusted, and everything that had happened this night told him that his terrible suspicions might be correct. Even Mrs. Hapsteade seemed to be concerned, a step ahead of the rest of them as usual. Isabel wanted to find Brian, spitestone or no spitestone. It was only logical. Brian could be in danger. They had to get back.

Horace crouched down in front of Neptune and opened his mouth to say the promised words again.

"But what if she can?"

CHAPTER THREE

One Day

ISABEL SQUEEZED JOSHUA'S HAND. "THE WARREN," SHE SAID, gazing around them. "It's smaller than I remember. I think." She released him and spun in a circle, scowling up at the walls. "My senses are still foggy. My memories, too. We have to find the spitestone. We have to destroy it."

"I don't know where it is," Joshua replied.

"You've been close to it already tonight. Mr. Meister's doba, maybe. Where is it again?"

Joshua looked—but didn't point—down deeper into the stone forest of the Great Burrow, where Mr. Meister's huge doba loomed in the golden shadows, largest of all. Isabel grabbed him again and pulled him forward, moving so fast that he had to jog to keep up.

Inside Mr. Meister's office, the round red walls towered over them, covered in shelves and cubbies full of wondrous things, amazing things: a book as thick as a chest, a floating cube made of floating cubes, an owl figurine with a single yellow eye that glowed like a torch. Maybe Joshua's Tan'ji was here, too. His heart skipped a beat as he noticed a white compass with a red needle on Mr. Meister's desk. Was this the Laithe? But he stared and stared at the compass, and felt nothing. Not that he knew what he was supposed to feel.

A couple of tiny birds fluttered down from above, chattering wildly around Isabel's head, obviously bothered. For a moment, Joshua forgot his instrument and thought of April, and Arthur. Isabel had put them in danger, he knew that for sure now. All so she could break into the Warren. With Joshua's help.

"Were you here tonight?" Isabel asked.

"Yes." He didn't bother to tell her he'd been here while the Wardens were figuring out how to save April.

"Your instrument won't be here, then," Isabel said. "Meister would have seen your talent, and before he brought you here, he would have hidden the Laithe deeper in the Warren. I think that's where we'll find Brian, too." She scowled fiercely. "But the spitestone is here. I feel it, like a shadow in a dark room. Do you see it?"

"I don't know what it looks like," Joshua said, frowning angrily at the compass. Why was he angry?

"It'll be yellow. That's my color. It might be glowing."

Joshua considered the furiously shining eye of the little owl, just beside the compass. It was right in front of her.

He looked away quickly. "I don't see anything like that," he said.

She cocked her head at him, eyes narrowing. "You're lying."

"I'm not."

She crouched down and grasped his hands. "I'm trying to help you, Joshua. You're going to be a Keeper at last, just like I always said."

"If that's true, then I'll become one anyway, even without your help. Mr. Meister will make sure I do. He said so."

Isabel hesitated, and then broke into a low, cruel laugh. "After what you've done? Helping the hated Isabel break into their precious sanctuary? You think they'll want you now?" She released him and stood straight. "Let's just wait for them to return, then. Let's see how it goes."

Joshua clenched his fists, his head and gut a tornado of fear and anger and doubt and regret. Would they forgive him? Would they let him become a Keeper now?

"I can fix it all, Joshua," Isabel said gently. "I'm going to take you to your instrument, and fix myself, and then they'll see. Then they'll understand. They'll forgive us both once they see." She clasped her hands together, pleading. "It's the only way to make everything right, Joshua. Help me. Where is the spitestone?"

His stomach full of lead, Joshua spoke. "It's here. It's right here."

"I can't see it," Isabel said. "What is it? Pick it up for me."

Reluctantly, Joshua took the one-eyed owl. It was warm to the touch. The gleaming yellow eye brightened, lighting up the room—but not, he noticed now, Isabel. It was like the light couldn't admit she was here. She cast no shadow in it.

"That's it," Isabel said, though her eyes wouldn't focus on it. "We need to destroy it. I think there's a . . . hole here in the Warren. Like a bottomless canyon. I remember but don't remember. Do you know what I mean?"

"You mean the Maw?"

"That's it," Isabel snapped greedily. "Take me there. Take me now."

Clutching the owl, his heart still heavy, Joshua led her back outside and deeper into the Great Burrow, where the chamber ended in darkness at the edge of a wide, deep chasm. The bottom of the Maw was so far down you couldn't see it. A narrow staircase led down into the gloom, carved out of the stone—the Perilous Stairs, a sign announced, and then in the fine print:

**Swallow up your fear,
or be swallowed up yourself.**

Joshua had never been invited down these stairs before, and he wasn't sure he wanted to be, but he'd come to understand that Brian did in fact live below.

"Throw it over the edge," Isabel said.

"What?" Joshua said.

"Throw the spitestone into the Maw. It's clouding me, and I can't help you unless we destroy it."

But Joshua didn't think he could do it. He would have to admit to Mr. Meister that he'd not only helped Isabel sneak into the Warren, but that he'd destroyed the spitestone too.

"You do it," he said, and he awkwardly shoved the owl into Isabel's hand. She shrieked, as if it had burned her, and jerked back. The little statue fell. It tumbled over the edge of the Maw and down the steep cliff. Once, twice it bounced, and on the third it shattered, exploding with a loud shriek into a sparkling cloud of startling gold. Joshua jumped. The shrill cry faded slowly as the breeze from below blew the cloud apart into nothing.

Isabel laughed with relief. "Better," she said, looking up and all around as if the lights had just been turned on. "Oh, much better. Now I see. I remember." Her dark eyes fell on him and widened. She grabbed him by the shoulders and leaned in so fast he flinched.

"It's here," she muttered hoarsely. "It's yours. The Laithe of Teneves."

Joshua froze. That name again. The Laithe. The Laithe of Teneves. But he shook his head, feeling like he might drown in the very idea of it.

"It's yours, Joshua," Isabel said. "I tuned the Laithe myself, years ago, and I know it better than anyone but its Maker."

Isabel had tuned his instrument? So maybe she *did*

know—maybe he *was* its Keeper, whatever it was. That sick flame of hope flickered in his chest again. He tried to ignore it. "I don't want it," he said, and it was a terrible lie. The worst lie ever.

"But you do," Isabel insisted softly. "All this time I've been promising you, and now you'll see I was right. Tonight you become a Keeper, Joshua. We just need to find it. You'll lay eyes on it, and then . . . everything will change. You will become who you are."

Isabel scanned the air around him. Joshua could barely breathe. She looked down at the ground, then spun about and spotted the staircase. "The Perilous Stairs," she breathed, with the voice of someone who has just discovered a long-forgotten thing. "That's our path."

She started down the stairs. Joshua stood there swaying for a moment. *You will become who you are.*

He looked back into the Great Burrow. Mrs. Hapsteade was back there somewhere, unharmed but helpless. Isabel could have cleaved her, he knew. But she hadn't. And what if everything Isabel was saying now was the truth? Wouldn't the Wardens understand? Wouldn't they forgive him?

He couldn't let himself answer. There were answers he couldn't bear. He turned and followed Isabel in a daze.

The Perilous Stairs were rough and terribly steep, and on one side the bottomless Maw yawned like the mouth of a giant beast. Joshua kept close to the wall, turning sideways to manage each high step as they zigzagged down the cliff face.

34

The breeze ruffled his dark hair and made him shiver. He told himself to keep his fear swallowed. He counted the steps to keep himself distracted from everything—Isabel breaking into the Warren, Mrs. Hapsteade severed and helpless, the deadly fall just inches away, the possibility of his promised instrument waiting for him below at last. The Laithe of Teneves.

As they rounded a sharp bend in the stairs, Isabel said, "Back when I tuned the Laithe, when I worked for the Wardens, I wasn't much older than you are now. I've never forgotten it."

Joshua nearly tripped, unable to ask her anything—all the things he wanted so badly to know.

She glanced back at him, her brown eyes full of dark excitement. "It's a globe, Joshua," she whispered. "Wait till you see. It's a living globe, a tiny earth. Every continent, every river, every mountain range, every forest—every *house*! All there to be found. All of it. That's how I know the Laithe is yours."

And now Joshua did stumble, so caught up in her words that he missed a step entirely. He plunged toward the edge, his heart frozen. But Isabel swiveled and caught him nimbly by the arm. She righted him and then continued down the stairs without comment.

"Every Keeper has a talent," she said. "And yours, of course—"

"Maps," Joshua breathed. Joshua loved maps. Reading

maps was his only hobby, the only thing he remembered always doing. He scoured them, memorized them easily. And it was his talent because he'd always thought of the world as a map he was standing on, walking across. He could hardly imagine *not* thinking this way. How did other people get around? Directions and distances and destinations—Joshua knew these things as easily as he knew colors. And this Laithe, this globe, it sounded . . .

"The Laithe is the greatest map that has ever been made," said Isabel. "More than a map—you'll see."

"And it's for me?" Joshua managed to ask. "You're sure?"

"It's already yours. It always has been."

At last they reached the bottom of the Perilous Stairs. One hundred and forty-seven steps, roughly—Joshua had missed a step or two when he'd nearly fallen. They were now almost two hundred feet below the Great Burrow. To the north, a great stone bridge crossed the Maw to a kind of balcony on the far side. To the south, the path they stood on cut into the rock face, into a narrow tunnel. Joshua squinted into the tunnel, confused. A little ways in, the passage darkened into a clean rectangle of total black. Impossible edges, impossible black.

Isabel tilted her head curiously at the darkness. "What's this?" She stepped into the tunnel, right up to the black. It was only a shadow, Joshua could tell, but its edges were so sharp that it looked more like a thing. Like a door. Isabel studied it, the wicker sphere pulsing and glowing again at her chest.

"Oh, that's clever," she murmured. "Something precious on the other side of this, no doubt. Something *and* someone, I think."

"Was this not here before?" Joshua asked. "When you were little?"

Isabel scowled. "Meister didn't allow me down here," she said bitterly. "He didn't let me do anything but the one thing he wanted from me. I came and tuned his precious unclaimed instruments, so that they'd be clean and ready when—if—their Keepers came to claim them. That's all the Wardens wanted me to do."

She stepped up to the edge of the shadow door. Miradel grew huge, its tangled strands spreading and spilling green light everywhere. "But I can do much more," she said, and then the shadow door seemed to shiver. It shuddered violently, and then suddenly it came loose, falling toward Isabel like a giant black domino. She didn't move, and looked as if she would be crushed, but the darkness was only a shadow and not a thing at all, and it passed through her like air. It vanished with a puff as it toppled onto the ground. Beyond, the tunnel stretched onward toward a bright light shining eighty feet ahead.

Isabel looked back at Joshua, laughing like she'd surprised herself. "There's not another Tuner alive that could do *that*," she said.

"Was it a trap?"

"No, nothing dangerous. Just a trick. The Wardens are full of tricks, you know."

"They've been nice to me," Joshua said.

A flash of fury slid across Isabel's grinning face, but then she tugged her red hair and smiled again. Not a real smile. "Of course they have," she said calmly. "You're valuable. They want to keep you for themselves. Just like April."

"They helped April. Brian fixed her."

"Yes, and now it's my turn. My turn at last," said Isabel. She gripped Joshua by the arm—not too hard, but not exactly soft—and looked into his eyes. "Brian is going to take some convincing. Don't be alarmed. I won't really hurt him." Without waiting for an answer, she pushed him gently into the hall.

When they reached the far end, Joshua paused at the threshold to Brian's workshop. He could see him at his bench, concentrating hard on an instrument, his eyes almost crossed.

"Go," Isabel whispered.

Joshua swallowed hard and then stepped through the doorway. Brian looked up and began to smile. A real smile. He looked goofy, not because of his ghostly pale skin or his ponytail, but because of the crazy goggles strapped over his glasses. He looked like an insect, or an alien. Almost as soon as his smile began, though, it vanished. He jumped up, knocking over his stool and dropping his equipment to the floor.

"You must be Brian," Isabel purred, right behind Joshua. "I've heard so little about you."

"Who are you?" said Brian, backing away.

Isabel walked up to him and plucked at his shirt. "'Beware

of Danger,'" she read. "Is that why they have you locked away down here? Danger?"

"You're Isabel," Brian said, his gaze falling to Miradel. "How did you get in here? Where's Mrs. Hap—"

"She's fine, totally fine," said Isabel with a wave. "We're old friends . . . or old somethings, anyway. I'm not here to hurt anyone."

Brian looked at Joshua, his face a question. Joshua could tell he was mad and scared. Joshua wanted to leave.

"Don't blame Joshua," Isabel said. "He's here for the same reason I am."

"But . . . the spitestone," said Brian. "How did you find us?"

"The spitestone is gone," Isabel said with a laugh, not really answering. "Finally gone, and it's like . . ." She pressed all ten fingers to her scalp. "It's like I discovered a box of old diaries." She held a finger in Brian's face, like she was lecturing him. "It's not just that I haven't been able to *find* the Warren, you know. All my memories of this place have been cloudy. It's like the spitestone—"

"I'm pretty up-to-date on how the spitestone works," said Brian.

"Yes, you would be, wouldn't you? You're the one that fixed April's Tan'ji. There's only one kind of Keeper that can do something like that."

Brian took off his goggles. Joshua just stood there, not knowing what to say or do. "I'm not a Keeper," said Brian. "I just tinker around down here in the basement."

"Tinker," said Isabel with a giggle. "Let's not waste time. You *are* a Keeper. Your Tan'ji is a Loomdaughter. I'd like to see it."

Brian shook his head. "No," he said. "No way."

Isabel sighed. Miradel began to swell and glow, a green haze lighting the space between Isabel and Brian. "You don't seem to understand. I need help. You are going to help me." Miradel throbbed, and Brian staggered, grimacing, his eyes glazing over.

"What are you doing?" Joshua cried, even though he knew. She was severing Brian.

Brian staggered numbly for a moment, and then straightened, his eyes clearing. Isabel had stopped, apparently, but Brian still looked like he was in pain. Joshua wondered if he'd ever been severed before.

"Just a friendly reminder of what a Tuner can do," Isabel said. "And severing isn't the worst of it, as I'm sure you know."

Brian swallowed so hard Joshua saw his Adam's apple bob up and down. Isabel was talking about cleaving, ripping apart the bond between Brian and Tunraden by force, all at once. Permanently. Joshua told himself she wouldn't do it. That she would never.

"Of course, there's no need for anything like that," Isabel said. "Not between friends. All you have to do is help me."

Brian eyed Miradel. Joshua thought he looked worried, but not as worried as he himself would have been. Something bright and thoughtful was burning behind those glasses. "Help you what?" Brian said calmly.

"Be what I'm supposed to be. I was meant to be a Keeper. And you, I think, were meant to help me finally become one."

Joshua wasn't sure, but it almost seemed like Brian hesitated—like the idea interested him somehow. But then Brian shook his head again. "That can't happen. No way. And even if I was willing to try—which I'm not—it would take hours. The rest of the Wardens will be back before then."

"Oh, you won't do it here."

Brian laughed. "You expect me to leave? With Tunraden? Forget it. Cleave me if you like, but taking Tunraden out of here is literally impossible."

"Tunraden," Isabel sighed. "That's a lovely name. And if I know Meister, I'm sure it's true you can't leave the Warren with her—not by the usual routes, anyway." She swept past him. She crossed the cluttered chamber to a tall cabinet against the far wall. She opened the door, revealing shelves full of strange objects—a black disk laced with red streaks like lightning, a cat head made of silver, a tiny brass top, a transparent rod with a long thin fish inside. Joshua stared, his eyes flicking wildly over these wonders. Tan'ji, they had to be—or technically, Tan'layn, instruments that still hadn't found a Keeper.

"Those aren't for you," Brian said, looking nervous.

"No, they're not." Isabel reached into the cabinet and pulled something out. A sphere as big as a grapefruit, blue and white and green. Joshua's mouth dried up, and his heart began to pound.

"What are you doing?" said Brian.

Isabel ignored him. She brought the sphere over to Joshua. He felt glued to the ground, pinned in place. "Here," she said, holding it out. "This is yours now, Keeper."

Brian gasped angrily, but Joshua barely heard him, frozen in place. The Laithe of Teneves. Here in front of him. Isabel had said it was a living globe, but Joshua hadn't understood what that meant until now. The little globe, wrapped in a glowing haze, was made of water and air and earth. Clouds moved across the surface. Currents rippled on the oceans. Africa and the Middle East were pointed at him, and he could see the grainy surface of the Sahara and the Arabian Desert. He could see the rugged brown of the Himalayas, the turquoise blue of the Caspian Sea, the fertile green of the Ganges Delta. He thought he could even see little splotches of giant cities—Mumbai, Cairo, Istanbul. It was a map like he'd never imagined, a map to erase all other maps, and it was all so perfect and real that he stood there thinking maybe he'd never—

"Here," Isabel said again, and she set the Laithe in his open hands.

Joshua had never been so terrified. He thought he might drop the Laithe from fear. The globe was small enough that he could almost wrap two hands around it. It felt like a stubborn cloud beneath his fingers, and he somehow understood that he couldn't actually touch the surface of the little earth. There was a copper meridian around the globe, too, a flat ring that circled it. He gripped the ring now. Lots of globes had meridians, all anchored at the north and south poles, but the Laithe's meridian had no anchors. The globe hovered inside the encircling meridian without touching it, like Saturn inside its rings. Gently he brushed a finger across the globe, and discovered that it could rotate freely inside the meridian in every direction. What was this thing? *How* was this thing? And no, he wasn't ready for it, not for this, it was too beautiful and perfect and . . . *important.*

The copper meridian was smooth and blank, which was strange. Normally, meridians had lines to indicate degrees, north and south. Joshua flipped the ring over, marveling as the globe inside stayed almost perfectly motionless, still centered on the eastern coast of Africa. The other side of the meridian was covered in strange markings—not degrees, no, but curious arrows that pointed in a clockwise direction. There were inscriptions that looked like words in a language he'd never seen. At the top, a small golden rabbit was attached to the meridian. It was curled up, as if asleep.

"Well?" said Isabel, watching him with her dark brown eyes.

Joshua struggled to speak, staring at the rabbit. "It's . . . too much."

Her eyes flashed. "It's yours, Joshua. I see that. It's a lot to take in, going through the Find—"

"Uh, this is *not* the Find," Brian said. Isabel rounded on him, but he only shrugged. "Speaking as the only Keeper in the room, just saying. This is not how the Find works. And if you don't go through the Find properly, you can—"

"It won't be up to the Wardens to decide what's proper today," Isabel snapped. "The Laithe is Joshua's. Surely you can see that."

Brian shrugged again, slowly this time. "I can see . . . things," he said, gazing at Joshua through his glasses. "But it doesn't matter what I can see. The Laithe is Tan'layn—one of the unspoken. You're going to speak for it?"

"It isn't Tan'layn anymore. It has been claimed. It is Tan'ji, and Joshua is its Keeper. Show him, Joshua."

Joshua thought he might cry. He wanted this wonderful globe, he did. But he felt sort of like someone had poured a thousand gold coins into his hands—an incredible treasure, but too much to carry. And now Brian was saying this wasn't the Find. "I don't know what to do," he said, and he meant it in all the ways it could be meant.

But Isabel impatiently reached out and touched the meridian of the Laithe. Joshua frowned. People weren't supposed to touch other people's Tan'ji, he knew that much. Isabel didn't seem to care. "Here," she said, pointing to the golden rabbit. "Slide this."

Hesitantly, Joshua took hold of the rabbit. He tugged it gently, and the rabbit began to slide around the meridian, as smoothly as a skate on ice. Instantly, the surface of the globe began to shift. Madagascar was still right in the middle, centered inside the Meridian, but as he slid the rabbit, the island began to grow. It swiftly tripled in size. Meanwhile oceans and continents around the edge rearranged themselves, drifting outward and shrinking.

Joshua released the rabbit, terrified. "I broke it!" he cried. "Look!"

"It looks the same to me," said Isabel. "You're zooming in, but only you can see it. You didn't break it—you're doing what it was made to do. You *are* its Keeper."

Only he could see. He *was* its Keeper. Trying to believe it, Joshua slowly slid the rabbit farther around the meridian. Madagascar continued to expand. The tip of India vanished over the horizon. Africa shriveled slowly away to the west. By the time the rabbit was a quarter of the way around the ring, the island nearly filled his view, a green swath of rainforest in the east, highlands in the middle, and drier land to the west.

Joshua kept going, moving the rabbit. Central Madagascar grew closer and closer. Off to one side, there was a lake he didn't know the name of and a city he did—the only city in Madagascar he knew by name, Antananarivo, a name that was fun to say out loud even if he wasn't sure how to pronounce it. When the rabbit reached the bottom of the meridian, Joshua realized there was nothing there to stop it, so he kept going on around the circle, back up toward where the rabbit had begun. He heard Brian say, "Whoa," but Joshua didn't look up. If it was true that no one else could see what was happening on the globe, Brian must be seeing something else—the Medium, probably.

On the globe, hills began to appear. A winding road, and river—a gray snake and a green. Blocks of buildings, and now the dots of individual houses. Trees, though many of them had lost their leaves. Joshua's mouth fell open. In real life, Madagascar was below the equator, which meant it was winter there now, especially in the highlands. There was farmland there too, not like the big square farms in Illinois, but sculpted in ledges across the hillsides. Terrace farming, it was called.

Joshua looked up. He blinked his eyes—he'd almost forgotten where he was. Isabel stood in front of him, her face eager. Brian was right there too, closer now, and Joshua turned to him.

"Will I see people?"

He wasn't sure why he thought Brian would know. Brian seemed smart, smarter even than Horace, maybe. And he knew about Tan'ji.

"Some," said Brian, his eyes darting through the air around the Laithe. But then he waved his hands like he was trying to erase his answer. "Don't ask me questions. This shouldn't even be happening."

People. Tiny people down there on this living globe. They couldn't be real people, of course. Could they? Joshua pushed the running rabbit farther, two-thirds of the way around now. The land beneath him continued to grow from the center and melt out of sight around the edges of the Laithe. He passed through a cloud. The view descended into a narrow valley of terraced crops between two forests. A farmhouse. Dirt lanes.

But then suddenly, as the rabbit reached three-quarters of the way around, the Laithe began to get fuzzy. Little blurry circles began to appear, like raindrops hitting a puddle. He pushed the rabbit farther, but the circles spread and grew. He couldn't see anything anymore, just ripples of brown and gray and green.

"I did break it," he whispered. "I can't see anything."

"What happened?" said Isabel.

In a panic, Joshua slid the rabbit backward. The ripples went away. The dirt lanes and the trees and the farmhouse reappeared, shrinking. The land farther out crept back in over the horizon too.

"Wait," he said, pushing the rabbit forward once more. But again, as he zoomed in, the rippling circles covered the surface of the Laithe. "I can't get close. I can't see all the way."

"You have to," Isabel said. "Try again."

"What do you see, Joshua?" asked Brian in a friendly way, leaning in over the Laithe.

"Like . . . circles. Ripples."

"And where are you now? Where are you looking?"

"Madagascar."

"Wow! That's pretty far away from where we are right now."

"Nine thousand miles," Joshua said automatically.

Brian whistled. "Super far. And have you ever been there?"

"What? No. When would I go to Madagascar?"

"I don't know. People go places. Some people, anyway. But if you haven't been there . . ."

"Enough," said Isabel, holding a hand up to Brian. "You've made your point."

Brian stepped back. "You can't expect him to master it in five minutes, zooming all the way in on a spot he's never been to, halfway around the world. If he were doing this the right way, he'd be in the Find for weeks before managing something like that."

"Weeks?" said Joshua.

"We do not have weeks. We have minutes." Isabel snapped her fingers at Brian. "Take me to the Loomdaughter."

Brian looked startled, like he had forgotten why Isabel was here. He frowned at Isabel's wicker harp. "If you think I'm coming with you, you're crazy," he said.

Miradel flared violently at Isabel's chest, spilling a forest of green light across Brian. He tensed, his eyes going wide.

"Don't, Isabel!" Joshua cried. "You said you wouldn't hurt him!"

Isabel's face was rigid with anger. After several frozen moments, it softened. The glowing green harp shrank and dimmed. "I'm not crazy," she said quietly. "I'm desperate."

Brian shook his head, breathing once more. "I get that. But I can't help you."

"You can," Isabel insisted. "You want to try, I know you do."

He looked away, but not before the strange fire in his eyes seemed to brighten. "I'm not . . . ," he began, and then started over, speaking slowly and carefully, holding his hands up like shields. "You're desperate for something that might not even be real."

Joshua's eyes darted to Isabel in alarm, but there was no anger, no burst of green light. Instead, she looked almost happy. "But it might be," she said. "Take me to the Loom-daughter. Show me. If you can convince me that you can't do what I want . . ."

"You'll let me go?" Brian asked lightly.

Isabel tilted her head in a way that wasn't quite a no, wasn't quite a yes.

"Just show her," Joshua pleaded with Brian, frightened by the conversation and wanting it to end, willing to worry about what came next when it came. "Just for a minute."

Brian looked long and hard at Joshua. At last he gave a single nod and abruptly turned away, walking deeper into the workshop without a word.

They followed him. In the back, Brian led them into a small, round chamber. It smelled like a rainstorm. There was a tall stone table there, and on top of it sat a big oval . . . thing. Joshua got up on his tiptoes to see.

"Tunraden," Brian said, his voice sullen and distant.

Tunraden was a great stone slab, almost two feet wide and six inches deep. It looked very, very old. There were no

49

markings on it, except for the top, where there was an engraved outline around the edge and two circles at each end of the oval. It looked very ordinary, Joshua thought, but it didn't *feel* anything like ordinary. Not at all. It felt like thunder.

"What does it do?" Joshua said, clutching the Laithe.

"It makes Tan'ji," Isabel said breathlessly, circling the Loomdaughter. "And he can use it to fix Tan'ji too. This is how he made April whole again, how he fixed the Ravenvine. And it's how he's going to help me become a Keeper."

"Well, two out of three, anyway," muttered Brian.

"You can . . . *make* Tan'ji?" Joshua said, not sure he heard right.

"On a good day, yeah."

Still studying Tunraden, Isabel said, "It's astonishing."

"Um . . . thank you?" Brian said, obviously trying not to sound pleased.

"It's bigger than I thought it would be," she went on.

"I get that a lot. Tunraden is one of the small ones, supposedly. The first few Loomdaughters were too big to even move. But you can see now why taking her outside is a bad idea. We can barely get around."

"I'll get you where we need to go," Isabel said.

Brian shook his head. "If the Riven discovered there was a Loomdaughter on the loose—"

"I can protect you."

"Says the woman who just threatened to kill me." Brian watched her with that dark and thoughtful light still in his

50

eyes. "I've been thinking," he said. "I don't think you really would cleave me. Why would you destroy the only person who could possibly help you?"

Isabel gave a smile that was more like a snarl. "If that person refuses to even *try* to help me, what would I have to lose by destroying him?"

Joshua stepped forward, his heart surging.

But Brian simply said, "Hope. That's what you'd lose. Nearly all of it, I think." When Isabel didn't reply, he said, "Let's wait for the other Wardens to come back. Let me talk to them. I can convince them to let me try and help you."

It was impossible to tell if Brian meant it or not. But Joshua certainly did not want to be here when the Wardens got back, when they learned what he and Isabel had done. They would take the Laithe away from him, he was sure of it.

"Please," Isabel spat. "Meister would never let you help me."

"I can't go with you, I'm sorry," said Brian.

"You've been down here a long time, haven't you?" Isabel said. "I doubt Meister ever lets you leave. How long has it been since you felt the sun? Breathed fresh air? Stood under a tree?"

Brian shrugged like he didn't care, but it didn't ring true. "How long since I got sunburn?" he asked. "Smelled car exhaust? Got pooped on by a bird?" He scrunched up his long face. "Actually scratch that last one. There are a surprising number of birds down here."

51

"How long?" Isabel pressed.

Brian scratched his chin. "Three years."

"Whoa . . . ," Joshua said slowly, trying to imagine living in a cave for three years. He could hardly even imagine three years of anything.

"And how many more years before Meister lets you go?" said Isabel.

Scowling at her, Brian said, "How many years since you've been trying to get your harp under control?"

Isabel scowled right back. "I have it under control."

"Mostly," said Brian. "Usually." He gestured at the air around her. "I can see it, you know. That thing is like a tornado in a bottle, and you've got your thumb squeezed over the spout, constantly."

It was obvious from Isabel's face—a smooth but guilty slab of shock—that he'd struck close to home. And Joshua knew that Isabel sometimes did lose control of the harp. But she shook her head stubbornly. "You don't know the first thing about it," she said.

Brian crossed his arms as if he had all day, and said, "Then tell me."

Isabel hesitated, leaning over Tunraden. "I can't *always* control it," she explained at last. "It gets away from me sometimes. It's gotten away from me in the past and . . . bad things have happened." She glanced at Joshua. "But nobody else could ever even use it at all. Not even a little. Besides, I was meant to be Tan'ji, and the Wardens robbed me of that. Then

Miradel came along, and . . . I was the only one for her. The *only one*. But it isn't quite right. Not yet."

"How is it not quite right?" asked Brian. "If I *were* going to try and help you—still a huge if—I would need to know."

Joshua couldn't help himself. Brian did need to know. "Sometimes she severs people on accident," he said.

"Rarely," said Isabel. "When I'm angry, or . . . upset."

Brian looked at her for a long time, chewing his cheek again. He said quietly, "Bad things have happened, you said. How bad?"

Isabel took a deep breath. She took another. "When Chloe was little, after she brought the Alvalaithen home but was still going through the Find, she was in the yard. She was playing with the dragonfly, going thin. I heard her screaming. I ran outside, and she was . . . sinking into the ground. It hadn't happened to her before—I guess she hadn't *imagined* it could happen."

Isabel paused, looking up at the stone ceiling, like she was imagining the surface of the earth hundreds of feet above them. "Chloe was in up to her knees, hanging on to a lawn chair like a life jacket, screaming. Like she was drowning. I panicked. I got upset, and—"

Little prickles of horror skittered across Joshua's skin. "You severed her," he said.

"While her legs were in the ground," said Brian.

Joshua remembered the Mordin on top of the car earlier in the evening, how Chloe had gone thin and put a crowbar into its leg. He remembered the scream. You couldn't put two things in the same place at the same time. Bad things happened when you did.

Isabel nodded. "I severed her. Just for an instant."

"But her legs would have been ruined," said Brian.

"She should have lost them," Isabel agreed. "But you've seen Chloe. She's a Paragon."

Brian's eyebrows shot up skeptically.

"What's a Paragon?" asked Joshua. It sounded like a shape.

"It's just a story," said Brian, and Isabel huffed and rolled her eyes. "But if you believe the story, each instrument—over its entire lifetime of perhaps hundreds of years—will only encounter one true Paragon. The one Keeper who can fully master all of its powers. The perfect Tan'ji."

"And that's Chloe," said Isabel. She sounded proud. "It's not just a story. I know it now like I knew it then. When she got herself out of the ground that day, her legs were broken. Shattered. But she shouldn't have been able to get them out at all. Only a Paragon could have done that."

Joshua looked down at the Laithe, at soft rings of clouds drifting over the Indian Ocean. Could *he* be a Paragon? Probably not, he decided. After all, he wasn't totally sure—not *totally*—that he was even supposed to be the Keeper of the Laithe. The thought filled him with an anger he had never felt before. All this talk about helping Isabel, and taking Brian out of the Warren. Isabel was using him, and Brian too. But no sooner had the rage flared up than it was gone again, washed away by a flood of confusion and uncertainty, of hope and desperation. He clutched the Laithe to his chest.

"So your daughter, the Paragon," said Brian. "Did you ever tell her it was your fault, the thing that happened with her legs?"

Isabel stiffened. "Not then, no," she admitted. "But now I have."

"Just the other day, you mean. Seven years after it happened."

"Yes. And you don't need to remind me that I didn't give up Miradel back then, either, even though I was a danger to Chloe. I left my family instead. That should tell you something about me and my harp."

"It does," Brian said softly. "It really does."

"I'm devoted to Miradel. She belongs to me, and I can't give her up, just like you can't give up Tunraden. But I want my family back."

"And you expect me to fix it all," said Brian.

"You fixed April," Isabel said. "And you made Meister's vest, didn't you? I can tell."

Brian didn't deny it. Joshua was confused—the red vest was Tan'ji? And Brian had made it?

Isabel held Miradel in her hand and pushed it toward Brian. The green light inside seemed to swirl and sparkle. "If you can turn a vest into a Tan'ji, why not a harp?"

Brian still didn't answer. His glasses shone emerald, two

copies of Miradel reflected across the lenses. And although it seemed to Joshua that every emotion was written on the older boy's face, fear didn't seem to be one of them anymore. And there was still that strange little fire in his eyes.

"Do to Miradel what you did to the vest," said Isabel. "Help me. Help my family. Fix me, and I'll become whole again, in all the ways. And you will have done what no Maker has ever done before."

Brian stood there, thinking. Joshua couldn't imagine what he himself would do, if he was Brian. Isabel was sad, and needed help. But Isabel was also bad, Joshua knew that—or at least, he knew Isabel did bad things. He tried to convince himself that the bad came out of the sad. He didn't understand quite how that worked, or if it was true. He only understood that it might be true.

Judging by the way he was looking at Isabel now, Brian seemed to be thinking the same sorts of things. He looked sorry for her, but sort of disgusted by her too, like the way a person might look at a badly injured animal.

After a long time Brian said, "Twenty-four hours. That's how long I'll give you. If I can't do it in one day, you bring me back and you give it all up."

Isabel bent her neck, pressing her forehead briefly against Miradel. She looked up at Brian, beaming. "One day," she said. "Thank you."

"And you have to take me someplace safe. Someplace with a leestone. If I use Tunraden for more than a few seconds without a leestone, it'll be like a dinner bell as big as a church for miles around. You have to protect me."

"I will. I have a plan." She glanced at Joshua.

"Okay," Brian said. "We're headed out, then." He stuck his fingers under his glasses and rubbed his eyes, then looked down at his own ghostly pale arms. "I don't suppose anyone has any sunscreen."

CHAPTER FOUR

The Departure

"BUT HOW WILL WE GET OUT OF THE WARREN?" JOSHUA ASKED, looking first to Isabel, and then to Brian. "You said it was impossible."

Brian pushed his glasses up onto his nose. "Yeah, well . . . that's not really a great word." He looked down at his feet, like he had something more to say but was afraid to say it.

Isabel laid a hand on Joshua's shoulder. "We need your help, Keeper."

Keeper. The word washed over him, but it didn't feel right. Not yet.

Isabel went on. "I need you to find something with the Laithe. Have you ever been to St. Louis? Anywhere around there?"

"St. Louis?" Brian said, sounding confused. But then he seemed to understand. He actually laughed. "You're thinking of Ka'hoka, aren't you? That's your plan? You won't be welcome there."

"There are sanctuaries there," Isabel said to Brian. "Lots of them. And most of them are deserted. We could find a safe place with a powerful leestone."

"What's Ka'hoka?" Joshua asked.

"You might know it as Cahokia," said Brian. "Cahokia Mounds."

Joshua did know that name. It was in western Illinois, near St. Louis, five miles east of the Mississippi River. There were mounds there, huge grassy ones. He didn't think anyone lived there. But he only knew where the mounds were, not what they were for. "I know where that is, but I've never been there."

"That's okay, dear." Isabel put on a smile he knew was fake. He could tell she was disappointed. "We'll just try it anyway—"

"Um, no," Brian said. "I'm not taking Tunraden anywhere near Ka'hoka."

Joshua closed his eyes. So much going on, and all of it so confusing. What was Ka'hoka, and why didn't Brian want to go there? And what did Joshua have to do with getting there? He didn't understand what kind of help he could be, or what Isabel wanted from him. He listened as the others argued briefly. Brian was saying Joshua couldn't go anywhere he'd never been, which sounded like a riddle, and then he heard Isabel say, "Joshua, have you ever been to a cloister?"

He opened his eyes. "Just the one by April's house. By the barn. You were there too." He wasn't even sure it technically was a cloister. The leestone was still there, sort of, and parts of the falkrete circle, but the wall that had surrounded it was long gone.

Isabel grimaced, apparently thinking the same thing. "That cloister has no walls. And we probably shouldn't go there right now anyway, because . . ."

Brian laughed. "Because you sent the bad guys there. Irony."

"I know where all the other cloisters are, though," Joshua said. "I saw the map."

Isabel turned and grabbed his shoulders, her eyes alight. "And have you been close to any of them? Besides the cloisters near the Warren, I mean?"

"Yes," Joshua said instantly. The map was as clear as a window in his mind. "I know a place."

"Where?"

"It doesn't matter where," Brian interrupted. "He's the Keeper of the Laithe. Let him choose."

Isabel nodded. "Go, then," she said thickly. "Find it, quickly."

Bewildered, Joshua obeyed. Holding the meridian in one hand and looking down at the globe within it, he spun the Laithe, finding North America. He centered his view on the tip of Lake Michigan, where Chicago was, and began sliding the rabbit. Canada and Mexico slid off the map to the north

60

and the south. The Atlantic and the Pacific melted away to the east and the west. The Great Lakes grew huge, blue, and shining. One by one they slid over the northeast horizon until only Lake Michigan remained. As the rabbit moved, the fat end of the lake, where Chicago was, got fatter.

Chicago, and all the suburbs, looked like the crater of an asteroid, or like something had exploded, with roads leading out in all directions like flying debris. But even so, how different the Midwest was from Madagascar. Beneath the spray of roads and rivers leading from the city, everything was made of squares, from downtown on out to the green farmland outside the city. Squares inside squares, like a screen door. So tidy, like a machine.

The journey they'd taken earlier that week was printed on Joshua's mind like a map. The walk from April's house, the car ride to Skokie Lagoons, the canoe trip down the river. He shifted the Laithe and slid the rabbit until the entire trip filled the hemisphere from top to bottom. He spotted the North Branch of the Chicago River—a thread of silver inside a finger of green that stretched into the city.

He zeroed in on a thick patch of green along the river, inside the gray patchwork of Chicago. There was a park area nestled between Interstates 90 and 94. A golf course. He aimed northeast of there, where the river made a big U-turn, like a thumb. He came in closer. A parking lot. A swimming pool.

The rabbit was three-fourths of the way around the

meridian now, headed for the top, just about the spot where things had gone wrong in Madagascar. But he tried to focus on his memories of this place, a little peninsula where the river swung from northward to southward.

Joshua was so wrapped up in his thoughts that he didn't realize his fingers were still pushing the rabbit. It was nearing the top now, and he could still see. He was doing it. The view through the Laithe was so close that he could see sticks floating in the water. The treetops were just below him. He saw a fuzzy, disgusting nest of bagworms in the branches of one.

Still he pushed the rabbit, and soon he was actually descending through the canopy of a maple tree. Pointed leaves, one after another, grew close enough to count their veins, filling the hemisphere before vanishing as he passed on by. Closer, and closer. He emerged from the green, just twenty feet off the ground now. And then he laughed—whether from happiness or just amazement, he couldn't say—as he saw a glint of silver up against the base of a tree. A canoe, bent and battered. He watched as it slid over the horizon.

Suddenly the rabbit came to a halt. It perched at the top of the meridian, just where it had started, but it had changed. It sat upright, ears alert, eyes open. They were blue. Somehow its legs had unfolded too. It looked like it was running now, which was strange because it couldn't move any farther. Joshua laughed again.

"I'm here," he said, and then shook his head. "There, I mean—I'm there." He looked up. He felt dizzy. He swayed, staggering, but Isabel steadied him.

She beamed at him. "That's good. That's very good," she said. "But we're not done yet. There's one more thing."

"What?"

"Just now you said, 'I'm there.' But you're not there, are you? You're here. And do you know the way from here to there? The shortest way?"

"As the crow flies," he said. He'd learned that from April.

"No," said Isabel. "As the rabbit runs. We can get there from here. From right here. Right now. You just have to open the way."

As the rabbit runs. The words tickled across Joshua's heart, up into his brain.

"I don't understand."

Isabel reached out for the Laithe. Joshua yanked it away. "No," he said, surprised by the strength in his own voice. "Tell me."

She nodded. "Tear the meridian loose. Tear through space and time."

And to his great surprise, even though he wasn't totally sure what those words even meant, Joshua didn't hesitate. He grabbed the meridian with one hand, cradling the globe in the other, and he pulled. Hard.

The meridian came loose from the globe as easily as a hat from a head. The globe instantly lit up, turning into a yellow sphere of light like the sun. Only this sun was cool to the touch. Joshua squinted, blinded.

"Whoa!" cried Brian.

Joshua looked down at the meridian in his other hand. There was something strange about the metal ring now. He held it up and examined it closer. And when he looked through the ring by the light of the tiny, floating sun, he saw a tumble of colors and unrecognizable shapes, a rush of movement, like it was speeding through a tunnel.

Somehow—though no one told him to—Joshua knew he should let the meridian go. He knew this was the way. He reached out and . . . placed the meridian into the air. That's what it felt like, placing it. When he let go, the ring hung there, motionless in the air like a little round mirror on a wall, with the rabbit perched at the very top and the hypnotizing tunnel of shapes still zooming within.

"Amazing," said Brian. "But is it supposed to look like that? And it's noisy, too."

Joshua frowned. He didn't hear anything.

Isabel waved Brian off impatiently. "Spin it, Joshua."

Joshua didn't move. The tunnel of shapes danced.

"Spin the ring," Isabel said. "Let the rabbit run now."

Joshua gripped the edge of the meridian and yanked it. It was a clumsy, bad spin, but the golden rabbit at the top of the hanging ring began to run in place. The meridian rotated beneath it, and as it rotated, the ring began to grow. From six inches wide, it grew to a foot. The flickering images inside seemed to slow down just a tiny bit.

But no sooner had the meridian started growing than it

stopped. The rabbit rocked to a halt atop it.

"Again," said Isabel. "Faster."

"He shouldn't have to do it this way," Brian mumbled.

"How should I do it, then?" said Joshua. But Brian only shook his head.

"Spin it again," Isabel said.

Again Joshua grabbed the meridian and spun it. The rabbit ran. The circle rotated and grew beneath it, and the tumbling tunnel of movement inside the circle slowed a little bit more. The ring grew to three feet wide, and the rabbit stopped running again. Joshua kept spinning. The circle grew wider and wider. The rabbit ran, rising into the air as the circle grew. The images inside the circle got slower and slower. Joshua started to catch glimpses of shapes that had names—a tree, a car, buildings. Or so he thought.

At last he gave the meridian the hardest spin he could. At the very top, the rabbit's golden legs were a blur. The ring grew wide open, eight feet wide at least, and the view inside started to drift into focus. The spinning meridian came to a halt with a deep thump that made Joshua's chest vibrate. Atop it, the rabbit was frozen, seated now, but ears still alert. It seemed to stare at Joshua with its shining blue eyes.

And through the wide-open ring . . .

The forest. The river. Roots and dirt.

The image flickered a bit, but it was definitely there.

"I can't believe I'm saying this," Brian said, staring, "but . . . I can't believe it."

Still holding the shining Laithe in his left hand, Joshua reached out with his right. He reached through the meridian. For some reason, he thought it might feel like reaching into water, but instead it felt like very faint static shocks, a ring of prickling surprise around his flesh, and on the other side, the air was wet and warm with summer, so unlike the cool air of the Warren. His hand was there. There, and not here.

Brian stepped up to the gateway, staring at the forest and the river. He stuck a hand through, too, and laughed happily. "Warm," he said dreamily. "Summer."

Joshua felt like he was in a dream. Or maybe like he was finally awake from a dream that had lasted his entire life until now. Maybe this was real, the most real thing he'd ever done. "But what did I do?" he whispered.

"You opened a door," said Isabel. "A portal. That's what the Laithe does."

Joshua stared. He stuck his hand through the portal again. He wiggled his fingers. What did it look like from the other side? Just his hand, hanging in midair?

"Let's go," said Isabel. "Joshua, you'll need to come last. The portal is only open on one side—whichever side the Laithe is on." She nodded at the golden sphere in Joshua's hand and then touched Brian on the shoulder. "Keeper?"

"Right." Brian tore himself away from the flickering portal. He went to Tunraden, cracking his knuckles. And then he dipped his hands right into the surface of the big, oval stone.

As he stuck his hands through the engraved circles, the

circles lit up, glowing as golden as the Laithe itself. With his hands buried to the wrists in the stone, Brian lifted Tunraden off the pedestal easily.

"You're strong," Joshua said.

"Gee, thanks," said Brian, raising his eyebrows at his own pale, scrawny arms. "But don't be fooled. Tunraden weighs over a hundred pounds. When I ask her to, she mostly lifts herself; I only steer."

"You look like a prisoner," Isabel remarked. And he did. He was handcuffed by the Loomdaughter, his hands still buried deep inside the stone.

"People have been saying that a lot lately," Brian said. He glanced at the dark forest through the hanging portal. "Maybe it's time for a change."

Isabel tipped her head way back suddenly, like she was trying to look through the roof of the chamber into the Great Burrow above. She frowned and said, "We need to hurry. Brian, you go first. I'll be right behind."

Brian took a deep breath. "I feel like I might regret this, but hey—at least it won't be boring, right?" And then he stepped into the portal.

But even though his hand had gone through easily, Brian seemed to be having trouble getting Tunraden through. The doorway sort of bent as Tunraden pushed against it, and for a second Joshua thought it wouldn't work, but then Brian pushed harder, and the portal slowly gave, and he was through. Joshua watched as Brian immediately set Tunraden down at his feet and freed his hands. Brian looked around the riverbank, and up into the trees, leaning way back, and thrust his fists into the air. No sound came through the portal, but Joshua got the feeling he was laughing. Or cheering.

Isabel wrapped her hands around Miradel, and without a word to Joshua, stepped through the portal after Brian.

Joshua was alone. Isabel and Brian turned, looking back at the portal, but he could tell by their eyes that they weren't seeing through it. They couldn't see him. They couldn't even come back without him. Isabel had said so, but even if she hadn't said it, Joshua knew it now.

For a second—just a few long seconds—he thought he might leave them there. He thought he might figure out how to close the portal, then take the Laithe someplace he could be alone with it. The Laithe was his. His to learn and his to use. He looked down at the glowing sphere, and up at the blue-eyed rabbit. They seemed to speak to him, to beg him to take them away. But where would he go?

Isabel stepped up to the portal. She gestured impatiently. She wanted him to hurry. Brian crouched down in front of Tunraden, looking worried.

And of course, Joshua couldn't leave them. That would be mean. Selfish. It was—and it startled him to think it—the sort of thing Isabel might do.

With that thought in mind, Joshua stepped through the portal, carrying the Laithe. Electricity crackled very softly across his skin as he passed, but he mostly felt nothing. No resistance. He emerged into the dark woods. It was hot. Bug sounds and the soft murmur of the river filled the air. He turned back to the portal. The meridian still hung there, the blue-eyed rabbit still sitting patiently up top. The silver canoe lay against a tree just beyond, but now, through the portal, he could see back into the Warren.

"*There* it is," said Brian, also looking.

"What did you see before I came through?" Joshua asked.

"Nothing. The ring was here, but it was empty."

"I told you," Isabel said. "The portal is a one-way door. It's only open on whichever side the Keeper of the Laithe stands. We can see in because you're here now, but no one can see through to us."

Joshua thought Isabel seemed rather satisfied with herself.

And then through the portal, movement. Two figures came running into Tunraden's chamber. Gabriel. Mr. Meister. The old man, obviously surprised, hurried over to the portal. He spoke words Joshua couldn't hear.

"Close it," Isabel said darkly.

"But I don't know how," said Joshua, his heart pounding.

"You do. The same way you opened it."

Through the portal, Mr. Meister leaned in close, his left eye huge and darting.

"I thought you said he couldn't see us!" Joshua said, backing away.

"He can't," said Brian, though his voice didn't sound so

sure. "But at least we know they got back safe."

"Spin it shut," Isabel said. "Now."

Joshua grabbed the meridian and spun it hard, in the opposite direction he had before. The rabbit flipped directions with a soft *snik!* and began to run back the way it came. The portal shrank. This time, though, the view through the ring stayed clear for a moment. Mr. Meister jumped back, startled by the shrinking ring. Then he gazed into the portal again. He looked sad, Joshua thought. More than sad. He looked betrayed.

The rabbit stopped. Joshua spun the meridian again, not looking into Mr. Meister's eyes even though he knew the Warden couldn't see him. And then Mr. Meister winked out. The view into the Warren was replaced by the tumbling tunnel of shapes. Joshua blinked back tears—sad tears or angry, he didn't know—and willed the rabbit to keep running. Faster and faster. The meridian grew smaller and smaller. The tumbling shapes accelerated. At last, with another chest-hammering thud, the rabbit reached the end of its run. It folded itself to sleep atop the now-tiny portal. The meridian was back to its normal size.

Joshua grabbed the meridian from the air. Almost without thinking, he brought the ring and the globe together. They returned to each other naturally, without him even having to try. As the little sphere settled into its place inside the meridian, the globe went dark for just a second and then slowly relit, shades of brown and blue and green and white, the familiar continents and oceans of the earth returning beneath a living patchwork of clouds.

"Very good," said Isabel, letting out a long breath. "Very good, Keeper."

But Joshua didn't need Isabel to tell him that. It *was* good . . . very good. He gazed down at the Laithe. Even with all the worries he had, even with the guilt he felt about closing the portal on Mr. Meister, this felt right. As right as anything he'd ever done. He wasn't even sure he cared what Isabel wanted, or what came next. His hands itched to make another portal.

CHAPTER FIVE

The Missing

Horace, Chloe, and Neptune stood on the shores of Vithra's Eye, deep beneath the city. The dark waters of the lake stretched out before them; on the far side of the cavern lay the Great Burrow. A brick pathway crossed the lake, a seemingly easy route that the three Keepers could not possibly hope to take. The heart of the Nevren was there, too strong for Tan'ji to pass through directly. But it occurred to Horace that if Isabel had indeed found her way into the Warren, she could have walked right across the bridge without difficulty.

He told himself she hadn't. She could never find the way.

Neptune stared across the water, shaking her wounded hand. "This has been a terrible night," she said. "Or is it nights? It's hard to tell after seventeen jumps, of course." She thought for a bit and then looked sheepishly at them both. "I think I remember saying things I shouldn't have. Back at the fifth cloister, before I fell asleep."

The Mothergates. In his worry and through his own fracturing journey back home, Horace himself had almost forgotten, but now the pit of dread grew strong. "We'll talk about it later," he told Neptune.

"We won't, though. *I* won't." Neptune shook her hand again. Her crooked pinky wobbled grotesquely. "Just . . . do me a favor. Don't tell Mr. Meister I said that stuff."

"Deal," Chloe said immediately. "I happen to specialize in not telling Mr. Meister things." She looked sturdy and impatient, probably the most immune of them all to the effects of falkrete travel. Chloe never seemed to doubt who she was. And she hadn't doubted Horace either, when he'd told her his suspicions about Isabel. About her mother. She'd been the first to lay her Tan'ji against the proper falkrete stone and begin the swift journey back to the Warren. And now they were here.

"Thank you," Neptune said, clearly grateful. Horace nodded.

"If you want to thank me," Chloe said, "hold still for a second." And she reached out and grabbed Neptune's mangled hand.

Neptune's wide eyes grew wider. "Uh . . . what are you doing?"

"I can't look at that finger anymore. I'm going to fix it."

"Are you—"

"On three," Chloe said, gently taking hold of the twisted pinky. "One . . ." And then she yanked the pinky hard, smoothly out and up.

"Gahhhh!" Neptune shrieked, snatching her hand away, her face white with pain. She flinched so hard she lifted off the ground a few inches and stayed there, tapping into her Tan'ji without seeming to realize it. She drifted backward through the air like a punched balloon. "Oh my—" She looked down at her hand as she floated, flexing it. To Horace's surprise, her pinky looked normal again. "Jiminy *joe* pants, you're bad at counting," Neptune said, frowning at Chloe. She dropped lightly to the ground, still flexing her hand.

"Better?" Chloe asked.

"Yes, but . . . ow." Neptune shook her hand out and gently probed at her finger. "Where did you learn to do that?"

Chloe shrugged. "School of life."

Suddenly a dark shape flew at them out of the shadows over the lake. At first Horace thought it was one of the peculiar little owls that patrolled Vithra's Eye, but this was much larger. The black shape swept in on noisy wings and landed with a flourish beside them, big as a cat.

"Arthur!" Horace said. A surprising rush of relief flooded him. If Arthur was here, that meant April was safe.

The raven looked up at him, cocking his head. He snapped his thick black beak, his eyes shining with intelligence. Horace had to remind himself that April's companion was only a bird—a smart bird, yes, but still just a bird.

"I guess they beat us here after all," Chloe said, squinting uselessly across the darkness over the lake.

Horace crouched down in front of Arthur. "What's up?" he asked him. "Everything okay?"

"*Watsup?*" the raven croaked. The raven couldn't really understand human language, of course, but he did sometimes imitate spoken words, like a parrot. "*Watsup?*" he said again, and then walked backward a few steps, watching Horace warily. He let out a high, rattling scream that made them all jump. He took furiously to the air and flew back over the water toward the Great Burrow.

"Whoa," said Chloe. "What was that all about?"

"Maybe you smell like brimstone," Neptune told Horace, referring to the foul, sulfurous stench of the Riven. "Birds don't like that."

"Maybe," Horace said.

In silence, Chloe led them across Vithra's Eye, dipping her scarlet jithandra into the water and letting the surface of the lake solidify into a path before them. The crystal, the calling card of the Wardens and the only way for a Keeper to cross these waters, shone like a glowing ruby ship cutting through a dark sea. They skirted the edge of the lake, where the terrible void of the Nevren was at its weakest, but still the pain of being severed from the Fel'Daera bit at Horace like frostbite, like a little death. In the nothingness of the Nevren, he forgot his instrument, forgot his friends, forgot even himself.

At last they emerged on the other side, a blessed relief.

The constant, comforting presence of the Fel'Daera surged back through Horace in a rush, and he drank from it deeply, his senses returning. Horace hated the Nevren, and struggled with it more than most, but it was a necessary trial. The same severing void that caused them so much pain helped protect the Warren from the Riven. The Riven bonded so tightly with their own instruments that they could not survive the Nevren. For human Keepers like Horace and his friends, meanwhile, the Nevren was still dangerous, but manageable. Barely.

His head clearing, Horace saw April on the far shore, in her clunky boots and sturdy dress. Arthur clung to her shoulder like a small, brooding bodyguard. As they stepped onto dry land, Horace could see something was wrong. April's prettily crooked face was tight with worry.

"You're here," she said. "You're safe."

"We're safe," Horace said. "You okay? Your brother?"

"I'm fine," she said. "My family's safe, thanks to you guys. We dropped them off at a friend's house. I'm not sure about my dog, but . . ." She trailed off, her mouth twisting. She glanced back into the Great Burrow. At her temple, Horace caught a faint golden glimpse of the Ravenvine, her Tan'ji. It occurred to him that with it, April might have seen them on the far shore of the lake, watching them through Arthur's keen eyes—or perhaps even listening to them through the sensitive ears of one of the lake's elusive owls. With her ability to eavesdrop on the thoughts and senses of animals, April might have heard them talking, might've even caught the bit about the Mothergates.

But Horace knew that was not what was troubling April now. And not her dog, either. He glanced past her. Down in the Great Burrow, Mrs. Hapsteade was talking intently to Mr. Meister and Gabriel beside her doba. Brian was nowhere to be seen. Or Joshua, for that matter. Horace's heart began to pound. Mr. Meister looked up at them, running the fingers of both hands through his bushy white hair.

"She was here, wasn't she?" Chloe said to April. "Isabel?"

April looked at Chloe with a kind of penetrating uncertainty, as if she couldn't bring herself to confirm it. Horace's stomach rolled over. He'd been right after all.

They ran down the great passage, Neptune leaping far ahead with long, bounding strides. She went straight to Gabriel's side and grasped the blind teen's face with both hands, murmuring soft questions to him. Gabriel clutched his Tan'ji, the long gray Staff of Obro, like a weapon.

"Where is she?" Chloe demanded, stalking up to Mr. Meister.

"Where's Brian?" said Horace, nearly on top of her.

The old man rounded on them and straightened his many-pocketed red vest. Behind his thick glasses, his gray eyes were huge and keen as ever. He was the Chief Taxonomer, leader of the Wardens here in the Chicago, as full of secrets as he was of answers. Horace feared the answers he might have for them now.

"Brian has been taken," said Mr. Meister simply. "Isabel

is gone, and she took Brian and Tunraden with her. Joshua too."

April gasped, and Chloe growled. Horace's head spun. Brian had told him Tunraden couldn't be taken out of the Warren. "But how?" he managed to ask.

"And how did she even get in?" Neptune asked, breathless.

Mrs. Hapsteade glanced at Mr. Meister. He gave her an almost imperceptible nod. She reached into the front pocket of her prim black dress, pulling out three small wooden crescents and a complicated black key.

Chloe blanched. "My key. My elevator key."

"But . . . the spitestone," Horace said to Mr. Meister. "You told me she'd never be able to find her way into the Warren."

"Plainly I was wrong. She devised a method to find her way through the spitestone's cloud." He reached into Mrs. Hapsteade's hand and arranged the three crescents so that they touched end to end, making a solid ring. A wooden ring.

"That's hers," Chloe snarled. "Is it a Tanu?"

"Not properly, no. I have never seen anything like it. As best I can tell, Isabel spun a loop of energy into the ring that was so subtle I failed to notice it. It was buried deep. Dormant. As I'm sure you are aware by now, this is a particular talent of hers. When the ring was brought near the spitestone, it came to life. It created a tiny obversion—a reversal—in the spitestone's power. Within a symphony intended to conceal the Warren, a single note instead *revealed* it. And because that note was attuned to

Isabel, she heard it clearly." He shook his head admiringly at the broken ring. "It was brilliant; I cannot deny it."

"I should have been more watchful," Mrs. Hapsteade said. "I had the wicker harp with me, and I let Isabel get right to my front door. Close enough for her to sense the harp—close enough to use it. She severed me before I even knew she was there. She tangled me."

"Severing sucks," said Neptune. "Isabel's severings *super* suck." Apparently, Isabel had a way of severing Keepers and then tying off the flows, so that the bond trickled back to life very slowly. Neptune, who had been severed by Isabel two nights before, said it was like trying to swim out of a bowl of spaghetti.

"Isabel's talents are obvious," Mr. Meister said. "Her objectives are less so. Come with me." And then, without another word, he turned and began marching deeper into the Great Burrow, clearly expecting the others to follow.

Horace walked in silence, his worry curdling inside him, fretting about Brian. Isabel's objective, of course, was to become a Keeper. How far would she go to try to make that happen? She'd already done the unthinkable, the supposedly impossible. He tried to stay logical. After several seconds, he said aloud, "If Isabel thinks Brian can help her, she wouldn't hurt him."

"Right," Chloe muttered scornfully. "And if she thinks he'll *never* help her, what will she do then? Just say 'Thanks anyway,' and pat him on the head?" When no one answered, she said, "I'm sorry, you guys. I'm sorry about all this."

April laid a hand on Chloe's magnificently scarred arm. "I don't believe in accepting apologies from people who've done nothing wrong."

"I want to know who brought the ring into the Warren in the first place," Neptune said.

"Joshua," Mrs. Hapsteade replied. "But I do not think he knew what it was."

"That's generous," said Chloe. "He's been traveling with Isabel, you know."

"So was I," April pointed out. "Joshua's just a little boy. I don't believe he'd do anything to hurt us. Not on purpose."

"I don't either," Mrs. Hapsteade said. "He came into my doba to confess about the ring, I think. But he was too late. He left with Isabel. She made him promises he couldn't resist."

Mr. Meister flourished his hand dramatically. "Promises, yes," he said. "Promises that have now been kept."

Gabriel, silent so far, thumped the tip of his staff into the ground as he walked. Once, twice, three times. His face was a storm.

Seeming not to notice, Mr. Meister added, "Oh, and Joshua is *not* just a little boy."

"Then what is he?" Chloe asked.

"He is one of us."

Mrs. Hapsteade gave him a sharp look. "Henry," she said, as if cautioning him.

"You mean he's a Keeper?" Horace asked.

"No," said Gabriel, even as Mr. Meister said, "Yes."

They had reached the top of the Perilous Stairs. The old

man paused here, his wispy white hair blowing in the breeze. His brow seemed to wrestle with itself, and then he said, "Joshua is the Keeper of the Laithe of Teneves."

Mrs. Hapsteade stepped forward. "Henrik!" she scolded, her voice like the swipe of a knife. Gabriel grimaced, grasping the Staff of Obro, looking as angry as Horace had ever seen him.

The Laithe of Teneves—the tiny living globe. Made by the same hands that had made the Fel'Daera. Horace gripped the box at his side.

"I saw it myself, Dorothy," Mr. Meister said. "Do you still doubt it? Even Isabel knew it to be true."

"She knew no such thing."

"How can you say that, after what has transpired here tonight?"

"That's not the point. There are customs to be followed. Rules to be obeyed."

"Yes, and I was honoring them long before you even went through the Find. But tonight—"

Bewildered, Horace held up his hands. "Wait, wait. Can someone please explain?"

Gabriel said, "Joshua now possesses the Laithe of Teneves. But if so, we believe it did not choose him. Neither did he choose it himself. Instead, the choice was made by another."

"By Isabel."

"Yes."

"And that's bad?"

"One does not meddle with the Find," Gabriel said stiffly. He looked furiously toward Mr. Meister, his ghostly blue eyes colder than usual. "And in the absence of a proper Find, one does not simply . . . *declare* that a candidate has become a Keeper."

Chloe made a small noise of surprise, and Horace didn't blame her. He had never before heard Gabriel utter a word of disagreement toward Mr. Meister.

If Mr. Meister was taken aback, he didn't show it. "And yet one might be forgiven for making such a declaration, after the fact," he told Gabriel calmly.

"There is no fact without the Find."

"The Laithe left here tonight in Joshua's hands," Mr. Meister said, fussing absently with his Möbius-strip ring. "It comes as no surprise. I knew he was the Keeper of the Laithe the moment I laid eyes on him."

"Forgive me," said Gabriel tersely, "but that is not for you to say."

"And yet I have said it." The finality in Mr. Meister's voice was unmistakable. He started down the steps, then paused and turned to Gabriel one last time. "One cannot turn a truth into a lie simply by refusing to hear it, Keeper. You of all people should know that." With that, he continued down the stairs, leaving the rest to follow in uncomfortable silence, wretched and surly. Neptune floated down lightly. Despite his blindness, Gabriel descended with his usual grace, aided by a faint whisper of the Humour of Obro that seeped invisibly from the tip of his great gray staff, allowing him to sense the hazardous steps.

Horace, Chloe, and April brought up the rear as Arthur took flight and coasted overhead.

"That was tense," Chloe muttered blackly.

"Like watching parents fight," agreed Horace.

April frowned and said, "I don't know how you guys usually do things, but as the new kid, I can tell you I'm a little freaked out that people are arguing about etiquette—whether the fork ought to go on the left or the right—when Brian is missing."

Gabriel cocked his head back at them sharply. "It is not merely a matter of etiquette," he said gruffly. "A Keeper who is forced through the Find is vulnerable."

"And dangerous," Neptune said, drawing a frown from Gabriel.

"Vulnerable to what?" Chloe asked.

"Outside influences," said Gabriel. "Promises of more power. Lostlings struggle to fully settle into their roles as Keepers. They struggle to truly embrace the completeness that is Tan'ji—the surrender, the belonging. And because they struggle, they are more likely to seek comfort in dark places."

"The Riven, you mean," said Horace. Immediately his thoughts went to Ingrid, the former Warden who had turned against them and joined forces with Dr. Jericho. Chloe said aloud what Horace was only thinking. "Is that what happened to Ingrid? Was she a Lostling?"

From several yards ahead, Mr. Meister spoke, as if he'd been listening all along. "Idle chatter feeds busy rumors. Let us focus on the task in front of us."

At last they reached the bottom of the stairs. They passed by the mysterious bridge that spanned the Maw, and entered the tunnel to Brian's workshop. Ordinarily the oublimort should have been here—a dark slab of woven shadow that was particularly tricky to pass through—but now it was simply gone. Horace knew Isabel must have removed it, a frightening thought.

At their feet, Arthur strutted past and suddenly took flight, his great wings hissing audibly in the air. He flew down the passageway ahead, his raucous cries echoing painfully. One by one, they followed the bird down the hallway.

They entered the workshop. The place was silent. Mr. Meister pointed at a curio cabinet across the room.

"The Laithe was here in this cabinet," he said. "I removed it from my office before bringing Joshua into the Warren, so that we could prepare for a proper Find when the time was right. But now it is gone."

A stool beside one of the workbenches had been tipped over. A box of rivets had been dumped onto the floor, along with a couple of unfamiliar tools. An object was lying there, made of leather, with thin, trailing straps. Arthur was plucking at one of them playfully.

"Something Brian was working on when Isabel arrived, I believe," Mr. Meister explained.

April crouched down and picked up the leather object, examining it. She slapped a hand over her mouth and let out a soft, sorrowful huff of surprise.

"What is it?" said Chloe.

"It's . . . it's for me." April stood and placed the leather object on her shoulder. She fumbled with the straps for a second, but then secured it in place. "For Arthur," she said.

It was a perch for the bird. To protect April from his sharp talons. Horace could see that Brian had even been engraving a vine around the edges, complete with a tiny flower just like the one that hung from the Ravenvine right in front of April's ear. But the flower was only half finished.

April looked to Mr. Meister, her sad hazel eyes seeming to catch fire. "Tell us where they went."

Silently, the old man led them deeper into the workshop, toward the back where a small, secluded chamber lay. This was where Brian kept his Tan'ji, where he used Tunraden to sculpt the Medium when creating and repairing Tanu. As they entered the little chamber, Horace sucked in his breath. Whatever had felt sacred here before had now faded, the space bigger and hollow and robbed of its weight. The usual electric bite in the air was barely noticeable. Tunraden was gone. But how?

Mr. Meister stepped up close to the far wall and stood studying it, his hands behind his back. He bent this way and that, craning his neck. Obviously, there was something there the others couldn't see. The left lens of Mr. Meister's glasses was an oraculum, a Tan'ji that allowed the old man to see the invisible Medium, to perceive things about instruments and their Keepers that others could not. After several moments, Mr. Meister said, "Tell me, Horace, have you ever contemplated the Laithe of Teneves?"

"Me?" said Horace, startled. "I guess so. A little."

Chloe stepped in front of Horace, as if protecting him. "What's Horace got to do with it?"

"I imagine he must be curious," said Mr. Meister, still looking up and around himself. "The Laithe was made by the same hand that made the Fel'Daera, after all. It was offered to him on the day of his own Find. And now it belongs to another, whose affinities are not unlike Horace's own."

Horace and Chloe exchanged a glance. Her fierce face was wrinkled with concern. "I've been trying not to think about it," Horace told Mr. Meister truthfully. "But I know that you guys had Joshua use the Vora. And I saw what he wrote—the ink was blue. The same as mine." The Vora, Mrs. Hapsteade's Tan'ji, was used on new recruits. Before they went through the Find, potential Keepers were invited to write with the great white quill, and the color of ink they produced revealed their talents and affinities, giving a clue as to what their Tan'ji might be.

Mr. Meister turned to face them. "His ink was *similar* to yours," he stressed, tapping his glasses. "Similar, but not the same. Just as the Laithe of Teneves and the Fel'Daera are similar, but not the same."

"But the Laithe is a globe. A map."

"Yes. The Laithe is the most astonishing map that has ever been made. A living globe, accurate down to the last tree, the last cloud, the last house. It is a marvel only Sil'falo Teneves could have devised—just like the Fel'Daera. Can you name for me another similarity between the globe and the box?"

Gabriel leaned over his staff. He didn't look particularly happy, but he seemed to be listening intently. Watching him, it occurred to Horace that Gabriel was only now hearing what the Laithe's powers were. Gabriel was so competent and so self-assured, so steadily formal about the ways of the Wardens and the responsibilities of being Tan'ji, but in this moment, he was just as lost as Horace was. And maybe Gabriel's naked curiosity in this moment was another reminder of how deep the rabbit hole ran, of how much there still was to learn. Horace would learn. He was learning right now.

Could the Laithe have been his? After all, he'd almost reached for it that day in the House of Answers, when all of this began. But instead he had become the Keeper of the Fel'Daera. And it was strange, because the Fel'Daera cut through time, but he didn't see what time had to do with the Laithe of Teneves. Why had it been offered to him? Besides the fact that both instruments had been created by the same maker, Sil'falo Teneves, how were the two instruments related? He churned through it logically, trying to find a way that the Fel'Daera was like the Laithe.

"I guess . . . the Fel'Daera is a map too," Horace said slowly. "A map to the future."

Mr. Meister straightened and tugged at his vest. "Excellent. But the Fel'Daera is not just a map. It has another power."

"Yes. I can send stuff through the Fel'Daera. So it's like a doorway."

The old man nodded hungrily, his face full of that familiar, eager light, urging Horace forward. "And?"

"And . . . and . . ." Just like that, it all fell into place. Easily, so easily. Horace felt not a trickle of surprise, not a sliver of confusion. Time and space, space and time. One was always part of the other. "The Laithe is a doorway too," he breathed.

Mr. Meister clapped his hands together in satisfaction. "When one travels through space, he must also travel through time, yes? And when he travels through time, he must travel through space. Like the Fel'Daera, the Laithe is a doorway. Or, to put it properly—a portal."

"That's how they escaped," Horace went on. "That's how Isabel got Brian and Tunraden out of the Warren—with Joshua's help."

"Yes. They opened a portal here in this very room, and escaped."

Gabriel grumbled ruefully.

"But where did she take him?" Chloe insisted. "Where does the portal lead?"

Mr. Meister clasped Horace firmly by the shoulders, his face lit with an almost holy wonder. His left eye loomed, as keen as a knife and as wild as a flame.

"That is what Horace is about to tell us," he said.

CHAPTER SIX

Door upon Door

"WITH ISABEL'S HELP, NO DOUBT, JOSHUA OPENED THE PORTAL," Mr. Meister said, gesturing. "Just here. They departed through it, taking Brian and Tunraden with them. I saw the portal closing from this side, yet even I cannot tell you where they went."

"But if the Laithe is a globe," said April, "doesn't that mean they could be anywhere in the world?"

"In theory, yes," said Mr. Meister. "But I doubt they went far. Even with Isabel's guidance, Joshua is still a neophyte. He would find it easiest, I think, to open a portal into a location he has been to before. And the greater the distance, the more difficult the gateway."

"So, what does that have to do with me?" Horace asked.

Mr. Meister eyed the Fel'Daera thoughtfully, looking at the silver sun. "The breach is very narrow at the moment, yes, Keeper?"

"Four minutes and thirty-four seconds," Horace said automatically.

"Narrow enough. Will you open the box, please? Look toward this wall and tell us what you see."

Chloe leaned in close to Horace, whispering. "Something about that wall going to change in the next four minutes?"

"If Horace will indulge me," Mr. Meister said with a bow.

Horace pulled the box from its pouch, bemused but preparing himself. Before opening the Fel'Daera—even to look at a blank wall—he had to orient himself and his companions in space and time. In order to see truly, he had to briefly consider all the recent paths that had led to the current moment, because the very act of opening the box to see the future *changed* that same future. It was a lesson Horace had learned the hard way, again and again. But by now, his preparations were smooth and automatic. He loosely plotted all the necessary trajectories as best he could—actions, positions, intentions—gathering them in his mind like strands of twine. When he felt grounded, he held the box in front of him and opened the lid.

Through the rippling blue glass, as expected—*nothing; the blank wall, unchanged from the present.*

"I see a wall," he reported dryly.

Mr. Meister stepped toward the wall, cocking his head and once more peering through the oraculum at what looked like nothing. He made a karate-chopping motion through a slab of air a few feet ahead of Horace. "Come closer, Keeper. Right here."

Still holding the box aloft, Horace moved forward. Nothing but wall. Whatever the old man was hoping for didn't seem to be happening.

And then as Horace pulled even with the old man, as the blue glass entered the invisible plane where Mr. Meister was waving his hand, a blast of static flickered inside the box—*a frenzy of wild movement, a rush of jumbled jagged shapes.*

It vanished as quickly as it had come. Horace blinked. The box had never done anything like that before.

Mr. Meister leaned in even closer, his looming left eye shifting back and forth between Horace's face and the empty air. "Ah, you've seen something," he said excitedly. "Back up, just a tiny bit. Hold the box quite still."

Horace stepped back cautiously, holding the box steady. And abruptly, there it was again: *a rush of movement, shapes flying at him, as if the box were moving at a tremendous speed.* He held the box rigidly, staring. None of the shapes were recognizable in any way, not at all real, just a hurtling tangle of lines and curves and planes. Still the sensation of immense speed was so convincing that he found himself leaning away. He leaned too far, and the vision vanished. He snapped the box closed and turned to Mr. Meister.

"Well?" the old man asked. "Have you anything to report?"

Horace's mind raced. "It's the portal, isn't it? The whatever—the residue of the gateway Joshua opened with the Laithe."

"Just so," Mr. Meister said proudly. "And what did you see?"

"Nothing. Just static. Shapes, flying at me."

"No more than that?"

"No. But why can I—"

"Shorten the breach, if you will. Make it as narrow as you can. Try again."

Horace glanced back at the others. Gabriel and Mrs. Hapsteade looked like statues, grim and motionless, Mrs. Hapsteade's head bowed as if in prayer. April's fists were at her mouth. She seemed not to notice that Arthur, perched on her leather-clad shoulder, was plucking at her hair. Chloe gazed back at Horace steadily.

"Do it," she said.

Mystified and exhilarated, Horace readied himself to try again, focusing on the silver sun emblazoned on the front of the box. He had only recently learned that this sun was a sort of valve, that he could adjust the breach by concentrating on it and narrowing or widening the flow of the Medium. The sun's twenty-four rays, one for each hour, meant that the farthest he could see into the future was a single day. When the breach was open that far, the entire sun shone silver. Right now, with the breach at less than five minutes, only the tiniest slice of the topmost ray glimmered. The rest of the rays were black.

Horace felt for the breach with his mind. He found it easily, felt the rush of energy blasting through the tiny gap. With effort, he closed the breach even further. *Three minutes. One.* The Medium seemed to howl as it poured through the shrinking aperture. The shining sliver on the topmost ray of the sun dwindled to a speck. Horace squeezed until he got where he wanted to be.

He pinned the breach in place—a kind of mental hammer blow—and released it. He blew out a breath. "Ten seconds," he said. Would it be enough? He didn't understand what was happening, why he should be able to see the leftovers of Joshua's portal. And he certainly didn't understand why shortening the breach might make a difference.

"Remarkable," said Mr. Meister. "Let us try again."

Horace opened the box, merging the glass once more with the ghost of Joshua's portal, a ghost only Mr. Meister's oraculum could recognize—or rather, the oraculum *and* the Fel'Daera, it seemed. What was this residue, exactly? What was the Fel'Daera showing him? He got the alignment right, and once more through the box—*a rushing jungle of careening shapes, swift and mad.* It seemed slightly slower now, and once or twice he imagined he recognized something—*a flicker of a tree-shape, a cluster of vertical lines so smooth they had to be man-made.*

"Still nothing," he said. "I can almost see something, but . . . I can't."

Mr. Meister spun away, clearly frustrated.

"It cannot be done," said Gabriel. "I wonder if it should even be attempted."

For some reason, this angered Horace. He'd always respected Gabriel, and thought of him as perhaps the most sensible and reliable of the Wardens. But now he closed the box and rounded on the older boy. "I don't know what's happening," he said, "or why I saw what I just saw, but I know Brian is out there. If the box can help find him, then I'll attempt whatever I like."

Gabriel stood silent for a moment, then nodded.

"I need someone to explain, though," said Horace. "Why can I see the residue of the portal? Is it in the future?"

"No," said Mr. Meister, and then corrected himself. "Yes, but no more than it exists in the present. The effects of the portal are lingering, like smoke from a fire. And because Joshua is a neophyte—because he made a messy fire—the smoke will linger for much longer than it should. Let us be thankful."

He pointed at the Fel'Daera. "As for why you can see anything at all, remember: the Fel'Daera and the Laithe have similar functions. Both were made by the same hand. Both slice through space and time, opening doorways where none could otherwise exist. And when those doorways intersect, new paths are revealed." He shrugged, then smiled ruefully. "No doubt Falo could explain it better than I can. She is the Maker, after all. Nonetheless, I understand the rudiments. With the proper alignment—and the proper mindset—the Keeper of the Fel'Daera could, in theory, see where the portal leads."

"The proper mindset," Horace repeated dryly. He was pretty sure that Mr. Meister was telling him that he had failed—that if he were a better Keeper, a stronger Keeper, he could use the box to figure out where Brian had been taken.

"It is only a theory," Mr. Meister said, shrugging again.

Chloe glowered at the old man, defending Horace. "Yeah, well, my theory is you ought to be able to figure out where they went yourself. You're the one who can see the threads."

"Indeed I am, but I—" Cutting himself off, Mr. Meister lifted his head, abruptly lost in thought. His mouth opened and closed, and his eyes roamed keenly back and forth.

Mrs. Hapsteade, silent so far, stepped forward. "Yes," she said softly.

Mr. Meister met her gaze. "Horace is not properly attuned. But perhaps the signal can be focused."

"It may be the only way."

Horace was at a loss, but Gabriel seemed to get it. He thumped his staff against the floor and said, "Would this be any better than what Isabel has done with Joshua?"

Mrs. Hapsteade sighed. "Honestly, Gabriel, consider our options."

"I'm sorry," said Chloe, raising her hand. "Would *what* be any better?"

April clutched at Chloe's arm. "Oh my god, thank you. I thought I was the only one who was lost."

"No, I'm lost too," said Horace.

"We need help," explained Mr. Meister. "Horace needs help. I can see the threads left by the Laithe, yes, but I cannot follow them to their final destination, any more than I can follow the threads of the Fel'Daera into the future. No one can.

But it might be possible to manipulate the threads so that *you*, Horace, might see more clearly. It might be possible to . . . *tune* those threads, if you like."

Tune. Suddenly Horace understood. "My mom?" he said lamely.

"Oh holy crap," said Chloe.

Mr. Meister nodded. "Jessica is a talented Tuner in her own right. She may be able to help us, if we can convince her to return, after all these years."

Horace hardly knew what to say. "Bring my mother here, you mean. Into the Warren."

"Yes."

"Tonight. Right now."

"Indeed."

Horace glanced at Chloe. Her eyes were wide and bright and her mouth hung open in a hovering, delighted O. Chloe adored Horace's mom—and Horace did too, of course, but . . .

His own mother. Here in the Warren with him.

Gabriel cleared his throat, almost apologetically. Reluctantly, he said, "Often when we have no other options, Keeper, we choose the most unexpected path."

"Okay," said Horace, before he even meant it. He cleared his thoughts, letting his doubts fall aside, and tried again. "Okay."

"Just so," said Mr. Meister warmly. "We will go speak to your mother, you and I. It has been long since I last saw her." He smiled, a hint of mischief on his lips. "Do you think she will remember me?"

The question brought a sharp memory to the front of Horace's mind. The story his mother had told him only yesterday about how she had become a Tuner, about what Mr. Meister had done to her. "She remembers you," said Horace, looking the old man steadily in the eye. "I think she even forgives you."

Mr. Meister's grin slipped. He managed to turn it into a pouting frown, nodding. "It is my sad lot in life that I often find myself hoping I am not remembered *too* well. Luckily for me, loyalty to our cause is far more important than loyalty to myself. Do you think she will help us?"

"She shouldn't, but she will," Chloe said. "I'll come with you. I want to tell her what happened."

"No," said Mr. Meister. "You cannot come. Stay here with the others."

"This whole thing is my mom's fault. I want to help."

"And help you shall. But let me repeat: you *cannot* come. Certain obstacles are more suited to some than to others. The path we take now is not for you."

Horace was sure that Mr. Meister was about to lead him out through the Warren's mysterious back entrance. But why couldn't Chloe come? Chloe opened her mouth to object— telling Chloe she couldn't do something was the surest way to make her try—but Horace held up a hand.

"It's okay. I'll be back. We'll find Isabel and fix everything. Okay?"

"We better," she said sulkily.

"We will."

"Just so," said Mr. Meister. "To Horace's house we go."

AFTER GOOD-BYES, MR. Meister led Horace out of the workshop. But instead of heading up the Perilous Stairs toward the Great Burrow, Mr. Meister stepped out onto the great stone bridge that spanned the Maw.

Mr. Meister paused. "You are aware that there is another way in and out of the Warren besides Vithra's Eye."

"Yes." The old man came and went from the Warren at will, of course, but he didn't go the way the others did. Horace had never known the old man to pass across the dark waters of Vithra's Eye, through the cold terror of the Nevren there. Chloe had suggested that Mr. Meister was physically unable to pass through the Nevren—a startling idea, since the whole purpose of the Nevren was keep out the Riven, while allowing Keepers through.

"Today you travel my way," Mr. Meister said now. "We go through Sanguine Hall."

Horace rolled the name over in his head, mouthing the words soundlessly. "And will there be a Nevren?"

"No."

"But then how is the Warren protected?"

Mr. Meister didn't reply, starting wordlessly across the bridge. Horace followed close behind. As so often happened in the Warren, the bridge seemed to be a danger unto itself.

Narrow, and without railings, it was a precarious walk. The cold breeze that always rose from the depths of the Maw became stronger the farther out they went, blossoming first into a sturdy wind and then, midway, a buffeting gale. Had the bridge not been made of stone, Horace might have sworn it was swaying. He crouched low, one hand on the Fel'Daera, inching his way across. Even Mr. Meister moved slowly, his wild white hair rippling madly. But he walked upright, and his gait was steady.

They continued on. The wind grew stronger, becoming so fierce that Horace almost lost his fear of falling. He reasoned that if he slipped off the edge now, the powerful gale from below might actually lift him into the air.

At last they reached the far side, where the bridge connected to an open stone balcony cut from the bedrock. As soon as they stepped onto the balcony, the hurricane wind subsided to a breeze once more. Mr. Meister straightened his red vest and ran his gnarled hands through his hair. Horace tried flattening his own tousled mane, but it was hopeless.

"You look fine," Mr. Meister said with a hint of a smile. "Come."

The balcony opened inward into a dark, rambling corridor. Mr. Meister reached into the collar of his vest and pulled out a shockingly bright white light. A jithandra. Horace had never seen Mr. Meister's jithandra before, but was unsurprised to discover that it was white.

"This is the Gallery," the old man said. "Stay close."

As they walked through the passageway, and as the light of Mr. Meister's jithandra slid along the corridor, doors began to appear upon the walls. It wasn't that they were becoming illuminated in the darkness, Horace realized, but rather that they were actually springing into existence. Doors materialized out of the stone as the full power of the white light fell upon them. As soon as Mr. Meister's light swept past, the doors flickered and ceased to exist.

"Are these doors real?" Horace asked, marveling.

"That depends. If you were here alone, walking by the blue light of your own jithandra, most of them would not be."

"Whoa," Horace said, craning his neck to watch as a battered iron door materialized on their right, then was deleted behind them. A bit farther on, Mr. Meister stopped in front of a thick wooden door suddenly blooming on the left.

"Here we are," said Mr. Meister, opening the door the moment it solidified. They passed through into a cramped stone chamber, barely six feet across. A little stab of panic jabbed at Horace as Mr. Meister tucked his jithandra away, his claustrophobia rising suddenly, but to his relief the door did not disappear behind them when the light winked out. Apparently, the doors of the Gallery were always real on the other side. And there was light here, too. Coming from above. Tipping his head back, Horace saw that the narrow chamber rose high overhead like a chimney. Many stories up, an amber light shone down on them like a September moon.

"Now we ascend," said Mr. Meister. "You did rather well

crossing the Maw—I gather you have no great fear of heights?"

Horace almost laughed, thinking how much easier his life would have been lately if he could have traded his real fear for that one. "Not really, no."

"Good. Follow me, then. For better or for worse, there is no elevator here." And the old man began scrambling swiftly up the wall to their left.

For a moment, it was as if Mr. Meister had begun to fly. But Horace looked more closely and saw a metal framework hugging the wall, spiraling upward. The framework was halfway between a ladder and a stair, steep enough that as Horace began to climb, he found himself using his hands to help pull himself up. The steps were very far apart, too—each one nearly as high as his waist. After just a dozen steps, his arms and legs were complaining hard.

Meanwhile, Mr. Meister was pulling away, scampering up the steep stairs like a goat, his white head bobbing in the darkness. Horace climbed after him, telling himself that this *was* better than the rickety elevator on the far side of Vithra's Eye. Surely the stairs would end soon. But the amber light above seemed to barely grow closer, and the distant floor below was nearly lost in shadow. And even though he was not afraid of heights, Horace began to think just how deadly a fall from this far up would be.

At last he reached the top, after sixty-seven giant-sized steps. He pulled himself up onto a wide stone ledge, thighs and shoulders screaming, knees and palms bumped and scraped, lungs heaving. Mr. Meister stood there calmly, looking down at him, apparently not winded by the climb.

"I regret to tell you your method lacks efficiency," Mr. Meister said. "If there is a next time, I will show you a better way to climb the ladder."

"Why wouldn't there be a next time?" Horace asked, sucking hard at the air.

"Most prefer the Nevren."

Horace rubbed his aching shoulder. "I can see why."

"Oh, not because of the ladder," Mr. Meister clarified. "Because of what still lies ahead. Because of Sanguine Hall."

Horace tried not to let his imagination run wild as his labored breathing continued to slow. "What's so bad about Sanguine Hall?"

Mr. Meister took a seat beside Horace with a sigh, his legs dangling over the edge like a child's. "Sanguine Hall is not bad. Merely challenging."

"Challenging enough that most people prefer the Nevren. The *bad* Nevren."

"Yes," Mr. Meister admitted.

Horace turned to look directly into Mr. Meister's huge gray eyes. "But not you," he said. "You prefer Sanguine Hall."

Mr. Meister began peeking into the pockets of his vest, one by one. After a moment he said lightly, "It is not a matter of preference for me, Horace. Surely you have already guessed as much."

Horace eyed the old man's red vest and his thick glasses.

The left lens of those glasses, the oraculum, was definitely Tan'ji, but so was the red vest. Through the pockets of the vest, Mr. Meister could extract items from his round red office in the Great Burrow, even when he was ten or fifteen miles away.

"You've got two Tan'ji, and—"

"Two that you know of," Mr. Meister interrupted.

Horace's mouth hung open. What else did the old man have in those pockets of his? "Okay . . . two that I know of. So I guess I figure if going through the Nevren is terrible for a person with just one Tan'ji, it must be extra terrible—maybe impossible?—for a person with more."

"Correct—terrible, impossible. I cannot pass through the Nevren. In this regard, I am like the Riven. The collective bond between myself and my Tan'ji is so strong that were I to be severed for even a few moments, I would be dispossessed. I would not survive." He said this simply, as if describing a book he might not enjoy reading.

Horace could barely respond to this. "Oh," he said stupidly.

Mr. Meister produced a warm smile. "It has not been an issue thus far, Keeper, I assure you."

"Right," Horace said. "Obviously. But okay . . . how can you even have more than one Tan'ji in the first place? I thought each Keeper could only bond to one instrument." No one had ever said that, exactly, but it seemed so obvious it didn't need saying. Horace couldn't imagine bonding—or even *wanting* to bond—with any instrument other than the Fel'Daera. That would be a betrayal.

"Ordinarily, yes," Mr. Meister said. "But my duties require a bit more . . . extraordinariness." He held out his hand. There on his finger was the glimmering ring Horace had noticed the very first time they'd met. It was a flat band with a single twist in it—a Möbius strip.

Horace, torn between fascination and revulsion, frowned at the ring. "Another Tan'ji?" he asked.

"No. Merely Tan'kindi—it does not take the bond. Yet it is powerful. This is a polymath's ring. The wearer gains the ability to bond to multiple instruments at once."

Horace shook his head, disliking the idea more and more. "But being a Keeper is special. Unique. How can you bond to all those things?" He meant *How is it possible*, yes, but not just that. He meant, *How dare you?*

If Mr. Meister noticed Horace's tone, he didn't react. "It takes some doing. You might say that the oraculum is my native Tan'ji. My first, my truest. The others have been . . . compelled to bond with me, with the help of the ring."

"Compelled. Like forced?"

"No. No more than a flower is forced to turn to the sun."

"I don't like it," Horace said, and then a terrible thought occurred to him. "Before I came along, could you have compelled the Fel'Daera to bond with you?"

Mr. Meister turned to him, his left eye huge and piercing through the oraculum. "If I could have, you never would have come along. You would not have been called."

"But did you try?"

A blink, slow and thoughtful. Horace was sure the old man would preach to him about the difficulty of these days, how the Wardens did whatever they must. But instead Mr. Meister simply said, "Yes. I tried."

Somehow Horace couldn't muster up the rage he was sure he should be feeling. Instead there was only a nasty twisting in his belly, sad and sick. He said the only words that would come to him: "You didn't have the right."

Mr. Meister smiled at him kindly. "Clearly I did not. Here you are, Keeper. The Fel'Daera is at your side. It answers to you and no one else." He slapped his knees and stood so swiftly that Horace flinched. "Enough. If you are quite recovered from your climb, we must continue. Sanguine Hall lies on the other side of this doorway."

Feeling surly but not wanting to show it—he *was* the Keeper of the Fel'Daera, after all—Horace staggered clumsily to his feet and looked around. *What doorway?* The ledge they stood on appeared to be a dead end. But in one place along the wall, he now saw a jagged, human-sized patch in the natural stone that had been bricked over. The bricks were dull and rounded with age.

Horace looked for a passkey, one of the kite-shaped stones that allowed the Wardens to pull a Chloe—to become like a ghost and pass through solid walls. But instead, Mr. Meister reached into his pocket. He removed a thin cylinder made of glass. It looked like an old-fashioned key, except that the key end was bristling and glittering instead of flat and dull. Mr. Meister held it up for Horace to see. At the bristling business end, the key split into three prongs, each of which split into three more, and each of those into three more, and so on, to what Horace imagined—illogically—was infinity.

"Another of my Tan'ji," Mr. Meister said. "Do not touch. It is quite sharp."

No Keeper ever touched another Keeper's Tan'ji without permission, of course, but Horace had been feeling the urge to do just that. "What is it?"

"The Riven call it a dashinti—a master key." He lowered the key and inserted it into the brick wall. The bristling glass tip slid in silently, like a twig into water. Horace had seen Chloe do similar things with ordinary objects many times. When Mr. Meister released the master key, it hung in place. "Go ahead," Mr. Meister said. "Pull it out it."

Startled to be given this permission, Horace nonetheless couldn't resist. He grasped the flat end of the key and tugged. He tugged again. The key wouldn't budge.

"Just so," Mr. Meister intoned. Then he took hold of the key and slid it easily from the wall and back in again. Chloe couldn't do that. "As I said, Tan'ji."

"You can pass through the wall with this," Horace said. "Any wall?"

"Essentially. I use it when I have the need—to enter, to escape." He chuckled. "On occasion, to impress. I used it the very first time we met, in fact. That day was so full of wonders, however, that perhaps you do not remember."

But Horace did remember. "You vanished into the wall. I thought it was a secret door or something."

"Everything is a door if I wish it to be," Mr. Meister said, and then shrugged boyishly. "Within reason, of course." He grasped the suspended key and twisted it—once, twice, three times. He nodded, satisfied, and glanced back at Horace, letting the key hang again. His face was creased with solemnity.

"Once we are in the Hall, do as I do," he said swift and low. "When they come, do not move. Do not speak. Let it happen. If you do as I say, there is little to fear."

The words sent a violent shiver through Horace. "When who comes?" he asked.

"Do not move or speak," Mr. Meister repeated. "No matter what. They will come, they will feed, they will leave. No harm will be done."

He took Horace by the elbow, and together they stepped through the brick wall.

CHAPTER SEVEN

Sanguine Hall

HORACE AND MR. MEISTER EMERGED FROM THE COOL SLAB OF stone into a still, brick-walled passageway, long and high—it stretched into darkness both ahead and above. There were glowing amber crystals here, too, embedded in the stone floor at regular intervals. The swirls of light rising from below turned Mr. Meister's face into a ghoul's face, casting cruel shadows on his cheeks and brow. The place appeared to be empty. Horace remembered Mr. Meister's words: *"They will come. They will feed."* He peered into the gloom overhead.

Behind them, the handle of the master key protruded from the wall; it had twisted around to follow them as they passed through. Mr. Meister pulled the key out swiftly and tucked it into a pocket. "Forward," he said, leading the way.

Their footsteps rang hollowly. Horace found himself nearly tiptoeing, his eyes and ears wide open. After twenty paces, Mr. Meister came to a halt, turning to face Horace, gesturing for him to stop. He backed slowly away, looking up and cocking his head.

"They come," he announced, still backing away.

And now Horace heard it. A rustling from the darkness above—a soft, glassy rattle. Horace's grandmother had a wind chime made of thin stone discs that clicked together in the breeze, almost musical but with no voice behind them, no throat. This sound was like that one, only thinner and higher, and fuller by far—a wind chime a thousand times as big. The sheer size of the sound made Horace's heart sink, because now it reminded him of another sound, one he never wanted to hear again: the golem.

A flickering cloud appeared overhead. A dozen yards down the passage, Mr. Meister said, "Don't move. Don't react, whatever happens." His voice was low and flat. He dipped the fingers of one hand into a vest pocket and held them there, waiting.

The cloud dipped into the light. Not the golem. Butterflies? Small and delicate, seemingly lighter than air. But these butterflies shone like polished steel, smooth and gleaming. And their wings weren't rounded. They were almost dragon-like, but backward—swept back in a curve, only to point forward again. And although the little creatures drifted in the manner of butterflies—wings held apart in a shallow V, slicing through the air as serenely as paper airplanes—they did not flutter. They seemed unable to flap their wings at all.

They glided down from the shadows in a great metallic flock, many thousands of individuals clinking lightly together and sailing blindly apart again. Horace held his breath as the swarm descended, as it began to fill the space between himself and Mr. Meister, dividing and circling them each with an unmistakable air of curiosity. Soon the old man was lost from sight.

Like a storm of tiny mirrors, the mass multiplied itself, becoming ever more uncountable. Their clattering wings were paper-thin, their bodies thin shining cylinders, no bigger than matches. As the swarm came lower still, some of the little creatures—not creatures, of course, but Tanu—drifted right past Horace's eyes. They were headless, faceless, no more than thin metallic rods with several rudimentary wriggling feet. But those wings . . . the wings were delicate and savage at the same time, fiercely curved, like scythes. The back edges were jagged.

Horace turned his head to watch one of the creatures as it drifted very close to his face. And then a sudden jolt of pain across his cheek, a trickle of warmth. He cried out.

He was cut.

Horace willed himself to stay utterly still. He understood now: he was buried in a swarm of ten thousand drifting blades. These wings were as deadly sharp as they looked, thinner and keener than any knife. *Don't move. Don't react.* Of course not, or you would be cut down to bone. With this realization came another, firm and sure and horrifying: although this swarm was not the golem, it was its kin.

Horace was afraid to even blink. The tiny things took up a swirling course around him, entombing him in a whirling wall of shine and sound and death. Through a break in the swarm, he caught a glimpse of Mr. Meister, and was horrified to see that some of the scythewings were alighting on the old man, coming to rest on his bright red vest. Horace looked down at his own brown shirt; only a few of the creatures had landed on him. But the creatures were alighting upon Mr. Meister, thick now, blanketing his shoulders and chest like a layer of silver snow. And not just his chest, but his hands, his face. They were clustering on the old man's glasses, like a ghastly shrub.

At his side, Horace felt a tingle across the back of his own hand. The tingle bloomed into a crawl, into a prickle of pain. Three scythewings were on his hand, roaming slowly. Now two more. It wasn't him they were interested in, he knew that now too. They wanted the Fel'Daera, snug in its pouch beneath his hand. He fought the angry urge to swat them away. He stopped watching, but felt them land, another after another after another.

Through the curtain of knives that surrounded him, another glimpse of Mr. Meister. The creatures crawled over his vest and glasses, his hand, serrated wings glinting. The oraculum was so thickly covered now that Mr. Meister looked like a monstrosity, a mute and bristling cyborg. The old man's mouth came open, teeth bared, and then Horace lost sight of him once again.

Agony swept over Horace, buckling his knees. He wasn't cut, no. This was something else. He looked down, horrified. The horde that had alighted on Mr. Meister was nothing compared to the throng that huddled and crawled across Horace's hip now, burying his hand almost to the elbow, along with the pouch that held the box. They were piled five and six deep, burrowing into their own mass, trying to get down to the Fel'Daera. The back of his hand stung from the hundreds of tiny feet working across his flesh, but he barely felt it. He would not have felt it had they begun to slice into him in their frenzy. He would not have felt it even if they had been sawing through his flesh to get to the box. None of this was the source of the true pain he felt now.

The box was screaming.

Screaming was the only word, even for this soundless cry. The box jangled with alarm and fear—panic and pain or something like them. These weren't quite the right words, no, because the box was not human, but these were the closest names Horace had for the sensations that burned inside him on the box's behalf. He felt his face curl into a grimace of torment, and recognized it as the same look he'd seen on Mr. Meister's face. The scythewings were destroying the box—no, devouring it. Or no . . . feasting on it. Yes. They were drinking from it. Like a plague of tiny vampires, leeching the life from it, feasting greedily on every ounce of the energy the box could provide. A bone-twisting torrent of the Medium barreled through the box and into a thousand voracious mouths.

They will come. They will feed. And they had and they were, and the box was a beacon of agony and when would they leave? Would it be too late?

There were so many of the creatures at Horace's hip now that the collective weight of them, tiny as they were, weighed him down. All of them mindless and insatiable, hungry for everything the box could provide. They drank so deeply that even though Horace could feel the box, he knew he would be unable to use it. There was simply no energy to spare. Maybe Mr. Meister had miscalculated, had not foreseen the appeal the box would have for this horde. Maybe they had never been offered a feast like the Fel'Daera. Maybe they would never get their fill.

Horace wanted to run, but could not. He tried to remain logical. Yes, he was half buried in blades, but the only cut he'd taken was when he had moved. And he got the feeling that any move he made now might be taken as an attack. It did not take much imagination to picture what the scythe-wings could do if angered. Instead he stuck to Mr. Meister's words of warning. He did not move. He did not cry out. He stood and let the anguish of the box course through him like electricity, turning every muscle in him to steel. He thought of Chloe, crawling through the inferno of her burning home, feeling the fire in her lungs, her heart, her bones, thinking her father might be taken or dead. This was nothing next to that. He told himself this over and over, trying to picture and feel the horror Chloe had described to him after the fire: the sight of flames inside her own eyes. *This is nothing compared to that. This is nothing compared to that.*

And then—after an eternity—they released him. The scythewings took flight all at once, lifting off like blown-free dandelion seeds. He staggered, nearly falling to his knees as the screaming of the box dropped to silence. But the box was there, yes, still there. The swarm unfurled from its orbit around him into a thick column again, rising like the smoke from the ruins of Chloe's house. And there was Mr. Meister down the hall, his sharp eyes on Horace and his glasses slightly askew. His fingers were still tucked into one of the pockets of his vest. The scythewings ascended into the shadows, out of sight, rising until at last they could be heard no more.

"Are you cut?" Mr. Meister called.

Horace touched his cheek. "I'm okay," he replied. The cut was deep but very fine—almost like a paper cut—and the blood was already drying. He undid the pouch at his side and removed the box. He examined it closely, turning it over in his hands. It was unmarked, not even a scratch. In his mind, it felt aching and raw, like a muscle that had been worked to exhaustion.

Horace felt much the same himself. But the box was safe. He could feel it gathering energy into itself again. Without waiting to ask if it was wise to do so, he twisted the lid open and looked through it down at himself—*blue floor, no feet, no Horace*. The future ten seconds from now. The box was working. He looked up to find Mr. Meister engaged in much the same activity—he'd taken off his glasses to examine the oraculum closely. He smoothed his many-pocketed red vest. When he was finished, he called to Horace again.

"Come. Let us leave this place." He spun and headed through the Hall.

Horace hurried to catch up. His legs ached and his cheek stung and his hand burned.

Mr. Meister glanced back. "I assume the Fel'Daera is none the worse for wear."

"Yes, but that was—what were those things?"

"Sa'halvasa, if you must know."

Horace repeated the word to himself, letting the sound hiss in his mouth. "They were dangerous."

"We are besieged by danger every day," Mr. Meister said curtly.

"Yeah, and it seems like half the dangers we face are right here inside the Warren."

"The Warren is a fortress, Horace, not a palace."

"But what are those things even doing here? They were like the golem—"

Mr. Meister spun around so abruptly that Horace nearly collided with him. The old man raised his hand, eyes flashing behind his glasses. "They are a necessity," he growled fiercely. "I thought I explained as much."

Horace reared back. But almost immediately Mr. Meister subsided, his stern gaze softening into concern. He glanced up into the air. "Forgive me, Keeper. This night has us all on edge. This place. Let us leave."

At the far end of the Hall, the passageway had partly caved in, long ago. They picked through the dusty rubble and, with the help of the master key, passed through another brick wall into utter darkness. Mr. Meister produced his jithandra again, revealing a cramped concrete tunnel running left and right. A narrow set of train tracks lined the floor.

"Trains?" Horace said, half to himself. But if trains came through here, they had to be the tiniest trains ever.

"Once," Mr. Meister said. "But no more. Either way, they do not concern us. We are out of the Warren now." He stepped across the tracks, carrying the light into an opening in the opposite wall. Horace followed through a locked iron gate, up three more flights of stairs. Another heavy door, and finally fresh air flooded over Horace, cool and invigorating. Light and sound from the city trickled down from above, through the leaves of two medium-sized ginkgo trees. A chain of falkrete stones traced a circle around a bird-shaped stone. A high, winding wall surrounded them.

"Another cloister," Horace said.

"Just so. Here we may rest for a moment. Beck will be here shortly."

Horace sank gratefully onto a stone bench, glad they would be driving to his house and not traveling by falkrete. He'd had enough for one day. No single part of him that could ache did not gnaw at him now, physical and mental. But he was safe. The box was safe. He licked his thumb and wiped the last of the blood from his cheek.

Mr. Meister took a seat beside Horace. He looked none the worse for the ordeal they'd just gone through. The muffled sounds of traffic outside were a novelty—how strange to think this world had been going noisily on its way while he and Mr. Meister had navigated the perils of the Warren and been held captive below by the swarm. How much difference a hundred feet made.

After a moment Mr. Meister spoke. "Horace, let me apologize again for my harsh words. Sanguine Hall can make one . . . testy."

"The Hall," Horace said. "I don't want to go through there again. Ever. The box was . . ."

"I know what it is like," Mr. Meister said grimly.

"Those sa'halvasa, they feed off the Medium, don't they? They force the energy out through our instruments. They suck the life out of them."

"Yes."

"The Riven wouldn't dare come through there."

"Even if they tried, they would not be able to stand and endure the assault the way you just did. And if a Tan'ji is activated in the Hall, even in defense, the sa'halvasa go into a frenzy so ferocious that the instrument—and its Keeper—will be drained dry."

Horace wasn't sure what that meant, exactly, but he at last understood the conversation back in the workshop. "That's why you told Chloe she couldn't come. You thought she'd try to fight them off."

"She is a fighter, is she not? If a traveler through Sanguine Hall cannot remain calm when the sa'halvasa come . . ." He shrugged, and pointed to Horace's sliced cheek. "Sanguine Hall is not for everyone. The Riven will not brave it, any more than they would brave the Nevren."

"But you brave it. You pass through Sanguine Hall every time you leave the Warren."

Mr. Meister waved his hand, flashing the polymath's ring. "It is a path I chose long ago. Do not feel sorry for me."

"I don't," Horace said, and immediately regretted it. "Or to be honest, I don't know if I do or not."

"There are reasons for what I do."

Horace had heard variations on this theme a dozen times before, and they could all be boiled down to the same two words: "Trust me." Horace wanted to trust Mr. Meister, he did. But every "Trust me" was no better than a locked door and a promise. And there were some doors, Horace knew, that the old man hadn't even admitted to yet.

"I know you have reasons," said Horace. "Everyone has reasons. But I don't know how good your reasons are. For example, did you have a good reason for not telling us about the polymath's ring? Or the scythewings?"

"Those matters were of no concern to you, until today. And today I told you."

Horace frowned, irritated. "Actually, you didn't tell me about the scythewings. You just said 'Be chill,' and dragged me in there."

"Some stories are better experienced than explained."

"Is that what you told my mom, too? About the kaitan?"

Mr. Meister seemed to wince. He studied Horace's face. "Even if your mother has indeed forgiven me for that, Horace, it seems you have not." He lifted his head as if hearing a sound. He stood. "Beck is here. Let us go." He began to stride across the cloister.

Horace fumed—on behalf of his mother, on behalf of Chloe and all the other Keepers, even on behalf of Isabel. Too many secrets. Too many doors. But as he watched the old man walk away, he realized maybe he wasn't angry. Maybe he was afraid. And the first step toward not being afraid, his mother always told him, was to *know*. Fear of the unknown was the one fear that could always be conquered.

Horace called out to the old man. "What about the Mothergates?"

The old man froze.

"Do you have a good reason for not telling us that they're dying?" Horace asked. "Is that something better experienced, too?

Mr. Meister turned toward him but still didn't speak.

Horace found that he was trembling. "I'm really wondering about that one. It seems like a big one."

"So it is," said Mr. Meister.

A confirmation. Horace held strong, pushing forward. "Do you know how it will feel if the Mothergates die? If our Tan'ji die along with them? Maybe it will feel like being severed. Or like being cleaved—I hear that's fun." Horace was standing now, but he didn't remember rising. "Or maybe it will feel like Sanguine Hall, like having the life torn out of us. Do you know? And would you tell us if you did?"

"I do not know," said Mr. Meister. "None of us know. We are all afraid."

"You don't sound afraid."

"It is my job to not sound afraid. *Fear is the stone—may yours be light.*' Yet I do not know how to lighten this particular stone, Horace Andrews."

"Tell me we can save the Mothergates."

Mr. Meister tipped his face to the sky. His jaw worked silently. His great gray eyes roamed the rustling deeps of the ginkgo trees overhead. Eight seconds passed. Twelve. At last the old man met Horace's gaze.

"The Mothergates can be saved," he said solemnly. "That is a fact."

Horace studied his face. He was almost sure he believed him. "Why did it take you so long to answer?"

"Why does the Fel'Daera sometimes lead you astray? Knowing that a thing can happen is not the same as understanding *how* it will happen. I do not want to give you false hope."

"It's only false if we fail," Horace said, the words coming out of him as though someone else had spoken them. He suspected he sounded much braver than he felt.

Mr. Meister opened his mouth to reply, but seemed to think the better of it and only nodded instead. "Just so," he said. "Well said. And speaking of hope, your mother is waiting for us. Let us see what help she may provide us in tracking down Isabel. Brian and Joshua must come before all else— even the Mothergates. Are we agreed?"

Horace took a deep breath and nodded. He wasn't sure he was ready for the conversation to come—it was hard even to imagine his mom and Mr. Meister in the same room together—but there was no one he trusted more than his mother. He knew no one more competent and sturdy. And frankly, sturdiness was just what he needed right now.

"Okay," Horace said, standing. "Let's go recruit my mom."

CHAPTER EIGHT

Friends Like These

"I DON'T KNOW WHERE WE ARE," SAID BRIAN, "BUT IT'S MOIST." His head was tipped up to the dark trees above them. Tunraden sat at his feet. Joshua watched as Brian reached out and plucked a leaf from a low-hanging branch. He sniffed it and ran it through his fingers. "The outside world is a lot stickier than I remember." Brian let the leaf fall and walked over to the river, standing on the muddy bank, watching the water flow by.

Isabel too was looking around. "That canoe," she said. "That's the canoe we rode in, two nights ago."

"Yes," said Joshua. "This is where April and I first met the Wardens." It was this very riverbank where Horace had pulled their canoe ashore, where the Wardens had been waiting for April. The Riven had attacked them almost at once, and only Isabel's sudden arrival had saved them. Joshua was relieved that the bodies of the Riven she'd cleaved that night were gone.

Brian examined the canoe, crumpled against the base of a tree. "What happened to this? It looks like it's been in a tornado."

"Dr. Jericho threw it at me," Isabel said lightly. When Brian stared at her with round eyes—Joshua guessed he'd never seen one of the huge, powerful Mordin in person before—she only shrugged. "He missed," she said, and turned to Joshua. "You said there was a cloister nearby."

Joshua nodded. The cloister was only a quarter mile away. Technically, Joshua had never been inside a cloister, but he knew that they were safe places the Wardens used, where the Riven's hunters—the Mordin—would not be able to detect them. He also knew from the cloister map that the leestone inside this cloister was a brown bird with a blue wing. Leestones were always birds. He had no idea why.

The walk was short, but it was slow going with Brian hand-cuffed by Tunraden, his hands again buried in the stone up to his wrists. Joshua led them over a bridge just downstream. They crossed a bike path and an open grassy area before diving back into forest again. At last, two hundred yards in, the high walls of the cloister loomed in the shadows.

Isabel laid a hand against the bricks. "This must be how Horace and Chloe got back to the Warren that night, after the fight on the riverbank. They leapt home from here through the falkretes."

"Where's the door?" Joshua asked.

"We have to make our own door." She began to circle the cloister, searching the wall for something. "I need to find the passkey. Ah!" She stopped and pointed to a small kite-shaped stone, high up on the wall.

"Oh," said Brian, as if he'd just realized something. "Oh my god." He started to laugh.

Isabel rounded on him. "What's the matter?"

"I'm an idiot." He shrugged and indicated his arms, his hands still buried in Tunraden. "I can't get in."

Isabel squeezed her eyes shut, groaning.

"What's the matter?" said Joshua.

Brian said, "The only way into a cloister is to press your fingers against the passkey. As long as you touch it, you can walk through the wall. Like Chloe. But I can't touch the pass-key and carry Tunraden at the same time. I can't get in."

"Can't you carry her with one hand?" asked Isabel. "You said she lifts herself, when you ask her to."

"She does. But it takes two hands. Just one of those design flaws, I guess."

Isabel shook her head angrily. "Not a flaw. It's a feature. It's made that way to keep you hobbled."

Brian grimaced and put Tunraden down, flexing his fingers. "I'm aware of that, but thanks for crushing my little delusion." He shook out his hands, like they had fallen asleep. He rubbed the tight bands around his wrists and glanced nervously into the dark woods around them. "I gotta say," he said, "I'm not crazy about Tunraden being out here without protection."

"You've been living in the Warren for three years," Isabel said. "The protection it gives you will linger with you for a while."

"For a while," Brian agreed. "But using Tunraden will burn through it pretty fast. I could drain a raven's eye in just a few seconds."

"I just didn't expect . . . ," Isabel began, and glanced at Joshua. "I thought we would have more options available to us."

Joshua wasn't stupid. He knew what that meant. "You think it's my fault," he said. "Because I can't take us wherever you want."

"It's not your fault," she said, but he knew she didn't mean it. "But if you would only just—"

"It's not Joshua's fault," Brian repeated, cutting her off.

Joshua frowned at the high cloister wall. Whether helping Isabel was the right thing to do or not, or whether any of this was really his fault, it was driving him crazy that he'd brought them all this way only to be stopped by something simple like a brick wall. "Maybe I can open a portal inside the cloister," he said. "Now that I've been here."

Brian shook his head, gazing at the Laithe. "Portals can't be opened into cloisters. Out, yes, but not in."

"Let me think," said Isabel. Without another word, she stalked off into the darkness, rounding the far side of the cloister.

Brian watched her go, then ambled closer to Joshua. He spoke low, sounding almost guilty. "Don't let us teach you anymore."

"What do you mean? You're not teaching me."

"We are. Mostly Isabel, but I've been doing it too. Isabel and I know more about the Laithe of Teneves than we have a right to—her because she tuned it, and me because of my abilities. But it's not good to tell you what we know. We can't take back the fact that you weren't given a proper choice with your instrument, but we don't have to make a bad thing worse."

In Joshua's hands, the Laithe was spinning slowly inside the meridian. The Pacific slid by, west to east, sparkling and blue. "Mrs. Hapsteade told me not to let Isabel fix my mistakes," he asked. "Is that what she meant?"

"Yes . . . look, you're supposed to Find your instrument and figure it out all on your own."

"Did you do yours alone?"

"Yes. I actually . . ." Brian sighed. "I was in the Find for like a year, living in the Warren, and I didn't speak the whole time. Literally. Mrs. Hapsteade brought me food. I ate it. And I thought about Tunraden pretty much every second. But nobody said anything to me, and I didn't say anything back. I was too busy thinking. Too busy figuring things out."

More and more, Joshua was feeling like Brian's life was just too strange to imagine. "But I don't want to not talk for a year," he said.

"That's not what I'm saying. I'm saying, if you really want to become Tan'ji—solid and true and self-sufficient—you've got to let the bond forge naturally. The Laithe is you. You and the Laithe are becoming Tan'ji. The more you let others interfere with that, the weaker you'll be."

"Weak how? Like I won't have powers?"

"They won't be as strong as they could be. But you'll be weak in other ways, too."

"What ways?"

"Just trust me. Figure it out on your own." Brian walked away. He knelt awkwardly on the ground beside Tunraden, obviously done talking.

Joshua wasn't sure he understood. How could he be weak? He had already made one portal. Still, even though he didn't want to spend a year in a cave doing it, it was true that he wanted to figure out the Laithe on his own. He didn't want anyone telling him what to do. And somehow, he knew that the Laithe felt the same way. The Laithe would help him help himself. He—they—didn't need anyone else.

Joshua wandered away. He fussed with the globe. He had noticed that it seemed to sort of float in his hands, and experimentally he let go of it. He felt almost no surprise when the Laithe simply hovered in the air, gleaming and beautiful, a softball-sized earth with a copper ring around it. He took a step back, and the Laithe drifted after him like a patient dog.

"It's mine," he said, loud enough for Brian to hear.

"No one's saying it isn't," said Brian without looking over.

More than anything, Joshua wanted to prove to Isabel that he didn't need her help. And they still needed to get Brian to safety. Without stopping to think whether it was smart, or even totally wanted, he took the Lathe in hand and centered his view on St. Louis. This was where Isabel really wanted to go. There were sanctuaries there, safe places for Brian. He slid the sleeping rabbit swiftly with one hand, zooming in fast. With the other, he nudged the globe so that he came down on top of Cahokia Mounds, just east of the city.

The site was easy to find, because of the very recognizable lake not even two miles to the north. Horseshoe Lake, it was called, but to Joshua it always looked more like a fishhook than a horseshoe. Now that he was seeing it through the Laithe, though, it looked less like a fishhook and more like a creepy, clawed hand. Sort of like the hand of a Riven, if he let his imagination run away from him, which Joshua sometimes did. The roads and farmland around the lake were bent along the curves of the shore, as if the giant hand were clawing at the earth itself.

But quickly the lake slid out of sight over the northwest horizon. Joshua could see the mounds now, like small grassy pyramids. He came in closer, feeling nervous as the rabbit started to rise toward the north pole. He tried to remember other maps he'd seen of this place, the positions of the biggest mounds. He imagined himself walking among them. The rabbit passed the nine o'clock position, halfway up the western meridian, and he started to really hope. This was better

128

than he'd done in Madagascar. But no sooner did he think it than the fuzzy rings started to appear, blurring everything.

"Stop," said Isabel. She stood nearby, hands on her hips, frowning at him. "A mishandled Tan'ji draws as much attention as a broken one. It was fine back in the Warren, but not here."

Joshua glanced at Brian. The older boy said nothing. "I'm only trying to help," Joshua said. "I'm doing what I'm supposed to do."

"I know. But if you want to help, take us somewhere we know you can go."

"Like where?"

Isabel looked up at the high cloister. "Like to a cloister without walls."

It took Joshua a second. "You mean the *barn*?"

Brian stood up. "Whoa, whoa, whoa," he said. "You're talking about the leestone near April's house? Where you sent the Riven?"

"It'll be safe by now," said Isabel. "We all saw Meister and Gabriel in the Warren. The rescue was a success. The Riven will be long gone. And even if they aren't, Joshua should be able to—"

"Fine," said Joshua, cutting her off just like Brian had a few minutes ago. "The barn."

Brian hesitated, and then gave Joshua a firm nod. "Okay. Fine. But you'll get us out of there if anything goes wrong."

"I will."

Isabel looked offended for some reason. Angry. But then she pushed another smile onto her face. "It's settled, then," she said. "Can you do it, Joshua? Are you ready to try again?"

And despite everything—despite Isabel, despite this plan he'd never asked for, despite not even knowing fully why he was even here, Joshua knew one thing: he was itching to use the Laithe again. He was aching to. And, of course, he also knew precisely where the barn was, twenty-seven miles to the north-northwest. He peered down upon the Laithe. He took hold of the golden rabbit.

"I won't just try," he said.

It turned out to be easy. With the Laithe, he found the meadow near April's house and swiftly zoomed in, sliding the rabbit. He came down near the back of the huge, abandoned barn, not far from the falkrete stones. When he was all the way in, and the rabbit awoke, he pulled the meridian loose and set it in the air. The globe in his hands became a golden sun, and inside the floating ring the tunnel of shapes appeared, flashing and tumbling.

Joshua gave the meridian a hard spin. The rabbit ran, faster than ever. He locked eyes with it, willing it to run. The portal opened swiftly, the tunnel of shapes slowing. When at last the portal was open wide—only two more spins by hand this time—and the rabbit had stopped running, the meadow appeared through the portal, an expanse of black under a starry sky.

"I'll go first," Isabel said. "I'll make sure it's safe."

"No arguments there," said Brian.

Isabel stepped lightly through. In the long grass beyond, she turned in a cautious circle, Miradel gleaming faintly at her chest. After a moment, she turned to them with unseeing eyes and gestured for them to follow.

Brian looked at Joshua. "Am I stupid for doing this? For trying to fix her?"

"I don't know," Joshua said. And he didn't. "Why *are* you doing it?"

"Oh, I guess a little teenage defiance, a little personal pride. A little fear for my own skin." He laughed and bent over, sticking his hands into Tunraden and hoisting her into the air. "What could possibly go wrong with a recipe like that?"

He entered the portal. It shimmered and bent as he pushed Tunraden through.

Joshua didn't hesitate to follow this time. He stepped through the portal, globe in hand, and into the wide-open meadow. Behind him, the big barn was a sagging black shadow against the night sky. He and Isabel had stayed in the barn for several nights earlier this week. This back end of it, he knew, was a maze of stalls and grain bins and low, slatted corridors. Above the barn, a million stars gleamed.

Brian lay down on his back in the long grass, Tunraden between his spread legs. He pointed into the sky with both hands and said, "So. Big. So freaky big."

Isabel, meanwhile, was squatting a little ways off,

examining what was left of the falkrete stones here, and the leestone in the middle that once upon a time protected this place—a flat stone, Joshua remembered, in the shape of a blue jay with black shoulders and a black crested head.

Neither Brian nor Isabel seemed very interested in Joshua's second portal. He was beginning to wonder if he actually needed to spin the meridian by hand at all. He tried now, concentrating his hardest as he stared into the blue eyes of the golden rabbit, high atop the open portal. He willed the rabbit to run back, the portal to close. Nothing happened. After ten frustrating seconds, he gave up and spun the meridian by hand. The portal shrank easily, the rabbit running smooth and sure. The riverbank winked out, replaced by the tunnel of shapes. *Go, go*, he said silently to the rabbit, and to his delight it ran and ran until there was nowhere else to run. It folded itself to sleep. Joshua snagged the shrunken meridian out of the air and nestled the golden sphere of the Laithe back inside.

"One spin, huh?" Brian said. He was sitting up now, watching.

"Yeah," Joshua said, embarrassed.

"You're getting better already."

"Thank you," Joshua said quietly, because it was important to be polite. But inside, he was a storm of pride. He was doing it. He was the Keeper of the Laithe of Teneves. He glanced at Isabel. She was prowling around the leestone now, Miradel leaking little sparks of green.

Brian lay back in the grass. "There are a lot of smells out here," he said. "Hey, did you know every time you smell something, that means a molecule of the thing the smell came from is actually inside your nose?"

"I don't know what a molecule is," Joshua said. And he didn't care.

"A lot of strange bits of the world are up inside my nose right now, is all I'm saying." Brian sniffed dramatically and pointed into one of his nostrils. "Cow poop. Right in there."

"That's gross," Joshua said. He turned away, cradling the Laithe against his belly. Isabel was still ignoring them both, muttering over the leestone.

Brian went over to her. Joshua followed. The leestone, as Joshua had remembered, was broken in two. It was dusty and weatherworn.

"You didn't mention it was broken," said Brian.

"*Physically* broken," said Isabel. "But it's still active. You can see that. Will it work?"

"It's not giving us as much protection as I'd like," said Brian.

Isabel clutched at Miradel. "I don't know how much is enough. I've never seen a Loomdaughter in action before."

"You said it was like a dinner bell," said Joshua. "As big as a church."

"Did I?" said Brian. "Well, like we also said earlier, I've been living in the Warren for three years—basically living *inside* a leestone. The remains of that protection, plus this leestone, should be enough. But we'll need to get star—"

He broke off. He turned and stared out over the dark meadow, cocking his head. He walked a few steps away. "Uh, guys?" he said. "Something's out there. Something's coming."

Brian was looking to the north, in the direction of April's house. And now Joshua could hear it, too. Something moving through the tall grass. Something . . . not small. He began to panic. Was it the Riven? Had they felt him using the Laithe wrong? This was like April's broken Tan'ji all over again.

Isabel hurried to Brian's side, Miradel blazing to life. "I don't feel anything. It's not Riven. Not a Warden, either."

"No," Brian agreed, and then he called out, his voice thin and high. "Hello?"

Joshua kept listening. He was a good listener. And the sound he heard told him that whatever was coming now wasn't walking on two legs. Was it an animal? It sounded large. Maybe a deer? If only April was with them. With the Ravenvine, she would have known right away.

And then, though it might have been a stupid thing to do, Joshua stood up and started walking toward the sound. He was a Keeper now, even if he didn't know yet what he was doing. Maybe one day he would be one of the Wardens, if they forgave him. And Wardens were brave. He was going to be brave. He would find out what was out there. If it was a deer, it would just run away.

He marched past Brian and Isabel, holding the Laithe by his side.

"What are you doing?" Isabel whispered.

"I'm going to see. You said it wasn't a Riven."

Isabel hesitated, then followed him. Joshua stomped through the tall grass. A pale shape moved in the darkness just ahead. Joshua heard a faint jingle. He stopped.

The creature came closer, and closer still. It stepped right up to him, and Joshua laughed.

A dog. A big, yellow dog. It was limping, but panting at Joshua in a friendly way.

Behind him, Isabel let out a little noise of surprise. "I think that's April's dog."

April's dog! Joshua bent and took the dog's jowls in his hands. The dog licked Joshua's face happily. He had never met April's dog, but he remembered his name—April had told him stories, one night in the Great Burrow when she was feeling sad for home.

"Baron?" Joshua said. The dog licked him more furiously, wagging his tail. "First Baron, it's you. I'm Joshua. I'm April's friend."

Isabel came closer, bending to pet the dog. She leaned in close, sniffing. "He smells like brimstone."

Now Joshua smelled it too. "He's limping. He was in a fight with the Riven."

Behind them in the darkness, Brian called out. "I don't hear any screaming. I guess everyone's okay? Hello?"

"Come on, Baron," Joshua said. "Come." He turned and headed back toward Brian. Baron followed, Isabel just behind.

When the dog saw Brian, he walked right over to him, sniffing his face. Brian leaned way back. "I feel like I remember I don't like dogs," he said.

"He won't hurt you," said Joshua. "He's April's dog. Tell him you're her friend."

"Hello, April's dog." Brian waved nervously. "I am April's friend."

"I'm glad he's here," said Isabel. "He can help keep watch while Brian gets to work."

"That's what I'm here for," Brian said as he hauled Tunraden over to the leestone. He set the Loomdaughter down beside it and sat cross-legged in the grass. Baron, who had maybe decided Brian was a friend, came over and lay down heavily next to him.

"I'll need the harp," he said to Isabel. When Isabel didn't move, he spread his arms. "I won't touch it. Not yet. Just put it in the grass here."

Reluctantly, Isabel slipped the cord from around her neck and put Miradel down in the grass, on the other side of Tunraden from Brian. She stepped back, but Brian stopped her. "You too," he said. "Sit here."

Isabel did as she was told. Brian leaned in deep over the harp, his nose almost touching it. He looked back and forth between it and Isabel several times.

"I have some ideas," he said, sitting up. "But I like to feel my way through things before I start. That way I'm not using Tunraden before I need to." He smiled at them like he was sorry. "You might want to get comfortable, though. This will take some time."

"How long?" Isabel asked.

"Long," replied Brian, drawing out the word. "But when I start—if I can do it—it should go fast." He hunched over, focused on the wicker harp. Twice he reached out, nearly touching it, but after a while—a long while—he just sat there motionless. Isabel sat motionless too, her mouth firm with worry and her eyes alight.

Joshua sat down. Baron wandered over to him, and after a while Joshua lay back, using the dog as a pillow. Baron snuffled at his hair, but let him be. Joshua listened to his pattering heart, watching Brian and Isabel sit silent. He closed his eyes and felt the comfort of the Laithe, spinning and drifting in above him, under the stars. A world between worlds.

Joshua woke to voices. To hot breath on his face. Stinky breath. Baron stood over him, panting. The Laithe was floating in midair by Joshua's side, beautiful and blue. He sat up, groggy, and tipped his head to the sky. Still nighttime, but the stars were different. A thin crescent moon was just rising over the far-off trees to the east.

"You awake?" Brian said. "I'm ready to try it now." He was moving his fingers through the air, as if practicing. Isabel sat up in the grass, her red hair in a comical tangle. Apparently she'd fallen asleep too.

"What time is it?" asked Joshua sleepily. "How long has it been?"

"Hours," said Brian. "I don't know. I'm not Horace."

"Can you do it?" said Isabel.

"I actually think I can. Maybe."

Isabel squeezed her eyes shut, her fists in her lap, her back as straight as a board.

"Just to be safe, Joshua, you should move away," said Brian. "You're a Keeper now, and I don't think you want to be near these flows."

Alarmed, Joshua got to his feet and hurried away. As he went, the Laithe followed him. He stopped, not turning around to see, but just *sensing* it. He knew right where it was. It was orbiting him slowly. It came around his front, and he saw it was tilted just like the real earth was tilted as it revolved around the sun.

"Is this normal?" he said, watching it.

"No," said Brian. "But it's pretty wicked. I wish Tunraden could do that. Now go."

Joshua kept on walking, another twenty feet, until Brian stopped him.

"Okay, son," said Brian, "that's far enough." He smiled goofily. "Get it? Son? Sun? Because . . . orbits . . ." He trailed off sadly, nodding at the floating Laithe. Joshua smiled politely. Puns weren't funny. Most jokes weren't funny.

"I guess my humor works better underground," Brian said with a shrug. "Isabel, you stay just where you are."

"What should I do?" she asked, her voice quivering.

"Absolutely nothing. Don't touch the harp, or draw on it, unless I ask you to. Okay?"

She nodded eagerly, like a little girl.

"Promise you won't use it," Brian insisted.

"I promise."

"This might hurt," he said. Joshua squinted his eyes almost shut, watching through slits, not sure he wanted to see. Brian practiced his gestures again, his fingers moving quickly through the air. He looked around nervously and turned to Isabel. "I feel like I'm about to get naked in public. You're sure it's safe?"

"We're alone," said Isabel. She seemed to be trembling. "Do it."

"You might want to cover your eyes," Brian said, but if he meant it as a warning, he didn't give them any time to obey. He shoved his hands into Tunraden, just like he did when carrying her. But this time, instead of only the circles lighting up, the entire surface of the stone oval burst into golden brilliance. A column of light shot into the sky. Joshua covered his eyes. Isabel rocked back and nearly fell over in the tall grass.

Brian started pulling out big, loopy strings of the golden stuff. It dripped from his hands like honey. His hands started to carve it into strange shapes, and the stuff—the Medium, it must be—seemed to obey him like an animal. Isabel gasped.

Then, suddenly, Tunraden went black. Brian cried out. The golden strings turned to ash and dropped back into the surface of the Loomdaughter. Brian went stiff and collapsed sideways, his hands bent painfully, his eyes crushed closed.

"Brian!" Joshua cried.

A low cry of pain slid out from between Brian's clenched

teeth. The cords of his neck stood out like cables, stretched tight.

Joshua ran forward. Isabel was still on the ground too, still looking dizzily at Tunraden. In the grass in front of her, Miradel was a swollen cloud of sparkling green light.

Isabel had severed Brian.

CHAPTER NINE

Shadows across Time and Space

MR. MEISTER SAT ON HORACE'S COUCH, AND SOMEHOW THE sight—his wild white hair, his gleaming red vest, his enormous spectacled eyes—was one of the most bizarre things Horace had ever seen. The Chief Taxonomer, here in Horace's house on Horace's blue couch, with Horace's cat, Loki, perched in his lap, and Horace's mother sitting beside him. The scene, in its own modest way, was even more unsettling than the sight of the Riven, the golem, the oublimort, the scythe-wings, every unbelievable thing Horace had encountered since becoming a Keeper. Simply put, every cell in Horace's body seemed to scream that the man simply shouldn't be here.

But he was. He had to be.

As for his mother, Horace still couldn't gauge her sur-prise. She'd been startled when she answered the door—in her pajamas and a huge T-shirt that read I READ PAST MY

BEDTIME—but hesitated only a tiny bit before inviting the old man in, with Horace following awkwardly, as if he didn't even live here. She was plainly relieved to see Horace. The last time she'd seen him, hours before, Chloe had been dragging him out the door on yet another unexplained mission. His mother said nothing now, only tousled his shaggy hair with a bit of extra verve.

His dad was at the door too, looking alarmed and almost comically ready for action. It was now 1:18 in the morning, after all. But his mother had simply said, "It's okay, Matthew. This is an old friend. From before." The way she stressed the word "before" made Horace wonder, not for the first time, just how much his father knew. Quite a bit, obviously. His father had gone back upstairs without comment, rims of worry crinkling his eyes.

Now Horace and his mother and Mr. Meister sat in the living room eating bagel chips—bagel chips! Horace's mother stared at Mr. Meister as he scratched Loki's lifted chin. She seemed to be having as much difficulty absorbing the old man's presence as Horace was.

"Did Beck drive you," she asked Mr. Meister, "or did you come by falkrete stone?"

"Beck drove us. We've had enough falkrete stones for one night."

"Good old Beck. Any address anywhere."

Hearing his mom talk so casually about the Wardens' secrets—secrets Horace himself had been keeping from his

142

mother—wasn't making any of this feel more real. "Yup," he said lamely, trying to go with the flow. "Good old Beck."

His mother took a bagel chip but didn't eat it. "So," she said to Mr. Meister cheerfully, "this was not a moment I'd bothered to imagine. You coming here. Ever."

"Why should you?" replied Mr. Meister. "Overpreparation is a waste of energy. Better to be nimble in the face of the unexpected."

"Ah, so you've come to see how nimble I am. Is Horace in trouble?"

"This instant? No, no more than usual. Considerably less, in fact, than in other recent instants."

His mother frowned, avoiding Horace's eyes. She folded her legs beneath her and nibbled at her bagel chip. "Look, I don't know if I seem very calm right now," she told Mr. Meister, "but there's a pretty big, confusing dance going on inside me, and you being here . . ." She crossed her eyes and spun her fingers in circles at her ears.

"My presence is disorienting," said Mr. Meister. "I understand."

"Disorienting to say the least. I'm trying to adapt." She plucked at her pajama pants. "You sent a very powerful leestone home with Horace, the day of his Find. I appreciated that." The leestone in question, a bulky sculpture of a raven atop a tortoise, had been sent home with Horace the same day he brought home the Fel'Daera. The statue, like leestones everywhere, protected the home from the attentions of the Riven.

143

"It was not a courtesy," Mr. Meister said with a wave of the hand. "It was a necessity."

"I was told it was a Mother's Day gift."

"Was it not?"

"You knew I would recognize it for what it was. You knew Horace was my son."

"Of course. And yes."

"Because you were still keeping tabs on me. After all these years."

"Yes."

"I never knew that. I assumed you might be, but never knew for sure."

"Good. Perhaps I haven't lost the step I sometimes fear I have."

"Oh, I imagine whatever steps you've lost have been compensated for." She glanced down at the polymath's ring on Mr. Meister's hand.

Mr. Meister laughed. "That is the Wardens' way, for better or for worse."

"Your way, you mean." To Horace's ears, these words sounded like they could have come out of his own mouth. For a moment, he glimpsed in his mother the young, rebellious teen she would have been all those years ago. His mother must have felt it too, because she shook herself off a bit and then said, "I wouldn't be thrilled tonight to act the way I acted back then. Not because I regret it, but because I'm different now. You, though—you talk the same. A half cup of mystery, a teaspoon of aphorism, a dash of blunt truth once in a while.

I used to dream about you talking."

The old man's eyes twinkled. "My condolences."

"What's aphorism?" asked Horace.

His mother said, "An aphorism is an apparent wisdom, wrapped up in a pretty package of words."

Mr. Meister laughed out loud, startling Loki to the floor. "Marvelous," he said. "Just so. And you say you're different now, Jessica, but it seems the best of you remains. And you still have your talents. You still have your harp."

"Of course. You heard that Isabel found it earlier, I'm sure. That she was messing with that spent raven's eye. Is that why you're here now?"

"Yes."

"What did she do? Is everyone okay?"

Horace nodded yes, but his mother didn't seem to be paying any attention to him.

"Was Isabel turned?" she asked the old man. "Is she working for the Riven?"

"I do not believe so," said Mr. Meister.

"I was stupid to let her come here."

"I imagine it was hard to resist the opportunity. Isabel's return was a shock—to Chloe most of all, no doubt. Yet not even Chloe can claim the connection to Isabel that you can, Jess."

A trembling silence fell. Into it, the soft wet sounds of Loki washing his face crept like tiny waves coming ashore. Hands in her lap, Horace's mother rubbed the knuckles of one hand against the nails of the other.

Mr. Meister scooted toward her gracefully, the oraculum glinting in the lamplight. He laid a knobby hand on her knee, his voice suddenly gentle. "Long ago, difficult decisions were made. Decisions in which neither you nor Isabel had a say. Do you wish me to apologize?"

Horace held his breath. His mother seemed to hold hers, too. Whatever else had happened all those years ago when his mother worked as a Tuner for the Wardens, an apology—if it was going to come—would be for one thing and one thing only.

The kaitan.

Only yesterday, Horace's mother had told him the terrible story of how she had become a Tuner. When she was Horace's age, and Isabel was younger still, the two of them, separately, had been drawn to a warehouse full of Tan'layn. But instead of being invited to return in order to go through the Find, as Horace had been with the Fel'Daera, the girls had been invited back only to be seated together in a terrible device called the kaitan.

Embedded within the kaitan, unseen, were two Tan'layn, one for each of them—instruments they could have bonded to, had they been allowed to go through the Find; instruments chosen by Mr. Meister and Mrs. Hapsteade with the help of the oraculum and the Vora. The instruments were weak, of course, expendable in the eyes of Mr. Meister—nothing like the Fel'Daera or the Alvalaithen.

They had to be, because as the girls sat there, somehow

the kaitan tore their bonds permanently loose from those undiscovered instruments, leaving the Tan'layn powerless and Keeperless forever. But instead of letting those broken bonds shrivel away, the kaitan instead wove the two girls together directly, binding them. The Medium flowed back and forth between their bodies. The process was ghastly, unthinkable . . . but that hadn't even been the end of it.

Now, in Horace's living room, they sat in the quiet for a full minute. At last, Horace's mother began to talk into it, soft and calm. "I'm sure you can't imagine how much it hurt—can't imagine the *way* it hurt," she said, looking at Mr. Meister as if he were an earnest child learning a gentle lesson. "Not the kaitan—what came after. You took us away, took us apart so that the bond between us would stretch and break and leave us raw. Leave us wounded. Leave us Tuners."

This was how it worked, Horace knew. Once the bond between the two was broken, the ruptured ends would linger, raw and exposed and sensitive. It was this sensitivity that gave Tuners their powers.

His mother continued. "I could feel the bond stretching, you taking Isabel away from me. I had only just met her, but for that hour or so, because of the bond, I *knew* her. You know? She was so scared, but excited, and was trying to crush her fear down deep. I could feel her moving farther and farther, and it just . . . *ached*." She wrapped her arms around her stomach, rocking gently. "I didn't know it then, but it was a motherly sort of pain. I wanted to stop, of course. Mrs.

147

Hapsteade said no. She told me the cure to the pain was ahead and not behind. And that was the truth, I guess, even if I had no idea what was happening. I remember I was crying and a woman on the street stopped and asked me if I was okay, and Mrs. Hapsteade said, sort of sad but sort of proud, 'These are tears of bravery.' And I was just thirteen and lost and, in that moment, I thought those words were so . . . kind. They seemed like the kindest words anyone had ever said about me. So, I kept walking, I don't know how many blocks more, all the while thinking about those words and Isabel moving farther and farther away, and when the bond finally ripped apart, it was like every muscle being ripped from every deep bone. I screamed. I fell onto all fours right there on the sidewalk. I could feel the Medium through every pore. It felt like hot water over a fresh burn. I just sat there, people walking by. Mrs. Hapsteade sat beside me. She didn't say anything. There was nothing to say."

She looked down, lifted Mr. Meister's hand still resting on her knee, and gently placed it into his own lap. She patted it before letting it go. "There is nothing to say." She exhaled loudly and looked over at Horace. She smiled thinly and gave him a tiny shrug, her eyes glistening.

Horace was fighting his own tears. The first time he'd heard her tell this story, she'd only let loose the facts, not the feelings—maybe to protect him, he realized. But with Mr. Meister here, old wounds had opened. He marveled at how strong his mother was, how wise, how . . . brave.

Mr. Meister removed his glasses and wiped them gingerly with a cloth snagged from a pocket. His eyes looked tiny without them. "You are correct that I do not know how it feels," he said. "I will apologize if you wish. I will apologize for what we asked of you."

"*Asked*," Horace's mother repeated with a bitter little laugh, wiping her eyes. But then she shook her head. "No. If you had it to do over, you'd do it again. I'm not angry, I just . . . I won't ask for an apology on those terms. And what happened to me then, what you did to me—it's been a part of me for twenty-five years. I'm not looking to change who I am."

Mr. Meister slipped his glasses back on. "Nor am I. And we needed you, back then. You and Isabel both."

"I don't want your apology, Henry. But I will remember that you offered."

Loki leapt up onto her lap. Horace's mother bent and nuzzled the cat's black flank. "Was that good?" she cooed to him. "Were you listening? I think that was good. I think that was important." She looked over at Horace, heaved another sigh. "You okay?"

He nodded.

"I'm okay," she said. "Everything is okay."

"I know."

"So," she said, sitting up straight. "You want to tell me why you're here now? Also important, no doubt."

"Yes," said Horace. "Very important."

"Isabel is on the run again," said Mr. Meister. "This time

with something of truly great value."

"Well, I can't find her. There's no bond between us anymore."

Mr. Meister gave a little half shrug, as if that might only be half true. "Regardless, you may be able to help us locate her. Will you come with us?"

Horace's mother ran her fingers through her hair, as if she were making up her mind, but he could see she'd already decided. There was never a question, really. She would come with them, into the Warren. She would help them track down Isabel.

She looked over at Horace, sighing. "You know, some kids just need their parents to make brownies for bake sales. Help them with their pinewood derby cars, take them to soccer practice, stuff like that."

Horace grinned. "And some parents just joined French club back when they were in high school. Sorry we're not more boring."

"It's not our fault. It's in our blood." She stood and stretched, dumping Loki onto the couch. "Okay, then. Better get my harp. Give me ten minutes—if I'm going to do this, I'd like to do it with pants on."

If it was bizarre seeing Mr. Meister in his home, Horace found it surprisingly unbizarre to see his mother in the Warren. Once they crossed Vithra's Eye, she moved through the golden-gray forest of the Great Burrow as if she belonged

150

there, her face lit with a comforting glow of memory, small sounds of recognition drifting from her lips. She pointed out Mrs. Hapsteade's doba, another doba where she and Isabel used to work and play, and a curving, secluded alcove at the top of a rock spill that she did not identify but that inspired a warm ripple of girlish laughter.

"Nothing's changed," she said dreamily. "Except it's smaller than I remember."

Chloe, who had been waiting impatiently for them on the shores of Vithra's Eye, looked up at the towering ceiling high above them. "You must remember it super huge, then."

At the back of the Burrow, they ran into a curious sight. The precarious edge of the Maw, and the Maw itself, seemed to no longer exist. Horace stopped, confused and disoriented, before he realized: Gabriel was here. The humour of Obro was up, just ahead of them, refusing to be seen from the outside.

"What's happening?" said Horace, alarmed. "Is something wrong?"

"Hardly," Chloe muttered. "This has been going on for a while. I chose not to participate."

From a ledge overhead, Arthur the raven squawked down at them. A second later, the humour vanished with a harsh shredding sound. Gabriel stood there holding his staff. Neptune and April stood a little ways off, staring like wide-eyed deer.

"What are you doing?" Horace said.

"We're helping Gabriel practice," said April.

Chloe grunted. "Is that what he's calling it now?"

"Some people like to practice *before* the danger comes," said Neptune.

"There are things I could have done better tonight," Gabriel said. "Things I hope to do better in the future."

"Yeah, well, I guess you should always try to be better than yourself," said Chloe.

"Good advice for everyone," Horace's mother said, with a gently chiding glance Chloe's way. She stepped forward to greet Gabriel and Neptune, introducing herself as Jessica. Gabriel only bowed and said, "It's an honor to meet you, Mrs. Andrews. Thank you for coming."

Neptune said, "We haven't met, but I've been known to hang around your house."

"Tourminda jokes," said Horace's mom. "Funny stuff."

Together, the five of them descended the Perilous Stairs. Horace's mother looked at ease even here, though she said she'd never gone down the stairs before. When they entered Brian's workshop below, the older Wardens were waiting. Mr. Meister looked as unflappable as always, even though Horace knew he had just returned through Sanguine Hall.

Mrs. Hapsteade swept up to Horace's mother, her stern face cracking, and drew her into a deep hug. They murmured inaudible greetings to each other. Mrs. Hapsteade gave Horace's mother a lightning-swift kiss on the cheek.

Horace's mother reached into her bag and pulled out her

harp. Folded up, it looked like a crude fish made from four curving arms of wood. "I guess we should get started. Where's the portal?"

On the drive in, Mr. Meister had explained to her what Isabel had done. Horace's mother remembered the Laithe of Teneves, of course. She'd been asked to tune it years before—it, and the Fel'Daera too. She'd even met Sil'falo Teneves, the Maker of both instruments, who'd delivered the two precious Tan'layn to the Warren. Isabel had ended up tuning both instruments, but Horace's mom had also plumbed the depths of both the box and the globe, and understood bits and pieces of how they functioned. She had seemed skeptical that she could do what Mr. Meister was asking of her, but her eagerness to try now lifted Horace's spirits a little.

The entire group retired to Tunraden's empty chamber. Horace's mother immediately approached the wall where Joshua had opened the portal earlier that evening. She held her hands out, groping like a mime, obviously sensing the residue.

"This is incredible."

"It is," said Mr. Meister.

She turned to Horace. "When you look through the box here, what do you see?"

"Just shapes, mostly. Moving fast toward me."

She nodded. "Opening a door with the Laithe isn't like falkrete travel. It's not instantaneous. It's more like movement. I think you're seeing the movement toward the destination Joshua chose."

"Let us try," said Mr. Meister solemnly.

"Right," said Horace, taking the Fel'Daera into his hands. Everyone watched him closely—except for his mother, who deliberately looked away. This was a kindness, he realized. He had never before used the box in her presence, and while he wasn't exactly embarrassed to do so now, still this part of his life had remained separate from her so far, belonging to Horace alone. It felt a little like being caught singing in the shower. But his mother, his good mother, was pretending not to listen. He oriented himself, grateful not to have her eyes on him. When he was ready, he opened the Fel'Daera.

"Show me where," he said, holding the box up and stepping forward.

His mother held out a flat hand, her face unreadable. Horace moved toward it, peering through the blue glass. And when he got the alignment right, the residue of the portal burst into view just as before—*hurtling shapes, a chaos of angles and curves rushing toward him.*

His mother gasped, clutching her head. "Whoa," she said. "Whoa."

"What's the matter?" Chloe asked.

"Nothing. It's fine. It just feels like . . . crossing the streams. Very intense." She touched Horace lightly on the shoulder and asked him, very kindly, "Can I help now? Can I try?"

Horace nodded, holding still. His mother moved to the pedestal where Tunraden usually sat and unfolded her harp.

The fish shape became a kind of bowl. From each of the four curving arms, shimmering sails made from ribbons of rainbowed light rose toward the center. The Medium. She began to pluck at these strings delicately, with the same sure fingers that had cut Horace's hair and pulled splinters from his palm. The strings vibrated and fluttered through brilliant cascades of color.

"That's a harp?" April asked. "It looks so different from Miradel."

"Every harp is different," growled Mr. Meister. "But none should be named."

Horace's mother shot him an irritated glance. "Mine is more harplike than most, April," she said, eight fingers poised like spider legs on the strings. "But I can still . . ." She pushed one pinky and pulled with the pinch of two other fingers.

Inside the box—*the tumble of shapes reversing itself, drifting away now.* Horace swayed, barely holding the box in place. "It's going backward. But I still can't see anything. What am I doing wrong?"

"Nothing," she said. "And that's a good thing. If the problem were inside the Fel'Daera, I couldn't help you. I can only do so much with the Medium inside a working Tan'ji. The portal is the problem." She looked up at Mr. Meister. "You said Joshua is the Keeper of the Laithe. I met him tonight, and I can believe it, but . . . did he go through the Find?" Before the old man could reply, she shook her head and answered her own question. "No, he couldn't have.

Isabel brought him to it. She's teaching him."

Horace's mother fussed with the strings again. "Joshua opened a portal—very messily—and when the Loomdaughter went through, it got even messier." A glint of yellow streaked across one of the sails of her harp. Inside the box, the receding tunnel of shapes spun briefly.

"Why messier?" Horace asked.

"Falo was smart when she created the Laithe—and the Fel'Daera, for that matter. She knew that Tanu might travel through them, dragging the Medium along. That can cause interference. Tangles."

Immediately Horace thought of the night in the Riven's nest when he had sent Chloe's dragonfly through the box. Chloe seemed to be thinking the same thing, because she watched him like a cat, twirling the Alvalaithen idly by the tail. "I tangled you," she mouthed at him. Inexplicably, Horace found himself blushing.

"Ordinarily," Horace's mother continued, "the Laithe and the box can handle Tanu. Clean opening, clean exit. But I would imagine if a Keeper is inexperienced, or compromised in some way, the passage of a Tanu could leave a terrible mess behind. That might be what I'm sensing."

Mr. Meister was nodding enthusiastically at every word. "This is marvelous news, then. You can help us. You can clean the residue and allow Horace to see."

"Probably. Maybe. I'm seeing patterns I don't recognize, and I've tuned nearly every kind of instrument there is. Well,

156

except a Loomdaughter." She looked at Mr. Meister. "Which one is she?"

"The eighth," Mr. Meister replied.

Now her eyebrows jumped. "Yikes."

"Yikes, indeed."

Loomdaughters, Horace knew, were so called because they were replicas of the Starlit Loom, the very first Tan'ji. Only nine Loomdaughters were made, each more powerful than the last—though none as powerful as the Starlit Loom itself. Every Tanu that had ever been made was created either with the Starlit Loom or one of the Loomdaughters. Most of the nine Loomdaughters had been destroyed, and Tunraden, the eighth, was the most valuable of those that remained.

"That explains this mess," Horace's mother said, bending over her harp. "But this is good. I can help." She pushed and pulled at the strings, using all ten fingers now, and then said casually, "I never tuned a Loomdaughter, but Falo did let me hold the Starlit Loom one time."

Horace's mouth fell open. The Starlit Loom. With it, Falo had made the Fel'Daera, and the Laithe. And long before that, some unknown earlier Keeper of the Loom had made the Alvalaithen—and another, of course, had created Tunraden.

To his surprise, Mr. Meister seemed equally shocked by this news. He actually sputtered before saying, "Falo showed it to you? Let you hold it?"

157

"Yes. It was very small. A little bit smaller than the Fel'Daera, I think."

Another surprise. Tunraden was the size of a sink.

"It would be smaller, yes," said Mr. Meister, as if he had never seen the Starlit Loom himself, but only studied it. "The Loomdaughters are crude replicas, similar in shape to the Loom but much greater in size. I am stunned that Falo actually let you touch it."

"I guess I was in the middle of some . . . teenage throes, so maybe she felt sorry for me. But the point is, I saw the Loom, and I think that can help me now. Most Tanu are like pipes, or drains. But looms are like fountains." She looked over at Horace. "Try again?"

Horace, listening and caught up in the notion that his own mother had actually *held* the Starlit Loom, had let the box fall to his side. He closed the lid, reset himself, and tried again, finding the invisible plane where the portal lay.

"Okay, let's see," his mother said. Her fingers began to dance. The strings of her harp quivered and shone. A muted rainbow of shadows flickered along the walls of the chamber. Suddenly, with a single thrust of his wings, Arthur leapt from April's shoulder and onto the pedestal, leaning toward the harp. April reached out for him, clearly embarrassed, but Horace's mother didn't so much as flinch. The bird stared at the strings and started to rock side to side, a little dance of encouragement. After a moment, April's eyes went cloudy.

"Wow," she breathed, clearly seeing the strings through the raven's eyes.

"What's he doing?" Horace whispered.

"Nothing. Just watching. He likes it. But the colors . . ." She shook her head in amazement.

Horace's mother twisted her hands, pressing the tips of all ten fingers together across five different strings. She pushed and pulled. Abruptly, four ribbons of golden light flared from the center of the harp out to the arms, where they vanished with a flash.

"Oh!" Jessica gasped, as the harp wobbled.

Inside the box—*no more movement; a motionless tangle of silhouettes.* "It stopped," Horace said. "But I still can't see anything. It's like a kaleidoscope."

"Here," said his mother. She caressed several strings, actually seeming to draw them from the center like thread from a spool. Green, purple, silver, mauve. And then, suddenly—

Trees. A forest. A shimmering ribbon through the leaves—a stream.

"I see it!" Horace cried. He was so excited that the box slipped out of alignment, and he lost it. He found the residue again and stared, reporting what the others could not see. "There's a stream. A forest by a stream, or more like a river. I don't see anybody, though."

"Remarkable," said Mr. Meister. "Well done, Jessica. Thank you."

Horace's mother looked flushed and bright-eyed. Young. "I missed this," she said breathlessly, and laughed. "I hate to say it, but I did."

"But now what?" said Chloe. "They went to the woods

159

by a river. What woods?"

"Mr. Meister, you said Joshua might be more likely to open the portal to a place he'd been before," Horace said. "I suppose this could be the riverbank where we fought the Riven the other day."

"We were at Skokie Lagoons the day before that," April said. "We spent the night in the woods by a river. And the next day, we were actually on the river for hours. Lots of woods. Do you see cars or bridges?"

"No, and I can't turn and look around," Horace said, frustrated. "I'm locked into this one view, like a telescope pressed against a window. I can see where they went, but I have no idea *where* the where is."

"I believe I can help," Mr. Meister said.

The old man reached into two of his many pockets, one with each hand. He dug deep with the left and he pulled out a familiar object—the compass that usually sat on his desk, its needle forever pointed at Mr. Meister. With two fingers of his right hand, he delicately plucked out a small metal object, a three-dimensional, six-pointed star—a jack.

"Jacks," April said. "I used to play jacks with my brother."

"As did I with mine," Mr. Meister said kindly. Horace wasn't sure he'd heard right. Mr. Meister had a brother?

Chloe's startled face scrunched quickly into mischief. She said, "I always assumed you would have eaten any siblings in the womb."

"Delightful, but no. We did not share that particular

residence. Now observe, please." Mr. Meister held the compass low for all to see, and slowly traced a path around it with the jack. The red needle of the compass, long and thin, swiveled smoothly to point straight at the jack, wherever it went. The needle moved with no lag or wobble whatsoever, as if it were connected to the jack with an invisible rod. It was so simple, yet utterly—Horace had to admit—magical.

"I always thought the compass was pointing at you," he said.

"So it usually appears." Mr. Meister held up the jack. "This little Tan'kindi is called a backjack, and I carry it with me wherever I go—in one of my ordinary pockets, of course. I leave the compass in my office, so that Mrs. Hapsteade can find me, should I wander off."

"As he often does," Mrs. Hapsteade remarked.

"But how does this help us?" asked Chloe.

Mr. Meister shrugged as if it were obvious. "We send it traveling, of course."

Traveling. Through the box. "Wait a minute, wait a minute," Horace said, feeling uncharacteristically slow. Maybe because it was so late, and so much had happened. "You mean you think I can send it through the portal? With the box?"

"Do you think you cannot? The merged doorway is open. If you can see, you can send, yes? The backjack will travel forward through time—a mere ten seconds, as determined by the breach—and sideways through space, to wherever the others have gone."

"But that seems crazy," said Horace.

Mr. Meister held out the backjack. Horace took it, watching the needle swing, and placed it inside the open Fel'Daera. He raised the box, careful not to let the backjack fall out, and once again found the portal. *The shimmering water, a bush rustling by the water's edge.*

"I guess if it doesn't work, we'll know in ten seconds," Horace said. If it didn't work, he assumed, the backjack would simply reappear here in the chamber ten seconds after being sent, falling to the floor.

Cautiously, Horace closed the lid. *Time and space, space and time.* The lid halves snicked closed, and the familiar tingle skittered through his hands. The backjack was gone.

"Goodness!" said Mr. Meister.

On his compass, the needle had disappeared. Or no, not disappeared—the formerly white face had turned entirely red.

"Did we break it?" asked Horace, alarmed.

"I do not think so. The backjack simply does not exist at the moment, and so it cannot be found. Keep watching."

In the back of Horace's mind, of course, he was counting. *Six seconds, seven, eight.*

At ten seconds precisely, an arc of whiteness began to bloom on the compass. The red portion narrowed swiftly, and began to shorten. The backjack had reappeared . . . somewhere. Within moments, the red had resolved itself into a squat arrow pointing nearly the opposite direction it had been before. The needle was short and fat now, the length of a fingernail, whereas before it had been as long and slender as a toothpick.

"But why is the needle short?" April asked. "What does that mean?"

Mr. Meister rotated the compass, experimenting. The needle stayed firmly pointed where it was. It reminded Horace of how Loki's eyes would stay locked on a bird in the backyard, even if you jostled his body around. "The needle lengthens as it gets closer to the backjack, shortens as it gets farther," Mr. Meister explained. "Our backjack is now . . . ten miles away? Fifteen?"

"And so we go get it," said Chloe. "We get them."

"Just so."

"But what if they're not there anymore?" April pointed out. "What if Isabel made Joshua open another portal?"

"Then we repeat the process," Mr. Meister said. "But the possibility of multiple portals raises another danger we have not yet discussed. Has it occurred to you, Horace?"

"What?"

"You are of course aware of Dr. Jericho's sensitivity toward the Fel'Daera."

"Yes."

All Mordin could sense when nearby Tan'ji were being used without protection. That was why they were called Hunters. But for reasons that had never been explained, Dr. Jericho had a particular awareness of the Box of Promises.

He was so sensitive to it, in fact, that he could sense it from the other side of the glass. Whenever Horace saw a future that included Dr. Jericho, Dr. Jericho—in that future—could sense that Horace had the box open in the past, watching him. It was a dizzying challenge.

Suddenly Horace gasped. The Fel'Daera and the Laithe were linked. Made by the same hand, and similar in function. "You think Dr. Jericho can sense the Laithe of Teneves too," he said. "Just like he senses the Fel'Daera."

"It stands to reason," Mr. Meister said, sounding not the least bit worried.

"But then Brian is in more danger than we thought! If Dr. Jericho can sense when a portal is being opened, even from the other side, the Riven will track them down in no time."

"It is a possibility we must consider."

"Let's go, then," said Chloe. She swiveled around to Horace's mother. "And you'll have to come with us, Jessica. I mean, I'm trying not to get too amped up about this whole mom-versus-mom thing, but if there are more portals out there, we'll need you."

Mr. Meister said nothing, his big gray eyes locked on Horace's mother.

His mother, chewing her lip, nodded thoughtfully. "Horace, do you remember when you lost your mind because I wouldn't chaperone your school's field trip to the aquarium? You know—that normal mom thing you wanted me to do, but I didn't?"

"Yes," Horace said, blushing. He'd been like nine years old. He had a vague memory of begging on his knees for his mother to come, blubbering at her.

She folded up her harp, still nodding, letting the glistening strings collapse into nothing. She got to her feet. "After tonight, we'll be even."

PART TWO

The Meadow by Night

CHAPTER TEN

The Call of the Laithe

BRIAN LAY RIGID IN THE GRASS, SEETHING IN PAIN. JOSHUA TRIED calling to him, but he didn't answer. Isabel couldn't see him, wouldn't see him. She sat there gazing at Tunraden while Miradel glittered on the ground before her.

"Stop!" Joshua shouted. When she didn't answer, he marched over to her, burning with anger. He took her by the shoulders and shook her. "Stop it! You're severing him!"

Isabel looked at him, dazed and alarmed. "What?" she said, and then she seemed to notice Brian. She cursed and grabbed Miradel. The wicker harp quickly faded and shrank.

Brian took a deep, sharp breath, like he'd been drowning but had crawled ashore. He rolled onto his stomach and lay there. "God," he said into the weeds. "Oh, god. Not severing. Cleaving."

"I'm sorry!" Isabel cried. "It was an accident."

169

Joshua stepped away from Isabel, pressing the Laithe to his chest, horrified. Cleaving. Ripping the bond apart by force. Severing was temporary, and only really dangerous if it lasted a long time. But cleaving was permanent. Deadly.

Brian lifted himself and laid his face atop Tunraden. "You're here," he mumbled into the stone surface. "Still here. I feel you."

"Brian, are you okay?" asked Joshua.

"No. Not okay. But better. Anything is better. Oh, god, my . . . . *existence* hurts." One of Tunraden's circles briefly flashed golden as Brian slipped a single hand inside her. He looked over at Isabel. "What the hell is wrong with you?"

"It was an accident!" Isabel said. "You were hurting me. And all those colors, all around and inside Miradel and me, they. . ."

Brian took another long breath. "The colors," he said to Isabel. "They scared you. So you started to cleave me?"

Joshua hadn't seen any colors. Only gold.

"I got . . . angry," Isabel said. "Something. It was too much."

Brian scowled at Miradel in Isabel's hands. "When you said you couldn't control her, I didn't know how bad it was."

"I've never started to cleave anyone by accident before. Never."

"I think maybe my heart stopped for a second," Brian said. "I think my brain forgot I *had* a heart." Baron came in and laid his slobbery muzzle on Brian's shoulder. Brian leaned away, then patted the dog awkwardly on the head.

"Try again," said Isabel. "Please. I can control her."

"You've got to be kidding," Brian said.

"It won't happen again. I didn't understand what you were doing. I couldn't even follow your flows, and they were hurting me, and I just . . ."

"Wanted to hurt me back," Brian finished.

"No," said Isabel. "Or yes, I guess. I just lost it."

"Why would you think you could follow my flows? You're not a Maker. You can't alter the foramen."

Joshua had never heard that word before, but Isabel obviously knew it. "Just try to explain what you were doing," she said. "See if I can understand, so I can be prepared."

"I told you it would hurt. I warned you."

"Explain it," Isabel pleaded. "Please. When it comes to the Medium, I . . . I'm not used to not knowing. I've never seen anything like what you just did."

Brian sighed. "Give me a minute. Let me think."

They sat in silence. Baron left Brian and ambled over to Joshua. The dog lay down, but after a few moments lifted his head sharply and looked out into the darkness to the northwest, perking his ears. Joshua watched and listened, and thought he heard music. A sweet whistling call. But no, not music, not here. Baron laid his head back down. Probably just an owl, or some other strange night bird.

Brian sat up, pulling his hand free from Tunraden. "Okay. No promises, but let me explain."

171

Isabel nodded obediently.

"There are two kinds of Tanu, right?" said Brian. "There's your basic Tan'kindi, which don't take the bond, and which will work for anyone . . . leestones, passkeys, dumindars, et cetera. And then Tan'ji, of course, which do take the bond and will only work for their Keepers. But harps aren't really one or the other. They don't take the bond, but they don't work for just anyone, either."

Isabel said, "So it should be easy to make Miradel Tan'ji. She's halfway there."

"Kind of. I've often wondered if I could turn a regular Tan'kindi into a Tan'ji, and I'm pretty sure I could. The foramen—" He glanced at Joshua. "That's like the operating system of the Tan'ji," he explained. "An anchor and a passageway for the Medium. What I was trying to do, Isabel, is tailor the foramen of your harp into more of a Tan'ji shape. It's sort of like turning a mitten into a tight glove. But the foramen—of any harp, but especially yours—is different. It's . . . bloody."

Isabel squirmed. She suddenly looked very uncomfortable.

"Maybe that's not the right word," said Brian. "There is no word. Look, there are other Tanu besides harps that don't fit neatly into a category. Jithandras, for example—not really Tan'ji, not really Tan'kindi. But jithandras are tailored to the talents of a particular Keeper. Your harp, meanwhile, isn't tailored at all. It's . . . spiky and raw and open. Like a vampire's mouth. It's hungry." He sighed again. "Hungry for the wound you received when you went through the kaitan."

Isabel scowled. She wrapped both hands around Miradel and pressed her lips against the twisted surface. A kind of painful growl rumbled in her throat.

Joshua, listening intently so far, couldn't help himself. "What wound? What's a kaitan?"

Nobody answered him. Instead Brian said to Isabel, "If I try again, it's going to hurt. And the hurt will get worse, if it's going to work."

"I can handle it," said Isabel. "I understand."

But Joshua did not understand. They were out here in this dark meadow, with only a broken leestone to protect them. And who would protect them from Isabel? This was no place for them to be. No place to be talking about wounds, or blood, or vampires. No place for Brian, especially.

"I don't want to do this anymore," Joshua said quietly. "Brian should go back to the Warren. I can take him."

Brian smiled and seemed to think about it for a few seconds, as Isabel watched silently. "No," he said at last. "I'm going to try again." He took his glasses off and wiped them clean on his BEWARE OF DANGER shirt. He laughed down at the words. "I guess I'm not heeding my own advice, huh?"

"I wasn't prepared the first time," Isabel said. "Now I am. And now at least you know—I really do need your help."

"You could always just give up the harp instead," Brian said. "Although I guess if you haven't given it up by now, even with what happened to . . ." He shrugged.

Isabel held her chin high. She hesitated and then announced, "If you can't fix me, I'll give Miradel up."

Joshua could hardly believe the words. And he wasn't at all sure he should. But he could tell by the look on Isabel's face that *she*, at least, thought she was telling the truth. And it occurred to Joshua then, in a way he couldn't completely grasp, that maybe that was the entire story of Isabel.

Brian looked as skeptical as Joshua felt. "I hear you," the older boy said. "But you need to hear me, too. Maybe you convinced yourself that I came out here tonight because I felt sorry for you, or because I wanted the challenge of fixing you, or . . . oh, I don't know . . . because I needed to be some kind of rebel. And okay, fair enough—none of those things are totally wrong." He leaned in, and his voice got soft and calm, almost kind. "But the real reason I'm here—the only reason I'm *still* here—is because you hurt people. You hurt Chloe. You hurt me. You put my friends in danger. And if I don't fix you, I think you'll keep on hurting people. Because *that's* who you are, whether you like it or not. Whether you even know it or not. I'm going to try again to fix you because I don't want the person that you are to be in the world anymore. Do you understand?"

Isabel looked up at the stars, blinking. Her throat worked up and down. Her lips were tight. She nodded and said, "I hear you."

Brian knelt in front of Tunraden again. "Ready?" he said.

Isabel laid Miradel in the grass and bowed her head,

174

folding her hands in her lap.

Brian tipped his head at Joshua, indicating that he should move back again. Joshua backed away, Baron at his side. Brian plunged his hands into Tunraden.

The fountain of golden light exploded back to life. Again, Brian pulled out thick, hanging ropes of the Medium. Joshua watched Isabel carefully. She stared like a statue, the Medium's light dancing across her eyes.

"Chloe saw the colors too, you know," Brian told her, gathering and twisting the Medium in his hands. "I guess she really is your daughter."

Isabel furrowed her brow for some reason. She sat back and clenched her fists, her eyes squinting with pain.

Brian began to mold the Medium, his hands fast and sure. The golden strings responded to his touch even faster than his hands moved, seeming to gather and organize on their own. Isabel arched her back, her shoulders rigid, her face aglow. Her mouth hung open. Miradel stayed dark.

Brian held an impossible honeycomb of light with one hand. With the other, he reached down to Miradel and pulled a golden spiderweb from its surface, flowing like a thousand rivers. Isabel lurched like she was going to vomit. Brian spread his fingers and parted the web, then carefully placed his honeycomb inside. His fingers flickered over and through the new structure. The threads rearranged themselves, found one another, melting into each other like wax. The web became a funnel, or a tornado, twisting and sinking into itself.

Joshua could hear Isabel breathing. She sounded scared.

"Halfway there," Brian said. As Joshua's eyes adjusted back to the darkness, he could see the boy's glasses gleaming under the stars.

Suddenly Baron leapt up, barking furiously into the darkness. A moment later, a rumble to the north, like an approaching train. No sooner had Joshua heard it than he felt it, beneath him. The ground was shaking.

Tunraden went dark as Brian pulled his hands free. Isabel grunted. "What is it?" Joshua cried over the clamor, blinded by the sudden darkness. A split second later, Miradel flared open wide, spilling green across the grass all around. Isabel started to stand, turning toward the approaching thunder, stretching out a hand for the harp. But before she could reach it, something monstrous—as big as a bus—roared out of the night and hit her, swallowed her. Something thundering and huge, a great black swarm of stones. Miradel winked out. Just a few feet away, Brian's shadow rose and then fell, yelling something Joshua couldn't quite hear. Isabel was swept away, eaten by the river of rock, carried off like a branch in a flood.

"Golem!" Brian yelled again, scrambling away on all fours. "Run, Joshua!"

Frozen with confusion and terror, all Joshua could think was that this thing was nothing like the golems in stories he'd heard. The golem roared past them, forty feet long. It crashed into a corner of the barn, not slowing down at all. A little section of the roof sagged, splintering into dust. Then the golem

176

turned and stood, rising high into the air like the neck of a shadowy dragon. Far above the ground, Isabel hung in its grasp, her arms and legs pinned inside. "No!" she screamed, thrashing around. "Let me go!"

Joshua realized he had grabbed the Laithe out of the air and was clasping it to his belly. Baron was dancing angrily in the grass, barking and whimpering at the same time. Brian waved and shouted at Joshua, telling him to run, but Joshua didn't know what to do. Brian wasn't running. Why wasn't he running? The golem just stood there like the trunk of a giant branchless trees, swaying a little, a million smooth stones crackling and shifting. Joshua dropped to his knees.

And then, over the thin sound of Isabel's shrieks and the low grind of the golem, Joshua heard footsteps to the east. Slow and heavy. Coming close. Baron whined and ran away into the darkness, tail between his legs. Joshua turned and saw a tall thin shadow coming closer, taking huge slow strides. Ten feet tall. Legs like lampposts. Hands as big as rakes.

A Mordin. One of the Riven, a hunter.

And Joshua knew this Mordin. He was taller than the others. He and Isabel had run into him before, and after the battle on the riverbank two nights ago, Joshua had learned his name.

Dr. Jericho.

The Mordin paused beside Joshua, grinning down at him. His beady eyes seemed to widen when he saw the Laithe. "Salutations," he said, his tongue licking over tiny, sharp teeth and cruel thin lips. His voice sounded like an evil song.

Dr. Jericho walked over to where Miradel lay in the grass, dark now. He bent to pick it up. The harp looked no bigger than a marble in his huge hands.

"No!" Isabel shouted, high overhead. "Put it down, you stinking cave snake!"

Dr. Jericho held Miradel up to his face, examining it closely. "Your proxy," he said. "How rustic. I don't know what hopes you were pouring into it just now, but I assume they were foolish—and I guarantee they were pointless. Funny— without you, your proxy is merely a bundle of sticks. Nothing more." He laughed, still peering at the harp. "Such a simple thing to create such fear, such destruction."

Joshua knew the Mordin was thinking of what Isabel had done to the Riven on the riverbank two nights ago. How Isabel had stormed into the battle late, using Miradel to cleave any Riven she encountered—two Mordin and an Auditor, at least. They'd died on the spot. Dr. Jericho had barely escaped with his life.

Dr. Jericho hoisted the harp up high, showing it to Isabel. "I pity you, Forsworn. You should never have been made what you are. But I cannot allow this to remain. This must end."

Isabel's eyes widened in horror. She lunged forward desperately, clawing at the air, struggling to reach the Mordin. "No!" she screamed. The golem held her like hardened concrete.

And then Dr. Jericho slipped Miradel whole into his mouth, and bit down.

The harp crunched sickeningly, splintering between his

teeth. Green light spilled briefly from between his lips, and then went out. He kept chewing, his jaw working hard. He raised his eyebrows at Joshua, who was staring in horror. Isabel was still screaming. The stones of the golem poured over her face and into her mouth, silencing her. The gruesome sounds of grinding, snapping sticks from the Mordin's mouth went on and on, until finally he swallowed and ran his pointed tongue across his lips. He wiped his mouth with one long finger and laid his hand across his chest.

"All gone," he said, his voice tinkling and cruel. "All safe."

He gestured casually, and the towering golem slowly collapsed, bringing Isabel down. It rumbled closer and dumped her in a heap on the ground. Her chest heaved like she was sobbing, but she didn't make a sound.

Dr. Jericho ignored her, instead looking into the darkness beyond Joshua. "All safe, I said."

More footsteps. Joshua spun around. A girl approached, a human girl with blond hair. A teenager, about the age of Neptune and Gabriel. She was pretty, but her face was sharp and sad. She held a small white rod in one hand—a flute? Joshua remembered the strange music he thought he'd heard earlier.

Brian stood up, mouth open, staring at the girl. "Ingrid," he said.

The girl—Ingrid—didn't look at all surprised to see Brian. She barely glanced at him.

"Ah yes, a reunion," Dr. Jericho crooned. "I believe introductions are in order." When no one answered, his eyes darted to Ingrid.

Ingrid pointed. "This one is Brian. He's not supposed to be outside."

"I might say the same about you," Brian muttered. Seeing Joshua's confusion, he said, "She used to be one of us. A Warden. Now she's just a traitor."

Ingrid ignored him, gesturing at Joshua and Isabel. "I don't know these other two."

Dr. Jericho leaned in so close to Joshua that his foul breath ruffled Joshua's hair. A splinter of Miradel was stuck to the corner of his fiendish mouth. "And you are?" he said.

For some reason, Joshua couldn't even think of not answering. "I'm Joshua."

"Joshua, Brian, and a Forsworn—a curious group," Dr. Jericho said. "None of you were present for the battle tonight, I think, yet here you are now, long after the battle is over. I was on my way back to the city when I felt the call of the Laithe. Quite a surprise, to say the least."

Joshua's heart pounded. *The call of the Laithe.* What did the Mordin mean by that?

"I expected to find the usual motley crew of Wardens. Chloe. Gabriel. Horace. But Ingrid played her flute from the edge of the meadow and told me there were three of you here, and none of you the usual suspects. Nonetheless, imagine my surprise when I arrived. I saw things I never thought to see."

Dr. Jericho turned and stood high over Tunraden. "There it is," he said greedily. "Oh dear, oh dear." He looked down at the Loomdaughter, stroking his chin with his long, terrible fingers. "So many failures tonight, and now this! Gifts beyond measure." He crouched down, his legs so long that when they folded, his knees rose over his head. He looked like an insect, like a praying mantis from some terrible nightmare. "A Loomdaughter and her Keeper, here for the having. Tunraden, unless I'm very mistaken." He leaned in toward Brian, his grin slipping away. "*Am* I mistaken, Tinker?" he purred. "I think not."

Suddenly Isabel rose to her feet and rushed at the Mordin, shrieking. Behind her, the huge shifting mountain of the golem rumbled, but didn't chase her. Dr. Jericho reached out, caught Isabel by the throat, and slammed her easily to the ground. She lay there gasping for breath, the wind knocked out of her.

"Let us not be silly," Dr. Jericho said to no one in particular. "There are no warriors among you now." He licked his lips, his thin tongue catching the sliver of Miradel stuck to his mouth. He swallowed it. "Not anymore."

"The other Wardens are coming," Brian said. "The warrior types. They know where we are."

"Oh, I doubt that very much. Let me see . . ." The Mordin pointed to Brian, Isabel, and Joshua in turn. "The valued Keeper of one of the most precious Tan'ji in the world, a Forsworn bearing a harp that would never have been given as a gift, and a Lostling."

Lostling. The word made no sense to Joshua, but apparently, that's what Dr. Jericho was calling him.

"The noble Mr. Meister would never have allowed any of this," Dr. Jericho continued. "Quite the opposite. You are . . . on the run, as they say." He pressed five long fingers against his chest and raised his eyebrows in surprise, like he'd been given a compliment. "Is it me you've come looking for? Should I be flattered?"

"Oh, absolutely," said Brian. He looked scared to death but was talking brave. "We heard great things about your club and can't wait to sign up. The pointy teeth, the creepy fingers, the caves that smell like rotten eggs." He looked back at Ingrid. "Was that the part of the brochure that got you hooked, Ingrid?"

"Better one night in a Riven nest that smells like brimstone than three years in a Tinker prison that stinks of surrender."

"Feisty," Brian said. "Speaking of nests, Gabriel and the new kids were trapped in one recently. The golem had him, but he got free somehow. You wouldn't know anything about that, would you? Because he told me a funny story I'm sure your new boyfriend would love to—"

"Enough," said Dr. Jericho. "We know what transpired that night in the theater. Old allegiances . . . old devotions . . . they sometimes linger. Ingrid followed her heart, but we in turn forgave her sentimentality. After all, it's only . . . *human*." He said the word like it was food. Joshua closed his eyes. He heard Dr. Jericho stand and walk away.

When he opened them again, the Mordin was standing

where Joshua's portal had been. He was examining the spot, peering at the air. "Crude," he said. "Just what one would expect from a Lostling."

Somehow the Mordin could sense the portal. Joshua himself could see nothing. "I'm not a Lostling," Joshua said stubbornly.

"You do not even know the meaning of the word," the Mordin replied. He turned to Isabel. "But *you* do. Why were you in such a hurry that you had to put the Laithe in his hands? And you gave him instruction too, it seems."

"Leave me alone," Isabel said miserably.

"You have disobeyed the laws of the Wardens."

"Why shouldn't I?"

Brian spoke up. "I didn't know the Riven cared so much about the sanctity of the Find."

"We do not. Your precious Find is already a stage show, a masquerade." Dr. Jericho gestured at Ingrid. Her face gave nothing away. "Mr. Meister's favorite recruits come to him at a vulnerable age, hungry for meaning, desperate for some-thing—anything—to tell them *who they are*. He lures them near, and presents their weak minds with the illusion of choice. He provides them an identity, and they gobble it up."

Joshua listened keenly. The Mordin disgusted him and frightened him, but if it was true that the Find was just an illusion, then maybe it wasn't so bad, what had happened to Joshua tonight.

"We Riven, on the other hand," Dr. Jericho went on,

"take our bonds long before we even have a sense of self." He removed his black jacket, big as a tent. He began unbuttoning the white shirt beneath. "We *are* our instruments, from the start." The Mordin turned away and pulled back the collar of his shirt, letting it fall, exposing his broad, pale shoulders. A thin forest of bristling hairs covered his back, almost like spines. And between his sharp shoulder blades, a bright bulge of metallic blue ran along his backbone from his neck to the middle of his back, buried in his flesh. It pulsed faintly from top to bottom, like a swallowing throat.

"This is Raka, my Tan'ji," said Dr. Jericho. The skin around the edges of the strange Tan'ji was scarred, burned. And that blue—deep and bright. Joshua immediately remembered writing with the Vora, and the blue ink that flowed from its tip. This blue was the same.

Dr. Jericho pulled up his shirt, covering the gleaming blue bulge. "Mine since birth. It chose me before I even understood the meaning of choice. With Raka, I—like all Mordin—can feel Tan'ji being used from miles away. But Raka is uniquely sensitive to a certain very rare kind of Tan'ji. The blue tells the tale: I am especially attuned to kairotics—abilities like yours, Joshua. Keepers who can pierce holes through space and time." He grinned and threaded his long arms back through his jacket. "My affinity for kairotics is a family talent, I'm told."

"That's why you felt the Laithe when Joshua used it," Brian said.

"Yes, from both ends. As I said, crude work. Loud. I would

have felt it from halfway around the world." He stalked back over to Joshua in two long strides and pointed at the Laithe. "This instrument did not choose you. Nor were you allowed to choose it yourself. The choice was made by another, forced upon you both. You are a Lostling." He shook his head sadly. "Your bond is poison. I can feel it."

"That's not true!" Joshua shouted, his voice sounding small and squeaky.

"Mr. Meister will hunt you down, you know," Dr. Jericho continued. "He will hunt you down and take your Tan'ji from you. He will seize the Laithe and tell you that you have no claim to it."

"Don't listen to him, Joshua," said Brian. "That's a lie."

"He took mine from me," Isabel said bitterly. "Mr. Meister took it and destroyed it. I never even laid eyes on it."

Joshua didn't want to hear any of it. No words from anyone. Every word was terrible. "But I already used the Laithe," he said. "I got us out of the Warren. I got us here."

"Here, yes," the Mordin laughed. "On the edge of a battlefield, mere hours after the battle ended. Could you do no better? Find no safer place, in all the wide world?" He reached out his terrible hand and laid it on Joshua's shoulder. It engulfed his entire chest. Joshua noticed a twisted black ring with a bloodred stone. "You are crippled, Joshua, through no fault of your own. But I can help you. If you truly are the Keeper of the Laithe of Teneves, we can give you refuge. We will leave you in peace with your instrument, give you time alone. Time to forge the bond and discover your powers."

185

And even though he didn't want to listen, the words made Joshua go weak. This was all he wanted: time alone. Time to sit with the precious Laithe and let it become a part of him. The Laithe itself seemed to want this too, and as he imagined it, he was sure he could hear it calling to him. If there really was poison in the bond, Isabel had put it there. It had to be cleaned. He had to be given time.

He looked up into Dr. Jericho's beetle-black eyes. He tried to think of something brave to say, but he didn't even know what would be the bravest thing right now. No words came. The Mordin nodded at him.

"You will come with me now," Dr. Jericho said.

"Don't do it, Joshua," said Brian.

Joshua didn't move.

But he didn't say no.

"Think on it, won't you?" Dr. Jericho said with a smile, releasing Joshua. "And then there is the matter of the Loomdaughter," he said. He turned toward Brian, holding up the hand with the black-and-red ring. In response, the golem rumbled across the grass toward them, a slow rocky avalanche. Joshua thought he saw something scarlet swimming inside the swarm, like a savage ruby fish.

Dr. Jericho grinned at Brian. "You are invited as well, Keeper."

"As if," Brian said.

"The choice is yours," the Mordin said with a shrug. "But I believe I have an invitation you cannot refuse."

The golem approached Tunraden. It poured itself around

her. Brian cried out and scrambled to reach her, but the golem simply built a rising, sliding wall that Brian could not dig through or climb over. He struggled helplessly, trying to fight through a black wave that had no end.

Dr. Jericho raised his hand, and the golem hoisted Tunraden into the air easily, like a very small child. Brian fell back, his teeth bared, his glasses crooked on his face.

"It would be a shame to destroy one of the last remaining Loomdaughters," Dr. Jericho said. "I wonder if the golem is up to the task?"

Joshua couldn't help himself. "Just go with him, Brian. Don't do this."

"No," Brian said, standing. "He's bluffing." His eyes flicked nervously to Ingrid, but Ingrid said nothing.

"You cannot survive the demise of your instrument," said Dr. Jericho, "however it comes to pass. I wonder—would a sudden death now be any worse than a slow death later on?"

Joshua didn't understand. Why a slow death later on?

"Wow, really hard to say," said Brian. "I can't remember the last time I died. Although I did come close just a few minutes ago."

Dr. Jericho smiled. The golem shifted, gripping Tunraden even harder. "I think you overestimate my patience for this night and this place. For you and your kind. For this war. You are the Keeper of a Loomdaughter, and therefore its slave." He nodded at the tight black rings around Brian's wrists. "I could simply take Tunraden away from here, you know. And you, slave, would be forced to follow—follow, or die. But I have not done that. I am still here, exchanging words with a Tinker who attempts jokes in the face of his own destruction, a silly boy whose stench I can barely withstand."

High above, the golem's stony grip seemed to tremble around Tunraden. Joshua held his breath.

"Do it, then," Brian said. He sounded brave, but his face was tight with doubt.

Dr. Jericho bent down. "You think I won't," he snarled through his teeth, little flecks of spit flying into Brian's face. One great hand dug at the ground like he wanted to rip the skin off the earth. The other, the one with the red-and-black ring, balled into a fist the size of Brian's head and trembled in the air. Overhead, the golem scraped audibly as it tightened around Tunraden, like gravel crunching under a giant's foot.

Brian had to hear it, but he didn't look up, continuing to meet the Mordin's gaze. "I'm waiting," he said quietly.

"You pretend to be as stubborn as the rest, Tinker," Dr. Jericho said. "If you truly are willing to lose everything you hold dear, then let us wait no more. It is one thing to feign bravery in the face of some distant dread." His massive fist shook harder, and his grin grew more savage. Tunraden seemed to groan. "But let us see how you fare, here and now, as everything you cling to is ground irrevocably into dust."

CHAPTER ELEVEN

The Where and the When

BECK'S CAB SLID THROUGH THE LATE-NIGHT STREETS OF CHI-
cago. It was ten past three, and the Kennedy Expressway was
all but abandoned. Mr. Meister and Gabriel sat in the front
with Beck, while Horace was crammed in the back between
Chloe and April, with his mother on the end. Arthur sat on
April's shoulder, looking out the window, and Horace could
tell by the faraway haze of April's stare that she was watching
the city pass by through the raven's keen eyes. Mrs. Hapsteade and Neptune had stayed behind in the Warren, with
good reason. "You be the bird tonight," Neptune had said to
April, clutching her injured pinky and hanging slightly cock-
eyed in the air to avoid her twisted ankle.

In the front seat, Mr. Meister held the compass, but he
wasn't bothering to look at it much anymore. It seemed clear
now where Joshua and the others had gone: the riverbank

where he and April had first encountered the Wardens. Isabel had actually killed some of the Riven there, cleaving them from their instruments and letting them fall.

It was hard not to forget that Dr. Jericho had almost become one of those fallen. Hard not to forget, because Horace himself had saved him. Through the Fel'Daera, Horace had actually witnessed Dr. Jericho's death seconds before it was about to happen. And he had immediately—impulsively, inexplicably—warned Dr. Jericho. Or threatened him, it was hard to say. "You're next," Horace had said, and the Mordin had reacted with lightning reflexes, fleeing the scene and saving his own life. Saved by Horace.

And the crazy thing was, Horace didn't feel a whole lot of regret. Was that stupid? Probably. As he sat here thinking about Joshua and the Laithe, he started to suspect that his regret was about to grow.

He leaned forward. "Mr. Meister?"

"Keeper?" the old man said, without turning around.

"I've been thinking about what you said. About how Dr. Jericho might be able to sense Joshua's portals. He can sense the residue of a portal, like you do, right?"

Now Mr. Meister did turn. "I am sure he can."

"Okay, so . . . let's imagine that I look through a portal with the box, and Dr. Jericho is already there in whatever place and time I'm seeing. He already senses the portal, but will he sense the box, too? Will he know I'm watching him, through the portal *and* through time?"

"Yikes," said Chloe.

"The mind reels, does it not?" Mr. Meister said. "I have underestimated Dr. Jericho's sensitivity to the Fel'Daera in the past. I am not inclined to do so now. We must assume that he would feel the box's presence." He studied Horace's face for a moment. "Why do you ask?"

Horace shrugged. "I was thinking about the breach. It's set to ten seconds. Let's say there's an open portal, right here and right now. If I look through that portal with the box, and Dr. Jericho is on the other side, he'll feel it, ten seconds from now. In other words, that only gives us ten seconds to do something before he knows he's been seen. And obviously ten seconds isn't long enough for us to get to wherever he is. It's not long enough for us to do anything about the future I just witnessed."

"That is true," Mr. Meister said, nodding.

"But if I look *too* far into the future, Dr. Jericho might already be gone, and I won't see anything useful at all."

"So, what do you suggest?" Mr. Meister asked.

"Maybe before I look through another portal, I set the breach wide. Then I look, and I slowly close the breach toward the present, moving backward in time. Once I see Dr. Jericho, I'll close the box."

"I'm sorry, but how does that help?" Chloe said.

"Well, I won't get to see everything that happens, but at least we'll know if he's there. And because Dr. Jericho will only sense the box *later*, he won't know we're coming *earlier*."

191

Mr. Meister turned to look at him, beaming. "Brilliant," he said.

"Wait, this is making my head hurt," said April.

Horace tried to explain better. He could barely hold on to the idea himself. "I need to use the box to figure out where Joshua went, but if Dr. Jericho is there—in the future—we don't want him to sense the box. Not too soon, anyway. So I'm going to check the future several hours out, and then rewind the box into the *end* of whatever's happening wherever Joshua is."

April just blinked at him.

"The point is," Horace continued, "Dr. Jericho won't know I've seen him until later in his own timeline, which gives us more time to get there and surprise him."

"Wow," April breathed. "You know, I used to think I was smart—"

"You're smart," said Chloe. "We're all smart here. Horace is just . . . so smart it's stupid."

"He's a Paragon," Horace's mom murmured. The pride and wonder in her voice were unmistakable. She was staring at him intensely, bright-eyed. Horace blushed even harder, though he had no idea what a Paragon was. His mother turned her gaze to Mr. Meister. "You didn't tell me my son was a Paragon."

Mr. Meister shrugged. "It's not a word I use lightly."

"What's a Paragon?" asked Chloe.

"Words do not matter," the old man said. "We all do our

best. Let me just say how grateful I am that when it comes to our little group, our best is *extraordinary*." He nodded at Horace. "Well done, Keeper. Well done."

Horace was as mortified as he was mystified. Proud to have figured this out, yes, but embarrassed by the compliments, especially from his mom. Fortunately, Chloe stepped into the awkward silence as only Chloe could.

"Does Horace get a badge or something?" she said. "A Paragon badge? I want a Paragon badge."

"I like badges," said April agreeably.

"Badges all around!" Chloe cried, raising a fist.

"No badges," said Mr. Meister. "Our work is our badge. And there is much work left to do this night."

Chloe shook her head sadly, feigning disappointment. "Work, work, work. Sorry, Horace." In the darkness between the seats, she pressed her foot against his. She was proud of him too.

Horace pulled the Fel'Daera from its pouch. The breach was still set to ten seconds, not nearly wide enough. "I might as well try and get it ready now," he said. He glanced at his mom. "Don't freak if I sort of . . . black out for a minute."

"I don't generally freak, do I?" she said. "But why might you black out?"

"It's the breach," said Chloe. "He can close it fine, but when he tries to open it—go further forward in time—he kind of zombies out."

"It's the silver sun," Horace admitted. "The Medium gets

away from me, and the breach slams all the way open, all the way to twenty-four hours. When it happens, I kind of lose track of time for a few minutes."

"It's creepy," Chloe added.

His mother's eyes fell to the Fel'Daera. She studied it silently for a moment. "No wonder," she said. "It's rusty."

Horace blinked. "I'm sorry—what?"

"No offense. Just a professional opinion. The box hasn't been tuned in twenty years. And in that twenty years it sat unclaimed, with the breach wide open to twenty-four hours. The box got used to it. Like a book that's been cracked open to the same page for too long."

There was almost no one on earth who could have criticized the Fel'Daera without making Horace mad. But this was his mother. She'd only have said these words if she really believed—*knew*—they were true.

He held out the box to her. "So fix it," he said.

His mom recoiled like he was trying to hand her a live bat. "Whoa, I didn't say that. I only work on instruments that have no Keeper. Besides, I told you, the Fel'Daera was beyond me even twenty years ago, when I was in my prime. And now—"

"It was not beyond you," Mr. Meister said from the front seat.

"Excuse me?"

He turned to look at her. "You believed it was beyond you because such tasks came more easily to Isabel. Isabel always succeeded; therefore your own failures were of no

194

consequence. You allowed yourself to fail."

Horace's mother let out a disbelieving, indignant huff. "Wow," she said. "Twenty years, but I guess we're picking up right where we left off. I'd forgotten how inspirational you could be."

Mr. Meister shrugged. "The truth is always inspirational once we fully accept it."

Horace's mom rolled her eyes so hard he thought she'd pull a muscle. But after a moment she said, "Okay, give me the damn box."

Horace let her have it, hardly wincing at all as she took hold of it. She laid the box in her lap and unfolded her harp, chattering in a pleasantly surly way. "I stand by my story, though. The box was a wreck. Full of knots and strains, and burst channels from when the last Keeper—" She stopped, glancing at Horace. Her fingers began to play across the strings of her harp. "But okay. That's all still clean. It's just the breach now. I understand the breach. It's a valve. A stubborn little valve." Her fingers danced. The threads of her harp sparkled like spiderwebs in morning dew.

"Oh!" she said suddenly. She curled her hand and took hold of three strings. "You'll feel this, I think," she said, and then she plucked the strings, very hard.

Horace swayed, dizzy, as if he'd stood up too quickly. The car seemed to lurch sideways. He shook his head, clearing it, only to find that his mother was already thrusting the box back at him.

"Try it now," she said.

"That's it?" asked Horace, taking the box. "What did you do?"

"Some flows were too tight, others too loose. I gave it a whack." She threw a sulky glance at Mr. Meister. "It was . . . easy, actually."

Mr. Meister chuckled softly.

Horace held the box. The twenty-four-spoked sun gleamed blackly. With his mind, he reached out for the breach. He found the fingerhold easily, the tiniest imaginable gate, the Medium thundering through it. He pushed his thoughts into the opening, willing it to dilate, wanting it to open to just a single hour. The breach began to widen with no resistance, and he panicked a bit—afraid it would slip away from him like it always did—but to his surprise it slid open steadily. The topmost ray of the box's blackened sun swiftly turned silver. A single perfect ray. The breach came to a halt, and he pinned it in place easily.

"Holy crap," Horace said.

His mother smiled. "Good?"

Horace pushed again, willing the breach to open just one hour wider. No sooner had he thought it than it began to spread. Silver slid neatly across the sun's second ray, another perfect sixty minutes. The breach stopped cold at precisely two hours.

Horace actually laughed out loud. "You fixed it."

"I *tuned* it," his mother replied.

Hungrily, Horace began to experiment with the breach, running it up and down. It opened and closed with ease, waves of black and silver sweeping back and forth across the face of the sun. Within seconds, he found that he could hold a specific time in his head—nineteen hours and six minutes, for example—and easily compel the breach to open to that exact position. It was so easy, so flawless. The box seemed to revel in this new simplicity, working with him as if they were one thing, one being. Horace could hardly get enough.

"This is amazing, you guys," he said. "Wait, wait. Let me try something."

He opened the lid, holding the box up in front of him. The breach was at five hours exactly, and it was now twelve past three in the morning, so he found himself looking not at the front seat of Beck's cab and an empty highway beyond, but into a bright morning full of traffic. The cab was traveling much faster than tomorrow's cars, so Horace was treated to the bizarre spectacle of catching up to a car, moving right through the rear window, and out the windshield. But Horace could change that.

While he watched, he slid the breach slowly open and closed. His view began to change marvelously. As he widened the breach, the events of tomorrow sped up massively, like a video being fast-forwarded. And as he closed it, those same events ran swiftly backward. He continued to swing the breach, first opening it—*an endless swarm of cars and trucks, hurtling over the horizon at blazing speeds*—and then closing it—*that same swarm now surging backward, a busy and flashing blur.*

And of course, the speed of this fast-forwarding and rewinding depended on the speed with which he opened or closed the breach. Carefully now, with his newfound control, he eased the breach open, slower and slower. Inside the box, tomorrow's zooming traffic—which appeared to be moving crazy fast because he was fast-forwarding through the morning—began to slow down. And it was slowing down because he wasn't fast-forwarding *as fast*.

On the heels of this tangled thought, Horace had an idea. A brain-busting idea so fragile and complicated that the more he thought about it, the more it fell apart. He could only get a glimpse of it, a snippet at a time. If he could manage to close the breach at exactly the right speed—

"Having fun?" asked April.

Horace snapped the box closed, tearing himself away. April flashed him a dazzling, crooked smile.

"Blowing my own mind," he said.

"Increased mastery is one of the great pleasures of being Tan'ji," said Mr. Meister. "But let us not get carried away. Save your energies, Keeper."

"Work, work, work," Chloe said again. She leaned into Horace's mother, twirling the Alvalaithen almost in her face. "Not that I'm worried," she said, "but there's no rust here, right?"

"Not a spot."

Mr. Meister murmured something to Beck. The cab took the next exit at a gallop, throwing them all to the left. Horace tried not to crush Chloe even as April lurched into him on the other side. Two minutes later, they turned again and found themselves on a road bracketed by forest. A mile down, they entered the park along the river, just as they had two nights earlier. They drove past the darkened swimming pool and into the parking lot. Beck swung the cab expertly into a space at the end, and they all tumbled out, glad to be free.

The night was still clear, and warm. Arthur rose into the sky at once, wings sweeping the air, squawking in what sounded like a happy way. He alighted heavily in a tree on the edge of the woods. His harsh calls echoed across the empty lot.

"I don't see anyone," April said, her eyes gray and distant. Then she bit her lip. "*We* don't see anyone."

Horace stepped up beside Mr. Meister. The red needle of the compass was longer and thinner again, pointing at the trees, toward the unseen spit of land where the river bent from north to south.

"Into the woods once more," Mr. Meister said.

They set out into the shadows of the forest. Gabriel and Chloe took their jithandras out, her red and his silver light casting an eerie metallic glow through the trees. Arthur kept pace, flying ahead and waiting for them to catch up. After a couple hundred yards or so, April said, "I feel the river. No one's there."

Gabriel rubbed his thumb across the dragonlike handle of his staff. "I was not aware you could feel rivers," he said.

"I can't, sorry," said April. "I'm still getting used to the vine being fixed." She reached up and touched the little black flower that dangled from the Ravenvine in front of her left ear. It was this piece that had been missing from the vine when she Found it, and that Brian had reattached only yesterday. "Everything in nature feels so . . . intertwined now. What I should have said is that I can feel river animals—fish, crawdads, turtles. Plus animals between here and there. Toads are awake. Squirrels are asleep. No one is disturbed. There are no humans up ahead, and there haven't been for a while." She lifted her chin prettily, frowning with concentration. "But there *were*. There's a raccoon, and I—*we*—can smell that there were humans here. I don't know how long ago."

"You don't have to say 'we,'" Chloe said. "We know it's not really you who can smell humans from hundreds of feet away."

April shrugged. "It just seems impolite not to give credit where credit's due," she said.

Soon Horace could hear the river, a murmuring drone just ahead. Mr. Meister, compass in hand, walked past a large silver thing lying against the foot of a tree. Horace realized with a start that it was the canoe, still lying where it had landed after Dr. Jericho had thrown it like a javelin at Isabel.

"What happened here?" Horace's mother asked, stepping around the fractured canoe.

"Horace was doing ninja stuff with the box," said Chloe. "Mordin. Auditors. Isabel came in and started mowing them down. General chaos." She elbowed Horace softly. "But it turned out fine."

Horace looked around the little clearing. Here was the tree Chloe had stepped through while battling the Auditor. Here was the branch where Dr. Jericho had nearly ripped Neptune down to the ground. And here was the spot Isabel stood when she cleaved—*nearly* cleaved—Dr. Jericho. "Yeah," said Horace. "Totally fine."

His mom rubbed her forehead but said nothing.

Mr. Meister stopped and held out a hand. "The portal from the Warren was just here." He bent down, picking something off the ground. "And here is our backjack."

"But where is Brian?" Horace asked.

Mr. Meister spun around slowly, peering into the woods. "If Joshua made another portal, he did not make it here. They left on foot." He tapped his chin thoughtfully.

"Great," Chloe said. "Now what?"

"If my dog were here, we could track them," said April.

Gabriel cleared his throat. He held out the Staff of Obro. "I hesitate to compete with a dog," he said, "but . . ."

Horace didn't understand what he was suggesting, but Mr. Meister obviously did. "Do it," he said with a nod.

Gabriel planted the tip of the staff, four curving silver talons that gathered into a point, into the mulch. A faint gray fog began to drift out from the dark hollows between them. But it wasn't a fog. "Since this is your first time, Mrs. Andrews," said Gabriel, "you may want to close your eyes."

"Oh, man, here we go," said Chloe.

Horace's mom looked puzzled, but closed her eyes.

"Steady yourselves," Gabriel said, and then the world vanished with a roar.

Horace kept his eyes open as the humour of Obro filled the forest around them in an instant, obliterating it. Nothing but a dimensionless gray, everywhere. Even though he was used to the humour by now, Horace's eyes still strained to see what could not be seen. No sky, no ground, no Horace. Not even the tip of his own nose—a constant, lifelong sight that Horace had taken for granted until the first time the all-swallowing cloud of the humour stole it from him.

The humour had swallowed the soft sigh of the river, too, and the drone of insects Horace hadn't even been aware of. But now Gabriel spoke, his voice thundering from everywhere in the directionless gray. "They were here," he said. "All three of them."

"But how do you . . . ?" Horace began, his voice trickling into the senseless void. And then he remembered again the first time Gabriel had demonstrated his powers, back in the Great Burrow. At first, he'd thought that the humour allowed Gabriel's blind eyes to see, but that wasn't quite right. Instead, the humour allowed Gabriel to *feel*, to examine his surroundings with a sensitivity far beyond any eye or fingertip. Down to the finest detail. That first time, Gabriel had actually read the dates on coins *inside Horace's pocket*. And now—

"Footprints," Gabriel said. "All around here." There was a pause, utter silence, and then: "They left to the east. There's a bridge across the river. I can't see the far side, but they crossed it."

Now Chloe's voice rang out. Gabriel could control sound within the humour, deciding which sounds reached which ears. He was letting everyone hear each other now, of course, which apparently took a great deal of effort. "The bridge," Chloe said. "Duh. I know where they went."

Another staticky roar, like a house-sized ball of tissue paper being crumpled, and the humour winked out of existence. Horace blinked and blinked, his eyes hungry to focus on something—anything. His saw his mother first, her own eyes wide and watery, her hands pressed against her lips.

She spotted Horace and blew a laugh out between her fingers. "So this is what you've been up to all summer?"

"Not every day," said Horace.

"Good."

Gabriel bowed his head, cradling his staff.

"The cloister," Chloe said. "Remember, Horace? It's across the river."

Mr. Meister actually slapped his forehead. "Of course. And young Joshua saw our cloister map. He knew it was there."

The old man led them over the river and across the field beyond. Horace had made this walk just two nights earlier, but he'd been in such a daze that he barely remembered it. He still didn't recognize the cloister when they found it in the woods beyond the meadow, the bricks of its high walls rounded and weathered.

"Dowsim, if I'm not mistaken," Mr. Meister said, naming the place. He stepped up to the wall, scanning it. "And here is the passkey."

"But why did they come here?" Horace asked. "Isabel isn't Tan'ji. She can't travel by falkrete."

"I suspect they sought the protection of the leestone within," said Mr. Meister.

"No one's inside," April reported, looking up at Arthur, who was perched on the wall above.

"They didn't go inside," said Horace's mother. "They went somewhere else." Everyone turned to look at her. She stood a little ways off, moving her hand through the air as if feeling an invisible shape. Mr. Meister hurried to her side, then beckoned Horace over.

A portal. Horace took the Fel'Daera in his hands. The breach was at five hours and twelve minutes, plenty wide enough for what he had planned. He prepared himself, gathering all the threads of action that had led them to this moment in time, and letting them drift into a future full of possibilities. When he was ready, he opened the lid and—with Mr. Meister's guidance—laid it against the unseen plane of the fading portal.

And there through the blue glass—*the tumbling tunnel of*

shapes, a kaleidoscope of motion. His mother knelt, opening her harp in the bed of leaves before her. She played the strings, and gradually the kaleidoscope began to slow, much more quickly than the last time.

"This one's not quite as messy," she said. "Joshua is getting better."

"As are you," said Mr. Meister.

After just seventeen seconds, the tunnel revealed by the box came to a stop, and a vision began to resolve—*a wide-open morning sky; an expanse of long grass; a half circle of stones on the ground.*

"It's the meadow," Horace said, hardly believing it. "By April's house."

"You've got to be kidding me," said Chloe. She glanced over at the high cloister walls.

"You are sure it is the same place?" asked Mr. Meister.

"Positive. I can't see the barn—it must be behind me— but I can see the falkretes and the leestone and everything." Not that Horace even needed to see those things. He wouldn't soon forget this place.

"Why is Isabel going back to all our recent battlefields?" said April.

"Mere coincidence," said Mr. Meister. "As I suspected, they are seeking a leestone. The leestone near the barn is damaged, but Isabel thinks it will protect them while Brian attempts to . . . *fix* her." He shook his head gravely. "But it is a foolish hope. I fear the worst."

"And this portal is only a few minutes older than the last one," Horace's mother said. "They passed through hours ago."

"Let me think," said Horace. "Let me look. I can't see anyone there now, but I'm five hours out. Let me dial it back." Still looking through the portal at the meadow, he focused on the breach and began to close it. Not too fast. It was now 3:31, so it was 8:43 in the meadow. And as he watched through the box, as he carefully rewound the morning still to come—*the morning sun, sinking in the eastern sky; a flock of birds streaking backward over the distant trees.* Seven o'clock. Six o'clock. Still nothing. *The sun dropping over the horizon, a sunrise in reverse; a paper-thin crescent moon, now revealed, chasing the sun down the sky.* Five o'clock. The breach was approaching an hour now, and still nothing in the meadow had changed. That was bad— he guessed April's house was at least forty-five minutes away by car.

Suddenly he saw a moving shape, but when he gasped and pinned the breach in place to see, he laughed to himself—*deer, a mother and a fawn.* He continued on. *A darkening sky; stars now, sliding down and to the left; the moon, a thin crooked smile, still sinking.* Horace's heart began to sink, too. Four o'clock, only a half hour in the future. It was hopeless. Even if he saw something now, it would be over before they could possibly get there.

Horace slammed the box closed. "I'm under a half hour now, and there's still nothing," he said aloud. "What if they're there, but I just can't see them? Maybe they're right behind me."

"Or maybe we're about to go get them," Chloe said, "and it'll all be over in a half an hour."

"Impossible," he said. "April's house is a long ways away. Even if we left right this second, we wouldn't get there until like four fifteen at best. But I already saw four fifteen, and we're not there."

Chloe squinted at him. "Don't you think it's weird you didn't see us *at all*?"

Horace frowned. That *was* weird. If they were going, why didn't he see them?

Chloe's face, meanwhile, split into a slow devilish smile.

"What?" said Horace.

"I'm just . . . I'm savoring this. Me getting it before you." She stepped up to the cloister wall and turned to April. "This cloister here. The leestone inside is a brown bird with blue on the wing, right?"

Arthur still stood atop the wall, his head darting to and fro. April's eyes went hazy, and she nodded. "Yes," she reported, looking through the raven's eyes. "A Eurasian jay."

"I still don't get it," said Horace.

"Maybe because you didn't make the trip between April's barn and the Warren *four times* tonight," said Chloe. She patted the brick wall like it was a horse. "This cloister was one of the stops."

"Oh holy cow," said Horace. She was right. He was so

207

focused on the time that he'd completely forgotten. From here, they could travel back to the barn by falkrete. Four or five leaps. They could be there in a matter of minutes.

Horace digested this news, letting it alter his perception of the path they were now on. What would they do, given this new information? What would Horace himself do? He didn't want to answer the questions he asked, exactly—making predictions was actually counterproductive—but he had to ask them, so that the right threads of possibility would plant themselves in his mind. One thing he knew for sure: he was ready to do whatever he could to help Brian.

It was 3:33 now. He opened the box and laid it against the portal again. The breach was at twenty-eight minutes. He began to close it as slowly as he could. Through the box, the future rewound itself, the crescent moon sinking slowly.

The breach shrank. Twenty-five minutes.

Twenty minutes.

Fifteen.

Still nothing. But that was okay—by falkrete, they could get there in less than five minutes, and he knew from experience that whatever happened there might happen very quickly.

Slower. He let his time sense zero in on seconds rather than minutes. He focused hard, closing the breach with the lightest touch he could muster, no more than a breath. He got it so slow that for every second he spent closing the breach, the breach shrank by five seconds—in other words, events in the future were rewinding at four times regular speed. The sinking crescent moon slowed to an undetectable crawl.

Twelve minutes.

Eleven.

And then, suddenly—*movement in the meadow; distant figures, running and clashing.* Riven. Mordin. But they were too far away to see clearly what was happening. Horace kept watching, and then he saw something new. *A distant black shadow, growing larger; a giant snake, rolling over the grass; a moving mass of stone coming closer.* It came straight at him, buried him. His view turned into a black sea of movement, and it was all he could do not to cower.

Horace swallowed. He didn't have the heart to tell the others—there was a golem in the meadow. It was rolling over the very spot where the box was now open in the future. Horace held his tongue, held his ground, still rewinding. Abruptly his view cleared. The golem had moved on. And once it was clear, he saw—*Mordin, many Mordin.* Moving in reverse, they backpedaled comically out of the meadow, slipping behind Horace where he could not see.

"The Riven are there," he reported now. "Lots of them." He didn't mention the golem. Not yet. He squinted into the box, but it was impossible to tell if any of the Mordin he could see was Dr. Jericho.

Horace kept at it, moving back and back through time, closing the breach as slowly as he could. And suddenly, there he was—*Dr. Jericho, facing away from Horace; barebacked and huge.* What was he looking at? No sooner had Horace wondered than a kind of fog swept over his view. This time, he understood at once what he was seeing—*a hazy curtain, drifting like gauze in the wind.* "We're there," he said. "Gabriel has the humour up, but I don't see him."

Now a wide ring, sprouting out of nothing right in front of Dr. Jericho and hanging in the air; and now figures—humans, four or five—stumbling in reverse out of the ring, appearing out of nowhere and bursting into the meadow just as Dr. Jericho slid backward, out of sight.

Horace blinked several times. The vision had gone by too fast. And backward, too. He pinned the breach in place and closed the box.

"What is it?" asked Chloe.

"I think I see a portal," Horace said. "Joshua opens a portal in the humour."

Mr. Meister hummed heartily. "He truly is its Keeper, then."

Horace had seen Dr. Jericho. Did he need to see more? Suddenly it struck him that something more important was at stake. If they were going to the meadow now, to face Dr. Jericho and the golem and a host of Mordin, Horace had now also witnessed the Wardens' escape. Sort of. He needed to get a better view, risk or no risk.

He settled himself quickly, and reopened the box. He let the future run for a moment. He watched—in regular forward motion this time—as Joshua opened the portal, inside the humour. Mr. Meister and Brian were there too—but no one else. Joshua pulled a metal ring free from the little blue globe and somehow hung it in the air. With a spin, the ring grew wide and opened onto a forest scene.

A freaky little burst of déjà vu stabbed at Horace—this new portal was open right back to the very place they now stood. He got dizzy just trying to follow all the loops of space-time he was piercing right now. Should he report this news, or not? He decided not. He kept watching.

Brian, carrying Tunraden like huge, heavy manacles, being pushed through the portal by Joshua; now Mr. Meister; and now a new figure, not a Mordin—a girl with blond hair, grabbing Joshua before he could escape. Horace almost gasped. It was Ingrid, the former Warden now working with the Riven. A traitor. And as he watched—*Joshua, tussling with Ingrid; the two of them fall-ing together toward the portal as a Mordin sprang at them; the portal going transparent, merely an empty ring now that Joshua had passed through; the Mordin falling, and a second later—Dr. Jericho, bursting onto the scene.*

Shortly after the Mordin's arrival, the humour came down, the night air clearing. Still no sign of Gabriel. Was he okay? And then Horace watched, horrified, as Dr. Jericho tore off his jacket and coat and reared back, roaring. Something was bulging from his spine, and Horace knew at once it was Tan'ji, actually imbedded in the Mordin's flesh. The portal spun closed, shrinking swiftly and vanishing.

Horace hardly knew what to think. The escape portal was

211

gone, but only three Keepers had gone through it. No Chloe, no April. No Gabriel. No Horace, for that matter. Where were they? Apparently they wouldn't be escaping through the portal. And Ingrid! All of this was news he felt he couldn't say. Not yet. Fair, or unfair? But maybe it didn't matter. This was the willed path, for him and for all of them.

Hoping he was making the right choice, he said, "Joshua opens a portal right back to this place. People get away."

Mr. Meister looked at him thoughtfully for a moment. "Just so," he said flatly.

If the old man knew Horace was withholding something, Horace didn't care. He cared about finding the others. He took hold of the breach again, closing it further, rewinding slowly, looking for the rest of the Wardens. It wasn't easy, since he couldn't look around. He had to hope the right things drifted across his view, like fish swimming past an underwater window. He rewound past the portal, back into the humour again, past Ingrid and Dr. Jericho, until a new figure appeared. *A human, curly haired, wandering blind through the humour; now turning toward him—Isabel, near and clear; looking angry but somehow hollow, her eyes empty.* Something was wrong with her. It took Horace a second, but then he realized—she didn't have Miradel. He didn't understand that at all. She'd stolen it back from the Wardens, and it was nearly impossible to imagine why she wouldn't be wearing it now. Sightless and aimless, she slipped out of view.

Horace kept rewinding, unsure where to stop. Still no

sightings of April or Gabriel, or Chloe or himself. And then abruptly, out in the meadow, far off in the meadow, so far he almost missed it—*a liquid tower of black, bursting high out of the shadows in the grass; a tiny figure hoisted atop it, far into the air, a gleaming dot of white at her neck.*

Chloe.

The golem.

No sooner had Horace seen the horrible sight than Dr. Jericho appeared, filling the frame, staring straight at him through the glass from just feet away—through the humour, through the portal and the glass, through space and time—his horrible face shifting and morphing horrendously, the way it always did when seen through the Fel'Daera. His many sliding faces grinned at Horace like ghouls.

Horace slammed the box closed, furious and frightened. Dr. Jericho had sensed the box, as Horace had feared he might, but Horace didn't care about that. That didn't matter. Only one thing mattered—an unbelievable, unmistakable thing.

The golem had Chloe.

"What did you see?" Chloe asked him softly. Chloe here and now. Chloe safe and sound.

"Lots of things," said Horace. Could he do this? Was this the way? And was he sure what he'd he seen? The golem, rising up from the ground like a geyser, carrying Chloe with it.

"Did you see Dr. Jericho?" Chloe pressed.

"Yes, and he saw me. Felt me. But that's not . . ." He trailed off, lost.

"What else did you see, Horace?" his mother asked.

Horace's mind raced as he tried to decide how much to tell them. Or should he look again? His head was tangled, his viewing a scramble—so much of it sped up, and backward. But Mr. Meister had cautioned him against making multiple viewings of the same future. At last he spoke, keeping it simple, trying not to meet Chloe's eyes. "I saw a golem."

Chloe groaned. Mr. Meister inhaled sharply. Gabriel gripped his staff in his hands so hard that Horace could hear his flesh rubbing against the wood.

"What's a golem?" said April.

"First," said Chloe, "picture a gigantic pile of creepy little rocks."

"Okay."

"Now picture it kicking your ass."

That was an accurate way to describe the golem. Horace remembered their first encounter with the living river of stone, when it broke into the House of Answers and nearly tore the place apart. On that occasion, Chloe had used the power of the Alvalaithen to actually go into the body of the beast. Horace couldn't bring himself to imagine how the golem in the meadow could possibly manage to capture her.

"What of Isabel?" Mr. Meister asked. "Did you see her?"

"Yes, but . . . she didn't look right. Miradel was missing."

All the anger drained from Chloe's face.

"Fascinating," Mr. Meister said. He looked thoughtfully down at his vest, his eyes far away. Horace could tell he wanted to ask more but knew that he shouldn't.

"Will there be a battle?" Gabriel asked. "Or do we simply slip away?"

Horace hesitated. "I did see . . . the Mordin and the golem heading down into the meadow. Like they were chasing something."

"Chasing us, you mean," said Chloe.

Horace shrugged. He couldn't say more.

"But we're not even there yet," said April, shaking her head in wonder. "This is so trippy. It feels like cheating on an imaginary test."

"How long, Keeper?" asked Mr. Meister.

Horace did the math. Altogether, he'd witnessed about three minutes of the future, from back to front. "We should probably assume the Riven are there right now, as we speak," he said. "We have six minutes before Dr. Jericho senses the box and realizes we've seen him. But I have no idea what happens in those six minutes—I didn't watch them, so that he wouldn't get his warning too soon."

"We need to go," said Gabriel. "Now."

Chloe turned to Horace's mother. To his surprise, she said, "Will you come? If there's going to be a battle, a Tuner could—"

"I'm not that sort of Tuner," his mother said firmly. "But I can't come anyway. Only Tan'ji can travel by falkrete stone."

"I'm pretty sure you're not the only one who can't go," April said sadly.

Chloe whipped around. "Why can't you—"

But April just pointed straight up, at Arthur still perched on the wall overhead. "*I'm* going," she said. "Try and stop me. But I don't think ravens can come along."

"Only Keepers," Mr. Meister confirmed. "No one else."

"I'll watch Arthur," said Horace's mom. "He can stay with me."

"I was really hoping you'd say that," April said, hurrying over to her, shoving a hand into a pocket of her dress. She pulled out a pile of dog food. "He likes you, Mrs. Andrews, but he'll like you even more now." She dumped the kibble into Horace's mom's outstretched hands.

Arthur swept down from the wall and landed heavily at their feet. He cocked his head and chirped curiously, rocking from foot to foot. April crouched down and said, "I'll be back. Be good, okay? Be good."

"*Begoood*," the raven crooned agreeably. "*Begoood.*"

Horace couldn't bear to tell her he hadn't seen her come back.

"Let us go," said Mr. Meister.

"Me first," said Gabriel. "I'll release the humour once I'm through."

"No, me first," said Chloe. "I'm the only one that can resist the golem. Plus, I don't know if anybody's noticed, but I'm pretty hard to kill."

Horace had to pretend he didn't hear Chloe's words. And he didn't want Gabriel to go first either—it wasn't clear just how much the humour could protect Gabriel from the golem. What was the proper path?

He held up a hand, remembering his last encounters with the golem and the night in the nest. "There's a ring that controls the golem, right?"

"In a manner of speaking, yes," said Mr. Meister. "As much as a string controls a kite. No doubt Dr. Jericho wears it now."

"And if we steal the ring? Can we control the golem?"

"No," said Gabriel. "There is a ritual involved. Each ring works only for a single golem, and proper introductions must be made."

There was no time to ask how Gabriel knew a thing like that—or to contemplate the idea that there was more than one golem in the world. Horace now had as much of an answer as he needed. And if Gabriel and Chloe and April were going to step into a danger from which he could guarantee no escape, there was one thing he could do for them. One thing at least.

"I go first," he said.

Chloe bared her teeth. "You didn't see that."

"I didn't, but I realize now . . . I think I was imagining it when I *did* see. The little glimpse of the future I got—it's dependent on me going first."

Mr. Meister shifted uneasily. "Perhaps a different future would be preferable in this instance, Keeper."

Horace was surprised to hear the old man suggest it. The old man had always frowned on trying to change or avoid the future the box revealed. Among other things, it led to thrall-blight, a fleeting but painful sickness that made Horace double over in pain. And according to Dr. Jericho, thrall-blight could spread through the Medium too, even to the Mother-gates themselves.

"I wouldn't prefer a different future," Horace said. "This is the path."

"But you can't even protect yourself!" Chloe cried.

"I've still got the phalanx," said Horace, crossing to the cloister wall. He took out his jithandra, and by its deep blue light he quickly spotted the passkey.

Mr. Meister said, "The phalanx might freeze Dr. Jericho in his tracks for few minutes, as you know, but it won't affect the golem."

"I don't plan to try."

"You're not planning anything!" said Chloe.

"My plan is for you to get the ring."

She scoffed. "The ring we can't even use?"

"If we take it, Dr. Jericho can't use it either," said Horace. "Look, we've been standing here talking for three minutes already. I'm going. Gabriel, you follow me quick. Then Chloe. Get the ring."

"Fear is the stone, Keeper," Mr. Meister intoned, settling the matter. "May yours be light."

"And yours." Horace paused, looking back. Chloe looked exasperated, but he knew—with a sick kind of fatality that he hoped was confidence—that she'd do what he asked. Beyond her, Horace caught his mother smoothing a knot of worry from her own face. "I'm going," he said again stupidly. It came out like a question.

His mother nodded. "Trust yourself. I do."

He searched for something better to say. "Please don't worry about me."

Her eyes shone as she shrugged. "Please don't make impossible requests," she said. Then she looked away and flapped her hand at him, like she was shooing a cat. "Go. Be brave and smart."

He swallowed through the sudden cinch in his throat, and managed to nod. Then he took hold of the passkey and stepped through the wall.

CHAPTER TWELVE

Gray Voices, Black Footsteps

JOSHUA WATCHED AS THE GOLEM REARED UP OVER THE MEADOW, a giant's hand threatening to crush Tunraden into dust. Dr. Jericho crouched over Brian like a giant insect that wanted to eat him, shaking his huge fist. No. This couldn't be. All Joshua's fault—he'd let Brian escape from the Warren, had brought him here, had called the terrible Mordin with the Laithe.

Suddenly a voice whispered in Joshua's ear. Isabel, on her knees behind him: "Someone's coming."

She pointed westward at the falkrete circle, over by the barn. No sooner had she raised her finger than a figure appeared there, out of nowhere—a shaggy-haired boy on one knee.

"Horace!" Joshua cried out, before he could stop himself.

"Behind you!" Ingrid shouted at Dr. Jericho. "Wardens!"

Dr. Jericho was already spinning around. Horace flung

his arm back, then forward, right at Dr. Jericho. There was something white in his hand, like a wand. A golden light burst from the tip with a soft *whump*, and then a ring of churning air flashed across the grass and struck Dr. Jericho in the chest. The Mordin stumbled back, nearly stepping on Brian as he fell, but then . . . he didn't fall. He hung there in midair over Brian, half on his back, his legs and arms flailing. He seemed pinned in place by his spine.

Brian scrambled out of the way. And then Dr. Jericho began to laugh, a high, screeching cackle that lifted goose bumps all along Joshua's arms, like a blade scraping against a bell. "Very good!" he shouted up into the sky. "Quite the surprise, Keeper! But I'll be free long before you are, I think."

The golem roared into motion. It released Tunraden. The Loomdaughter fell from the sky right through the body of the golem, scattering a spray of stones as it fell. Tunraden hit the soft ground with an earthshaking thud as the golem roared over the grass toward Horace like a tidal wave.

Someone grabbed Joshua by the collar and began to drag him away. He clutched the Laithe to his chest and looked up, expecting to see Isabel, but it was Ingrid. She looked furious. A second later, though, Isabel tackled the girl with a growl. Ingrid lost her grip on Joshua as Isabel took her to the ground.

Joshua rolled onto his side. He spotted Horace running from the rumbling heap of the golem, out into the meadow. But the golem was twice as fast. Just as it seemed to sweep over him, another figure appeared from nowhere inside the falkrete circle, tall and dark, a long gray staff in his hand.

An instant later, a tearing sound like slow distant thunder rolled across the grass. A gray void swallowed Joshua, erasing the world, a featureless sea of nothingness.

The humour! Gabriel was here!

Joshua could hear Dr. Jericho roaring faintly in the void, and the golem too. They'd all been swallowed. But then Gabriel's voice rang through the fog, deep and calm. It was a voice, Joshua knew, that would only reach the ears Gabriel wanted it to. "Brian. Joshua. Are you all right?"

"Oh, thank god," said Brian. "Gabriel. I'm . . . I'm experiencing a lot of regret, to be honest."

"Joshua, can you open a portal inside the humour?" said Gabriel.

The question came so fast Joshua hardly understood it. "I don't . . . I don't think so. I need to see the Laithe to—"

"Get outside the humour, then," Gabriel said. "Get to the barn. Hide. Ingrid is here in the humour with us, playing her flute and searching. I can mute her for a little while, until you get free. The others are coming. Let us do the fighting."

"And the barn is . . . where, exactly?" Brian said doubtfully.

This, Joshua could do. "I can take you," he said. "Wait for me at Tunraden."

Joshua had been in the humour only once before, during the battle on the riverbank, but he knew the gray fog didn't confuse him as much as it did the others. He was just as blind as they were, but his sense of direction and his memory of where everything was remained intact. He still knew exactly where Tunraden had fallen, thirty feet to the northwest. And from there, the barn door was eighty feet to the south.

A hand grabbed his ankle, hard. Isabel or Ingrid, he didn't know—and didn't care. He knocked his attacker loose with a vicious kick, striking a solid blow, and crawled away toward Tunraden. Ten feet. Twenty.

"Where is it?" cried an angry voice, somewhere in the humour. "I can't see anything!"

Joshua thought it was Isabel at first. But no—it was Chloe. They really were coming, all of them. The Wardens would save them.

Gabriel spoke again. "Dr. Jericho has the ring, here in the humour. Horace pinned him. Now's our chance."

"Where is he?" Chloe yelled.

"Over here!" Joshua cried. But of course that meant nothing in the humour.

"This way, Chloe," said Gabriel. "Don't flinch." There was a pause, and then Gabriel said, "Good. He's straight on, fifty feet ahead. When you get there, I'll—" Suddenly his voice became a roar. "Joshua, get down!"

A sharp pain streaked across Joshua's arm, a handful of knives grazing his skin. Joshua dropped onto his stomach, surprised to find that he was more angry than afraid. He had forgotten his surroundings. Dr. Jericho was right above him in the humour, swiping at him blindly, still pinned midair by Horace's weapon. Joshua squirmed forward on his belly through the grass, the Laithe pressed against his neck.

Ten feet on, safely past the hanging Mordin, he groped and quickly found Brian's bony hand.

"Whoa!" Brian cried.

"It's just me," said Joshua. "Do you have Tunraden?"

"She's here. She's fine. Can you get us to the barn?"

"I think so." Joshua got to his feet. He reached out and felt cold, rough stone, buzzing with power. It was Tunraden, hanging at Brian's waist. "Sorry!" he said, yanking his hand back.

"What happens in the humour stays in the humour," Brian said. "Just get us to the barn."

Joshua found Brian's elbow and pulled him southward. His shoulder burned. Brian had a hard time moving over the lumpy ground without being able to see, with Tunraden handcuffing his arms, but Joshua knew the way. He led him in a straight line. Joshua didn't know where the edge of the humour was, but they must be getting close.

Suddenly, sight filled his eyes. Nighttime. The old barn, just in front of them. They had made it out of the humour.

"You did it," said Brian.

But Joshua just looked back at the humour. Or he tried to. There was nothing to see. The humour wouldn't let itself be seen from the outside. He couldn't see the golem, either—it must have been on the far side of the humour. Joshua's guilt wrapped around him like a scarf. His friends were fighting inside the humour because of something he'd done. He'd been so stupid tonight, done so many stupid things. He would try not to be stupid anymore.

Brian elbowed him and nodded. They hurried inside the back entrance of the huge, gloomy barn. Joshua had been in the barn at night before, but it felt different now. Broken walls and low, slanted ceilings and shadow upon shadow upon shadow. He tried to stay brave. They went farther inside and found a crooked hallway with a series of narrow stalls. Ducking into one of them, they moved to the very back and sat, pressing themselves against the wall. Brian freed his hands from Tunraden, flexing them.

"Now what?" said Joshua.

"Now we wait," Brian replied, catching his breath.

"I don't understand why we left the humour."

"Ingrid is in there," Brian said. "She would have found us. Her flute—if you can hear it, she can find you, even in the humour. Gabriel was pinching off the sound of it for us while we were inside, so she couldn't find us, but he can't keep it up forever."

"So we hide here. And hope she doesn't get out."

"Gabriel's good at keeping people lost in the humour, but yes. We hide and we hope." Joshua could hear both of them breathing. It sounded loud against the silence in the bar. But outside the barn, out in the meadow, it was totally quiet, too. Joshua shifted uneasily.

"We shouldn't have left the Warren," Brian whispered after a while.

"No," Joshua agreed.

"It was stupid of me to go along with it. I thought I was doing a good thing. And you shouldn't have Found the Laithe like this. I'm sorry."

Joshua gazed at the little globe, hovering back and forth in front of him. "I'm a Lostling. That's what Dr. Jericho said, but I don't know what it means."

"It's just a word. Don't listen to him. You really need to not listen to him. You . . ." Brian shook his head. He sat silently for a long time, and then whispered, "Anyway, if we get out of this, maybe Mr. Meister can help undo whatever damage Isabel has done." Joshua didn't like the word "damage."

"I'm getting better already," he said.

"I know."

"But I'm still not good enough. Not good enough to open a portal inside the humour."

Brian shrugged. "I doubt that. It's your Tan'ji. You can feel it, if you try. The humour is a tough place to be—to even think. You just have to . . . use the force."

"What's the force?"

Brian stared at him like he was crazy. "Never mind."

Suddenly Joshua heard a voice—faint and far away. He couldn't hear the words, but it sounded like a woman. Or a girl. Crying? Laughing? And now he heard footsteps crunching across the grass outside the barn. More than one person, it sounded like. Coming closer? He looked up at Brian.

"I hear it," Brian whispered.

They listened for several seconds, and then they heard

distant shouts, farther away. There was no doubt about this one—it was Chloe, calling Horace's name. She was outside the humour. Joshua shot to his feet.

"Sit, sit!" Brian hissed.

"They need our help," said Joshua.

"We're the ones that need help. Quiet now."

Joshua sat back down. Chloe had gone silent, but the approaching footsteps were louder than ever. *Not a Riven*, he thought. Too stealthy. But it was definitely more than one person. His throat itched to call out. Was it a friend? At his side, Brian seemed frozen with fear, staring at Tunraden.

Whoever it was entered the barn. Their feet scuffed across the gritty floor.

"They're coming closer," Joshua said.

"Open a portal," muttered Brian. "Get us out."

And then a voice called out to them. Joshua thought he would collapse with relief.

"It's me," said the voice. Sweet and kind.

April.

CHAPTER THIRTEEN

Into the Humour

CHLOE WAS YANKED THROUGH THE FINAL FALKRETE STONE AND into the blind gray void of the humour. Quickly she drank from the Alvalaithen, going thin. Horace and Gabriel were already here, she knew. And April and Mr. Meister would be coming behind her. But Chloe's job was to get the ring that controlled the golem.

She shouted into the terrible, hated gray, looking for guidance.

Gabriel's gigantic voice rose around her at once. "Dr. Jericho has the ring, here in the humour. Horace pinned him. Now's our chance."

"Where is he?"

Another voice cried out. Joshua. "Over here!" But inside the humour, he could have been anywhere.

"Face this way, Chloe," Gabriel said calmly. "Don't

flinch." Chloe felt a gentle pressure on the left side of her belly, like a fist pressing against her. She swatted at it, but nothing was there. It was Gabriel, manipulating the humour, creating something out of nothing. She didn't like it much, but she thought she understood. She turned, and the gentle pressure—remaining stationary as she spun—slid across her belly. She turned until it was dead center, a few inches above her navel. "Good," said Gabriel. "Dr. Jericho is trapped straight on, fifty feet ahead. When you get to him, I'll—" Suddenly his voice became a roar. "Joshua, get down!"

Chloe had no idea what *that* was all about. Hopefully nothing. Glad for about the hundredth time that she didn't have Gabriel's troubling powers, or its burdens, Chloe started moving forward, clinging to her determination. Distantly, she heard Joshua and Brian talking about getting outside the humour to the barn. She tried not to think about Horace, or what might have happened to him. She tried not to think about Isabel. She thought only about the plan, meager as it was.

Get the ring.

The golem wasn't really alive, of course. It was a Tanu, a machine. And the ring that controlled it was on Dr. Jericho's finger now, trapped somewhere ahead inside the blank expanse of the humour.

Moving straight ahead in the humour, though, was its own challenge. Even with Gabriel's phantom guidance, it was easy to drift left or right. Chloe kept on slowly, putting one foot in front of the other, keeping Gabriel's pressure point centered.

Suddenly Gabriel called out April's name, startling Chloe.

April's voice drifted out of the gray. "Tell me what to do. How can I help?"

"Look outside the humour, if you can," Gabriel said. "The golem was chasing Horace when I arrived, but they're beyond me now."

"Let me try."

Chloe walked on, pretending she hadn't heard. The golem was chasing Horace. Had it caught him? And why had Gabriel let her hear?

She almost forgot what she was doing when Gabriel's voice slammed her, commanding, "Chloe, stop." She rocked to a stop. The pressure on her belly disappeared. "Dr. Jericho is just ahead of you," Gabriel said.

"I can't see in this stinking fog," she complained. "How am I going to get the ring if I can't see? Take the humour down."

"I can't do that." Gabriel's words were piercing and clear. She got the feeling they were coming only to her ears. "Dr. Jericho still holds the golem's leash, but he won't risk bringing the golem into the humour while he himself is inside. And then there's Ingrid. The humour is protecting all of us now."

"So I just grope around and hope I get lucky."

"I'm going to try something. I'm going to . . . thin the humour out around you. I can lower the density enough so that you should be able to see faint shadows nearby. For a little while, anyway."

This was utterly new. But Chloe's surprise was followed by a queasy wash of guilt. "That's what you were practicing, back at the Warren."

"Yes," said Gabriel dryly. "Trying to be better than myself, as you pointed out."

Chloe grimaced. "Sometimes my mouth gets ahead of my . . . head."

"You may need your mouth now. You'll only see shadows, and remember—the Mordin will see you too. You'll be able to speak to each other, but you won't hear anything else unless I think you need to. And you'll only have a minute or so to get the ring."

Suddenly April spoke again, sounding hopeless. "It's no good. I can't—"

Her voice cut out. Another voice cried out April's name—*Joshua*, Chloe thought.

She barely had time to wonder what had happened before Gabriel's low voice thundered against her ears again. "The ring is on his left hand. Are you ready?"

Chloe nodded. Instantly, magically, her useless eyes began to work. A shadow slowly resolved out of the nothingness up ahead. A huge shadow, long limbed and suspended in midair—Dr. Jericho, thrown half onto his back, pinned in place by a blow from Horace's phalanx. And now a faint, nasty trickle of brimstone wormed into Chloe's nostrils.

Chloe stepped forward. The Mordin, just a faint silhouette in the gray, tipped his head toward her.

"Ah," he sang happily, as if being trapped here didn't trouble him at all. "A glimmer in the gloom. A visitor—young Chloe, by the feel of it."

Dr. Jericho's great left hand hung in the air just a few feet in front if Chloe, his fingers like the gnarled limbs of a dead tree. She couldn't see the golem's ring, but she knew what it looked like, a twisting black band with a scarlet stone. Deep inside the body of the golem, she also knew, there was a jagged crystal that same exact color that swam among the golem's stones like a ruby fish in a black sea. The heart of the golem. But Chloe had no idea how to actually get the ring away. And she didn't know how long Gabriel could keep this up, or how long the effects of the phalanx would keep Dr. Jericho pinned.

"I'm not really here to visit," Chloe told the Mordin.

"Come looking for your mother, then?"

Of course he knew about Isabel. She hated him for knowing it.

"I freed her, you know," Dr. Jericho continued. "I took the Forsworn's proxy and swallowed it up myself."

Swallowed it. Miradel. Somehow Chloe knew he meant that literally. She couldn't see his face but could practically feel him grinning in the shadows. "Good for you," she said. "Where's Horace?"

"Ah, I see. Friends before family. Don't worry—he's safe in the golem's embrace." Dr. Jericho flared his great hand and then balled it into a giant fist. "For now."

If she could lunge for him, and reach the ring, she could make it go thin and slip it from his hand. But she knew from experience that the Mordin's reflexes were far quicker than any human's, even hers. "Let him go," she said, knowing he wouldn't.

"Oh, goodness—did he not want to be caught? It was foolish of him to come alone, if he had no idea what the future held."

Chloe thought quickly. The Mordin was acting calm, as he usually did, but she knew a fierce temper always lurked just beneath the surface, and something in his voice told her that his rage was boiling extra hot tonight. Maybe she wasn't quite as logical as Horace was, but she was prepared to do anything. And being prepared to do anything meant that more options became logical. If she couldn't grab for the ring, maybe she could let the ring come to her. Possibly not smart, but smart was for people with time. It was Horace's job to be reasonable. Chloe's job was to be fearless.

Chloe released the Alvalaithen, knowing Dr. Jericho would sense it. The dragonfly's wings went still. She sauntered closer to the Mordin, just outside his reach.

"Horace always knows what the future holds," she said. "He saw all of this." That was a lie, but she had to hope it would work.

"Did he? How strange. I haven't felt the Fel'Daera's gaze upon me."

She took a step closer. "I don't know anything about that,"

she said. "But Horace saw me take this ring from you." She stretched out casually for the Mordin's filthy hand. He yanked it out of her reach. She shrugged as if it didn't matter, and took another step forward. "He saw me controlling the golem with it," she said.

The Mordin cackled. "Impossible. Even with the ring in hand, you cannot make the golem obey."

This was just what Gabriel had said. The golem wouldn't listen to her. But she wanted the Mordin to underestimate her. She stepped even closer, as if still trying to reach the ring. The Mordin's huge, insectlike shadow grew darker, resolving. She tried not to recoil from his long, shadowy fingers and his sharply pointed nails.

"If that's true, then why are you afraid to let me see it?" she taunted. "Are you afraid a Tinker has some talents you don't know about? If so, I don't blame you. It's been happening to you a lot lately." She took another step.

The Mordin struck so fast that Chloe didn't even have time to flinch. His arm shot out like a snake, clutching her around the torso, his hand so huge that it pinned her arms to her sides. His strength was swift and immense, as if he hoped to crush the life from her before she could go thin. She felt a pop as one of her ribs broke.

Chloe gasped and gurgled. A rush of blood surged into her head, dimming her vision. But this was what she wanted. She drank deeply from the Alvalaithen. Its music filled her, and the dragonfly's wings whirred to life. She willed its power to spread, to carry out from her own body and into everything that touched her—every last thing but one. She'd learned to do this with her own clothes, with small objects she carried, and once—in a moment of great need—with Horace's entire body. She summoned up some of that same need now.

She couldn't make Dr. Jericho's entire body go thin; he was far too large for that. But she didn't need the whole body. She only needed a bit of it, the flesh and bone of his hand. Everything but the golem's ring. It took less than a second for the Mordin's fist to become as much of a ghost as she was.

The awful pressure crushing her body faded.

And the ring fell free.

Chloe ducked out of Dr. Jericho's grip—unholdable now—and neatly caught the ring just before it hit the ground. The Mordin roared and swiped at her. This time she didn't flinch because she didn't have to. His huge clawed hand swung through her. He flailed furiously at her, raging.

"Well done, Tinker," he spat. "Now that no one wears the ring, the golem sleeps. With Horace deep inside. You've gained nothing."

Chloe scowled, her heart racing. Her rib ached, but she refused to grab at it. Was it true? Was Horace now trapped inside the golem? She clutched the foul ring. It was as big around as the lug nut of a tire, the misshapen scarlet stone faintly warm.

"I'll just destroy the ring, then," she said. It would be easy, after all. Make it go thin, stick it deep into the ground.

Let it meld with the earth and cease to be.

But Dr. Jericho inhaled sharply, as if in genuine fear. "Destroy the ring, and the golem destroys itself. Quite violently. None of us will survive, least of all Horace." He reached out with a hideous finger and stuck a sharp nail directly into the ghostly Alvalaithen. "Correction. None of us will survive except you."

Suddenly his immense shadow shifted. He started to slip out of the air. He reached nimbly for the ground, catching himself. The effects of the phalanx had worn off. Slowly Dr. Jericho stood to his full height, a shadowy ghoul towering over her.

"Ah," he sang merrily. "Better."

CHAPTER FOURTEEN

Eyes, Ears, and Nose

FOR APRIL, THE FALKRETE STONES WERE EASY.

Mr. Meister had explained how to do it, to get quickly back to the meadow and help save Joshua and Brian—she had to lay her Tan'ji against the proper stone, and suddenly she would be in two places at once. Part of her would remain where she was, but another part of her—another April entirely?—would be in the next cloister along the line. From there, it was simply a matter of believing that she was there in that second cloister, rather than here in the first one. If her belief was strong enough, true enough, then suddenly she would travel. If she had faith, the new April would be the only true April, and the old one would be left behind. Mr. Meister had led her to think that finding that faith might be difficult, that believing might be a challenge.

But for April, it was no challenge at all.

Maybe it was because she'd always imagined there were other Aprils out there, in this universe or another. Other versions of herself—but still herself, of course. An April in a universe where her uncle Harrison wasn't fat and crude. An April in a universe where Uncle Harrison was much *worse* than fat and crude. An April in a universe where she and her brother, Derek, lived happily alone, or sadly alone. An April in a universe where her parents had never died in the first place.

It wasn't that she was unhappy being the April she was. Not at all. She just assumed all the other Aprils, along all those other lines of existence, were no more or less happy than she was. April didn't believe in looking back.

And so with each jump, it was easy to commit herself to that next new April. Easy to commit to the notion that the April she'd left behind was no one worth clinging to.

Naturally she was worried about what she would find in the meadow—and also about what she *wouldn't* find—but first and foremost she'd been worried about losing her way. Each falkrete circle had a dozen stones or more, and only one stone led along the right path, the path to the meadow by Uncle Harrison's house. But as Mr. Meister had promised, the proper stones were still marked with mints from the rescue mission they'd sent for April earlier in the evening. Chloe's mints.

April jumped from cloister to cloister with no troubles whatsoever, taking her time so that she wouldn't catch up to Chloe, who was traveling the falkretes just ahead of her. One tricky aspect to the falkretes, Mr. Meister had explained, was that a jump could not be made while anyone was watching you. If someone was watching, you were locked in place by their observation, and you couldn't split and make the jump. He hadn't bothered to clarify that *animal* observations didn't count—only people and, apparently, Riven—but April wasn't surprised. People generally didn't bother to include animals when they talked about awareness. And the falkretes didn't seem to include them either.

And so she jumped from stone to stone, even as possums and cicadas and other night creatures watched her. Five jumps, Mr. Meister had told her. After four jumps, she found herself in a cloister far from the city, with a leestone colored like a Steller's jay. All the leestones had been birds, she noticed—and not just any birds, but corvids. Jays and magpies. Crows and ravens. Some of the smartest birds—the smartest animals period—that there were. She tried not to think about Arthur.

She found the last falkrete, the one that would take her to the barn, the white mint still atop it. The falkrete was shaped like a bear asleep in the earth, or a dog. She crouched in front of the stone, the Ravenvine in her hand. Here, at last, she felt doubt. What would she find at the barn? What could she possibly do to help the Wardens? The golem sounded frightening, and without Arthur, she wasn't sure how much good her powers would do. There would be other animals in the meadow, but she would be lucky to discover something useful.

She took a deep breath. "It doesn't matter," she said. And

239

it didn't. She couldn't *not* help, couldn't stand the thought of staying behind while poor Joshua was out there, lost and way in over his head. Not while Brian, who had fixed her precious Ravenvine and made her whole at last, was lost and in danger. Not while Horace and Chloe and Gabriel did the fighting for her. She would find a way to help them. And although she'd been trying hard not to fret about it all night, she had another reason for wanting to go back: First Baron.

Her dog had been injured earlier that night as he tried to attack Dr. Jericho. The Mordin had struck Baron, sending him flying; April had felt the crackling pain in her own ribs. A painful injury, but not fatal. Still, she'd had to leave him there, pulling away with the vine, before the dog could make his escape—if he had even tried to escape. He was a good dog. He would fight to protect her, just like good dogs did.

She blinked away an unwanted swell of tears. Probably she would not even get the chance to go looking for Baron tonight. And that was okay. Baron was strong. Independent. Probably he didn't even need her, right?

She gritted her teeth and touched a golden curve of the Ravenvine to the stone. Immediately, with a wrench she hadn't felt before now, she vanished from where she was. She materialized in a new place, but for a moment it didn't feel like anyplace at all. She was blind and lost inside a thick and endless soup of gray. Had something gone wrong?

Then a deep voice rang at her, coming from all sides.

"April!"

Gabriel. She was in the humour. She was in the meadow by the barn after all.

She drew back her hair and tucked the Ravenvine around her left ear, snugging it against her temple. "Tell me what to do," she said, her voice drifting into the humour like a coin into water. "How can I help?"

"Look outside the humour, if you can," said Gabriel. She thought his voice sounded strained, but he was trying to hide it. "The golem was chasing Horace when I arrived, but they're beyond me now."

"Let me try." Through the Ravenvine, April reached out into the cacophony of animal minds all around—insects, mostly, by the thousands. She set their busy drone aside and reached for something closer to human. She sensed a family of mice in the grass nearby, but they were in the humour, as blind as she was. Farther out, beyond the edge of the humour, she briefly felt a bat flicker by. It flitted out of range before she could even borrow its eyes. She searched for more, but all she felt were bugs buried sightless in the grass, the world huge and meaningless around them.

"It's no good," she said, trying to reach even farther. "I can't—"

And then a new mind. Warm and intelligent. So deep and familiar and startling that the tears she'd beaten back moments before now welled up and overflowed, pouring down her cheeks.

First Baron. He was here, trotting past, apparently circling the edge of the humour. Worried and confused.

April turned without saying a word to Gabriel and went to Baron, still crying. She wondered if Gabriel could feel her tears. The dog stopped and sat, whining. Through his eyes, out in the night beyond the humour's edge, a wide swath of the meadow simply didn't exist. That's what the humour looked like from outside. April was in there, of course, hidden by the unseeable humour—but Baron didn't know it. Not yet. All he knew was that the bad things were back. Their stink filled his nose. One of them had hurt him. His left flank was tender and sore. April reached up to her own side, rubbing the spot.

There was a sound, too, crisp and huge in the dog's keen ears, a sound not exactly like any April had ever heard before. It reminded her of the trucks that dumped gravel and tar on the country roads every year or two, an endless liquid slide of tiny rocks.

The golem.

She couldn't see it. Judging by the sound, it was on the far side of the humour from Baron. And it was huge. Baron was afraid of it. She opened herself to that fear, letting it fill her, letting the dog's memories come to her.

The dog was mere feet away from her now. That meant she was nearly at the edge of the humour. She forced herself to stop.

Gabriel's voice surrounded her. "What do you see?"

"The golem has Horace, farther down in the meadow, on

242

the other side of the humour."

"Is he harmed?"

"I don't know. I can't actually see him. My dog is—" It was so impossible to explain. How was she supposed to describe knowledge acquired through memories stolen from another mind? Baron had seen the golem pour over Horace, burying him. The sight made no sense to the dog, of course, but remains of the images were still there, loose shapes to be reassembled and understood. It was harder to tell how long ago it had happened—a minute? Two minutes? "The golem ran him down," she said. "That's all I know."

"Chloe is working on it," Gabriel replied. Again, she thought she could detect a note of effort in his voice, as if he were lifting something heavy while he spoke. "Can you see Brian and Joshua? I sent them out of the humour. To the barn."

"I don't see them. Maybe they're already inside. Why did you send them out?"

"Ingrid is in the humour. She's playing her flute."

"I don't hear anything."

"That's because I'm not letting you. But I can only hold her off so long. I'm . . . I'm juggling a lot here at the moment."

That explained the strain. It was easy to forget that the humour was full of activity, unseen and unheard, and that Gabriel was like the spider at the center of the web, a finger on every thread.

April nodded, keeping it simple for Gabriel's sake. She

opened her mind to Baron's again. His nose was filled with brimstone. But she dug through that sharp bite and found other scents, too. Human scents. One of them was faintly familiar to Baron, a stranger he'd met only once or twice before. Instinctively April understood that the scent, herbal and biting, belonged to Isabel. It was a bit embarrassing to recognize something so personal about the woman.

But the other two scents were unfamiliar, new to Baron. Or no—newish. She drank the emotions attached to those smells. *Curiosity. Kindness. Happiness.* Recently made friends, then. She let the dog's mind slip farther into her own, and almost as if by magic, new little bridges of memory began to form, connecting sense to sense. This smell, sweaty and strong, belonged to this boy—long hair, glasses. Brian. And this smell, slightly spicy but not nearly so pungent, belonged to a small boy with dark hair. Joshua.

These sights and sounds were recent, too. Baron hadn't seen them, she thought, but had definitely smelled them. Baron swung his head and looked back at the rear of the barn, and she grasped that Brian and Joshua had gone that way. And now she heard voices talking low. Whispers.

"They made it to the barn," she reported. "They're hiding, I think."

"It's clear, then?" Gabriel asked.

"I smell brimstone. But it's everywhere. I don't see anyone."

"Chloe has the golem's ring. She'll help Horace. Go to

Brian and Joshua. Be their eyes and ears. It won't be safe in here soon."

"What about you? What about Mr. Meister?"

"He hasn't arrived yet."

That was worrying. Mr. Meister was supposed to be traveling right behind her. He should have come through the last falkrete a minute or two ago.

"Help them," said Gabriel. "We'll find you."

April nodded weakly—and she didn't know if Gabriel could read the doubt and worry on her face, but suddenly he spoke words that she hadn't even been aware she needed to hear.

"I will not leave without you, April," he said solemnly.

April nodded again. Firmly this time. Joshua and Brian needed her. Everything would be okay.

She stepped out of the humour. Through Baron's eyes, she watched herself emerge out of nothingness into the dark night. Her own girlish scent flooded her nose. And there Baron was, frisking and wagging his tail at her, flooded with a happiness that almost brought her to her knees. He wiggled so hard it made his wounded ribs ache—and hers too—but he didn't mind. And neither did she.

She sank to her knees, burying her face in his fur. "Good boy," she said, her own too-high voice looping through her ears. "I'm sorry I left you. Good boy." He licked her face. She felt it from both ends—the rough tongue on her cheek, the taste of her own sweat.

She struggled to her feet, still clinging to Baron's fur. "Come on," she said. "Friends." He gave a single, sharp bark of agreement, making her throat jump.

She strode across the grass toward the barn, Baron at her side. As they came closer, they crossed the scent trail of Joshua and Brian. The dog's nose was so sensitive, she could even tell which direction they'd been traveling—the trail was ever so faintly stronger in one direction than the other. Thanks to Baron, she could still hear them whispering. And now she heard another voice too—tinny in her own ears, but loud and clear in Baron's.

"Horace! Horace!"

April spun around. Chloe, somewhere out past the unsee-able humour. April's eyes wouldn't fix on anything, but above the wrinkle of the humour, she thought she saw the top of a dark tower, looming over the meadow. The golem?

Baron was watching too. He let loose a little whine bark, tickling her throat. He was worried.

"It's okay," she murmured softly. "Chloe has it under control." Saying the words didn't help her feel any better.

She kept on. She crept in under the collapsing eaves at the back of the big barn. Lots of insects here, and more. Spiders. Lots of them. She didn't mind spiders—she admired them, actually. But now that the Ravenvine was repaired, she sensed them in a whole new way, reminded that they weren't insects at all. Insects were mostly oblivious to human activity, but the spiders here in the barn were much more . . . aware. Wolf spiders, probably. And with a start, she realized they could actually hear her. Not with ears, exactly—spiders didn't have ears. But they were hearing her footsteps, vibrations in the air felt through the hairs on their bodies, their legs. It tickled her as she walked. She suddenly felt very loud.

She tried to shake it off, letting Baron's mind wash the spiders out. Through him—through the vine—the whispers coming from up ahead were plainly audible now, the words clear.

"They're coming closer," she heard Joshua say. He was definitely frightened.

"Open a portal," said Brian. "Get us out."

She opened her mouth. "It's me," she said. "April."

She still couldn't see them, but she knew right where they were. She knew the barn well—here at the back end, there were stables and storage rooms, grain bins and pens. Some walls were broken open or collapsed, while some corridors were blocked by fallen timber, so this end of the barn was a bit of a labyrinth. She passed through a crooked doorway into a leaning hallway lined with narrow stalls. Baron swept past her, tail wagging madly, and trotted into the first stall—right over to the boys, who were cowering against the cobwebby, broken slats of the far wall. Tunraden lay on the lumpy ground in front of Brian, looking monstrously out of place. A faint blue orb was floating near Joshua's head, shining and casting crisp shadows. April nearly gasped at the sight of it—a tiny, perfect earth. The Laithe of Teneves.

"Oh, thank my dry pants," said Brian when he saw her. "We thought you were the Riven."

"I don't want to take that as a compliment, but it's nice to be scary for a change."

Joshua stood up, facing April like a schoolboy who'd done something bad. "Did you find Horace?"

"In a way. The golem caught him. But Chloe is going to save him, don't worry. Gabriel sent me to find you guys."

"I'm sorry," Joshua said stiffly.

April's heart broke a little for him. She wrapped him in a hug. His posture was as stiff as his words. "Don't be sorry," she told him. "It's going to be okay. You're a Keeper now."

Joshua looked away.

"I'm sorry too," Brian said. "I don't know what I was thinking."

"Isabel forced you," April said. "You didn't have a choice."

Now it was Brian's turn to look away. What exactly had happened here tonight?

"Where *is* Isabel, anyway?" April asked. "I smelled her outside—or Baron did."

"She was in the humour, fighting with Ingrid," Joshua said. "Dr. Jericho ate Mirabel."

April shook her head. "Wait . . . what?"

"Ate it," said Brian. "Swallowed it. It's gone."

"But Isabel's alive?"

"Last time I checked," said Brian. "I was about to—" He shook his head, looking guilty and confused. "She'll be fine.

248

But you said Chloe was going to save Horace. How?"

"Chloe was looking for a ring," said Joshua.

"The golem's ring," said April. "The golem has Horace. Chloe's trying to save him. But what about the Riven? How many are there?"

"We only saw Dr. Jericho," said Joshua.

April frowned. Horace had reported seeing lots of Riven, and Baron's nose seemed to confirm that Dr. Jericho wasn't alone. But where, then, were the others?

"I am in way over my head," Brian muttered, watching her. "Aren't you?"

"I can swim," April told him. "And so can you. Gabriel sent me to find you, to be your eyes and ears. He's got his hands full in the humour, but he said he'd come for us."

"He will," said Joshua firmly. "And Chloe will rescue Horace. And then I'll open the Laithe so we can escape—all of us."

April rubbed his head. "I know you will," she told the boy. Horace had seen it happen, after all. "I know you will."

The ground shook slightly, startling her. A huge rumbling erupted far out in the meadow, beyond the humour. Joshua flinched and put his hands over his ears. April forced herself not to cringe in pain. It was loud in her own ears, and through the vine—through Baron—it was a rocket blast. It had to be the golem. Baron danced in place, excited and terrified. April bore the clamor as best she could, and in the midst of it, she heard a tiny voice cry out.

"I think I just heard Chloe," she said. "Calling for Horace again."

As quickly as it had come, the clamor died down. Silence returned.

"The golem has them both now," Brian groaned. "We're screwed."

But April could hear faint voices out in the meadow. Chloe for sure, and . . . was that Horace? "Chloe can't be caught," said April. "And anyway, I think I hear her." She frowned and cocked her head to hear better—pointless, since she was using Baron's ears now and not her own.

Abruptly, a new shiver of alarm coursed through her. Her throat rumbled as Baron began to growl. He growled not out into the meadow, toward the golem, but deeper into the barn, toward the front, where—beyond the half-collapsed labyrinth of the barn's back end—a wide-open loft soared high and the barn's crooked front door stood jammed slightly open. Open enough for a human to get out, or a dog. Open just enough for a Mordin to get in.

She felt pain inside her nose. A stinging that came as a surprise. This was Baron's pain, but instead of running away from the sulfurous stench, the dog hurried toward it, his hackles rising, still growling low. She hissed at him, but he ignored her, disappearing into the deeps of the barn, headed for the front.

"What's the matter?" whispered Joshua.

"Brimstone," April whispered. There were Riven inside

250

the barn, coming from the other side, opposite the way she'd just come in. "We're not alone in here. Be quiet."

Joshua's eyes got wide and watery. "What are we going to do?" he whispered.

April shook her head. She couldn't leave Baron—he was her eyes and ears—but obviously couldn't leave the boys either. Or maybe she should. If they all just sat here, they were sure to be found. If they went back out the rear of the barn, they risked the golem. But April alone had the power to track and avoid the Riven in the darkness of the barn. Maybe she could lure the Riven away, keeping the boys safe, and find a way back here with Baron. Above all, she knew she had to keep Brian and Joshua safe.

"Don't move," she told them. "I'm going to distract them. I'll be back when I can." She glanced at the gleaming blue Laithe. "Keep it covered. Stay dark." And then without waiting for an answer, she slipped into the shadows after Baron.

CHAPTER FIFTEEN

The Sky Falling

JOSHUA WATCHED AS APRIL LEFT THEM, TIPTOEING AFTER
Baron. She vanished into the maze of the dark barn before
he could stop her. He could smell the brimstone now too. He
grabbed the Laithe and buried its dim light in his arms. He
dropped into the corner beside Brian.

"I'm scared," he whispered.

"Don't be," said Brian, his knees snugged to his chest. "I
won't be if you won't be. Quiet now."

Joshua tried to be as quiet as he knew how. He got so
quiet he could hear his own blood, sloshing through his ears.
Maybe the leestone Brian had repaired would protect them. It
didn't work against Dr. Jericho, no, but Dr. Jericho had been
watching them all along. Now they were hidden. Maybe the
leestone would help them stay that way.

Seconds passed. And then a terrible sound crept out of

the shadows. A hollow grinding sound, long and slow, rattling in Joshua's teeth. Something sharp being dragged through wood. A nail. A claw. And now a footstep, far too heavy to be human. Another, not twenty feet away, inside the barn. The rotten-egg smell of brimstone burned in his nostrils.

A Mordin appeared at the entrance to the stall, stooped over beneath the low ceiling like some nightmare dinosaur, like the skeleton of a raptor. Its knuckles dragged on the ground. Joshua held his breath, hugging the Laithe of Teneves hard. For a split second, he thought the Mordin would pass them by, but then it paused at the opening, took a half step back, and sniffed the air. Once. Twice. Long, rumbling sniffs. It turned its head.

Suddenly Baron began to bark, out on the front side of the barn. The Mordin spun around. In the same instant, from the opposite direction, a huge *crack!* pounded the air. The Mordin went flying like it had been hit by an invisible train.

"Whoa!" cried Brian.

Joshua knew that sound. It was the weapon he'd seen Mr. Meister use once before, on the riverbank. Sure enough, Mr. Meister himself came sprinting into the stall a moment later, his brilliant white jithandra hanging from his neck.

"Keepers," he said breathlessly. "Gabriel told me I would find you here. Are you quite all right?"

Joshua nodded, shielding his eyes, not too stunned to notice that Mr. Meister had called him Keeper. And Mr. Meister wasn't alone. Isabel stood behind him, looking miserable.

Sad, or mad, or both. She held something in her hands—a small white circle laced with glittering strings.

Brian stood up, looking worried. "I've been rather dumb," he said.

"Agreed," said Mr. Meister, "but no doubt brave too. Where is April?"

"She went after Baron," said Joshua, pointing deeper into the barn. "Her dog."

"Was she using the Ravenvine?"

"I think so."

Mr. Meister frowned. "If Dr. Jericho senses her, I fear he may go after her."

"But Dr. Jericho was pinned, inside the humour," Brian said.

Mr. Meister shook his head. "No longer. Chloe was—"

Abruptly, the rotting wall of the little room exploded into splinters. A Mordin burst in, bellowing angrily. It knocked Mr. Meister to the ground and then swiped at Brian, grabbing him by the leg. It lifted him into the air. It grasped one of Brian's dangling arms as if it meant to tear Brian in two.

But then it stumbled, dropping Brian as it clutched at its head in obvious pain, crashing through what was left of the wall like a wrecking ball. Joshua dove out of the way. He looked over to see Isabel on her knees, fumbling with the white circle in her hands.

"It's no good!" she cried. "I can't cleave. I can only sever for a second."

Joshua understood. She had a new harp—Mr. Meister

must have brought her one. But it was weak. She couldn't sever the Riven long enough to . . . well, to kill them. The Mordin shook his head groggily and started to rise, but Mr. Meister rolled over and fired his weapon again—something small and unseen in his hand. Joshua's hair flew up as the blast zipped past him. It struck the Mordin head-on, throwing it back against a thick wooden beam. The beam cracked, buckling a little bit, and the Mordin fell limp to the ground in a shower of dust from above.

Mr. Meister stood, brushing off his vest. He turned to Isabel. "Find April. Bring her back. You owe her that, at least."

Isabel frowned at him, but then nodded. She hurried off into the darks of the barn.

Brian struggled to his feet. "You brought her a new harp?"

"A weak one, yes," Mr. Meister said. "Something that could be of use, but nothing that would be a danger. I thought it best to keep her close."

"But how did you know that Miradel—"

"Horace saw Isabel through the Fel'Daera," Mr. Meister explained. "He saw that something was amiss, that the wicker harp was gone. Before I came here, I dug through the pockets of my vest. It took me a while, but I found a suitable substitute."

"Horace saw her before you came?" Brian said dreamily. He was clearly figuring something out, but Joshua didn't have any idea what it was.

"Tell me, Keeper," said Mr. Meister, leaning close to Brian, "how did you and Tunraden fare, attempting to fulfill Isabel's wishes tonight?"

255

Brian opened his mouth, then shut it again. At last he said simply, "I was close. But that's over now."

"When I found Isabel in the humour, she told me about Dr. Jericho. About her harp's demise. But when Horace first reported that the wicker harp was missing, I confess I rather wondered if . . ." He trailed off.

"If I had blown it up or something?" Brian asked. "No. No, I was doing it. It was doable. I think." He shook his head. "But now all this calamity. My fault. And I am not equipped for this kind of stuff," he said.

"On the contrary," Mr. Meister said. "You seem to be handling it quite well. Tunraden has survived. Now we must ensure that she returns to the Warren, where she belongs. Prepare yourself. When the others return, we will go."

"I'm on board, believe me," Brian said. He stooped and slipped his hands into Tunraden's surface, lifting her.

Mr. Meister crouched down in front of Joshua. "Very soon, we will need you to make a portal, Keeper. Can you do it?"

"I'm not even sure I *am* a Keeper," Joshua said. "I think I'm a Lostling."

"Did Dr. Jericho call you that?"

"Yes."

A loud crash shook the barn, far away toward the front end. Mr. Meister ignored it, smiling kindly at Joshua. "Don't tell me you would let the word of a Mordin cast doubt on what you *know* yourself to be, in the purest waters of your deepest heart."

Joshua gazed down at the Laithe. It sounded like Mr. Meister was forgiving him. It should have brought him relief, but it only brought another worry—could the old man *help* Joshua? Would he let Joshua do what he needed to do? He wasn't sure he had those pure waters, and even if he did, he needed room to find them. Joshua forced himself to nod, just once, his throat bunching up. The barn shook again, louder and closer this time.

"Whoa," said Brian, as a shower of dust rained down on them. He slid to the doorway, peeking out.

"Now listen," said Mr. Meister. "In a moment, Isabel will return with April. Then we will enter the humour again, and there you will open a portal for us. Understand?"

As he spoke, strange sounds began to echo through the barn's walls. It sounded like hammers on a pile of gravel. It had to be April, and Isabel. They were in trouble.

"Do you understand, Joshua?" Mr. Meister said again. His huge left eye leered at him, and now Joshua thought he saw, deep inside that eye, a tremble of worry. Mr. Meister was hearing those sounds too, and he was afraid.

Somehow, it was a comfort. Joshua told him the most honest thing he could think of. "I don't know if I can do it."

"You can, and will. Horace witnessed it."

Joshua stopped breathing. "Through the box, you mean? He saw me opening a portal in the humour?"

"Indeed he did."

"But where *is* Horace? And where is Chlo—"

Another rumble interrupted him. Shouts at the front of the barn, the earth shaking, the walls trembling.

And then the sky fell in.

CHAPTER SIXTEEN

A Sending Seen

CHLOE REARED BACK AS THE SHADOWY SHAPE OF DR. JERICHO loomed over her, freed from the phalanx's powers now. But on the instant, the humour thickened around them with a soft *whump*, and sightlessness returned.

Gabriel thundered at her, sounding breathless. "Out in the meadow, behind you. Horace is there."

This time, Chloe didn't think. She spun and dove away from Dr. Jericho, into the ground, letting the earth swallow her up. She was still blind here, but it was blindness on her own terms. The ground was cool and gritty, full of stones. Her broken rib burned and complained. She ignored it. She swam through the dirt, the ring still clutched in her hand. She couldn't say how she moved, exactly—she didn't even want to know—but the effort happened at the tiniest levels, cell by cell, molecule by molecule, a willful act of matter pushing back at matter.

She fell into a rhythm with it, and found an astonishing speed. She didn't go deep—there was no need. She had to get free of the humour, had to find Horace.

She streaked onward until she was sure she was well clear of the humour. She dipped a little lower and then curved back up toward the surface, like a dolphin. She found a final burst of speed.

Chloe shot high into the air, into the warm night with stars overhead. She hit the ground at a run, releasing the Alvalaithen's sweet song and looking back. Fifty yards behind her, the humour was a dizzying stitch in her vision, invisible. Beyond it, the roof of the barn hung as if floating. Somewhere in that direction, a dog barked. April's dog? But just here, out in the field, not thirty feet away—a hulking mass of rubble, dark against the night sky. The golem, asleep, with Horace inside.

She'd gotten lucky. She ran up to it. The golem had taken the shape of an enormous slab, an obelisk like a giant domino standing on end. It was as tall as a house, as thick as a redwood.

She pounded her fist against the wall. Divots appeared briefly under her hand, bits of the golem shaking loose beneath her blows, but the stones fell back into the mass, defying gravity, and slithered back together.

"Horace!" she cried. "Horace!" She dug at the stones, but got nowhere. The holes repaired themselves as quickly as she could scoop them out.

Chloe opened up the dragonfly's song and plunged into

the body of the golem. She swam through the dense sea of stones, groping, blind yet again but searching for the telltale sign of flesh inside her flesh. She felt nothing. She went higher, up the tower of the golem, weaving to and fro. Ten seconds into her search, a scorching burn slashed through her hand. She knew from experience what it was—the heart of the golem. Somehow the jagged red crystal could burn her even while she was thin. She veered around it with a curse, and continued upward.

At last, high off the ground, deep in the golem, she found him. Horace. Her hand entered his, their bloodstreams crossing like passing currents. Horace twitched, his fingers flexing. He was alive.

Quickly she moved up until her mouth was at the side of his head. Her lips entered the curls of his ear.

"Horace!" she called softly.

The stones around them in the dark shifted and rattled as Horace took a labored breath. "I'm here," he said, his voice trickling through the black mass. "I'm okay."

"You're not okay," Chloe said, knowing how terrified he must be. He'd been buried alive before, but not like this. This was not a coffin; this was thick black quicksand, tight and choking. It would have been a nightmare for anyone, but Horace most of all.

"Having trouble," Horace wheezed, "breathing."

"I've got the golem's ring," she said. "I'm getting you out."

"I know you are."

But she had no idea how to get him out. Possibly she could make Horace go thin and carry him with her. She'd done it before—but only for the briefest slice of time, and only through the slimmest of barriers. If she made him go thin now and dragged him through the golem, stones would fill his formless body just like they filled hers now. And if she couldn't keep him thin until they were clear, he wouldn't survive.

"I thought I would destroy the ring, but I can't," she said. "The golem will . . . explode, or something."

She expected him to ask how she knew this—and *did* she know? —but instead he said simply, "You're going to send it."

"Send the ring? What do you mean?"

"Traveling."

The box. He wanted her to send the ring through the Fel'Daera. "Will that work? Is sending the ring any different than destroying it?"

"It's what happens."

Chloe tried to piece it together. Sending objects through the box didn't destroy them, of course—if it did, the Alvalaithen wouldn't be here—but it did make them utterly gone. What would happen to the golem?

"Take the box," Horace said, and took another labored breath. "Try."

Take the box. An incredible thought. It was an effort even to imagine that she deserved that kind of trust. "I'm not its Keeper, though. How do you know I can even send anything?"

"I saw you do it. I know that now."

"That's crazy. The box never even—"

"Trust me. You can't see, but you can send." Horace wheezed and shifted, his breath trembling. "Or maybe you'd like to chat about it awhile."

"Okay," said Chloe. "I get it." She reached into Horace's pouch and found the Fel'Daera. She concentrated on it, letting it go thin with her, and pulled it slowly free. She'd never before touched the box, and she cradled it carefully now, as if it were her own.

"Don't do anything stupid," Horace mumbled.

"It's way too late for that," she said.

She left him. She went up instead of down. She quickly emerged through the roof of the golem's body and clambered out atop it, three stories above the meadow. She made sure the Fel'Daera—and everything else—was fully clear, and then let the dragonfly's wings go still.

From up here, she could see over the patch of unsight that marked the humour, all the way to where the lumbering, rickety barn stood beneath the starry skies. With any luck, Joshua and Brian were safe in that barn, and maybe April too. And who knew who—or what—was inside the humour right now.

There was no time to wonder. Chloe struggled to open the box. She'd seen Horace do it a hundred times, and he made it look easy, but the lid was a funny thing. It was like two insect wings, folded together along a curving seam in the middle. At last she got them apart. They swung open smoothly, exposing the rippling blue glass within. Through it, of course, she saw only her own feet, here and now. She was not the Keeper of the Fel'Daera. She couldn't see the future.

But could she send?

She laid the golem's ring gently inside the box. For a brief, surreal moment, she found herself hoping that the box wouldn't work for her. This wasn't what Tan'ji were supposed to do. But she shoved the thought aside with a guilty flush, and spun the lid closed.

She felt nothing. For a second, despair flooded through her. What would she do now?

And then the world collapsed beneath her feet.

The golem began to fall apart with a clattering roar. Chloe fell with it, into it, riding the avalanche downward. She tucked the Fel'Daera into her gut, protecting it. Below her, she glimpsed Horace's face, gasping for air, his arms pinwheeling through the falling shower of stones. He was yelling something, but she couldn't hear him over the din of the golem's collapse, like a hailstorm on a metal roof.

"Horace!" she shouted as she fell, trying to keep her feet beneath her. The stones swallowed Horace.

A split second later, Chloe landed with a jolt, her legs plunging into the loose pile of the golem's body. Her rib screamed at her. The thunderous rain of stones trickled slowly to a stop, and everything went quiet. The golem was—what? Dead? Unconscious? Either way, Horace's plan had worked. She had sent the ring. It was nowhere now, and the golem was nothing.

Horace. Chloe wormed her way free and scrambled over the pile. She spotted an arm sticking out of the rubble and yanked at it, slipping and sliding on the mountain of slick stones. With her help, Horace clawed his way out, still breathing hard, and collapsed on the slope of the pile, his head downhill against her knee.

He lay there a moment, chest heaving, and then held out his hand. "Box," he said.

Quickly Chloe laid the Fel'Daera in his palm. He clutched at it, eyes closed. "Let's not do that again," he said.

"Which part?"

"All of it." He looked up at her, upside down. His shaggy hair was a wreck. Then he rolled over and struggled to his feet. "We should get down," he said.

They half walked, half skated down the slippery slope of the expired golem, headed away from the barn and the humour. Once they reached the bottom, hidden behind the heap, Chloe cautiously sipped from the Alvalaithen and stuck a finger inside her torso to feel her broken rib.

"You okay?" Horace said.

"I'm fine," she said. She could feel the fracture, a coarse seam. But there were no jagged edges, and the bone was in place. More or less. She *was* fine. "Let's go," she said, pulling her finger free. "We have to get Brian. Dr. Jericho is—"

"They're leaving," said Horace. "Without us. Joshua's going to open a portal in about . . . two and a half minutes. He's leaving with Brian and Mr. Meister."

"That's what you saw? They leave without us?"

"Yes."

To her great surprise, he started walking away, deeper into the meadow. Just then, a dog started barking, far behind them. It sounded like it was coming from the far side of the barn, around front. What was he barking at? More Mordin? And now a sharp crack rang across the meadow—Mr. Meister, firing his mysterious weapon somewhere inside the barn. So it *had* been him she'd seen, after all. Chloe turned to look, back past the limp golem and the unseen wrinkle of the humour. Was it her imagination, or was the humour sliding? All she could think was that Gabriel must be on the move inside it. "They're fighting up there," she called after Horace, who hadn't even bothered to turn around. "What about Gabriel? And April?"

"I didn't see April. We have to trust that Gabriel keeps her safe. That they keep each other safe."

"What about Mr. Meister? And my mom?"

Horace stopped and turned to face her. "Look, here's what I know. We don't leave through the portal. Neither does Gabriel, or April, or your mom. The humour comes down. And . . . there's another golem. It's going to come down into the meadow in a few minutes. And Mordin, too."

A second crack from Mr. Meister's weapon rang out. Chloe hardly heard it.

"*Another* golem? Why didn't you say that before?"

"I didn't realize. When I opened the box back at the

cloister, I was closing the breach, so everything I saw was moving backward, and sped up. Like a video rewinding. I'm trying to make sense of it."

Chloe stood there for several seconds, trying to digest it. More noises at the barn, faint crashes and rumbles.

"Is that the second golem?" she demanded.

"I told you, I couldn't see the barn. But what else could it be?"

"I don't know." She pointed back at the motionless heap of the first golem. "Did you see *that* happen?"

"Yes, from far away. I saw the golem rearing up, lifting you. That's when I closed the box. I thought it had captured you. But I was watching it backward. The golem wasn't rising—it was collapsing beneath you."

"That's how you knew I would be able to send the ring."

"Yes, once you showed up with it," he said.

She stomped her foot. He was so *reasonable*, even now. "You should have told us, Horace. You should have said only a few of us would be escaping through the portal."

"You know I can't say everything. Nobody wants that."

"Yeah, well, nobody wants to be stranded in a meadow full of Mordin and golems, either."

"You would have come anyway."

"I know that! Could you just stop being logical for a second and let me be pissed? I mean, what are we supposed to do now?"

Just then, a truly enormous clamor filled the night air, a thunderous cracking and splintering. They both flinched, staring. A cloud of pale dust rose into the night sky beyond the humour. From what Chloe could tell, the ancient barn had collapsed. It had to have been the golem.

Horace looked shocked. He hadn't seen the barn through the Fel'Daera, she knew, so he couldn't have known this would happen. "Joshua and Brian were in there," she said. "And April was headed there too, I think."

Horace shook his head. "If they were, they got out. I told you, I saw them leave through the portal."

"You didn't see April. We need to do something."

Horace shook his head and opened his mouth, but nothing came out.

"What do we do, Horace?" Chloe insisted.

Before he could answer, another voice spoke out of the darkness, a man's voice . . . but not a man. The words had the unmistakable hissing music of the Riven, somehow slippery and brittle at the same time.

"You must come with me, Keepers. That's what you do."

CHAPTER SEVENTEEN

Every Bad Thing

APRIL CREPT THROUGH THE BARN AFTER BARON, TRYING TO ignore the bite of brimstone in her nostrils. She wasn't at all sure she should be doing what she was doing. If there really were Riven here in the barn, she had to distract them, lure them away from Joshua and Brian's hiding place. But also, she had to find Baron. She had to keep him safe too.

She snuck down the narrow corridor and deeper into the mad shadows of the barn, trying not to get lost. Although April knew the barn well, she'd never been in it so late at night. It was very dark, and the ground was packed high from years of manure and compaction, so all the doorways seemed freakishly low.

Baron was somewhere closer to the front of the barn, moving slow. She couldn't see him, couldn't figure out what *he* was seeing. Frustrated and frightened, she let his vision drop out of her mind—her own night eyes were better than his any-way, plus she really shouldn't be using the vine like this. The Riven might detect it, and locate her. Isabel had explained that empaths like April were hard to detect so long as they didn't draw too hard on their instruments, so she tried that now. Quickly she let Baron's presence slip even farther out of her consciousness, sipping at the vine—quiet enough to stay undetected, she hoped, but still loud enough to be useful.

The flow of senses from the dog dropped to a trickle. His mood was still clear, though. He was furious. Frightened, too, and his fear was making him angry. The fear and the smell. *Biting. Stinging. Bad.* She didn't dare call out for him, and it struck her that leaving Joshua and Brian behind was probably not what Gabriel wanted her to do. But if she was their ears and eyes, this was how she could protect them. Warn them. Watch their backs. Find the enemy before the enemy found them.

She crept around a blind corner, through a splintered opening no more than four feet high. There were sounds with her in the barn, she realized. Footsteps, cautious but heavy. With the vine muted, and Baron's keen senses dulled, it was hard to tell—were they near, or were they far? She whipped her head this way and that and then tripped, tumbling to the ground. As she fell, she heard the horrid sound of a sharp claw being dragged along wood, back in the direction she'd come. By the sound of it, it came from the narrow corridor where Brian and Joshua were hiding. Her heart dropped. They were going to be found. She'd messed up.

"Hey," she called out weakly, trying to draw the creature's attention. "Over here."

And then sound exploded around her, inside her. Her throat leapt as Baron started barking, somewhere at the front of the barn. *Fury. Fear.* And on the heels of that, back toward Joshua and Brian, an ear-shattering *crack!* Then the sound of splintering wood, and a large body hitting the ground.

She hardly had time to register that Mr. Meister was here, that he was fighting alongside them now, when Baron's barking cut off violently. He was in trouble. Pain in her jaw, her neck—but again, not really her pain. Without meaning to, she opened the floodgates to the Ravenvine again, to Baron. Through the vine, she felt a huge iron grip seize around her jaw, her midsection. The stench of brimstone in his nose—her nose—was so heavy it made her eyes water. She saw a cruel face, tiny sharp teeth. She understood—a Riven had captured Baron. Grabbed him and hoisted him off the ground, forcing his muzzle shut.

She was on her feet before she knew it. She ran for him. She stumbled through another opening and into the towering loft at the front of the barn. As she ran across the open vault, Mr. Meister fired his weapon again, back at the barn's rear. She had to hope he had things under control. She squeezed out through the barn's huge front door, wedged slightly ajar, and found herself outside beneath the stars.

Her heart nearly stopped. A handful of Mordin stood there. One of them held Baron prisoner against his chest.

He was squeezing the dog's muzzle with one hand while the other was wrapped completely around the dog's gut like a noose. *Terror. Agony. Bite.*

But Baron couldn't bite. He couldn't escape. The Mordin's grip around him was so tight that April herself could hardly breathe.

And now footsteps, thunderous and swift. April fell back as Dr. Jericho rounded the corner of the barn at a full gallop—a terrifying sight. He ate up the ground like a horse, occasionally planting one of his hands as he ran. When he reached the group of Mordin, he slowed and straightened, glancing at Baron and striding right up to April. He smoothed his shirt prissily, almost comically—as if April could forget the beast he'd been a mere second before.

He breathed heavily down at her for several seconds, his great chest heaving. "Our little empath," he sang at her at last. "I thought it might be you. So good of you to return."

He'd sensed her using the vine. No doubt they all had. She'd been stupid.

Dr. Jericho turned to the other Mordin. They exchanged words; he seemed to be interrogating them. One of them handed him something, and he turned back to April, extending a hand as he slipped a huge ring onto a gruesome finger. A red stone glittered.

"Before we go on, let me explain the situation," Dr. Jericho said. "There is no hope for you. You will come with us now."

April saw herself through Baron's crazed eyes. She looked and smelled as frightened as she felt. She tried to settle herself. But now, through his ears, she heard the rattling rustle of a hundred thousand tiny stones, coming from behind her. And through his eyes, a monstrous shape looming over her shoulder. Bigger than a Mordin by far. It stood, rising as high as the barn roof, undulating like a tight flock of birds, a murmuration. She didn't need to turn around. This, she knew, had to be the golem. She was surrounded.

"I've already lost one golem tonight," Dr. Jericho said. "It's always good to have a spare, don't you think?"

"I didn't know you were a pet owner," April said. "That's nice."

"*Na'tola ni chenthi,*" said one of the other Mordin. Except this was not a Mordin's voice. This voice was like daggers and silk, honey and poison. "There is nothing to discuss. Let us convince her."

"Quite right," said Dr. Jericho. He lifted his hand, and the Mordin holding Baron reared back. Pain exploded along April's neck and spine.

And then she felt Baron no more.

April squeezed her eyes shut. The Mordin had killed Baron—torn him in two, maybe. She couldn't feel him.

But something was wrong. Something was . . . off. It wasn't just Baron that was gone. The Ravenvine itself was gone. April couldn't reach it. She wasn't severed, she just . . . couldn't get hold of it. She realized there was a presence in her way, a presence she hadn't noticed in the terror of a few moments ago.

Something had taken control of the Ravenvine. Something she'd felt before.

April opened her eyes. In the Mordin's arms, Baron squirmed helplessly. He was alive. A figure stepped forward—one of the Riven, but not a Mordin after all. This one was shorter, and curvier. Pale blond hair pulled back into a tight braid. A cruel, perfect mouth and bright blue eyes. A triangular red stone gleaming high in a smooth white forehead.

An Auditor.

A mimic. A hijacker. Auditors had no Tan'ji of their own, but instead had the ability to draw on the power of any Tan'ji around them. And this one had done so now, taking control of the Ravenvine so thoroughly that she'd pushed April clean out of it.

"You were right, Ja'raka," said the Auditor to Dr. Jericho, slinking closer like a tiger. Her blue eyes flashed. "Our little empath, back again."

"So many tasty morsels tonight," said Dr. Jericho. "Some slip away. Others do not."

April was not prone to anger. She was a reasonable person who believed in more constructive emotions. But sometimes, being pissed off was the right thing to be. She bundled her rage and reached for the vine. The Auditor was ready for it, though, and too strong. She kept April at bay, maintaining her stranglehold on the vine's power. Meanwhile April could hear the golem behind her, slithering closer. It swept over her feet, gripping her ankles in a liquid vise.

And then, inexplicably, the Auditor staggered back, her blue eyes widening. April felt a loose spot in the Auditor's grip on the vine—almost as if it had been pried open from the outside—and she poured herself into it, back into the Raven-vine. She tried to oust the Auditor from it completely, but couldn't. The Auditor held on with an angry shriek, still cling-ing to a share of the vine's powers.

At almost the same moment, the Mordin holding Baron cried out and crumpled, clutching at his back and falling to his knees. He spilled Baron onto the ground, even as April opened her mind to the dog's again. *Fear. Shame. Hurt.* Baron scampered a few steps away and then rounded on the Auditor, snapping at her, more out of fear and desperation than any-thing else. The Auditor drew back.

And now Dr. Jericho sank awkwardly to one knee, shak-ing his head. The golem's grip around April's legs loosened and fell away. Two other Mordin staggered back, groaning. What was happening?

"Run!"

April turned toward this new voice. Isabel stood in the barn door, her red hair ghostly copper in the starlight. She glared at Dr. Jericho, her face crumpled with fury. She held an unfamiliar white disk in her hands. Her eyes flicked to April.

"Run!" she yelled again. "I can't do more than I already have!"

Dr. Jericho was already getting back to his feet. April ran toward the barn, toward Isabel. Baron sprinted past her. She could hear the golem gathering itself behind, the Auditor shouting, footsteps pounding. Just as April reached the barn door, the golem swung a mighty arm at her, tripping her heavily. But in the same motion, it tore loose a section of wall. The doorway began to collapse. April and Isabel dove into the high loft of the barn, with Baron scooting ahead, just as the heavy beam above the door and a section of wall thundered to the ground behind them, sealing the narrow way in with a thick tangle of wreckage.

April clambered to her feet. A few hundred slick golem stones had been cut off from the rest. They lay scattered across the floor, lifeless. Meanwhile Dr. Jericho and the other Riven roared and pounded outside, tearing at the timber, but they couldn't get in.

"I came to get you," said Isabel, rising. "We're leaving. Joshua's going to—"

April pressed her hand against the woman's mouth, laid a finger against her own lips. She tipped her eyes meaningfully down at Baron. The Auditor was still inside the Ravenvine, and therefore—infuriatingly—still inside Baron's mind. She could see and hear everything.

"Go," said April, tipping her head.

They turned to go. They hadn't gone twenty feet when the roof high above them splintered. Baron scrambled back as a fist the size of a boulder, seemingly made of smoke and stone, pounded into the ground just in front of them. Debris rained down on April's head. The golem had broken through the roof.

Stretched from the floor to the high ceiling like a tree, the golem began to sprout tentacles, thick fingers of rock that grew swiftly like airborne rivers of oil, surrounding them. Isabel grabbed a loose plank and swung at one of the tentacles. She knocked a gaping hole in it, stones flying in all directions, but the writhing tendril healed itself instantaneously. It wrapped around her legs. She swung again and briefly broke loose.

April scrabbled in the dirt at her feet and found a heavy length of some old farm implement, a huge pipe thick with rust and jagged at one end. She swung wildly, struggling to keep her balance, fighting off the golem's ever-encroaching arms. Meanwhile, the main body of the golem loomed thirty feet overhead, rising up to the ceiling like a black wave. Why didn't it just swallow them up?

April fought on. Baron barked and leapt. They would never get away. This was a battle April wasn't prepared for. This was Gabriel's territory—or better yet, Chloe's. She looked up into the rafters, sure that at any moment the golem would crash down upon them, overpowering them. Through the vine, she caught wind of a pair of mourning doves up there, frightened out of their slumber by all the commotion. As she fought, she opened herself to the eyes of one of them.

From that vantage point, high above the ground, she saw

that the roof was in shambles. Already decrepit, the golem had smashed it beyond repair. In fact, it looked like the golem was holding the broken roof aloft. April wondered if the towering golem might not be the only thing keeping the barn standing at all. But why would it bother? Why not let the barn collapse and crush them all?

"They want us alive," April shouted.

"They want *you* alive," called Isabel.

April hardly knew if that was true—or *why* it would be true—but it gave her a fiendish idea. A crazy idea, but the only one she had. She beat the golem back from her legs and lurched away. She raised the rusted pipe to her own throat and pressed the jagged end against her flesh. "They won't take me alive," she said loudly, hearing her voice through Baron's ears, knowing the Auditor would hear it too. "I'm ending it. Now."

Isabel froze. In a flash, the golem coalesced and went for April, striking like a snake. It swarmed over her, seizing her arm and knocking the pipe free. And as it did—as it withdrew from the roof high overhead—the barn gave out a slow, screeching wail. Something massive snapped, like the limb of a tree in a deep freeze. And then with a splintering, thundering bellow, the barn came down.

It was the golem that saved her—that saved them all. The body of the thing took the brunt of the collapse. April was thrown sideways, carried with the golem's body as easily as a stick down a river. A river of blinding, crushing mud. As she slid, she reached out for Baron through the vine. The Auditor was gone—had she been crushed? As for Baron, he too was buried and sliding, just feet away, but he was okay. With effort, April cut off the vine entirely, hoping the Riven would think she was dead.

She bumped up against something hard, banging her hip painfully. The rocky current twisted her, pinning her arm behind her back. At last they came to a stop. The golem's stones were loose around her, and she began to dig her way out. Baron was on her in an instant, snuffling around her face. A slab of timber had pinned her legs, but she was mostly unhurt. She wrenched her legs free and dragged herself into the long grass.

Dr. Jericho was roaring angrily somewhere beyond the rubble at the front of the barn. He, at least, had not been crushed in the collapse. And what about Isabel? For that matter, what about Joshua and the others? Had they gotten out the back of the barn in time, or had she made a terrible mistake?

But there was no time to fret. She had to get away. She crawled on her belly as quickly and quietly as she could. She'd spilled out onto the west side of the barn, where there was a little stream lined with trees fifty yards ahead—Winding Creek, it was called. If she could get to it, she could hide.

Baron seemed to understand the need for quiet. He slunk low at her side as she crawled. She desperately wanted to reach out to him, to use his nose and ears, but was too afraid.

She would remain blind—or human, anyway—until she got farther away.

She kept her own ears open as best she could. Briefly, she thought she heard voices around the back of the barn, human voices—surely the others had gotten out, right? But she also heard Mordin running. The best she could say about that was that none of them came her way.

She kept crawling. At last, after maybe a full minute, and without any signs of pursuit, she reached the creek. Although it was true that Winding Creek did in fact wind in places, here beside the meadow it ran almost straight north and south. Though the water was barely a foot deep and only a few feet wide, the banks were just steep enough, and the grass tall enough, to completely hide her. She hunkered down at the water's edge, peering back over the meadow. Baron lay down beside her, exhausted. Her eyes slid over the spot where the humour sat. Gabriel was still there. She had to hope the others had gotten out of the barn and were safe inside the humour now.

From this angle, she could see past the slippery blur of the humour and deeper into the meadow. Almost straight in that direction, a half mile to the north, was her house. It seemed almost too incredible to imagine. No one would be there now, her brother and uncle having taken refuge with a friend of the family. She could hardly imagine how Uncle Harrison must be explaining all this to himself. As she stared past the humour into the night, thinking about the word "family," she realized she saw light. A distant dot of bright rich blue, moving very slightly like a hovering firefly, deep in the dark meadow. She stood up without thinking, peering at it, but almost at once she lost sight of it. The gleaming blue dot winked out.

Her skin tingled with a desperate hope, threatening to melt her. Horace's jithandra. What else could it be? That must be him, out there in the meadow. She squinted to catch a glimpse of it again.

Suddenly a massive crumpling sound tore through the air, much closer by. The humour vanished, and the huge swath of meadow at the back of the barn sprang into sight. April dropped to a crouch, her heart a hammer. In the newly exposed patch of meadow, she saw the shadows of several Riven—including Dr. Jericho, who must have galloped around from the front of the barn after it collapsed. Another Mordin lay on the ground at Dr. Jericho's feet, wailing in pain.

Mordin, yes. Six or seven by April's count.

But no humans.

No one at all.

CHAPTER EIGHTEEN

Leavings

MR. MEISTER GRABBED JOSHUA AND HAULED HIM TO HIS FEET. "Run!" he cried, as the barn began to collapse around them.

Mr. Meister dragged Joshua behind him and pushed Brian ahead, out of the stall. Joshua didn't know an old man could have such strength. They stumbled clear of the little room just as it caved in, then staggered out the corridor in a rush, heading toward the back entrance of the barn, the way they'd come in. The walls began to buckle too, and the doorway began to lean, threatening to trap them. Brian struggled, half shuffling, handcuffed as he was. Tunraden banged against his knees.

The noise around them pounded at Joshua's ears. A huge beam crashed down, nearly striking them. With a groan, the doorway they were sprinting for suddenly gave way, tumbling like a badly built tower of bricks just as they were nearly upon it. It was so loud, Joshua barely heard the crack of Mr. Meister's weapon as he fired it for a third time. The slumping debris in the doorway exploded outward. Together they stumbled through the newly made opening. Brian fell into the grass painfully. Joshua skipped over him and turned to watch as the entire barn went down in a cloud of dust.

"It is time," Mr. Meister said, even as the dust still rose into the sky. "Our hand has been dealt to us." He picked Brian off the ground and turned to Joshua.

"Use the Laithe, Joshua. Get us out. Take us anywhere."

"But I—"

"Anywhere. And you must be swift. Dr. Jericho is attuned to the Laithe, do you understand? Sensitive to it. That's how he found you in the first place. He will sense it when you use it, and he will come running. With or without Ingrid, he will find us in no time."

Joshua nodded, as frightened as he'd ever been. He fumbled with the Laithe, but he was so nervous he couldn't get the sphere to center on North America.

A Mordin came around the corner of the collapsed barn. And then another. But instead of firing his weapon, Mr. Meister shoved Joshua and Brian forward into the nothingness that lay in front of them—into the humour.

All sight dropped away. Mr. Meister kept pushing them on, deeper into the silent gloom. But it wasn't silent. There was sound here now. A shrill melody that grabbed Joshua, seeming to crawl across his skin. Ingrid's flute.

"Gabriel!" Mr. Meister called.

Gabriel's voice came at them, from everywhere at once. He sounded exhausted. "Here. I'm nearly done, though. I can't stop her any longer."

"It doesn't matter. We have what we need."

"Keep moving," Gabriel said. "There are Mordin behind you. Two of them. No—three now."

"Dr. Jericho?"

"Not yet."

"He will come soon enough. Joshua is going to open a portal. Have the others returned?"

"No. I've been alone in the humour with Ingrid, keeping her lost, keeping her busy. Dr. Jericho was after me for a while too, but then he left in a hurry. What happened to April?"

"I do not know. I fear that Dr. Jericho went after her, but I sent Isabel to help. Let us hope she does."

"And Horace and Chloe?" asked Gabriel.

"I have seen no sign, and do not expect we will. We must leave without them."

There was a pause. Joshua thought his heart would break. *Leave without the others?*

"We cannot leave," said Gabriel. "Horace said he saw—"

"Horace told us what he wanted us to know, and no more," Mr. Meister said sternly. "His exact words, I believe, were 'People get away.'"

People, Joshua thought. *But not everyone.* He waited for someone to say something else. The humour was silent except for the clinging, searching melody of Ingrid's flute. Mr. Meister wanted Joshua to open a portal here, so that he and Brian could escape. But there was no sign of Horace, or Chloe, or April. If Joshua opened a portal now and left, he'd be leaving them behind.

At last Gabriel spoke. "If the others stay, I stay," he said firmly. "You go. Get Tunraden and the Laithe away."

"But the Riven are everywhere!" Joshua cried, unable to help himself.

"All the more reason for me to stay."

"I can't do it," Brian said suddenly. "I can't leave them. I can't leave Gabriel."

"You will send help," Gabriel said. "Now move. Keep moving. Ingrid is with a Mordin. They are coming for you."

They shuffled forward again, fast as they dared. Joshua rubbed his arm, as if he could rub the sound of Ingrid's flute away.

"Behind you!" Gabriel cried. "Here!"

The crack of Mr. Meister's weapon rocked through the humour.

"One down," said Gabriel. "But two more have joined us. You must hurry."

Mr. Meister's unseen hands gripped Joshua by the arms. "Get the portal ready, Joshua. Think of a place. Let the Laithe *be* that place. Gabriel will tell us when we're clear."

But Joshua, panicking, could only think of *every* place. A frozen lake in Canada, a desert in South America, a farm in Madagascar. Nowhere he could actually take them. Why wouldn't his brain work?

"Tell me where," he said.

"No. You are the Keeper of the Laithe. You decide. Only you can get us away."

His mind still wouldn't focus. But as he thought of a thousand places they could never go, his eyes straining uselessly to see the Laithe, he realized that the Laithe was listening to him. It was shifting with his thoughts, spinning, trying to find the destination he wanted it to find.

"I am the Keeper of the Laithe," he mumbled to himself. "Only I can get us away." But he wasn't sure he believed it.

And suddenly the obvious solution came to him. He would take them back—back the way he'd come. A place he could go, a place he had been. He was stupid not to think of it sooner. No sooner had he thought the thought than he felt the Laithe shift again. It was over North America now, over the Midwest. He fumbled for the golden rabbit and grabbed it, sliding it around the unseen meridian. It seemed to almost want to move on its own, to listen to him.

In his mind, Joshua saw what he knew the Laithe was now revealing—Illinois, endless grids of cornfields, Chicago. On and on he slid the rabbit, around the bottom of the meridian. Block after block of houses, growing closer. A winding river in a blanket of green—the north branch of the Chicago River. And now a park, with green trees, a ribbon of water inside. A particular grove of trees beside a green meadow. Down and down, under the canopy. A cloister, and leafy ground.

At last the rabbit reached the top again. Joshua had done it. He knew he was there. *They* were there, he and the Laithe both.

"I have it," he tried to say, but the words would barely form. "I have it," he said again.

"Open the portal," said Gabriel. "They're coming for you."

"Now, Joshua!" Mr. Meister shouted.

Joshua tore the meridian free. He set it into the air and, in the same motion, spun it. Not hard, not hard at all. But *perfectly*. The rabbit ran. He could see it in his mind, feel it in his flesh. The rabbit ran, and the portal widened. He heard a gasp of wonder, like a rush of wind, and realized it was Gabriel. Was he seeing now as the portal opened? What could he feel?

One spin was enough. Joshua knew it would be. The portal slammed open wide, and he almost imagined he could see the blue eyes of the rabbit, high atop it.

"Go," Joshua said. "Here." As he spoke, Ingrid's flute got louder. It was in his ears, in his brain. He reached out blindly and found Brian's arm. He yanked him toward the portal and pushed him rudely through with all his might. He felt him go, felt Tunraden pass through the barrier.

"Mordin!" Gabriel shouted. "Go, go!"

Joshua groped until he caught the wrinkled hand of Mr. Meister. Joshua had to go last. He was the Keeper of the Laithe, wasn't he? He shoved Mr. Meister through.

"Jump!" Gabriel shouted.

Just as Joshua jumped, someone grabbed his arm. Not a Mordin, though—this was a human hand. It had to be Ingrid. Joshua fumed with rage. Ingrid filled him with rage. Why would she do this? He swiped out, and caught a handful of hair. He pulled with all his might, swinging. He tripped, but she tripped too, and let him go. He felt another pulse from the portal—she'd fallen through. He dove after her, trying to steer his own fall through the portal, the Laithe tucked under his arm. The electric tingle of the portal washed over him. In the split second before he made it all the way through, another hand grazed his foot. Joshua tucked into a ball, tumbling, escaping. He fell into a quiet forest, green and soft. He hit the ground and looked back.

The portal hung in the air, opening back into the meadow, into the humour. But for some reason the humour wasn't there. Or maybe it was—a kind of smoky curtain across everything, like a thick silver fog, but not so thick that Joshua couldn't see. A Mordin knelt on the ground, clutching his hand. Joshua looked down at his own feet—here, on the forest side—and scrambled away. Three long fingers lay on the grass like dead snakes. Fingers. Sliced clean by the closing portal. Mr. Meister swept in and scooped the awful things up, shoving them into a pocket.

"Close it," the old man said. In his other hand, he held Ingrid's white flute. Ingrid herself lay at his feet, breathing hard, shocked and furious.

"He'll find you again," Ingrid said. "He always will." She lay on the ground beside Joshua, nodding up at the portal.

Joshua looked. Dr. Jericho stood on the other side, breathing hard. His eyes simmered like angry black suns, but of course he couldn't really see them—still in the humour, he couldn't even see the portal itself. But he could clearly feel it.

"I told you," Ingrid said. "He'll find the friends you left behind, and then he'll find you. All this—"

"Shut up," said Brian. He stood a little ways back, Tunraden at his feet.

"Seconded," said a new voice. Joshua rolled to see. There was a woman here in the woods. Horace's mom, of all people. "My son isn't coming back this way," she said to Joshua. "Close the portal."

"Horace is alive, Jessica," Mr. Meister said gently. "He is with friends. Powerful friends."

Ingrid laughed.

"This was the future he saw," said Horace's mother. "You heard it as well as I did, Henry." She looked down at Joshua. "Close it now, Keeper. Close it."

Joshua got to his knees in front of the portal. Dr. Jericho was still glaring at it, a tower of fury now, just inches away. Miles away. Joshua spun the meridian, letting the rabbit run. As it shrank, the humour winked out of sight on the other side—Gabriel had taken it down. Dr. Jericho reared back, letting out a bellow of rage that Joshua almost imagined he could hear. The Mordin tore off his jacket and shirt, seeming to grow, suddenly looking a foot taller and twice as savage as he had a moment ago. He roared and roared as the portal shrank. Too slow, too slow, but Joshua couldn't move.

Beyond Dr. Jericho now, more movement. Half a dozen more Mordin loped into view. An Auditor. And then, from the wreckage of the barn beyond them all, movement. The rubble began to shift. A golem rose slowly from it. Horace's mother watched, her face like stone.

At last the tumbling tunnel of shapes appeared, and the horrible scene at the meadow vanished. The rabbit finished running. Numbly, Joshua plucked the meridian out of the air and brought it home to the Laithe. A nugget of hurt swelled in his gut then, so heavy and hard he thought he might collapse into it, into a ball of nothing.

"We have to go back," he said, gripping the Laithe.

Mr. Meister shook his head. "We cannot risk it, Keeper. Even if you open another portal, no one can come through it from the other side unless you go back yourself. But Dr. Jericho will reach the portal—and you—long before any of our friends."

"*Very* long before," Ingrid muttered coldly. "He hears you coming like a train."

"Kind of like your mouth," said Brian.

Joshua glared at Ingrid. She had dirty blond hair and blue eyes. She had a bloody nose, too. Joshua was pretty sure he'd done that, kicking out in the humour. He was glad.

"I don't care," Joshua said. "I need to go get them."

289

"I will not allow it," said Mr. Meister.

"I doesn't matter. I'm not a Warden."

"Joshua," said Horace's mother gently. "Keeper."

He looked up at her. She wasn't alone. Arthur the raven stalked at her feet, watching Joshua with his black marble eyes. Joshua wrapped his arms around his knees and buried his face.

April.

Horace's mom knelt down in front of him. "Horace knew what he was doing, Joshua. He went there knowing he wouldn't come back this way—him or the others. Not at this time or in this place, anyway."

Joshua shoved the Laithe away. "Well if he knew what he was doing, I sure don't."

"You will. And soon. Do you know why?"

Joshua shook his head.

"Because when the time is right, you will find Horace, and our friends. And you will bring them back home."

CHAPTER NINETEEN

The Stranger in the Field

"YOU MUST COME WITH ME, KEEPERS. THAT'S WHAT YOU DO."

Horace whirled around in the long grass to face the slippery, whispering voice. A tall dark figure in a long black robe stood there in the meadow—far too tall, with long sinewy limbs.

Horace fell back, scrambling to pull the phalanx from his pocket. He and Chloe had escaped from the golem only to be found by one of the Riven—a Mordin, by the look of it, though it was short for a Mordin. Horace laid the tip against the Fel'Daera, drawing power from the box and filling the phalanx. He drew back his hand to fire at the Riven, to pin it in place, but then suddenly the Mordin shifted and . . . split.

There were two Riven now, identical. They stepped swiftly apart in unison, covering ground as only the long-legged Mordin could. In an instant, they were twenty feet apart, flanking Horace and Chloe left and right.

"Oh, what the hell?" Chloe snarled, crouching low, her angry eyes darting back and forth between the two intruders. But a moment later, one of the shadowy figures shimmered and winked out of existence.

"Peace, please," said the one that remained.

Horace clutched the phalanx, but didn't fire. "How did you do that?"

The figure spread his enormous arms. "How does any Keeper do what they do?"

Horace realized that something was missing. The stranger had no smell—no stench of brimstone. He squinted at the figure, trying to make sense of it.

"You're not a Keeper," Chloe said. "You're a Riven."

"So it may seem," the newcomer said, "but I assure you I am not." He stepped forward, arms still spread and huge hands open in a gesture of truce. "I am what the Riven once were."

Horace straightened, the words catching him like a forgotten memory. He pulled his jithandra out of his shirt, releasing its blue light. The tall figure crouched down gracefully in the grass, letting the light illuminate him.

Horace's mouth fell open.

"Oh, mother," Chloe breathed.

He was . . . beautiful.

Pale skin, porcelain smooth, and high chiseled cheeks. His mouth was a delicate slit with a faint—and friendly? —curve to it. His hands, hanging between his legs, were the size of magazines. Just like the Riven, he had an extra knuckle on each finger. But whereas the deformity looked hideous on the likes of Dr. Jericho, here the fingers seemed unspeakably graceful and dizzyingly functional, as if they were the perfect dreams of stubby, useless little fingers like Horace's. And on one of those long fingers sat a gray ring with a wide green stone, unmistakably Tanu.

But most of all . . . the eyes. His eyelids had not one but two extra folds of skin, each one angled in the opposite direction of the other, in a way that made him look both happy and cross at the same time. And the eyes themselves were bigger than a Mordin's beady ones, but just as black. Yet around that blackness was a startling ring of brightness—white? blue? silver?—that caught Horace's gaze and held it fast.

"If you've gotten your fill, douse your light," the stranger said.

Horace tucked his jithandra back into his shirt. "You're Altari," he said breathlessly.

"I am. I'm a Warden. My name is Dailen."

"*You're* a Warden?" Chloe asked incredulously.

"We're Wardens too," said Horace.

"I gathered," said Dailen. "Where is the Laithe?"

"Joshua has it," Horace said, confused. "He's going. He's going right now." If Horace had his times right, the portal was now open. In another few seconds, Joshua would be following Brian and Mr. Meister back to the riverside cloister.

Dailen didn't even ask what Horace meant by that. "You are not the Keeper of the Laithe?"

"What? No, I'm . . ." Horace lifted up his shirt, revealing the Fel'Daera at his side. Dailen looked puzzled, clearly not recognizing it. Horace, embarrassed, hardly knew what to say.

"It's the Box of Promises," Chloe said. "You know. Horace is the Keeper of the Fel'Daera."

Now Dailen's brows shot up high. His eyelids disappeared, his mesmerizing eyes growing round and wide.

"The Fel'Daera," he whispered, and then his gaze grew sharp again. He leaned in close to Horace. "We must get you away. Come with me."

"Not likely," said Chloe.

Horace ignored her. "Come with you where?"

Just then, a crumpling tear crackled across the meadow, from up near the barn. Gabriel had taken the humour down. Two loud cries instantly sprang to life, laid bare now that the humour was gone. A long, wailing shriek that sounded like a Mordin in pain. And then an animal roar of anger that Horace knew in his bones was Dr. Jericho. This, he had no doubt, was the roar he'd witnessed through the box. The other Wardens were gone. The portal was closed.

"Gabriel and April are still up there," Chloe said. "We need to help them."

"There is no time," Dailen said. "Come with me if you want to escape."

Chloe shook her head. "I don't want to escape. I want to

help my friends. And I don't even know who you are."

Now there were shouts from up at the barn, the rasping calls of the Riven. There was a low clattering rumble, big as a train. Horace watched in horror as the second golem, unseen until now, rose out of the ruin of the barn. Gaunt shadows crept across the grass, at least a half dozen, and now some of them turned and headed into the meadow, coming this way.

"Chloe, come on," Horace pleaded. "He's Altari. He's a Warden."

Chloe gritted her teeth. "Fine," she said. "But if we're abandoning people, I'm not leaving them with two golems to fight." The wings of the dragonfly became a blur, and she spun and sprinted back toward the silent pile of the fallen golem.

"What is she doing?" Dailen said sharply.

"What she always does," said Horace, watching Chloe, his heart a hammer in his chest. Just as Chloe reached the pile, a Mordin leapt over the top of it, directly at her, arms outstretched like a great bat. She didn't even flinch. The Mordin pounced on her, clutching at her uselessly. It passed right through her and rolled to a stop, scattering stones across the grass. Chloe vanished into the pile at a run, and the Mordin scrambled after her, digging out huge scoops of stones with his shovel-sized hands, like a badger trying to dig out a rabbit. Hardly thinking, Horace whipped the phalanx at it, releasing its power—a burst of light, and a soft *thup!*

Dailen cried out in surprise. The Mordin, crouched on

its hands and knees like a nightmarishly giant cricket, wailed and arched its back as it was pinned in place. It flailed angrily, spitting out foul-sounding words.

Horace put the tip of the phalanx against the box again, drawing power for another shot. Meanwhile Dailen was already surging toward the pinned Mordin. With three great strides, he nearly covered the distance, just as another Mordin rounded the pile at a run. And then, so smoothly Horace didn't really see how it happened, Dailen split again, his single tall form becoming two. One Dailen veered swiftly across the path of the running Mordin, luring it leftward, while the other leapt at the Mordin pinned beside the golem.

With an angry roar, the running Mordin swerved and lunged at the Dailen on the left. It tackled him, diving, but Dailen's figure vanished, leaving the Mordin to tumble to the ground empty-handed. In the same instant, the other Dailen—the real Dailen?—landed hard, with both feet, on the back of the Mordin Horace had just pinned. There was a sickening, fleshy crunch as the Mordin was driven to the ground. It lay there motionless.

Chloe shot out of the pile, something wrapped in the hem of her shirt. The golem's heart. She stopped when she saw Dailen standing atop the fallen Mordin. Her face wrinkled with distaste. The other Mordin, meanwhile, found its feet and began to charge. Horace fired the phalanx again, sure he would miss the moving target, but he got lucky. The Mordin slammed to a halt with a fierce grunt, head and limbs snapping forward violently, as if it had reached the end of an invisible chain anchored to its spine.

"No more bravery," Dailen told Chloe. "Run." And then he stepped off the fallen Mordin's back—both to the left and the right, doubling again.

Chloe ran past him, racing to Horace's side. He frowned down at the glint of scarlet peeking out of her bundled shirt. "I had to," she said, seeing his expression. "The ring is coming back."

The two Dailens looked back at them. "Run," they said again, the word coming out of both mouths at once. "Now."

No sooner had he spoken than the pile of the golem exploded, slick black stones showering into the air. For a moment, Horace thought it was destroying itself because Chloe had stolen its heart, but then a huge dark figure waded powerfully out of the heap, swinging its massive arms like wrecking balls, spraying stones in great black waves.

"No more!" the figure thundered. *Kal nadra!*

Dr. Jericho.

But this was Dr. Jericho as Horace had never seen him, darker and more horrifying by far. His mouth, always frightening, had become a terrifying shark's mouth, wide and cruel and full of dagger-sharp teeth. Curls of smoke seemed to trail from his coal-black eyes. He wore no shirt or jacket, and bristling spines rose from his back like poisonous thorns. He stormed through what was left of the golem and stood heaving in front of the two Dailens, looming two or three feet taller than the Altari, and twice as broad. Horace's chest wouldn't loosen to let him breathe.

"*Dak shinti Altari peshtu,*" Dr. Jericho snarled at the two Dailens.

"*Muk'levra gosht, Kesh'kiri,*" the Dailens replied in unison. "*Mikanti fro'da ji kota.*" And then the Dailens leapt back, both mirrored figures in perfect harmony. But as they leapt, they each split again.

Four Dailens now stood in an arc around the raging Dr. Jericho, crouching warily just out of the Mordin's reach. Which one was the *real* Dailen?

"*Ta'lendra vox,*" Dr. Jericho sang, swiveling his fearsome head on his long neck as the Dailens began to circle him, moving haphazardly this time instead of in unison. And now Horace had to blink—suddenly there were *eight* Dailens, spreading out around the fearsome Mordin.

"*Akhentra!*" Dr. Jericho spat, lashing out with heart-stopping speed at one of the Dailens. His great clawed hand raked across Dailen's chest, and seemed for a split second to catch flesh, but the Dailen winked immediately out of existence.

"This is heavy stuff," Chloe whispered, the tremble in her voice unmistakable. "I think we're seeing the big boys play now."

Horace couldn't speak. He tugged her sleeve and forced himself to turn and run.

Chloe followed him. They stumbled through the long

grass. Horace did his best to ignore Dr. Jericho's blade-sharp howls, and the growing rumble that told him the second golem had joined the battle.

And then suddenly Dailen was with them—one of him, anyway, loping easily alongside. "Head for that tall willow tree at the meadow's edge," he said, pointing. "There's a creek. Hide and wait for me there. Don't use your instruments."

"What are you going to do?" Horace asked him, breathless, but before he even finished the sentence, Dailen winked out of existence.

"How does he do that?" Horace asked, marveling.

"Don't know, don't want to know," Chloe said.

They ran for the creek. It was farther than it looked, the willow Dailen had pointed to much taller than it seemed. At last they reached the creek, a spindly little thing. A farm field lay beyond it, acres of soybeans stretched out beneath the starlight. They hunkered down beneath the dangled crown of the great willow, breathing hard.

"Now what?" said Chloe.

"Now we wait. We hope for the best."

"Professionally speaking, Horace, that's a terrible comment coming from someone who can see the future."

They'd come a long ways, far from the battle behind. Horace couldn't see a thing. But by the sound of it, the Riven were spreading out across the meadow. Suddenly, something came running at them from up the creek bed. Horace whirled around just as April's dog trotted up. He splashed happily across the water, wagging his tail and snuffling at them.

"April's dog," Chloe said.

"Baron," said Horace. "Hey, Baron. Where's April?"

Chloe peered around, as if April might be close by.

Horace didn't think so. He and Chloe had made a commotion, sprinting over here. But it occurred to him that April might be in the dog's head right now. And if she was, she'd be able to hear them.

"Hello?" he said to the dog, feeling a little insane. "Can you hear us?"

Chloe frowned as if he really were as insane as he felt, but then her mouth became an O. "I get it. Walkie-talkie dog." She leaned over Baron. "April? Are you there?"

"We're being dumb," Horace said. "The dog can't talk. Questions won't help." He grabbed the dog gently by the jowls, turning its head to and fro. "We're in the creek," he explained. "Under this big willow, if you can see it. We found a friend. Get here if you can."

Baron tolerated it for a few seconds, but then he wrenched his head away, staring back up the creek. He gave a little whine, and then sprinted off the way he'd come.

"You think she's okay?" said Chloe, watching him go.

"I don't know."

Out in the meadow, the battle sounds had died away, but he could still hear the golem rumbling over the grass. Twice, a Riven's shout cut through the night air.

"You told that dog we found a friend," Chloe said.

"He got us away from the Riven. What would you call him?"

"You trust him?"

"Why wouldn't I?"

"He killed that Mordin," said Chloe. "He slammed it to the ground, but its Tan'ji was still pinned in the air. It tore clean out of its body."

Horace tried not to imagine it. "Seems like that should make us trust him *more*," he said, half to himself.

Chloe didn't respond. He let silence fill their waiting. Thirty seconds. Forty-five. At last footsteps approached, crunching through the grass. The stride was far too long and heavy to be human. Horace gripped the phalanx hard.

"Keepers?" said a soft voice, questing. Dailen.

Horace stood up, stepping out of the shadows. "Here."

"You are safe? And your instruments too?"

"We're fine," said Horace.

"Across the creek, then. Not far now."

"Not far till what?" said Chloe.

Dailen didn't answer. He stepped across the little creek in a single stride. Horace and Chloe followed, wading into the leafy green soybean plants beyond.

"What happened with the Riven?"

"I scattered them as wide as I could, luring them in different directions, but they'll figure it out. They will find our trail soon enough."

"What about Dr. Jericho?" Chloe said.

Dailen shook his head. "I cannot defeat Ja'raka Sevlo alone, even when I diverge," he said. "I can only mislead him—for a little while, at least. And I ran into other difficulties, too. There is an Auditor with them. And the golem."

Horace looked back, half expecting to see a white-haired Auditor looming out of the darkness, or perhaps the thin man's gaping mouth and bristling shoulders. "Why did Dr. Jericho look like that?" he asked. "I've never seen him look so . . . horrible before."

"He revealed himself as he truly is. He was too angry to keep up even the semblance of a disguise." Dailen touched a great hand to his chest as he walked, then looked down at his palm. "Far too angry." When he dropped his arm again, Horace saw a dark stain on his fingers.

"You're hurt," he said, remembering how Dr. Jericho had seemed to swipe the Altari's chest. "But . . . that wasn't really you, was it?"

"I am always really myself," Dailen replied absently, waving Horace off. "But sometimes I do not stop being myself quite quickly enough." He came to a halt. "We are there."

"We're *where*?" said Chloe. There was nothing ahead of them but wide-open field, acre upon acre of low, leafy soybeans.

And then an enormous rustle hissed in Horace's ears, like a whispering crowd. Just ahead, the ground seemed to come to life and lift into the air. A mossy green mass rose to the top of the soybeans, a kind of latticework forty feet long and forty feet wide. Swiftly it resolved itself into a kind of platform, filling in the gaps and rippling like water in slow motion.

Horace, mesmerized, went up close. The shifting slab,

two feet thick, was made of tiny not-quite-round shapes, thousands of them. It whispered swishily, like a forest full of leaves rubbing together. For the second time tonight, Horace was reminded of the golem. But this time—unlike with the scythewings in Sanguine Hall—Horace felt no sense of dread. Far from it.

Dailen strode past him and stepped up onto the green platform. It seemed to give just slightly under his feet, but held firm. He walked to the middle and sat, folding his great legs beneath him. He watched them with his brightly ringed eyes, waiting silently.

From far behind them, harsh shouting. Unmistakably the Riven again, speaking in their own slashing tongue. Now distant footsteps, and the crashing rumble of the golem, coming closer.

"Are you going to fight the golem?" Chloe asked. "You and this . . . thing?"

"The mal'gama was not made for fighting. Hurry now. Come to the center."

Horace climbed onto the sliding blanket of stones. They were slightly fuzzy, almost furred. He crawled across them on his hands and knees to Dailen's side. Chloe, meanwhile, marched onto the platform and then refused to sit, looking back at the approaching Mordin behind, their dark swift shapes visible now. Out in front, the golem was a thundering brute, surging toward them like a giant molten bear.

"They're coming," Chloe said. "Is this thing going to

protect us, or what?" At her chest, the Alvalaithen came suddenly to life, wings blurring madly.

"The mal'gama will protect us, yes," Dailen sang. "But just to be safe, I recommend not using your particular Tan'ji just now. I also recommend sitting."

Chloe scowled. The dragonfly's wings went still, but she remained standing. Behind them, the golem crashed through the little creek, spraying water and flinging mud. The towering form of Dr. Jericho ran at its side, eating up the ground with huge, furious strides, his monstrous teeth bared.

"You better be right about this," Chloe said.

"I think he is," said Horace.

"Thank you, Keeper," Dailen said calmly. "I believe I am."

The next instant, the mal'gama launched itself into the air, taking them with it in a burst of speed that shoved Horace's breath down into his chest.

CHAPTER TWENTY

Stranded

APRIL CROUCHED ON THE CREEK BANK WITH BARON, NOT SURE what to believe. The humour was gone, and there were no humans inside—no Joshua, no Brian, no Gabriel. The Mordin on the ground was still crying out in pain. Beside him, Dr. Jericho stood tall, seeming to stare intently at something right in front of him.

And then April spotted it. She could barely see it. A glittering ring of gold, hanging in the air. She knew at once it was a portal.

As she watched, the portal began to shrink. Suddenly she understood—whichever of her friends had been in the humour before it came down, they were gone now. Escaped through the portal. Dr. Jericho watched the portal shrink too, apparently unable to stop it, and then he threw his head back, tearing off his jacket and shirt. He let out an enraged roar that made her cower, even here, far away. She caught a glint of blue on his back. Somehow he seemed to grow even taller. Meanwhile the portal kept shrinking, and before long April couldn't see it at all.

The portal was closed. The others had vanished. She'd been left behind.

Dr. Jericho, towering and mad, went on roaring.

April wanted to roar too. The others had left without her. Joshua, at the very least, had escaped from the barn and gotten out through a portal in the humour. Probably Brian too, and Mr. Meister. And even Gabriel—had the humour disappeared because he was gone now?

She wasn't sure if she was outraged at being left behind, or relieved that at least someone got away. She watched as the Mordin advanced into the meadow, some of them at a run. She saw the hated Auditor among them. There were almost a dozen Riven headed deeper into the meadow now, and she found herself hoping that the blue light she'd seen out there hadn't been Horace after all.

Two of the Riven, including the injured one, stayed behind near the barn. April realized with a sinking heart— losing a hope she hadn't even thought to have yet—that they must be guarding the falkrete circle. She didn't have much chance of getting home that way.

The wreckage of the barn began to creak ominously. Slowly, terribly, the golem April and Isabel had battled rose up out of the remains, like smoke out of the remnants of a

306

fire. Baron lifted his head and let out the tiniest bark. She laid a hand on him, watching the golem gather itself and tumble into the meadow after the Mordin. As she watched it creep, the sounds of battle broke out, downstream and far out in the meadow. The Riven were shouting and roaring, their strange harsh language slashing across the field. But who were they fighting?

Baron whined. His tail thumped against her leg. April turned just as a shadow leapt down into the creek bed beside them. She flinched so hard she rolled halfway into the water, drenching her legs.

Isabel crouched down to peer at her. "You got out of the barn," she said, not even bothering to apologize for scaring April. Her cheek bore a nasty, fresh scrape, and her tangled red hair was a briar patch.

"Yes," April managed. "So did you. I'm glad." The words came out easily, even if April wasn't sure how true they were. "Thank you for saving me back there." She owed the woman that much, at least.

"I was just doing what I was told," Isabel murmured. "I'm only sorry I couldn't do more harm to that beast. There's no death too cruel for him." April knew she meant Dr. Jericho. Isabel turned her frantic, wounded eyes to April. "I was close. Brian was fixing me. It was happening, but then . . ."

April had no idea if that was true or not. But she found a pool of pity stirring in her gut, despite everything Isabel had done. The woman was desperately—or angrily?—clutching the round white object April had seen earlier. A harp, she realized now. "I heard what happened to Miradel," said April. "At least you found a replacement pretty quickly."

"Replacement," Isabel laughed bitterly. "A consolation prize from Mr. Meister. I can't do anything with it. I can't cleave. My severings last only a second, not long enough to even down a Mordin. The best I can do is stagger them."

Being severed for too long, April had learned, could lead to dispossession and death. Human Keepers could endure being severed for a matter of minutes, an hour at most. But for the Riven, whose Tan'ji were literally a part of them, being severed for only a few seconds might prove fatal.

"Well, you saved me," April said. "That's all I'm saying."

Isabel gazed out over the meadow. "Meister left, didn't he? He took Joshua and Brian with him, I'll bet. What about Chloe?"

"I don't know. I thought I saw Horace down in the meadow, but . . ."

"We need to find Gabriel," said Isabel.

"I don't even know if he's still here."

"*You're* still here," said Isabel firmly. "*He's* still here."

And then April remembered the words Gabriel had said to her just before she left the humour. "*I will not leave without you, April.*"

Brave Gabriel. He'd saved her once already tonight.

And it made sense—maybe the humour hadn't vanished completely, but had just been made tiny. Gabriel would be huddled inside, blind to the outside world, using just a trickle of the Staff of Obro's power so as not to be detected by the Tan'ji-hunting Mordin. But she knew from experience that if the humour was very small right now, she had no chance of spotting it. Not with her human eyes, anyway, or with Baron's.

"Use the vine," Isabel said, seeming to read her thoughts.

"That's crazy," April said, nodding at the two Mordin fifty yards away.

"Be quick. Be quiet. Eyes only. If you can spot the humour, and we can get close to it, I'll be able to sense it."

That was a bit of a surprise, but April had learned not to underestimate what Isabel could do, even without Miradel. She collected herself, trying to forge the next step. All in all, she was impressed by her own calmness. She wasn't sure who, exactly, had let her down the most on this long evening, but it wasn't herself. And she believed that the best way to feel better about things having gone against you was to bring them back *for* you.

Carefully, she accessed the vine. Just a thin stream to see who or what was around. Baron was here, nearly spent. And there were plenty of crawdads. Toads too, lots of them. Before the vine, she'd never realized how many toads there were in the world. But she needed something else, and within seconds she found it. A surly, slow-moving mind, high in a tree fifty feet downstream. She focused on it, opening the vine just a little wider. Yes. A possum. She just needed to borrow its eyes, very gently.

"Quiet now," said Isabel.

April ignored her. She let the possum's senses come into her own. Taste and smell came first, foremost on the creature's mind. He was eating something, wet and foul. She stuck out her tongue and pushed the sensation away. She closed her eyes and narrowed the stream, letting his vision swim up in her mind instead. It was stunningly bright—she'd known possums had excellent night vision, but of course had never experienced it before. In his busy hands she saw his meal now, a pile of wet innards. A toad, she was pretty sure. *Terrific.*

From the possum's perch, she could see out over the meadow. Possums were stubborn creatures, a personality trait that she usually admired, but she had never cared for possums much. She thought of them as zombie raccoons. But now she was glad this pigheaded specimen had elected not to be disturbed by all the night's calamities.

Sadly, although the possum's wide pupils drank in the starlight as though it were sunshine, his distant vision was lacking. She could see the meadow, could see figures moving around it—far more than she would have thought possible— but it was so blurry she couldn't tell whether she was seeing humans or Riven. She guessed Riven, based on the smell and the sound. But she was really on the lookout for just one thing. One unseeable thing.

The telltale stitch of the humour.

She'd seen the humour this way before, earlier tonight,

but that had been through Arthur's keen eyes. To spot it now, she'd have to get—

Lucky.

There it was, a stitch in the possum's sight, a strange sliver in the meadow. A patch of unsight, scarcely bigger than Gabriel himself. The possum himself was unaware of it, still hungrily devouring his meal.

"I found him," she whispered. He wasn't terribly far, either, less than a hundred feet away, about halfway to where the Mordin were guarding the falkretes. He wasn't moving, and with good reason. If he moved, he would be—to use an expression—traveling blind, wholly unaware of what transpired outside the confines of the humour. She had wanted to find him for her own protection, but as she saw his tiny, lonely shelter out there, she realized she maybe had it backward. Gabriel needed her. With her help, the vine's help, he could see outside. He could move the humour safely away.

The shouting continued, out in the meadow. Riven— louder by the second, agitated. And the rustling thunder of the golem. For some reason, though, they seemed to be spread wide across the meadow, battling or pursuing multiple mysterious foes. What was happening?

Baron lurched to his feet. He'd heard something, she realized. Voices, farther downstream along the creek. Whispers. She couldn't make them out at all, but before she could speak or get a hand on the dog, he trotted off to investigate. *Sound. People.*

People? Could it possibly be—

"That's enough," Isabel said. "If you found Gabriel, note the spot and get me close. Enough with the vine."

Reluctantly, April pushed Baron from her mind. Taking one last look at the humour's location through the possum, she let him go too, releasing the vine completely.

Isabel was clearly listening to the sounds of battle out in the meadow. "Who's fighting out there?" she asked worriedly.

April realized she must be thinking of Chloe. But first they had to get to Gabriel. "Come on," she said. "Before I lose my mark."

April crept slowly across the grass toward the spot where she'd seen the humour, Isabel behind her. She kept her eyes on the Mordin up by the barn. She was so distracted trying to stay quiet and low, willing herself to not be seen, that she nearly jumped when Isabel touched her arm. April turned, and there was the humour. A slippery little crease in the dark. She nodded at Isabel, and together they plunged into it.

The gray nothingness of the humour swallowed her. The meadow sounds fell away. She expected Gabriel to be stoic about their sudden appearance, as always, but to her surprise he let out a huge sigh of relief.

"Oh, thank goodness," he said from everywhere. "I've been lost at sea out here. Not a lot of landmarks in a meadow."

"Well, you might want to find some," April said. "We need to move. There are Mordin outside, too close for me to start groping around with the vine anymore."

"Can we go back the way you just came?" Gabriel asked.

"Yes. Perfect," said April.

"Good, then. Footprints. Stay low."

Gabriel took April's hand firmly. He took her surely over the grass, using the humour to follow her trail back to the creek. To distract herself from the possibility that they might be seen, she talked to him.

"The others are gone, aren't they?" April asked.

"Mr. Meister and Brian, yes," said Gabriel. "They escaped through a portal with Joshua."

"So back in the forest, when Horace said—"

"Horace said what he needed to."

They walked on in silence. They managed to make it to the creek. April instructed Gabriel to keep heading straight. They crossed the creek—a difficult and wet task in the humour—and kept moving. Beyond the creek was a soybean field, April knew, and though she couldn't see it she could feel the low plants brushing against her ankles.

"I have no idea where I'm going," Gabriel said. "All this flatness."

"Let me check," said April. Tentatively, she reached out with the vine—just a trickle again. Almost at once, with a surge of relief, she felt Baron again, very close by. He seemed happy, excited. *Friend. Nice.* But he was alone. She could see now that they were a good ways out into the soybean field—farther than she thought—and the tree-lined creek was screening them from the Riven over in the meadow. The sounds and scent of the ongoing battle weren't exactly distant, but distant enough.

"We're good," she reported.

The humour dissolved slowly, with a soft rustle. Baron heard her and smelled her at once, and trotted over, his wagging tail swatting the soybean plants with soft *thwaps. Friend,* he was still thinking, and there was a hopeful kind of questioning attached to it. *Your friend too?* Or at least, that was the only way April could translate his mood.

Cautiously she took his memories. Someone had just petted him. Said kind words to him and called him by name. That meant friend. And they'd said another name too, the only other word he'd really understood. It clung to his memories like a good scent.

April.

Horace and Chloe. It had to be. She pulled at the dog's ears, but the sounds coming from over in the meadow—the golem, muddled voices—were too distant to hear clearly. April dug deep, opening wide, searching through Baron's fading sights and smells, trying to figure out where he'd been. Where Horace and Chloe were.

"You're doing too much," Isabel warned. "They'll feel you, even from this far away."

"I've got it under control," she said. But Isabel was right. Reluctantly, she eased off on the vine. "Where are they, boy?" she said.

"Where is who?" said Isabel.

And then their voices started up again. Talking in the distance, straight ahead in the soybean field. Too far away for April to hear at all, and too far for Baron to understand what they were saying. But it was Horace. And Chloe. No doubt about it. Her heart leapt, except . . . someone was with them. Someone with a strange voice.

"Horace and Chloe are out there," she said, pointing. "But they're not alone." Isabel sucked in a sharp breath.

The three of them hurried together through the field, heading north toward the voices. In the meadow on the far side of the creek, meanwhile, the Riven were perhaps two hundred yards off, but coming closer. April could hear the golem's distant rattle and roar through her own ears, and now she caught a glimpse of it through the trees, a black sea serpent cruising through an ocean of grass. April's dread grew. She realized her own little group and the small army of Riven were converging on the same point—hers from the south, and the Riven from the east—all of them headed for Horace and Chloe. It was obvious Dr. Jericho knew precisely where April's friends were.

Suddenly Gabriel pounded to a halt. "Stop," he said softly. "Listen."

April couldn't hear a thing with her own ears, but apparently Gabriel's were sharper. She still had to rely on Baron, the vine barely a trickle, and through him Chloe's voice rang out thinly. "They're coming. Is this thing going to protect us, or what?"

Another voice answered her. It wasn't Horace. It wasn't even human. April couldn't make out the words, but the voice was singsongy, lilting. A Riven? What was happening? At her side, Gabriel went stiff, and then launched into an awkward run. April went after him, catching him by the hand. Isabel followed behind.

They'd gone no more than a hundred feet, still a hundred feet or more away from the voices, when—up ahead and off to the right—the golem pounded across the creek and into the soybean field, spraying water, headed straight for Horace and Chloe. Dr. Jericho ran at its side, looking every bit a beast.

Gabriel dove to the ground, dragging April with him and gesturing for Isabel to do the same.

"Down," April whispered to Baron, releasing the vine. "Lie down." The dog obeyed, burying himself in the leaves.

April buried herself too. Through the leaves of the soybeans, she thought she could see movement straight ahead, but barely. She realized Gabriel was refraining from using the humour so she and Isabel could see what he could not. But why were they simply watching and not acting? "What are you doing?" she whispered in Gabriel's ear. "We need to get to closer to them, get them inside the humour."

"If I'm not mistaken," Gabriel replied, "I believe they have found a better plan."

Up ahead, Chloe spoke again. She was close enough now that April could make out her words. She sounded as alarmed as April felt. "You better be right about this."

Horace answered her, sounding much less dismayed. "I think he is."

Then finally that singsongy voice, most relaxed of all.

"Thank you, Keeper. I believe I am."

April frowned, forcing herself to stay low. Whatever Horace and Chloe's better plan was, it had better happen fast. The Riven were nearly upon them. She could hear Dr. Jericho roaring, feel the ground thundering beneath the golem, smell the brimstone in the air. April reached for Gabriel, about to insist that he run to the others and let the humour loose.

And then suddenly a great rustling arose. A section of the field, green as leaves and as wide as a house, lifted into the sky. April craned her neck to see, her mouth dropping open. The wide green carpet rose swiftly, leaving the Riven and April and Gabriel and everything helplessly behind. In seconds, it disappeared into the sky's sea of stars, taking Horace and Chloe with it.

CHAPTER TWENTY-ONE

Destination Unknown

THE SURFACE OF THE MAL'GAMA SHIFTED BENEATH HORACE, cupping him as the entire structure rocketed up out of the field. Chloe, still standing, toppled over with a howl. The mal'gama swelled up and caught her gently, cradling her. Faster, and higher. Behind them, far below—two hundred feet?—the dark cloud of the golem swirled and stormed in a fury. Dr. Jericho screamed up at them, his massive fists clenched with rage.

Wind whipped through Horace's hair. Chloe rolled onto her side, grimacing. "This was unexpected!" she shouted. Horace could hardly hear her over the rush of wind. The front of the mal'gama folded itself into a kind of cone, and the gale subsided. It was like being inside an airplane without a roof. Horace had the sense they were still accelerating.

They continued to rise into the night, speeding away.

The meadow was far behind now. The meadow and everything in it, and that included—if events had unfolded the way the Fel'Daera had foreseen—April and Gabriel. They were still down there somewhere. Horace tried to calm his guilty, churning gut by hoping that in all the commotion, his friends had managed to slip away under the cover of the humour. Or even better, maybe they'd gotten away through the falkrete stones.

He sank back into the mal'gama, trying to catch his breath and clear his thoughts. A close call—several of them—and now this most unexpected escape. If only April and Gabriel had been with them. He looked over at Chloe. She still had the golem's heart wrapped in the hem of her shirt, but she was peering out over the edge of the mal'gama. She glanced back at him, her face brimming with wonder and worry.

The worry was inescapable. But so was the wonder. The mal'gama was obviously related to the golem, made of tens of thousands of small pieces working together. Horace couldn't stop himself from wondering if it had a heart too, buried somewhere in the green carpet beneath them. How did it work? It could defy gravity, like Neptune. But also it was propelling itself forward, at great speed. How?

Dailen watched them calmly, still sitting upright, a faint smile of amusement on his angelic face. "I envy you," he said. "Your first ride on the mal'gama."

"What is it?" asked Horace. "It's not Tan'ji."

"No. The mal'gama is Tan'kindi, though I'm told I have

319

a flair for it." He held out his slender hand, indicating the green-stoned ring. "I've been lucky to have the opportunity. This is the last mal'gama in existence."

"It's like the golem," Horace said.

"Yes, but quite a bit more tame. And it flies, of course."

"It's a flying carpet," said Chloe.

Dailen shrugged elegantly. "If you like. You would not be the first to suggest it."

Horace reached out and plucked experimentally at a single green piece from the undulating whole. To his surprise, it came away easily in his hand. He shot a sheepish look at Dailen, but the Altari only nodded at him encouragingly. The chunk was soft and smoothly fuzzed, about as big and heavy as a large marble. He peered at it closely, turning it. It wasn't perfectly round, but instead had cleanly chiseled faces—six squares and eight hexagons.

"I've seen this shape before," Horace said.

"Perhaps," said Dailen. "It tessellates in three dimensions." Abruptly, a patch of the mal'gama in front of Horace began to rearrange itself with a whispering sigh, the little balls coming together and climbing over one another, rotating and pressing tight, building a short tower. The balls fit rigidly together like a puzzle, up and down and left and right, leaving absolutely no gaps between them.

"Go ahead," said Dailen. "Try to bend it."

Horace grabbed the little tower. He tugged at it with two hands, gently at first and then as hard as he could. Whereas the golem was constantly shifting, like quicksand or tar, the mal'gama was as firm as bedrock. He released it, and the stones melted back into the whole, becoming part of the soft, supple carpet again.

"And it's strong," said Dailen. He pointed at Chloe. "Lay the golem's heart down, and I'll show you. It's not a souvenir for keeping, anyway." Chloe bit her lip, then lowered her shirt and let the bloodred crystal fall out onto the green stones. It was jagged, pointed at both ends, made of razor-thin flakes. It was almost painful to look at. The mal'gama shifted to envelop it, and then began squeezing it like a vise. After a moment, the foul red crystal shattered into a cloud of scarlet dust. It scattered into the wind and vanished.

"I thought you said this thing wasn't made for fighting," Chloe muttered, watching intently. She wrapped her arms around her knees, a wary look in her eyes.

"It's a matter of temperament," Dailen said. "Think of the mal'gama like a whale. It endures. It travels far. The golem, meanwhile, is a tiger."

"Speaking of traveling far," Horace said, "where are you taking us?"

Dailen hesitated, looking troubled. He casually plucked three green stones from the mal'gama. "I do not know," he said. The stones began to weave around one another in his palm, a kind of horizontal juggling act, but the look on Dailen's face said his thoughts were far away.

"You must have had a plan," said Chloe. "Where did you

come from? Were you going to take us back there?"

Dailen sighed. "I'm not sure now how wise that would be."

Chloe scoffed, clearly frustrated. "How wise does it need to be?"

But Horace thought he was beginning to understand. When Dailen first encountered them he had asked about the Laithe, not the Fel'Daera. "You didn't come here for us," he said. "You came here for the Laithe."

Dailen dropped the stones back into the mal'gama, where they were absorbed at once. "That is true."

"But the problem isn't just that you didn't find the Laithe. It's what you *did* find."

The Altari looked at him, his eyes brighter than ever. With his curious double eyelids, he looked both furious and deeply apologetic. He glanced down at the Fel'Daera. *"Do Fel'Daera lekta Tan'ji,"* he murmured, and then smiled sadly at Horace for several seconds. "What is your name, Keeper?" he said at last.

"Horace. Horace Andrews."

"My name is Dwen'dailen Longo, Keeper of Floriel. I come from Ka'hokah." He let his eyes fall to the Fel'Daera again, and left them there. He sighed and said, "I am a companion of Sil'falo Teneves."

Sil'falo Teneves. Maker of the Fel'Daera. Maker of the Laithe of Teneves.

"Oh, crap," said Chloe slowly. "This is happening."

Horace's shoulders and chest began to tremble. He told

himself it was only the chilly breeze this high up, but that was a lie.

Dailen leaned in close. He clasped his great hands together as if in prayer. "I intend to help in whatever way I can, Horace Andrews," he sang. "But I regret to inform you that you are not supposed to exist."

PART THREE

Into the Havens

CHAPTER TWENTY–TWO

Seeking Shelter

APRIL LAY IN THE SOYBEAN FIELD, PEERING INTO THE NIGHT SKY, looking hopelessly after the giant flying carpet that had carried Horace and Chloe away.

"I don't believe it," she whispered, though she wasn't sure what she didn't believe—the fact that Horace and Chloe had left them here, or the *way* they had left them.

"What did you see?" said Gabriel.

"They're gone," April said. In the darkness ahead, Dr. Jericho roared, shouting at the other Riven in his own tongue. He sounded furious. "There was a . . . thing. Like a flying carpet. Like the golem, but not. It took them away."

"Then they are in good hands," Gabriel said, hardly sounding surprised. "Now brace yourselves—I'm bringing the humour back." A moment later, the cold, silent expanse of the humour surrounded them once more.

"Now what?" Isabel said. "Do you plan to just sit here?"

"The Riven won't give up," Gabriel said. "Dr. Jericho must suspect I didn't leave through the portal. They'll return to the meadow, the barn. They'll look for us where they last saw us. Then we must move."

Baron whined. He didn't like the humour, not at all. April reached out for him and dug her fingers comfortingly into his thick fur. He licked her, panting nervously. "Horace and Chloe," she said. "Whose good hands are they in now, exactly?"

"The Altari," Gabriel said.

Isabel laughed. "The Altari?" she said, clearly not believing it. "What would they be doing here? They don't fight. They pout in their sanctuaries, waiting for the end of days."

"Horace and Chloe left here on a mal'gama," Gabriel said. "Only an Altari could have been holding the reins."

"So you say," Isabel said, but she sounded worried.

"Sorry, who are the Altari?" asked April, utterly lost.

"Friends," said Gabriel. "I'll tell you the story when we are clear."

Baron struggled beneath April's hand. She clutched at him, but he squirmed away.

"He's outside the humour," Gabriel said, alarmed. "He'll be seen."

Very cautiously, through the vine, April reached out for Baron. *Freedom. Sounds. Smells.* Through the dog, she could tell that the Riven were leaving the soybean field. She could hear the golem, crossing back in the meadow now. The smell of brimstone had grown fainter. "You were right," she reported. "The Riven have moved away."

"We should move too, then," Gabriel whispered. "But which way?"

April thought. She'd been in this field before—especially in those years when the farmer that owned it grew corn, purposefully losing herself in the sea of tall stalks. To the north, the field butted up against the strip of woods behind her own backyard. "My house isn't far away. But I suppose the Riven might look for us there. They know where I live. They were actually inside."

"But there is a leestone there," Gabriel said thoughtfully. April thought she heard Isabel make a small noise of surprise. "Despite what happened earlier tonight," continued Gabriel, "the leestone—in time—will make the Riven forget that your house even exists."

"How much time?"

"Hours, perhaps."

"It's been hours. A few, anyway."

"If the Riven were in your house, no leestone could make them forget it so soon," Isabel said.

April wished the humour was down, so that she could have served Isabel with her most skeptical stare. "I want you to ask yourself if you're really somebody we'd trust with a judgment like that," she said. "You're the one that sent the Riven there in the first place."

"You think you know me," Isabel said, her voice strained.

"I really don't," said April. "That's the problem."

"I saved you. You said it yourself."

"From yet another danger that you yourself caused. And anyway, you said you were only doing what Mr. Meister told you to do. Maybe you hope he has a stronger harp back at the Warren for you—one he's set aside especially for his most obedient pets." April bit her lip, almost embarrassed to be talking like this. She sounded just like Chloe. It must be rubbing off.

"None of this is helping," Gabriel said. "Either we try the house, or we need to leave this place entirely. But I can't go far, not yet. I've asked the humour to do a lot of things tonight it doesn't normally do—keeping the humour small, thinning it out, silencing Ingrid's flute. Exhausting things. I'm not sure how much longer I can keep us hidden."

"I vote we stay in the open," Isabel said at once.

That made April want to argue for the house, but she checked herself. Was she being sensible, or just acting out her annoyance with Isabel? Was it smart to return to the house?

"I vote . . . house," she said slowly. "Even if the leestone isn't totally working yet, maybe the house is actually the last place the Riven would look for us." This, even as she said it, struck her as the kind of thing people in movies said, right before the bad guys caught them. The truth was, she had no idea what to do. "Or maybe it's the first place they'd look, I don't know."

"The house," Gabriel said firmly. "I can bury the entire thing in the humour if I need to."

April nodded. "This way, then," she said. "Are you coming, Isabel?"

Silence for a moment, and then Isabel said, "I have no choice."

April led the way. Baron, still standing patiently just outside the humour, jumped a little as the humour began to move. He could see the wrinkle of it, and though he didn't understand what was happening, he could smell April and the others on the ground after they passed by. April wasn't sure what he would do—whether she would have to step out of the humour and call to him, or grab him—but after snuffling along their trail for a few seconds, he settled into an easy lope beside the humour, seeming to know where they were headed. He glanced nervously over at the meadow across the creek now and again, where the Riven still roamed, but for the most part his thoughts were simple and clear. *Home. April. Happy.* These weren't words, of course—never words—but abstract ideas that April's mind translated into words. His idea of April, for example, was rich and complicated, made of a dozen tiny little parts that each had their own little translation: *girl, sweat, dirt, spice, hair, flower, food, touch, peace, breath, friend.* She let herself swim in the feel of it as they walked, feeling both more and less like herself than she ever could without him.

After they had gone a few hundred yards, Gabriel's deep,

tired voice rolled through the humour. "I'm spent. Are we clear?"

April tested the air outside. The brimstone stink was faint and distant. And they were nearly to the woods that cut through to her backyard. "It's fine," she said, and Gabriel brought the humour down slowly—slower than she'd known he could—with just a soft, rippling sound. The older teen stood there, sagging, leaning on his staff.

"You okay?"

"Fine. like I said, I just . . . exercised some muscles I didn't know I had."

"It was the thinning, wasn't it?" She'd helped him practice, back at the Warren. But apparently it was exhausting.

"I'll get better."

"You will."

Baron was already loping into the woods toward the house, along a game trail they'd walked a thousand times. April followed, the others in tow. When she emerged on the far side, at the edge of her yard, she was swamped with a wash of sadness she wasn't expecting. Just hours before, she'd been here in the yard with her brother, Derek, showing him the astonishing power of the Ravenvine, and trying to explain the unexplainable world of the Keepers. And now Derek and her uncle Harrison were gone, run from this place by the Riven. She could hardly imagine that Derek was sleeping right now. He was no doubt lying awake in some strange room, worrying himself half to death about April.

"Are we changing our minds?" Isabel said.

April startled. "I'm not. Let's go."

They crossed the lawn to the back porch. Baron stopped to drink noisily at his water dish—his tongue darting messily into the bowl, his jaws snapping frantically around the airborne water he drew out. It was distinctly distracting. April let him slip from her mind and crept through the backdoor of the house.

The lights were still on. The house smelled faintly of brimstone. Otherwise everything seemed normal. As she came through the hallway into the foyer, she noticed that the front door was open. Two sets of huge scratches were gouged into the wood on either side of the doorframe, as if a Mordin had been clinging to it for dear life. She slammed the door shut and ran upstairs to her bedroom.

The leestone was still there atop her bookshelf, a green stone laced with gold, carved into a raven's skull. It was quite lovely if you didn't mind skulls, which naturally she didn't. She took it down now and hid it under her pillow. She didn't quite know why.

As she came back downstairs, Uncle Harrison's grandfather clock began to strike four a.m. April was stunned that so much had happened in so little time—barely twenty minutes had passed since she'd come through the falkretes! It felt like hours.

Isabel was peering at the clock, and April noticed that the clock's glass face was cracked. Now she saw other signs of the earlier battle, too—a couple of chairs knocked over in the dining room, the china hutch leaning precariously into the corner. Most disturbing of all, though, was the wide, still-sticky patch of black-red blood on the parlor floor. It smelled foul—not human. Within that patch, two strange sights: the fireplace tongs and the poker, sticking straight out of the floor, embedded like sticks stuck in snow. April grabbed the poker, tugging at it experimentally. It didn't budge, buried at least a foot deep.

"Looks like Chloe was here," she said.

Isabel frowned. "How long do we have to wait here?"

April, annoyed, sprawled comfortably out onto the couch like she'd just gotten home from school. She rolled her eyes up to look at Isabel upside down. "We're not waiting. We're resting. We're thinking." None of that was strictly true, of course. They were hiding. And what came next, she hardly knew.

Gabriel took a seat in Uncle Harrison's fat rocking chair. He tapped his staff against the fireplace poker. It twanged dully. Isabel turned away. She glanced up the stairs for a moment, making April tense, but then she wandered into the kitchen, hugging herself.

"I'm feeling sort of rejected," April said.

"By Isabel?" Gabriel said, not even bothering to lower his voice.

"Okay, you're making jokes now. You must be tired. But no." She wiggled a rising hand through the air. "By Horace and Chloe, flying off with the shiny Riven, leaving us behind."

"The Altari," Gabriel corrected. "And they had no choice. Dr. Jericho nearly caught them as it was."

April glanced at the gouges on the front door. "I know. I'm not bitter. I just got a little . . . melancholy."

"Melancholy," Gabriel said with a laugh.

"What's so funny?"

"When I first became the Keeper of the Staff of Obro, that was the name used for the humour. The melancholy."

She flopped over to look at him. In the little time she'd spent with Gabriel, he hadn't been much of a sharer. "Seriously?"

"Yes. I hated the word. It comes from the Latin. It means 'black bile.' Something that causes depression."

"Well, it *is* kind of rough in there. For us, I mean."

"I am aware. But it didn't seem necessary to draw attention to the fact. I started calling it the humour instead. The name stuck."

"Wow. You rebranded your Tan'ji."

Gabriel looked puzzled. "I don't know what that means."

"It doesn't matter. Humour is much better." She sighed. "But here's the other thing, maybe the real thing. Horace let us all think we were going to get away through the portal tonight."

Gabriel banged the poker again, softly. *Twang, twang, twang.* "It's not easy being a Keeper. Least of all, I think, the Keeper of the Fel'Daera. He can't tell us everything— *shouldn't* tell us."

April had no doubt that was true. And she wasn't mad at

Horace, not exactly. It seemed to her that there was something dishonest in what had happened, something sort of cruel about witnessing another person's future and then lying about it—even if it was a lie by omission. Still, she asked herself what she would have done if Horace had told them all the truth, and she knew—without question—that she would have come anyway. And maybe, in his own wise way, Horace had known that too. About all of them.

April looked up at the ceiling, at the cobwebbed corners and the cracks around the ceiling fan. She ran her finger around the golden curves of the Ravenvine, down the little black flower that dangled in front of her ear. "I am happy with who I am," she said. "I mean, I've been chased out of my home, and there's a pool of Mordin blood on my parlor floor, but I am generally happy with who I am. I'm the Keeper of the Ravenvine."

Gabriel grunted noncommittally. She didn't really want to ask him what he meant by that.

Isabel came back into the room, fiddling mindlessly with the little white harp. April thought she might apologize for the house, for what had happened here, but instead she said, "What would the Altari want with a person like Chloe? What would they do to her?"

"You don't need to worry," Gabriel said. "She'll come to no harm."

April sat up. "Okay, explain, please. Who are these Altari?"

Another twang on the poker. "The Altari are the Makers," said Gabriel. "They are the ones who first made the Tanu,

336

who made nearly all of the instruments we still use today."

"But . . . Brian is a Maker, isn't he? And he's human."

"Brian is an anomaly. The Altari are the true Makers."

"And they just happen to sound exactly like the Riven when they talk," April said.

"That's what the Wardens don't want to tell you," said Isabel. "They're embarrassed to admit it. The Riven and the Altari—they're the same, down deep."

"They are not the same," Gabriel said.

"Two twigs on the same branch," Isabel insisted.

April held up her hands. "You're saying these Altari are related to the Riven?"

"They are the progenitors of the Riven," Gabriel said. "The ancestors. The Riven broke ties with the Altari millennia ago. They became twisted, lost in shadow. They became the dark things we fight to this day."

"Why did they break ties?"

"Because of us," Isabel said. "Because of you."

"It's true," said Gabriel. "Long ago, the most powerful Altari were friendly with humans. They shared their creations with us. They embraced those few rare humans that could become Tan'ji. But most Altari did not feel this way. They separated from the elite, renaming themselves the Riven. They dedicated themselves to hunting down human Keepers and waging war with their Altari brethren. The Altari, outnumbered, retreated into secrecy, almost completely severing their ties with humans."

"In other words," said Isabel, "the Altari left them—left

you—alone to wage the war against the Riven. Just like they've left you now."

Gabriel said nothing. April tried to get a grasp on it. "The Altari helped Horace and Chloe tonight. Maybe they'll come back for us."

"It is . . . unlikely," Gabriel said. "Isabel is right—the Altari do not often choose to meddle."

"But they *did* meddle," April pointed out. "What were they even doing here?"

"They came looking for something," said Isabel. "They must have found it."

"I do not think so," said Gabriel. "There are no Altari strongholds within two hundred miles of this place. Even with the mal'gama, it would have taken hours to get here. What they sought was here in this place long before Horace and Chloe arrived."

Isabel shifted uneasily, and suddenly April knew. "Joshua," she said.

"Possibly," Gabriel said, and then shrugged. "Probably." He cocked his head in Isabel's direction. "What was done to him tonight . . . might have caught their attention. He is a Lostling."

"He's no such thing," Isabel said. "He's the rightful Keeper of the Laithe."

"And yet he did not claim that right on his own. The Laithe did not choose him." Gabriel pointed his staff at Isabel like a spear. His voice grew hard. "The choice, and the claim, were made by you."

Isabel spun and stalked out the front door, all but stomping her feet. She slammed the door shut behind her.

Gabriel lowered his staff calmly. "How deep is your distrust of Isabel?" he said quietly.

"Pretty deep at the moment. Like, she's at the bottom of my list—of humans, anyway."

"Should we have left her to the Riven, then?"

April hesitated. With all Isabel had done, all the danger and damage she'd created, still it was hard not to imagine— even to wish—that there was a corner just ahead for Isabel. A corner she might turn, and somehow set everything right for herself. And for her family, too. "If I were on a sinking ship with her," April said finally, "I wouldn't want the sharks to eat her. But I wouldn't give it much thought if she just drifted away."

Gabriel nodded as if he understood perfectly. "I brought her here for a reason."

"Here to the house?"

"Yes. Out in the open, I suspect she could have called the Riven down on us if she wanted, with that little harp of hers. Here, I think the leestone would stop her."

"Do you really think she would do that?"

"Do you think she would not? Her only allegiance is to herself. At any rate, it seemed to me that either we had to bring her here, or abandon her altogether."

"And you couldn't abandon her. Couldn't throw her to the sharks," April said.

"Oh, I could have. But I didn't think *you* could."

April didn't know what to say to that. She didn't even know if it was a compliment or an insult. "Where did she get that new harp, anyway?" she asked. "She said Mr. Meister brought it to her."

Gabriel nodded. "He did. After Horace reported that the wicker harp had been destroyed, Mr. Meister found that harp in one of his vest pockets—in the Great Burrow, actually. He took it, came through the falkretes, and gave it to Isabel in the humour. That's why he showed up late."

"Why would he do that?"

"The new harp did help us tonight," Gabriel said, and shrugged. "Any port in a storm—that's what Mr. Meister would say."

"But what would *you* say?"

"He wanted to demonstrate that he still has a little faith in her."

"How could he possibly still—"

Gabriel held up a hand. He cocked his head, seeming to listen at the front door. "Mr. Meister is a complicated man with a complicated job," he said quietly. "He and I do not always agree, but that does not mean he does not have his reasons."

Faith in Isabel. It seemed dangerously mad. Still, the woman *had* saved her from Dr. Jericho and the Auditor. And as for Mr. Meister, there was no question that disagreeing with the man wasn't an easy proposition. Even when his rationales were lacking, he managed to make it seem like he had secret motivations—perfect motivations—that he simply wasn't willing to share. She lay silent for a moment, mulling it over, trying to push Isabel from her mind.

"You were arguing with Mr. Meister in the Warren," she said to Gabriel. "About Joshua."

Gabriel frowned. He didn't seem to appreciate the reminder. "Briefly. I understand his position."

"You called Joshua a Lostling. I'm guessing that's someone who didn't go through the Find. But what's the big deal? He's clearly the Keeper of the Laithe."

Gabriel leaned back, his ghostly blue eyes drifting toward the ceiling in thought. He laid his staff across his broad chest. "I'm a traditionalist, and I freely confess that some of my thoughts on this matter might be considered . . ." He searched for a word.

"Stubborn," April finished.

Gabriel smiled. "Yes."

"People say the same about me sometimes. I refuse to agree."

His smile became a soft laugh. "Joshua is the Keeper of the Laithe. I do not deny it. He opened a portal in the humour, blind. It was impressive. But because he did not have a proper Find, the bond of Tan'ji is tainted."

Isabel again. "Tainted how?" April asked. "He's using the Laithe. It's working for him."

"To a degree, but the Laithe's powers have been handed to him, rather than being discovered by him. He's only parroting what he's been taught. He may be slow to master his Tan'ji—if he ever masters it at all. He has sprinted forward, yes, but the ground is turning to mud beneath his feet. The next steps will be difficult."

"Difficult. But not impossible."

"No."

April frowned. "Then what's all the fuss about?"

Gabriel thinned his lips and shifted, clearly unsettled.

"There's more," April said. When Gabriel hesitated, she pressed. "Tell me the more."

"It's not easy to explain," Gabriel sighed. "To be Tan'ji is to surrender. During the Find, we give ourselves to our instruments. Wholly. Unconditionally. You may have felt this change in yourself less than others do—being an empath, you are naturally more . . . connected. To everything. Bonds come easily to you."

April supposed that was fair. Still, although she would not have thought to use the word "surrender" to describe her bond with the Ravenvine, she understood that she had embraced a kind of unconditional acceptance of it. An acceptance that was both greedy and helpless. Like a sail permanently unfurled in a volatile wind. She let her thoughts trickle through the vine, through the power that coiled there. Did that power belong to her, or did she belong to it?

"Do you understand me?" Gabriel said.

"I think so," said April. "I do know that I am . . . changed."

Gabriel hunched forward intently, tapping the Staff of

Obro softly against the floor. As he spoke, his voice and face lit with a kind of dreamy, fiery fervor. "In our world—the world of the Keepers—there are forces at work beyond us all. The Medium. The Mothergates. The Starlit Loom. We cannot truly comprehend these things—not their histories, not their functions, not their fates. And because we cannot comprehend them, we can only serve them when we surrender to them—to them, and to the arcs of their existence." He lifted his face, clearly struggling to put words to a thing that lived wordless inside him. Watching him, April felt a stirring in her chest, fluttery and frightening. She sat back, the Ravenvine burning at her temple like a bared thread of her soul. She understood nothing Gabriel was saying, and yet she understood everything he meant.

Gabriel pressed the silver pommel of his staff to his forehead. He closed his eyes. "To be Tan'ji is to . . . *become*," he said thickly. "We become. For better or for worse. Do you understand?"

April could only nod. "Okay," she said, her own voice hoarse. "Okay."

"But as for Joshua . . ." Gabriel grimaced, his face creased with pain. "Ingrid was a Lostling, you know. Chloe had that right."

"Ingrid!" April exclaimed. "She didn't choose her Tan'ji? She was taught?"

"That's right. She never went through a proper Find. She never fully surrendered to her Tan'ji, or to everything from

343

which her Tan'ji flowed, and so when certain choices were presented to her—*difficult* choices—she . . ." He shrugged.

"You're saying she joined the Riven because she was a Lostling. That's why she turned?"

"Yes."

"And you're worried Joshua might do the same?"

"His bond is tainted," Gabriel said. "Joshua is weak, through no fault of his own. And if the right words are whispered into his ear—or the wrong ones—he may not have the strength to stay with us."

"How do we fix that? How do we make him strong?"

Gabriel shook his head and took a deep breath. "We do not," he said, and April could hear years of knowing sadness threaded into those words. "He either finds that strength himself, or he is lost."

The front door flew open. Isabel rushed in. "We've been found."

For an instant, April's hopes soared. The Wardens had returned, or maybe the Altari, here to rescue them. But Isabel crossed to the window and peered frantically out into the darkness. Not the Wardens, no. Not a rescue.

Isabel turned, her eyes wild and furious. "They're here," she said.

CHAPTER TWENTY-THREE

The Lostling

"IF YOU WILL, KEEPER," SAID MR. MEISTER, "EXPLAIN TO ME exactly how you came to possess the Laithe."

Mr. Meister sat at his desk in the Great Burrow, his stern face focused on Joshua. Or at least, he seemed stern. It was hard sometimes to read the old man's expression behind his thick glasses. And Joshua was tired, as tired as he could ever remember being—tired in his body, his heart. He'd slept in the cab on the way back to the Warren, slumped over on the lap of Horace's mom. She put off an air of comforting motherness he'd never felt before. She needed nothing from him, so unlike his own mother, who—as Joshua had understood even when he was a very small child—had needed so many things Joshua didn't have.

The Laithe floated silently beside him now, a perfect little earth. Joshua wondered if the sun had risen outside. He wondered if it had risen over the meadow by April's house, and he hoped beyond hope that all the friends he'd left behind there were alive to see it. April. Chloe. Horace. Gabriel. And Isabel too. It seemed like everything always came back to Isabel.

Mr. Meister wasn't saying anything about the missing Wardens, though. Instead, he wanted to talk about the Laithe. "Are you going to take it away from me?" Joshua asked.

"Certainly not," the old man said. "You are the Keeper of the Laithe of Teneves. I cannot change that, and would not if I could."

"But I'm a Lostling."

"Are you?"

Joshua didn't know. All he knew was, he felt lost. He looked up at the shelves of the round red room, filled with wonders. The little birds were here, comforting at first, but soon they made him think of April, the way all animals always did now. On one of the shelves high overhead, he spotted the gleaming white mouthpiece of a flute. Ingrid's flute. It was here, and so was she, held prisoner in a doba farther up in the Great Burrow. She seemed disoriented in the Warren the same way Isabel had earlier tonight, which meant there had to be a spitestone here, just for her. She hadn't spoken a word since arriving. He wasn't sure he wanted her to. Somehow, she was as scary as a Mordin—a human, working with the Riven. He wasn't sure he could imagine it. Not completely.

"I didn't Find the Laithe on my own," said Joshua. "Isabel did it."

"Ah, yes." Now Mr. Meister leaned forward, his big left eye wide as a ping-pong ball. "Let us discuss that for a moment. Isabel gave you no choice in the matter? Nor the Laithe?"

"No. She opened a cabinet. There were a lot of . . . instruments in there, I think."

"Tan'layn."

"Yes, I guess. She brought me the Laithe. She handed it to me."

Mr. Meister grimaced. "What did she say?"

"She said it was mine now."

"And did you feel that it was yours? When you laid eyes on it?"

Joshua tried to remember. "I don't know. Mostly I felt scared. I was afraid I would break it. And I didn't know how it worked, so Isabel showed me—"

"What did she show you, exactly? What did she say?"

"She showed me . . . the rabbit." He pointed to it now, sleeping atop the meridian. "She told me to slide it. She touched it, actually." He felt himself frown. "I didn't like that."

"Nor should you. Nor does any Keeper." Mr. Meister tapped his fingers thoughtfully on his desk. "When you left the Warren here tonight with Isabel and Brian, you opened a portal along the riverbank where I first met you. Do you remember our meeting?"

"Yes."

"Do you remember what I said to you?"

347

Joshua did, word for word. "You said, 'I believe I know why you are here.'"

"Precisely. I knew even then—as much as I can allow myself to know—that you would become the Keeper of the Laithe of Teneves. Just as I knew Horace would become the Keeper of the Fel'Daera." He tapped the left lens of his glasses, the oraculum. "It is my job to know such things."

"Thank you."

"Do not thank me. Only remember the words I said to you then." He leaned in close, peering at the floating Laithe. "Who chose the riverbank as your first destination?"

"I did."

"Not Isabel?"

"No. All she said was I should choose someplace close by. Someplace I'd been recently."

"Why did she say that?"

"Well, she wanted to go someplace else. But I couldn't do it. I couldn't make the Laithe do it."

"Where did she want to go?"

"Cahokia Mounds. She thought we could find a safe place with a leestone there."

Mr. Meister sat back, clearly surprised. One of the little birds flew down and circled the Laithe like a huge, flapping moon, twittering. It landed on Mr. Meister's desk. The old man held a finger out to it, and it nipped at him gently. "Describe to me what happened when you tried to steer the Laithe to Cahokia Mounds."

"It wasn't just Cahokia Mounds. The same thing happened in Madagascar." Joshua got flustered, feeling like he was explaining it badly. "I mean, Isabel didn't want to *go* to Madagascar. I was just messing around."

"I understand. And what happened?"

Joshua shrugged. "I couldn't get there. I zoomed in, but when I got close—"

"How close?"

"Two thousand feet." Joshua surprised himself, saying that. How had he known that? But it was right. "When I got down under two thousand feet, things got messy."

"Messy how?"

"Like . . . raindrops on a puddle. It got worse the farther I went. I couldn't see anything, couldn't get to the ground."

"Have you ever been to Cahokia Mounds in person?"

"No."

"Do you think that matters?"

"Brian said—"

"Brian is not the Keeper of the Laithe. You are. I ask you again—do you think it matters whether you have been to a place or not, when it comes to the Laithe? Would that have been the Maker's intent?"

"I don't know, I—"

"Where is Cahokia? In the real world, I mean. Point to it," said Mr. Meister.

Joshua's arm shot out automatically. He pointed almost exactly southwest by south, directly at Cahokia Mounds.

"I have no idea whether that's right or not," Mr. Meister said. "Yet I trust you implicitly. And how far away is it?"

"Two hundred and fifty-seven miles, as the crow flies." *Or the raven*, he thought miserably.

"What does Cahokia look like?"

"It's a park. A couple thousand acres, I guess. It has . . . you know . . . mounds. Big grassy ones. There are fields and forests, and a couple of ponds. A visitors' center."

"The visitors' center has a parking lot, I assume. On which side?"

"South, mostly. A little west."

"But you've never been there."

"I told you, no."

"If you were to walk to Cahokia Mounds from here in a perfectly straight line, are there any towns you might pass through, once you left the city?"

Joshua walked the route in his head. He was, to be honest, surprised at how easily it came to him. There were a handful of towns directly along the way. "I guess . . . Fairbury, Clinton, and Mount Auburn."

"In order, I assume."

"Yes. Eighty-nine miles away, one hundred and thirty-seven miles away, and one hundred and sixty-eight miles away. Mount Auburn is the smallest. It's very small. Only eight blocks by four blocks."

The old man threw his hands up. The bird on his desk fluttered into the air with a startled chirp. "Have you any idea of the absurdity of what you've just done? I've been to Cahokia many times but can only give you a passing idea of where it lies. Somewhere to the south and west, one or two hundred miles away. I couldn't name a thing along the way, except for corn."

"But I've studied the Midwest the most," said Joshua. "I don't know as much about other places."

"Nor do I. Madagascar, for instance. I can tell you it's an island, a rather large island—"

"The fourth largest in the world, if you don't count Australia."

"—a *very* large island, located on one side of Africa or the other."

Joshua spit out a laugh. "There are no big islands on the *west* side of Africa. Just the Canary Islands, and Cape Verde, and the islands along the Cameroon line. But all of them put together aren't anywhere near as big as Madagascar."

"You continue to make my point for me," Mr. Meister said with a smile. "Admittedly, I don't get out much, but I am positive that in all my many years, I have never heard anyone even utter the words 'the Cameroon line.'"

"Okay, so I'm smart about maps. So?"

"You are more than smart. You are preternaturally skilled. You are as talented with maps as Horace is with time. Do you know I once gave Horace a watch, so that he would know the time down to the second, should he have the need? But he did not have the need. Not because the occasion did not arise, but because he *already knows the time down to the second*. I have neither seen nor heard mention of that watch since I gave it to him." His smile turned to a thoughtful frown, and his eyes got faraway. "Indeed, if he does not want it, I would like to have that watch back. It was quite nice."

Joshua crossed his arms and slumped down even farther into the couch. "I know what you're trying to do," he said seriously. "You're trying to build up my confidence."

Mr. Meister roared with laughter. "That I am, yes. Is it working?"

"Not in the right way. I already know I'm good with maps, and directions, and distances. But what I'm not good at is the Laithe."

"So you say. I happen to disagree."

"I'm a Lostling."

"Everyone who goes through the Find feels lost at times. But a true Lostling is different. When a Keeper receives his Tan'ji from another—as opposed to Finding it on his own—a stagnation sometimes occurs. The Keeper becomes a Lostling."

"What's a stagnation?"

"A slowing down. A dulling. A loss of will and motivation, particularly when it comes to the new Tan'ji. This stagnation is often made worse by outside forces, who—seeking to help, or perhaps giving in to impatience—interfere with the natural process of the Find. The Lostling, in turn—being stagnated—may welcome this kind of interference."

"Well, *I* don't."

Mr. Meister's bushy eyebrows shot up. "No?"

"No. I don't even want to be talking to you right now."

"But I could teach you so much." Mr. Meister scooted closer. Behind the oraculum, his left eye leered at the Laithe. "I know all about the Laithe, after all. I can see things even you do not. I could tell you everything you need to know."

Joshua grabbed the Laithe out of the air and yanked it away, hugging it to his chest. "No."

"You do not want me to teach you?"

Joshua shook his head. He just wanted Mr. Meister to go away. He just wanted to be left alone with the Laithe, pretty much forever. And maybe that was stagnating, but he didn't care. "I don't want you to teach me."

"It would be so easy, though," Mr. Meister crooned. "I can teach you, and within the hour, you could be opening a portal back to the meadow, to rescue our companions."

Joshua caught his breath. Was this what the old man wanted from him? But Joshua had been ready to do that right away, back in the forest, and Mr. Meister had stopped him. "I can do that anyway," Joshua said. "I told you. I can open a portal back in the meadow right now."

"Certainly you could. Just as you've been taught already. But are our companions still in the meadow?"

Joshua hadn't thought about that. "I don't know."

"Let us imagine they are in the general area, at least. Let us imagine that our friends have taken refuge, and that you—through sheer luck, or intuition—open a portal a mere quarter mile from them. Will they see it?"

"They might."

"And there will be no Riven around, of course."

Joshua squirmed uncomfortably. "There might not be."

Mr. Meister snapped his fingers, as if he'd remembered something disappointing. "Oh, but even then—there is still the small matter of Dr. Jericho. Sensitive to any portal you might open, and swifter than any of us, by far. Shall we hope he has given up the hunt, and gone home?"

Joshua said nothing. Mr. Meister got louder, his eyes wild. "How close would you need to get, Keeper?"

"Closer," Joshua mumbled, unable to even look at him.

"How close? An eighth of a mile? Two hundred yards?"

"Closer, I guess."

"The Keeper of the Laithe does not guess. He knows. And he opens the portal precisely where he means to. Anywhere he wants to."

"I'll figure it out."

"It's easy. Let me show you. All you need to do is—"

"No!" Joshua shouted. He shot to his feet, still clutching the Laithe.

Mr. Meister leaned back. His face melted into kindness again. He watched Joshua silently.

"Stop it," said Joshua. "Just stop it."

"I have stopped," said Mr. Meister, holding up his hands.

"I said I don't want you to teach me."

"Good, because I will not." Mr. Meister stroked his chin, his eyes as sharp as ever. "Dr. Jericho made you an offer tonight, I believe," he said. "He asked you to join him."

Startled by this sudden shift, Joshua felt his anger fritter away. "No."

"Come now," Mr. Meister said, his voice full of gentle doubt. "That is his very purpose. To lure Keepers away, to bring powerful instruments into the Riven's fold. And the Laithe is very powerful. A great prize. There are few Tan'ji that the Riven desire more."

"Dr. Jericho didn't say anything like that to me."

"He offered you a kind of refuge. An assurance. A clean path through the Find."

It was true, of course. And it made Joshua sick to think it, but . . . he'd listened to the Mordin. He wasn't sure he'd actually considered the offer, but he hadn't *not* considered it either. He'd never be able to say that out loud, though. It was too terrible, and too true, to ever admit out loud. "It doesn't matter if he said that or not," Joshua muttered. "I'm here now."

"And is that what you want? To be here?"

"Is it what *you* want?" Joshua shot back.

Mr. Meister looked astonished. "Absolutely," he said. "Do not doubt it for a moment. I only press the matter because you are a target now, Joshua. If Dr. Jericho believes you are a Lostling, he also believes you are weak. Ripe for the picking. Easy to turn."

"But I'm not," Joshua said, as if trying the words on. "I hate the Riven."

"I'm sure you do, but be warned. The Find is always filled with despair, and the quick start you've been given likely means your finish line is all the more distant. You will encounter hours and days of deep misery and doubt—even long after such trials might seem behind you. And Dr. Jericho hopes that your desperation will lead you to consider paths you might otherwise ignore. Paths that you might, even now, insist you would never take."

"But I never would," Joshua insisted.

Maddeningly, Mr. Meister shrugged. "That is not for me to say. But I will say this—I have known true Lostlings, Joshua. Indeed, I played my own lamentable part in creating one, once."

"You . . . made a Lostling?"

Mr. Meister waved his words away, his face cloudy. "A story for another time. The point is, I feel compelled to tell you: you are no Lostling."

Joshua wanted to believe it, but wasn't sure he did. He wasn't even sure Mr. Meister believed it. "How do you know?" he asked.

"For one thing, you are far too curious."

"Why does that matter?"

"Only the curious can make their way through the wilderness of the Find. Only the curious will reap the rewards of discovery. Only the curious ever fully embrace becoming

Tan'ji." He cocked his head, looking at Joshua suspiciously. "You are a curious man, are you not?"

Joshua nodded, not even able to say yes. He nodded as hard as he could.

"Then it does not matter that Isabel put the Laithe in your hands. What matters is that you must put your mind into the Laithe. Embrace your questions. Discover the answers. This is the fire within which the bond of Tan'ji is forged. And when that bond is true, you will discover that you can embrace your fears, and your doubts, rather than hiding from them in the shadows. Do you understand?"

"I think so."

"I will not teach you to master the Laithe, but will answer questions you may have, if I can. Simple things."

Joshua was bursting with questions, but none of them had words. He looked at the Laithe, its moving clouds and ocean currents, its shining poles and rustling forests. He let the sight push aside thoughts of Lostlings, and the Riven, and days full of misery. "Just one question," he said. "How does the Laithe . . . *know*?"

Joshua wasn't even sure the question made sense, but Mr. Meister chuckled gently. "I ask for simple and you give me back an ocean. Perhaps one day you will meet Sil'falo Teneves, and she can answer that question herself." He bent forward, close to the floating Laithe, so close that his nose almost touched it. The shining globe threw sky light across his glasses, his wrinkled skin. "For now, remember this. The

Laithe is alive, Joshua. Or at any rate, it is a living projection of the earth as we know it. As we walk it. As we breathe it. It has limitations, yes. Limitations that are yours to discover. But you must not imagine that those limitations lie within *you*." He pressed a bony finger against Joshua's chest.

"Okay," Joshua said. "I'll try."

"Just so. Anything else?"

"No. You can leave me alone now."

Mr. Meister got to his feet at once. He laid a friendly hand on Joshua's shoulder. "Quite rude of you, Keeper. And quite proper."

Joshua nodded politely. "Thank you," he said. It seemed like the only thing to say.

"Experiment all you like. The Laithe is yours. But you must not pass through any portals you may open, under any circumstances. Are we agreed?"

"Agreed." Just saying it made Joshua feel older. Responsible.

The old man went to the door. He paused, as if thinking. "One last thing, Keeper. Not a lesson, but a point of trivia that might intrigue you. When Horace came to our warehouse for his Find, just two months ago, we offered him the Laithe."

Joshua stopped breathing.

Mr. Meister hummed, as if trying to remember. "He nearly chose it, I believe. He seemed quite interested in it."

"Why are you telling me this?" Joshua managed to ask. His hands were fists.

"Because of the only fact that ended up mattering." Mr. Meister gazed down at the hanging, spinning globe. "The Laithe was not interested in him."

And then he flashed Joshua a quick smile, and left them there alone.

CHAPTER TWENTY-FOUR

Up in the Air

HORACE SLEPT. HE DREAMED OF THE FEL'DAERA.

In his dream, the box was as big as a bed, and Horace lay down in it because the box had something to show him. It made him nervous, because he knew the box was meant to be empty—always empty—but the blue glass was cool and smooth and inviting. In his dream, Horace knew that if he fell asleep in the box he would wake up very small, and everyone would be able to crush him. People were already waiting to crush him, people as tall as trees—Dr. Jericho, Mr. Meister, a willowy figure that both was and was not Sil'falo Teneves. And so instead of sleeping in the box, he stayed awake and sat in it and drove it between the towering figures like a flying carpet, and everywhere he flew, great hands swatted at him but could not hit him. The box kept him safe.

Meanwhile, far below through the glass bottom of the

box, he could see a tiny blue earth. He drifted lower. He saw ocean, and cliffs, and island rocks covered in grass. He was sinking toward them, and he didn't know why. He tried to cling to the box, but it had become small again, and as he sank he knew that although the box couldn't carry him, it still meant to slow his fall, and that they must try to land on one of the soft islands on the little blue earth below, instead of the jagged rocks in the waves. But the box grew smaller and smaller. It became so small that he could barely grip it, until at last he hung by a single finger, and then that finger slipped—

Horace woke up, half choking on a sucked-in breath. He rolled over, and the mossy ground beneath him rippled, cushioning him. But not the ground, no.

He sat up. He was surrounded by nothing but pink early morning sky. He wasn't falling, of course. He was on the mal'gama.

Dailen sat a few feet away, watching him with those strangely ringed eyes. Chloe slept at Horace's side, curled into a ball.

"I trust you slept well, Keeper," Dailen said. "I always sleep best aboard the mal'gama, even a thousand feet in the air."

A good sleep, yes, except for that dream. Horace rubbed his arms, trying to shed it. He looked for the sun, wondering how long he'd been out. But even without the sun, he knew the time—6:45 in the morning. He'd only been asleep for a couple of hours.

Horace got up on his knees, the wind tugging at his hair. He could see the hazy horizon all around, far below. The sun was low to the east. He saw no recognizable markers—no Lake Michigan, no Chicago.

"Where are we?" he asked.

"Nearly there," said Dailen.

"There," Horace repeated. "You mean Ka'hoka?"

"Yes."

"So you're taking us after all."

"So it seems." Dailen had explained very little before Horace passed out, exhausted, revealing only that the mysterious Ka'hoka—a place neither Horace nor Chloe had ever heard of before—was another sanctuary like the Warren. Dailen hadn't been clear about just who or what that sanctuary held, but Horace gathered it was another stronghold of the Wardens. A group of Wardens somewhat different, he assumed, from the small, ragtag crew in Chicago.

"You're taking us to Ka'hoka even though I'm not supposed to exist," said Horace.

Dailen grimaced. "I should choose my words more carefully," he said. "What matters is that you *do* exist. The Fel'Daera has taken a Keeper. I can think of worse surprises."

"Thanks, that's . . . encouraging."

"Don't take offense. It's nothing to do with you."

"Is it because I'm human? Is that the problem?"

Dailen's perfect face spilt into a radiant smile. He laughed, a tinkling chorus. "You've been spending too much time with

362

the Riven," he said. "We Altari don't second-guess the Find, regardless of who it may come to."

"Then why were you so shocked when you saw the Fel'Daera?"

Dailen didn't answer right away. When he did, it was Horace's turn to be surprised. "I've met your Chief Taxonomer," the Altari said.

"Mr. Meister?"

"Yes. He strikes me as a man who chooses his words *very* carefully."

"You can say that again."

"And do you admire that about him?"

Horace wasn't sure how to answer. It seemed to him that Mr. Meister's job required a certain amount of caution—a large amount, to be fair—but it was hard not to resent certain secrets the old man had kept. Certain very big secrets, especially. "I'd rather know things than not know them," he said. "Even if knowing is hard."

Dailen's eyes seemed to glow. "Good," he said. "Then you should be aware your arrival at Ka'hoka will be . . . tumultuous."

"How do you mean?"

"You know the name Sil'falo Teneves."

Horace caught his breath. "She made the Fel'Daera. And the Laithe. She was the Keeper of the Starlit Loom."

"She *is* the Keeper," Dailen corrected.

"Wait . . . the Loom still exists?" Horace asked.

"Yes. As does Falo herself. And like all Makers, she has a bond with every instrument she's created. The bond isn't as strong as the bond of Tan'ji, but we like to say the bond of the Maker is lavro'dorval—the first bond and the last. It endures."

Horace couldn't help reaching out for the Fel'Daera in his mind, wondering if he could somehow feel the presence of Sil'falo Teneves there. He felt nothing . . . not that he knew how he would know. "What kind of bond is it?"

"Nothing you can feel. Or at least, nothing you would not have always felt. What matters in your case is that a Maker always knows when one of his or her creations has been Found."

"But that means . . . you're saying Falo knows I have the box." Horace felt suddenly naked. Like he was on a stage in front of an audience he had only just discovered. Could Falo feel him using the box? Feel his mistakes? He cringed at the thought.

"Falo certainly must know that someone possesses the Fel'Daera," said Dailen. "Just like she also knew last night that the Laithe had been . . ." His face went sour as he searched for a word, and then he shrugged, clearly looking for Horace to fill in the blanks.

"A boy named Joshua has the Laithe, but he didn't go through the Find," Horace said. "It was given to him."

"That explains it," Dailen said, his face growing even more sour. "Falo knew something was wrong and sent me to investigate. But instead I found you."

"And I was a surprise," said Horace. "Not the worst surprise you can think of, but not the best either."

Dailen ran three long fingers thoughtfully through the mal'gama. The stones flowed around them like obedient fish. "I don't know about good or bad," he said. "All I know is that Falo lied to me. She lied to all of us."

"Lied to you how?"

"There's no easy way to say this. To you, of all people."

"Then say it the hard way," Horace said, pushing a strength into his voice that he didn't feel at all.

Dailen cleared his throat, a melodic little drumroll. "Falo told us—she *assured* us—that the Fel'Daera had been destroyed."

Horace closed his eyes. The mal'gama rippled almost imperceptibly beneath him, coasting over the steady winds. *The Fel'Daera, destroyed.* An almost unthinkable thought. And that word—"assured." Dailen made it sound like the destruction of the Fel'Daera had been a desired thing. Horace felt suddenly, horribly alone.

He reached down and grasped Chloe's shoulder. Dailen watched in silence. "Hey," Horace said. "Wake up."

"Slumberbum," she mumbled.

"That's not a word," said Horace. "Wake up. I need you."

She opened her eyes. "What's happening?"

"I need you to hear. I need you to talk."

Chloe struggled to sit up. A splotchy red imprint of the mal'gama's stones had branded her cheek. She tugged gruesomely at the corners of her eyes, looking around. "You okay? Where are we?"

"Sky," said Horace impatiently. "Listen, Dailen and I have been talking. Sil'falo Teneves has been spreading the story that the Fel'Daera was . . . destroyed. And I get the sense . . ." He stopped, swallowing away a sudden hitch in his chest. "I get the sense it was generally considered good news."

Chloe frowned. "Why would she say that?" When Horace didn't—couldn't—answer, she turned to Dailen. "Why would that be good news?"

Dailen wrapped his arms around his long legs, looking sheepish. His head sat literally between his knees. "The Fel'Daera was created for a singular purpose. If it is not being used for that purpose—or so the reasoning goes—it has no reason to exist."

Horace looked away, but strained to hear every word. Chloe, perfect Chloe, asked the question he would have asked if he could have.

"And what is that singular purpose?"

"To help safeguard the Starlit Loom. The Fel'Daera was meant to always stay by the Loom's side. But when Falo last returned to Ka'hoka with the Loom, the Fel'Daera wasn't with her. She said it had been destroyed."

"Obviously, she lied," said Chloe. "And not only was the box not destroyed, but Falo actually left it with Mr. Meister. So he could find a new Keeper for it."

"As has come to pass," said Dailen, his eyes dropping again to Horace's side. He didn't look angry, or frightened. He looked disappointed. But in Horace, or something else? "We knew that Falo left the Laithe with Mr. Meister. But not the Fel'Daera."

"You sound pretty bummed about it," Chloe said. "What's the big deal? Why would it be good news if the Fel'Daera were destroyed?"

Horace looked at Dailen now, feeling as if he stood on the edge of a cliff, as if the mal'gama might open up beneath him and let him plummet to the earth below. There were answers to this question; he knew it in his bones. Answers that weren't wrong. He suddenly thought he might vomit.

Dailen, grimacing reluctantly, took a long time answering. "No doubt you'll hear the arguments when we reach Ka'hoka. You must understand that for some among the Altari, Falo is our Oppenheimer."

"Who's that?"

Horace rocked himself back and forth. "He was the father of the nuclear bomb," he muttered.

"That's insane," said Chloe. "The box is a time machine, not a bomb."

"I don't wish to debate the point," Dailen said. "Falo is my friend. But just to make the thinking clear, imagine for a moment that the Riven got hold of the box. What might they be able to achieve, once they know what the future holds? For instance, would we have made it out of the meadow last night if some box-wielding Riven with the proper talent had seen our escape in advance?"

"But they won't get the box," Chloe said stubbornly. "Ever."

Dailen raised his thin, graceful eyebrows. "Truly?" he said, and turned to Horace. "Is that what the future tells you?"

Horace, awash with shuddering emotion, hated and believed every word the Altari spoke. The truth was, the Riven *had* nearly stolen the box. On one occasion, in fact, Dr. Jericho had actually taken it from Horace, and only the Mordin's arrogance had allowed the Wardens to prevail, saving the Fel'Daera.

Or no.

Not quite right.

It was only because of the future the Fel'Daera revealed that Horace had brought the box to Dr. Jericho in the first place. The box was never in any danger that Horace himself had not foreseen, and permitted. He had witnessed the future and then walked the willed path, the path upon which the box was lost . . . and then *found*.

He straightened and looked Dailen in the eye. "If the box is as powerful as you're suggesting," said Horace, "I won't lose it."

Dailen studied him for ten long seconds, nodding almost imperceptibly. "How skilled are you?" he said at last.

"Compared to what?"

Abruptly, the mal'gama began to slow. Horace and Chloe braced themselves, trying not to topple over. The mal'gama came to a complete halt, suspended in the air. Dailen stood up, towering above them. He backed away. Beneath them, the mal'gama began to shift. The protective cone at the front dismantled itself and the floor slid and spread. It rolled beneath them like a tide of fuzzy marbles. Soon Horace and Chloe were seated in the middle of a green circle with no walls, fifty feet across, surrounded by nothing but pink-blue sky overhead and the perfect hazy circle of the horizon all around.

"Stand," said Dailen.

Horace stood, getting it at once. He was ready. He pulled the Fel'Daera from its pouch.

"Have you mastered the breach?" asked Dailen.

The question surprised Horace, but he didn't let it show. Falo must have been a good friend indeed to have shared a detail like that with Dailen. "I have," Horace said.

"Six seconds?"

Six seconds was at the lower limit of what Horace had managed with the breach. He'd never gone below four. He nodded, and took hold of the silver sun with his mind. He found the opening of the breach quickly, and began to close it with the newfound ease his mother's tuning had provided. From nine minutes and forty-four seconds, he effortlessly shrank the opening down to six seconds exactly, and pinned it in place.

"Done," he said.

If Dailen was impressed, he didn't show it. "Now me," he said, his curious eyes glowing. He split in two—a second

Dailen splitting off from the first, the new one beginning to trot in a circle around Horace and Chloe. As he moved, the running Dailen split again, leaving another stationary Dailen behind. Again and again he split, a new Dailen springing into existence every thirty degrees or so. At last, twelve Dailens stood there, forming a complete ring around them.

"You know I'd never give up the Alvalaithen," Chloe murmured to Horace. "But if I *had* to trade . . ."

The Dailens began to speak. The words came out normally, fluidly. But as if by magic, each Dailen spoke only a single word, so that the single voice that spoke to them—out of a dozen mouths in turn—seemed to be whizzing around them. "When you are ready, open the Fel'Daera and look into the future." Twelve words, twelve mouths. When the last Dailen had spoken, he started again, and the voice swept in the other direction. "In the next several seconds, one of me will cease to exist." In unison, the twelve Dailens all turned around, facing outward. "Witness the future, and then point to the Dailen that will vanish."

"One of you is going to disappear, and Horace just has to see which one?" said Chloe. "This is too easy."

All twelve Dailens looked back over their shoulders at Horace, smiling. "Go," they said together.

Dizzied by the display, but not wanting to appear more impressed by Dailen than Dailen had been by him, Horace readied himself.

"When I say go," he said.

The Dailens nodded and looked away.

Horace gathered the threads of the moment together—this path, this chain of events, these moving ripples on the river of time. Dailen's challenge, his power, Horace's own power. When he was centered, Horace raised the box. "I'm looking . . . *now*," he said, opening the lid. He began to spin slowly, watching the encircling Dailens through the glass. And through that glass—*Dailen after Dailen, tall and still, crisp and clear.* The future looked certain, at any rate. Three seconds passed. Four. Suddenly, more than halfway around the circle—*a Dailen disappearing, winking out of sight.* There was no mistaking it. "I see it, no problem," Horace said calmly, pointing with one hand. With the other, he flicked the box closed and dropped it to his side. "Right there."

Less than two seconds after he spoke, the Dailen in question vanished as if deleted.

"Was that supposed to be tricky?" said Chloe, watching.

Horace started to shake his head, but in that very moment, someone snatched the Fel'Daera from his hand.

He whirled around, shocked and fuming. The Dailen from the opposite side of the circle stood there, having sprung forward and grabbed the box with ease. He held it high in the air, smiling down at Horace with a kindly look of apologetic triumph.

"Forgive the trespass, please," Dailen said, and handed the Fel'Daera back to Horace at once. "Merely trying to make a point."

Horace seized the box, embarrassed and outraged. "But that wasn't fair."

The other ten Dailens evaporated, leaving just the one, pressing a hand to his injured chest in mock offense. "Fair? I've never known Ja'raka Sevlo to be fair. Does he give you do-overs?"

"No, but . . ." Horace kicked at the ground. The Altari had outsmarted him, and he knew it. "No. He doesn't."

"That was pretty sneaky," said Chloe. "Are all the Altari this sneaky?"

Dailen knelt down. "My apologies, Horace, please. I hope you'll see nothing but friendship in this little show. When we get to Ka'hoka, expect the Wardens' Council to test you far more harshly than I just did."

The Wardens' Council. Horace didn't much like the sound of that, but he was too frazzled to ask. He slid the Fel'Daera back into its pouch. "I'd like to think that if I'd known how sneaky you were, I'd have seen what you were planning to do."

"Me too. All the more reason to be prepared for the Council. Not every Altari is sneaky, but some are downright devious."

Now Horace had a terrible thought. If this Council was glad that the Fel'Daera was gone, what were they going to do when they found out it still existed? "Wait a minute," he said. "Am I in danger going to Ka'hoka? Is the box in danger?"

Chloe stepped up beside him. He could practically feel her bristling protectively.

"In what way?" asked Dailen.

"The obvious way," said Chloe. "The same way that Frankenstein's monster would be in danger if he wandered into a frightened village."

"No, no," said Dailen. "There's a big difference between being concerned about an instrument's power and wanting to destroy it. Willfully destroying a Tan'ji is criminal."

"Then is there some other way Horace might be in danger?" Chloe insisted.

"I won't say that. But I will suggest that you do your best to pass whatever tests the Council gives you."

Chloe balled her fists. "Or else what?"

Horace was hardly listening. Despite what had just happened, he wasn't worried about passing some test. He was the rightful Keeper of the Fel'Daera. He was distracted by something the Altari had just said. "You said destroying a Tan'ji is criminal," he told Dailen. "But you guys thought it already *had* been destroyed, so Falo must have invented some kind of story. Who did she say destroyed it?"

Dailen took a deep breath and let it out slow. "I won't tell you that."

"Why not?" Horace objected. "You said knowing is better than not knowing."

"Actually, you said that. And I do agree, but I can't really give you any knowledge here. The story Falo told us, even though it was a lie, has to be partly true. And since I don't know where the truth ends and the lies begin, we would only be guessing."

"Why does her story have to be partly true?" Horace asked.

But Dailen shook his head, his face dark. "The history of the Fel'Daera is not mine to tell." He turned away. The mal'gama began to move again. The breeze strengthened, coursing over them. The front edge folded once more into a cone.

"It was the last Keeper, wasn't it?" Horace asked. Just admitting that the Fel'Daera had once belonged to another was still hard for him. But he'd gotten plenty of little hints, dark suggestions. Something bad had happened. And logically speaking, it must have been something so bad that the destruction of the precious Fel'Daera might very well have been a part of it.

Dailen said, "If no one has yet told you that story, I won't do it now. And I already told you, I don't know the truth. But I will say this." He turned to face Horace again, his sad and hopeful eyes full of worry. "Some tales are better left unheard."

CHAPTER TWENTY—FIVE

The Well of Giving

CHLOE WASN'T WORRIED. NOT EXACTLY.

Sure, she was a thousand feet in the air, riding a giant flying carpet piloted by an eight-foot-tall Altari who could multiply himself, and she and Horace were headed to a mysterious new place where the Fel'Daera wouldn't exactly be welcome. Still, she wasn't worried. Concerned? Maybe. Alert? Definitely.

She watched Dailen, trying not to be too obvious about it. Although she didn't normally think in these terms, he was magnificent to look at. He was every bit as pretty as the Riven were revolting. Maybe more. She sort of hated it about him. And he was different from the other Wardens, too, not because he was Altari, but because he was a fighter. His power wasn't meant for hiding or observing. It was meant for getting dirty. She couldn't help but admire the way Dailen had stood his ground with the Riven in the meadow, fending them off single-handedly. Well, not quite single-handedly, but still. Maybe if there were more Wardens like Dailen, this whole war would have been over by now.

Of course, she would never have said any of this out loud. Not in a million years.

"So this Council you were talking about," she said. "What are they going to do to us? Pass judgment, or whatever?"

Dailen turned to her. The circles of light in his eyes seemed to glow. "No, not really," he replied. "The Council will likely want to see you demonstrate your powers. And as with all visitors, they will decide what you can and cannot see in Ka'hoka, where you can and cannot go."

Chloe grunted. She didn't much like people telling her where she couldn't go—not that they could stop her anyway.

"What about Falo?" Horace asked. "She'll definitely be there?"

"She will. I'm sure she'll want to meet you."

"Is she on the Council?"

"Falo is the Keeper of the Starlit Loom. She does not answer to Councils."

"Then why should *we*?" asked Chloe.

Dailen laughed. "Why indeed?" he said. "Tell me, Keeper, what is the name of your Tan'ji?"

Startled by the question, Chloe stuck out her jaw. "The Alvalaithen."

"The Earthwing," Dailen said, surprising her again. But

apparently he was only translating, because then he added, "I have never heard of it."

"What's the name of *your* Tan'ji?" she shot back. "I've probably never heard of it either."

"Few have," said Dailen. "But I'm not beyond sharing." Dailen stood and unbuttoned the top two buttons on his torn, high-collared robe. He bared his lean shoulders. The three deep scratches from Dr. Jericho had made—slashes, really—looked shockingly red against his pale skin. Chloe got yet another surprise as she glimpsed a jithandra, hanging from the usual long chain. But that obviously wasn't what he wanted them to see.

At the bottom of his neck, a segmented band made of battered black metal wrapped tightly around his throat. It was plainly Tan'ji, plainly ancient. Each section was a rectangular slab about the size of a domino, each one etched with a different symbol, inlaid in fading gold. Horace, predictably, moved closer to get a better look.

"This is Floriel," said Dailen. "Forged over the Starlit Loom, long before Falo's days."

Chloe wouldn't let herself be impressed. It seemed to her that practically everyone she knew had a Tan'ji made with the Starlit Loom. She held out the dragonfly. "Likewise."

Now it was Dailen's turn to look surprised. His strange eyes roved over Chloe, taking in the mottled skin around her throat and the large dark patches on her forearm. She didn't mind. She wasn't ashamed of her scars. But then Dailen rolled up his own sleeve, uncovering an enormous red welt, a foot long and raised. "It seems you and I have something else in common, Keeper," he said. "Floriel has brought me more than my share of scars."

Chloe considered him, then lifted up one side of her shirt just high enough to reveal yet another wound, a permanent red welt—much like Dailen's—across her torso. She'd gotten this one weeks ago, while battling through the golem in the House of Answers. "Again, likewise," she said.

"Whoa!" said Horace. "You're hurt again. What happened?"

Chloe looked down at herself. Horace wasn't talking about the old wound; he'd been there when that happened. Instead he was looking at the purpling bruises on her ribs, obviously fresh and shaped suspiciously like long fingers. She yanked her shirt down, wincing. "Oh, yeah. Dr. Jericho popped a rib last night. But don't worry, I set it while you were sleeping."

"Set it?"

"Yeah, you know." She let the wings of the dragonfly flicker. She made a pinching motion at her side. "Everything's back in one piece now."

Horace just stared at her like she was crazy. So she'd melded her own rib back together again, reaching into her torso while thin. It was easy, once she got the alignment right. Just the very edges, not too much. There'd been a lot of pain the moment she released the Alvalaithen, and the bone actually knitted together—like a tiny punch hitting her at a

378

hundred miles an hour—but it felt much better now. Mostly.

Dailen, meanwhile, seemed unconcerned. He watched her with genuine interest. "Tell me, Keeper," he sang. "Can you be killed?"

"Wow, is that your icebreaker? Very charming."

"I mean it. What if, for example, you were to fall from the mal'gama down to earth?" As he spoke, a hole as wide as a bed suddenly broke open in the mal'gama, a few feet away from Chloe. Wind blasted through it, ruffling her hair. "Could you survive?"

Chloe barely glanced at the hole, at the quilted green countryside hundreds of feet below. "Yes," she said. "I mean, I've never done it, but I'm pretty sure I could survive any fall. Go thin before I hit, slow myself inside the earth, wing my way back up."

"Holy creeping cow," said Horace, sounding horrified. Frankly, she was surprised he'd never thought of it.

"What about you?" Chloe asked Dailen. "You can be injured while you're doing your doppelgänger thing. Let's say a train hits one of you, or a tree falls on one of you. Do you die?"

"I can vacate a variant more quickly than you could pull a hand from a fire. It's a reflex, like a flinch. I'm usually out before any serious damage can be done."

"What if you got hit by lightning? Even you aren't that fast."

"If one of my variants were to die, a part of me would die too."

Horace spoke up. "But that's never happened, right?"

"Floriel has sixteen stones, each one named. With each, I can produce a variant of myself." Dailen turned slowly, revealing the rest of his Tan'ji. The black tiles went all the way around, but just at the neck of his nape, a single tile was gleaming white. "Last year I lost Ne'vele. I wasn't fast enough. Now that variant is gone forever."

"Gone," Horace said hoarsely. "Like dead. And a part of you died too."

Dailen turned back around, buttoning his robe again, covering Floriel. "Yes. I lost certain memories. A skill or two." He smiled again. "I'm told I also lost some of my caution, which I didn't have in abundance to begin with."

"But how do you . . . how can you even . . ." Horace was stammering. Not for the first time, Chloe wondered how exhausting it must be to be filled with so many questions all the time. "Sixteen variants," Horace said. "Or fifteen, sorry. And they're all you."

"All me."

"And you can keep track of all those versions of yourself," said Horace.

"Yes. It's like juggling. Or to put it better, if this makes sense, it's like playing several games of chess at once, but moving so quickly between the boards that you're hardly ever missed at any of them."

Chloe couldn't help herself. "Were you away from the board when you lost Ne'leve?"

"Briefly. It's a mistake I won't make again." The tone of Dailen's voice suggested he didn't want to discuss it further.

But Chloe pressed on. "How did you die?" she asked. It was a strangely delicious sort of question, one she'd probably never have the chance to ask anyone again.

Dailen hesitated, then broke into another luminous smile. "Tree fell on me."

She let herself smile back at him. "Did it hurt?"

"Very much."

"Good," Chloe said matter-of-factly. But then, realizing how that must sound, she tried to clarify. Reluctantly, she found herself liking this Dailen, wanting to trust him and wanting—as much as she hated to admit it—him to like her. "I mean, of course it did. I've had my share of trees."

Dailen bowed. "I've no doubt that's true." Then he looked down through the hole still yawning in the mal'gama. "We are there."

Chloe leaned over. Below, she saw part of a lake, and a highway, and thick clumps of forest surrounding fields lined with trails. There were hills there too, strange-looking hills.

A lurch in her stomach told her that the mal'gama was beginning to descend. It was some kind of park they were approaching now. She saw what looked like a visitors' center, and a parking lot, and people walking trails below.

"It seems like somebody might notice a giant flying carpet coming down out of the sky," she remarked.

"Don't worry," said Dailen. "The mal'gama can't be seen

from below if I don't want it to be."

The hole in the mal'gama closed itself with a rustle. They continued to descend. Eventually they dropped below the tops of trees, into a forest. The mal'gama rearranged itself smoothly, sliding silently down through the branches like melting snow. They landed in a small clearing on the edge of the woods, away from the trails and the cars. The mal'gama became a soft green carpet again, spread throughout the trees like a blanket of moss. Dailen stepped lightly off onto the ground.

"Welcome to Ka'hoka," he said.

"Where?" said Chloe. There was nothing here but trees.

"All around us. Beneath us, actually. It's not the city it once was—most of the smaller sanctuaries are abandoned now—but it's still the largest gathering of Wardens anywhere in the world."

Horace was gazing off through the trees. In the distance, beyond the woods, two of the strange little hills Chloe had seen earlier rose out of a wide flat lawn, like noses on a face. Definitely not natural.

"Wait a minute," said Horace. "I know this place. This is Cahokia Mounds."

"That's another name, yes," said Dailen.

"My parents brought me here. It's like an old Native American site. A city, or something."

"For a while it was. Long ago, it was the largest city on the continent. But it's been ours alone for nearly seven hundred years now."

Chloe had read about Cahokia Mounds. They were still in Illinois, just on the other side of the Mississippi River from St. Louis. But yikes. "Seven hundred years," she repeated, trying to grasp it. "And the Altari have been here all that time?"

"Yes," said Dailen. "And actually, we were here long before that. The humans who lived here came and built their city on top of us. They . . . had dealings with us. But then the floods came. Famine. Disease. The city above was abandoned, but we remained below."

"You say that like you were actually there when it happened," Chloe said.

"Don't be silly. How old do you think I am?"

"I honestly don't have the slightest idea. You might as well ask me how tall I think God is."

"I'm barely an adult," Dailen said. "Basically still a teenager, by your way of thinking."

That was a surprise. And not a terrible one. "How many years is that?"

"We don't usually talk about age. We don't celebrate birthdays. But if numbers make you feel better, multiply human years by four or five to get Altari years. Roughly."

"So, you're like eighty or ninety," said Horace. "Roughly."

"I told you, we don't keep track. I'm young. If you want to see *really* old, wait till you meet Falo." Half of Dailen's face wrinkled doubtfully, and he added, "Don't tell her I said that." Then he turned away, heading off through the woods. "There's an entrance just ahead. Let's go."

They moved deeper into the trees. The mal'gama gathered itself and moved behind them like a great green ghost. In short order, they came upon a small, shallow lake. A weak, wispy fog hung over the morning water. A black island stood dead in the middle of the water, bristling with tall, spiky evergreens. Dailen didn't speak, but the mal'gama slid past them and laid itself down over the surface of the water, making itself long and narrow, creating a bridge. The Altari led the way.

The island was even smaller than it looked, barely as big across as a small house, and perfectly round. The ground was spongy under Chloe's feet. Passing through the dense trees that ringed it, they came upon a round pool at its center, deep and black and perhaps twenty feet across. The island forest, tall and straight, rose high overhead, surrounding the pool like a stockade.

Gracefully, Dailen pulled out his jithandra. Its crystal, longer than the ones on the jithandras they used at the Warren, glowed with a reddish-purple light, a kind of vibrant magenta. And instead of emerging from silver flower petals, this crystal was mounted in a miniature cluster of bare, black tree branches.

"Follow me," Dailen said. "Do as I say. This may seem familiar at first, but then it won't." He dipped the crystal into the pool, and the water—just like in Vithra's Eye—began to solidify around it with a crackling gurgle. He stepped out onto this new surface, moving the dangling jithandra into open water ahead. Horace followed him, and Chloe came behind, inching out onto the walkway.

After just a few steps, Dailen halted near the center of the pool. "Now the fun part," he said. He leaned forward, and with a graceful, practiced sway, swung the jithandra in a wide circle through the open water ahead. In the crystal's rippling wake, the surface of the water solidified, creating a ring in the center of the pool with an even smaller pool inside, three feet across.

"*Koltro sis'koltro,*" said Dailen. "Rings within rings." After a moment, there was a rumble and a thud beneath them somewhere. And all at once the water inside the newly formed ring dropped away with a deep gurgle. No swirling, no sloshing. The water just fell, revealing a dark shaft that plunged straight into the ground.

"Wow," said Horace. Chloe, unable to find a way to be unimpressed, said nothing.

"Quickly, before the walkway dissolves again," said Dailen. "There are handholds in the wall. They'll be slick, so be careful. When you get to the bottom, make room for the mal'gama." He swung his long legs over the edge and disappeared swiftly into the hole.

Horace hesitated, peering into the dark shaft.

"We could bail, you know," Chloe said, watching him. "You don't have to do this." She knew he was going to do it, but as a matter of practice she felt Horace needed to be reminded now and again that options were available. Just knowing other choices were there made the main thing that much easier.

But Horace simply pulled his jithandra out of his shirt. "I can't bail," he said. "And neither can you. There's a Mothergate here." And then, before Chloe could respond or even react, he climbed awkwardly over the edge and disappeared into the earth.

A Mothergate. One of the three mysterious artifacts that powered all Tanu. And supposedly it was dying—whatever that actually meant. Chloe remembered Horace's mom explaining how she could feel the Mothergates. She'd even pointed at them. Two of the Mothergates were far away—halfway around the world—but one was much closer. A couple hundred miles, she'd said. Could she have meant here? Horace obviously seemed to think so. And when Horace sounded sure of something, he was almost never wrong.

Chloe scampered to follow him, annoyed with him for dropping his little bombshell without giving her a chance to answer. The shaft down through the pool was not quite as cramped as it looked, but she could hear Horace nearly wheezing below her. The rungs were cutouts in the stone, wet and cold. They descended thirty feet, maybe, until the shaft ended in a tunnel running left and right. The passageway was tall but narrow—built for Altari, obviously.

As she alighted, Chloe gazed meaningfully at Horace. He avoided her eyes. *Fine*. If he wasn't going to ask Dailen about the Mothergate, she could go along with that for a little while.

But eventually someone would have to say something.

"Make way," said Dailen, backing up. They stepped away, and the hazy sunlight streaming in from overhead winked out, eclipsed by the mal'gama. Their jithandras—red, blue, magenta—lit the huge Tanu as it poured slowly into the tunnel after them, like lumpy green molasses. Moments later, there was another *thud* from above, and the sound of rushing water. Dailen's ring-shaped walkway had dissolved, and now the pool was refilling itself, hiding the entrance once again.

Dailen turned. "This way."

The floor of the passage sloped gently downward as they walked. The ceiling, though, remained level, so that as they walked, it got higher and higher until it could no longer be seen by the light of their jithandras.

Horace, walking steadily in front of Chloe, gazed up into the shadows. "Is the Nevren here in Ka'hoka?" he asked. "Or will there be something else?"

Dailen cocked his head. "Something else?"

"You know, like . . ." Horace trailed off, and glanced back at the mal'gama coursing through the tunnel behind them. "In the Warren, there's a . . ."

"A what?" said Chloe. She had no idea what he was getting at.

But now Dailen apparently understood. He stopped and turned. "So it's true," he said. "The Chief Taxonomer has embraced the sa'halvasa."

387

"What are you guys talking about?" said Chloe.

Horace told her the tale. Mr. Meister's multiple Tan'ji. Sanguine Hall, the Warren's elusive back entrance. A swarm of tiny, deadly Tanu. The Fel'Daera, screaming as the sa'halvasa feasted on it. Chloe hoped her face looked as horrified as she felt. She looked up into the shadowy heights overhead, as if the little scythe things would come after them here.

"I confess I've always wanted to witness the sa'halvasa," said Dailen. "It's related to the golem and the mal'gama, as you might have guessed, but it's the wildest of the three. It has no heart. It takes no leash." He shook his head. "But to actually *remove* the Nevren . . ." He sounded not so much worried as disgusted.

"So, there used to be a Nevren in Sanguine Hall?" Horace asked.

"Yes."

"Is it safe using the sa'halvasa instead of the Nevren?"

Dailen shrugged. "It's hard to imagine any Riven being able to endure the sa'halvasa. And of course, they'd have to find the Warren first. Still, the Nevren is the surest way to keep out the Riven. We would never rely on the sa'halvasa here in Ka'hoka. We have several Nevren scattered throughout the city, in fact. But we'll only have to pass through one to get where we're going. Goth en'Sethra, it's called."

Chloe checked Horace's face. It was stony. "Great, it's got a name," she said. "Probably just a tiny little Nevren, then."

"Goth en'Sethra is the most powerful Nevren in existence," said Dailen.

"Oh," said Chloe. "Or that."

"Goth en'Sethra," said Horace. "What does that mean?"

"It doesn't translate exactly—the Well of Sacrifice, the Well of Giving. I should warn you that it's a bit different than other Nevrens you've encountered. And it's ungated, so you may find it shocking at first."

Horace and Chloe exchanged a confused glance. "Ungated?" said Horace.

"Yes, it's—" Dailen began, then frowned. "You know what the Nevren *is*, yes? How it works?"

"It's some kind of energy field," Horace said.

"But you don't know what creates that field?"

"We never got the handbook, sorry," said Chloe.

Dailen seemed to consider it, then actually knelt on the ground, so that his face was level with theirs. He didn't invite them to do the same, apparently wanting to look them in the eye. "I assume you know that the bond of Tan'ji can be destroyed in many ways," he said.

"Dispossession," said Horace. "Cleaving."

"Yes, to name just two. One slow, one swift. Either the bond withers away because of prolonged severing, or it is forcibly torn apart. But certain Keepers find another end. A sort of end."

"What else is there?" Horace asked. Chloe suspected he was thinking about the Mothergates again. Or maybe the last Keeper of the Fel'Daera.

Dailen bent his head and said, almost reverentially, "Fusion."

"Fusion?" Horace repeated. "Like nuclear fusion? Things being put together?"

"Not nuclear, no. But yes—being put together. It's when a Keeper and his Tan'ji get fused into one. One entity. One being. One . . . instrument, if you like."

No one spoke for a moment. Chloe twirled the Alvalaithen madly. What was Dailen saying?

"You mean physically?" Horace asked. "Like the Riven?"

"No, it's like a permanent and irrevocable bond with the Medium."

"But *how*?" said Horace.

"Essentially, the Tan'ji—the unified Keeper and instrument, that is—starts drawing in great quantities of the Medium. Massive amounts, dangerous amounts, looping from Keeper to instrument over and over without release. Eventually the whole system basically implodes. It collapses on itself. It forms a kind of loop, and this loop is actually a hole—you might imagine it as being kind of black hole. It's so powerful that it sucks into itself every last bit of the Medium nearby. Any Tanu that come close to the fused Tan'ji cease to function." Dailen watched them for a moment, letting them digest it, and then said, "Sound familiar?"

Horace said, "Wait, so are you saying this hole—this collapsed Tan'ji—that's the Nevren?"

"That's what makes the Nevren, yes. It consumes the Medium all around, like a black hole consumes light. And without the Medium, no Tanu can function. No Keeper can even connect to his or her instrument." Dailen shrugged. "And there's your Nevren."

Chloe hardly knew how to respond, fascinated and horrified at the same time. "But what about the Keeper?" she said. "Does the Keeper die?"

"No. But after the fusion, it is hard to say that they live, either. Not in the way you are used to thinking of it."

"Then what happens?" Chloe demanded.

"The Keeper . . . remains," Dailen said. "Kept in a kind of stasis by the Medium. Outside of knowing, outside of time." He watched them warily, his strange ringed eyes sad. "Wherever you find the Nevren, that's the source. There's a Keeper at the core, usually kept in a chamber underground. Fused for all eternity."

Chloe strode forward, hardly thinking, red with rage. She stepped up to Dailen, reared back, and slapped him, hard, right across the face. The sound of the slap echoed smartly through the tunnel. Dailen left his head where the slap had thrown it, curled against his shoulder, looking strangely childish. A red welt began to bloom across his white cheek.

"Chloe," Horace said low. "That's not what anybody here deserved."

Chloe whirled toward him. "Don't you think I know that?" she shouted, and then she spun back to Dailen. "Don't *you* think I know?"

She couldn't even name her anger. Not that she needed to. She thought back to the first time she and Horace had passed through the Nevren, behind the House of Answers. She remembered walking across hollow metal plates in the floor. And now she was afraid she understood—there had been a Keeper beneath those plates, fused to her instrument, imprisoned forever in the dark, outside of time and light and knowing. The thought made her want to puke.

"I know it sounds dreadful," said Dailen. "I won't try to convince you to understand this gift the way we Altari do. But only a willing Keeper can be fused."

"You're right," said Chloe. "You shouldn't try to convince me."

Horace spoke, his own voice shaky too. "Wait, so the lake in the Great Burrow—Vithra's Eye. There's a fused Keeper out there in the center of that?"

Chloe pictured it—the forbidden brick walkway that led across the center of the lake. Somewhere out there in the darkness . . . what? Another pit covered in steel plates? A cage? She hated to imagine.

"Yes," said Dailen. "But just to be clear, Vithra's Eye isn't the name of the lake. It's the name of the Nevren."

Chloe said, "And Vithra is name of the Keeper who's trapped there."

"Vithra remains there, yes. She fused herself. She . . . gave herself, and her Tan'ji. She became the Nevren."

"To protect the Warren."

"Yes. To protect those who took refuge there."

"When did that happen?"

"I'm not sure. Well over a century ago. Before the American Civil War."

"And ever since, she's just been . . . there. Remaining."

"Yes. But there is no suffering. It's a kind of sleep, a meditation. A oneness."

Chloe looked over at Horace. She recognized the look on his face at once, a sort of tightly bundled thoughtfulness that meant he'd figured something out before she did. "What?" she said.

"Ungated," he murmured, and turned to Dailen. "This Nevren up ahead. The Well of Giving. The Keeper there isn't caged, is that what you're saying? We'll see him. Or her."

Dailen stood, his face stony and smooth, his reddish-purple jithandra swinging in the dark. "Them," he corrected. And then he turned and continued down the passageway.

Horace and Chloe followed him in silence, each wrapped in their own thoughts. The mal'gama tumbled after them. If Chloe was understanding Dailen correctly, there was more than one fused Keeper in the Nevren up ahead. And they would be visible. She couldn't explain to herself why the idea angered her so much, why she'd slapped Dailen. She wasn't opposed to sacrifice, not at all. But dead was supposed to mean dead. Gone was supposed to mean gone.

She had no idea how long they walked. It was hard knowing such things underground, where you could only see twenty feet ahead and twenty feet behind. It was like walking a treadmill, with no sense of progress. But gradually she became aware that the passageway had widened and that they seemed to be in a natural cavern now. A big one, the walls and ceiling all lost to shadow, the echoes of their footsteps coming back slow and tinny. Dailen had pulled far away, a spindly but graceful silhouette inside a cloud of magenta light. At last he stopped. A moment later, just beyond him, four amber lights like those in the Warren began to glow, forming the corners of a broad, dark square that seemed to almost shine in the new light.

"I think maybe we're here," Chloe said.

They caught up to Dailen and found him standing by the edge of a square pool, fifty feet across. The water was as smooth as the water in Vithra's Eye, but whereas that water was black, this had a more silvery sheen. And there was something else, too. A massive chain, thick as a man's torso, descended from the shadows above and plunged down through the center of the square pool, into its own faintly rippling reflection. Chloe stepped right up to the edge of the water, which was paved with broad, flat stones. Each of the stones, she noticed, was engraved with a ferocious-looking bird. Leestones, undoubtedly. She stood on one and peered into the water. Her own face shone back at her, quivering dreamily, reflected on the gently undulating surface of the pool.

"Welcome to Goth en'Sethra," Dailen said. "The Well of Giving."

"Are we supposed to swim, or what?" Chloe said.

Dailen laughed kindly. "There is no water here." He

stooped to pick up a small rock and tossed it into the well. The rock hit the water with a thin clatter, skittering and sliding over the surface.

Not water. Glass. Glass or something like it. Dailen stepped out onto it, onto his own gleaming reflection. He strode out halfway to the huge chain, and beckoned them to follow.

Chloe frowned at the glass, and the massive chain. "Is this like an elevator?" If so, it was the biggest elevator she'd ever seen, big enough to carry an entire house.

"In a way," said Dailen. "Come on. Let me show you."

She and Horace walked out onto the glass. Their footsteps made delicate ripples, as if they really were walking on water. But the glass felt as solid underfoot as steel.

"What is this stuff?" asked Horace.

"This is a mir'aji," said Dailen. "It forms the mouth and the belly of Goth en'Sethra."

"Sounds very gastronomical," said Chloe. "Not very comforting."

"Oh, were you looking for comfort?" Dailen said. "Because sanctuaries that chose comfort over security have long since been overrun by the Riven."

"I get it, I get it," Chloe said. "Let's get it over with, then. Where's the down button on this thing?"

"I have it." Dailen removed his jithandra once again, letting it dangle over the mirror. "Ready?" he said.

Chloe glanced at Horace, feeling a sudden burble of

dread. "This is going to suck, isn't it?" she asked Dailen.

"Yes," said the Altari. He lowered the jithandra. Horace made a little noise of surprise, and Chloe thought she knew why. Dailen's purple-red crystal cast no reflection in the mir'aji. "Close your eyes if you like," Dailen said, watching it. "If you can." The tip of the crystal touched the strange glass and then pierced it silently, like a needle into flesh. The entire expanse of glass shimmered crimson for an instant . . . and then vanished beneath their feet.

They fell.

Chloe shrieked, pinwheeling her arms, as she plummeted into the suddenly open well. The massive chain stretched far below them—very, *very* far below—where a distant square of golden light glowed in the impossible depths. Chloe drank from the Alvalaithen as she fell, panicking, but no sooner had she gone thin than she went bone-cold, and the Alvalaithen was wrested from her. It was gone, utterly gone, her powers unreachable.

The Nevren.

The loss was so sudden that she almost forgot she was falling. Her skin tightened painfully in the cold. Or someone's skin, anyway. She couldn't close her eyes, not because of fear but because they weren't hers to close. Whose eyes even were they? But there were still sights here in the frozen dark—tall shapes, strung from the central chain. Bodies. Long limbed and pale. They seemed to be sleeping, curled into balls, each one clasping an object to its chest. She began to see faces—long and lean, smooth and peaceful, eyes mercifully closed.

She curled into a ball herself as she fell, clutching at her own chest. She had something too, she knew. Or she once had. Something that was absent now. Despair choked her. The Nevren had taken everything she was. But still the greedy force pulled at her, tore at her as she sped past the motionless, sightless forms. And was she falling, or were they rising? Was there a difference?

The string of dangling figures—a dozen, two dozen—rose into the growing heights overhead, the depths below. She would die here, she knew it for a fact, the only fact she knew. Die here in this bottomless, roofless pit. Die in a way these suspended bodies would never die. She was already dead, not flesh or bone or energy or even thought. Just a hollow husk of stone. A streaking meteor, going nowhere. She would orbit this place forever, through ten thousand famished moments just like this one. And this one. And this.

Suddenly the chain was bare. Just as quickly as the cold had come, warmth flooded her. Her skin went slack. She sucked in a great breath and pulled at the power throbbing at her chest now, reborn. The Alvalaithen. She was Chloe, and she went thin, filling herself with the dragonfly's sweet, exuberant song.

Off to one side, moving with her through the shaft, she saw Horace. The Fel'Daera was in his hands, and he had his forehead pressed against it. His eyes were squeezed shut. And then, abruptly, a kind of electric shiver flashed through her body. It felt like falling through a thin plane of effervescent bubbles. Her stomach did a violent flip-flop, and her hair too. Somehow she was rising now. She and Horace were in a new shaft, dark and bottomless. There was no chain here. She spotted Dailen, beneath them, his robe flapping elegantly. They were all rising very fast but slowing, approaching their zenith.

"Release the Alvalaithen," Dailen called. "Get your feet beneath you." Chloe stilled the dragonfly and swung her arms, struggling to turn herself upright. She glanced up, and saw that they were rushing toward a flat, smooth ceiling. She threw her hands over her face and cried out.

But instead of crashing into the ceiling, she found herself awash in golden light. The walls of the well disappeared. An instant later, she reached the peak of her ascent and began to fall again, landing almost at once on a hard surface, dropping to all fours. Breathing hard, she stared down between her hands and saw her own pale and panting face, reflected up at her. She crouched now on a mirrored surface just like the one at the top of the well. A mir'aji.

But this was a new place, bright and clean. Slender arches stretched to the heights above. A hundred feet directly overhead, the bottom end of the Well of Giving yawned darkly. The great chain dangled motionless from the well's mouth, a massive triangular weight at the end, pointing straight down at them like a titan's javelin. Farther up, darkness hid the heart of the Nevren they'd just fallen through, where the fused figures still hung suspended, unseen but unforgotten.

Chloe struggled to her feet. Off to one side, Horace lay atop the mir'aji, his cheek pressed against his own perfect reflection, still clinging to the Fel'Daera. Beyond him, Dailen stood easily, graceful as always, watching them with worried eyes.

"Are you okay?" the Altari asked.

Horace rolled to his knees, hugging the Fel'Daera against his gut. "Fine," he said hoarsely. He lifted his eyes to the open mouth of the well far above them, and then to the silver glass below. Chloe could see him trying to figure out how the whole thing worked.

"You said it would suck," Chloe said to Dailen. "But you didn't quite explain just how much."

"I told you more than most would have," said Dailen.

"Those fused Keepers. They were Altari."

Horace looked over at her sharply. "You saw them?" he said. "You watched?"

So, he'd had his eyes closed the whole time. Chloe was glad he hadn't seen what she'd seen . . . but not a hundred percent glad. He'd left her to witness it alone, to remember it alone.

"Mostly Altari, yes," Dailen said. "But two or three human Keepers as well."

"Why so many?" she said. "Why do you need a Nevren like that? What are you hiding here?"

"Who are you to ask?" said another voice, deep and sono-rous, rolling through the cavern like a cascade of massive bells.

Chloe spun around. A dozen Altari stood beneath one of the delicate arches, watching them. They were beautiful. They varied greatly in height, the shortest barely taller than her own father, the tallest nearly as tall as Dr. Jericho himself. The tall one held a massive weapon, like a staff with a huge scimitar blade on the end. The blade, two feet long, seemed to be made of blazing blue light.

All the Altari had the same ringed eyes that Dailen did. And although their smooth white skin had no wrinkles that she could see, somehow they all looked older than Dailen, who by comparison now seemed terribly young—something in the cast of their eyes, maybe, or a slight stoop in the shoul-ders. Most of the newcomers were male, but a couple were female. Again, though, Chloe could not have explained quite *how* she knew that.

The Altari out front, medium height but very broad, began to approach them. His face was stern and luminescent, except for a clean slit of a scar that ran down the center of his forehead, nearly black. He walked out onto the mir'aji, right up to Chloe. He crouched down in front of her, glanced at the Alvalaithen, and then stared her solidly in the eye. "I am Mal'brula Kintares, called Brula. Who are you to come to this place, asking after our secrets?"

Chloe looked over at Dailen. He stood erect, his head slightly bowed. Brula caught Chloe's chin in a gentle but inescapable grip, and turned her face back toward himself. A hot blossom of rage billowed in her chest.

"I do not ask Dwen'dailen Longo," the Altari said. "I ask you. Who are you?"

Chloe went thin. Brula's grip on her face slid loose, and she backed away very slowly, just a single step. "I'm a Warden, thanks for asking. My name is Chloe Oliver. I'm the Keeper of the Alvalaithen."

If the Altari was surprised, he didn't show it. He let his eyes drop to the dragonfly again, and then he stood. He turned to Horace. "And you?" he sang.

Horace simply stood there, his hands still pressing the Fel'Daera to his belly. He didn't look afraid.

Brula crossed over to him, not bothering to crouch down. "Visitors to Ka'hoka must announce themselves."

Horace craned his neck to look up at him. "I'm here to see Sil'falo Teneves."

A musical murmur washed through the remaining Altari. The tall one holding the blue blade took a single step forward. Brula silenced them by holding up an elegant hand.

"No one sees anyone here—or anything—except by the will of the Council," he told Horace.

"She'll see me. Whether you allow it or not."

Chloe thought her face would burst as she suppressed a wild smile of pride. Dailen too seemed to be hiding a pleased grin behind his smooth face.

"Indeed?" said Brula doubtfully. "And why is that?"

Horace opened his hands, revealing the Box of Promises. "Because I am Horace Andrews," he said. Brula gazed down at the box. His eyes flared open wide. He actually took a step backward. Horace took the box into his hand and held it up. He thrust it out at the Altari shrinking before him, at the others watching from afar. He held his chin high.

"I am the Keeper of the Fel'Daera," he said.

CHAPTER TWENTY—SIX

As We Breathe

THE LAITHE OF TENEVES HOVERED OVER JOSHUA'S FACE. HE LAY on the couch in Mr. Meister's office, gazing up at it. He'd been watching it for hours, and only touched it once. He didn't really need to touch it.

He was both very happy, and very discouraged. He was happy because he'd solved one of his problems with the Laithe. He didn't know how he'd done it, exactly, but he had.

He could go anywhere.

He'd tried three different places, faraway places he'd never been—Tokyo in Japan, Stubbsville in Vermont, and Watership Down in England. A huge city, a small town, and a grassy hill in the countryside. All places he'd read about, but never been. He'd zoomed in on each of them easily—so easily in fact, that he hadn't even needed to touch the sleeping rabbit. He'd just . . . asked it to move without thinking about it, and it had moved. He didn't even realize what he'd done until later.

But each of those first three tries, the same thing happened to him that had happened in Madagascar the night before. When he got too close to the ground, somewhere below two thousand feet, ripples like raindrops began to spread across his view, clouding it.

The Laithe had limitations, Mr. Meister said. And he'd seen that. For example, he hadn't seen any people in Tokyo, or moving cars. That was a limitation, and it made sense to him. Sort of. But the raindrops? That had to be his fault. Each time—or so it seemed to Joshua—he got a little closer to the ground before the raindrops appeared. That was encouraging.

And so he had tried again. Someplace wilder yet, someplace far from humans. He brought the Laithe around to northern Africa, to the depths of the Sahara, and slid the rabbit once more. Quickly, hundreds of miles of shifting sand filled his view. The desert was so empty, so featureless, that it was hard to tell how close he was getting. He'd been trying to convince himself that it didn't matter whether he'd been to any of these places, but now he took that one step further.

He *was* in this place.

As he got closer to the huge desert, a few little ripples began to appear. But this time, he refused to see them. *It's sand down there*, he told himself. *Only sand. I know sand. I have been to sand. I am going to this sand now*. And as he pushed closer, the ripples didn't grow. In fact, they stopped altogether.

He kept looking, not watching the rabbit as it slid.

And then suddenly, he was there. The rabbit stopped. Joshua was so close to the ground, he could see individual grains of sand. They were a little blurry, though, shifting jerkily, like they were being moved by the wind, but he couldn't actually *see* them move.

He tore the meridian loose and hung it in the center of Mr. Meister's office. The blue-eyed rabbit came to life, and Joshua wanted it to run, so it ran. The ring opened quickly under its feet. The tunnel of shapes appeared, but it was slowing fast and didn't last long. Before the gate was half open, he could see. Sand. Hints of blue sky. Ripples of heat in the distance. He was getting better.

And then the portal was open wide, and Joshua stood looking out over the remote Sahara. It stretched before him for miles upon miles, an ocean of sand. It was like nothing he'd ever seen before.

He had promised Mr. Meister he wouldn't go anywhere, and he was going to keep that promise. But still . . . his hand wasn't exactly *him*, was it?

He reached through the tingling portal. The air was so hot and dry on the other side, and the sun so instantly warm, that it felt like reaching into an oven. He squatted down and scooped up a little handful of sand, not at all sure he should be doing this. The sand was hot at first, but it cooled in his palm, and he brought it into the Great Burrow. This was something worth learning—that even though he and the globe were on this side of the portal, meaning no one on the other side could get through, he could still reach through and bring back things himself.

The Sahara sand was duller than beach sand, not quite as bright, but otherwise it felt the same, which was surprising. He poured the sand into a neat little pile on Mr. Meister's desk. A gift. A prize. He had done this. He, Joshua, had reached six thousand miles across the world and brought back sand from the Sahara Desert.

He could go anywhere. But he hadn't.

There was only one place he needed to go. The meadow. April and Gabriel. Horace and Chloe.

He gazed up at the Laithe, thinking about it hard. He had been thinking about it hard for a long time now. Because yes, it seemed he could go anywhere, but as Mr. Meister had suggested, that still wasn't good enough for what he needed to do. He had to get as close to the missing Wardens as he possibly could—within a few yards, ideally.

But he didn't know exactly where they were.

Joshua's first plan was a bad one. He thought maybe he would just make a portal somewhere near April's house, step on through, and go looking for them himself. But of course, for one, he had promised he wouldn't do anything like that. And for two, if Dr. Jericho was still in the area, he would feel the portal and find Joshua in no time.

Then he had a second plan. He would just open up portal after portal, all around the meadow and the house, hoping to get lucky. But again, if he didn't like opening up even one portal with Dr. Jericho around, lots of portals seemed lots worse.

Then he didn't have a third plan.

His fourth plan was to just lie here and worry. He glanced over at the pile of sand on the desk once in a while, just to remind himself how well things had been going. He had done that. He had.

But it was nearly noon now, and lying around was not the answer. Not for a Keeper anyway. He had to think like a Keeper—whatever that meant. But then Joshua thought some more. The first thing a Keeper would do to stay safe was to think like a *Mordin*. If he was a Mordin, and there were Wardens on the loose, away from home, what would he do?

First things first, he'd keep guard over the falkrete circle by the barn. That was how the Wardens got in, and it was the quickest way out. The Riven were smart enough to do that, for sure. So maybe Joshua would just take a look. He would open up a portal there beside the barn, just for a second. If he saw any Mordin, that was actually good, wasn't it? It meant they were still probably looking for the Wardens, that they hadn't found them yet. And if he didn't, well . . . he wasn't sure what that would mean.

It was a good plan, he decided. The *only* plan, but a good plan.

He spun the globe to North America, over the Midwest. He let the sleeping rabbit slide. Down and down he went, into northern Illinois.

Within seconds, he was over the meadow. The barn was there, a squat slab of black and gray. And there was another black blob out in the meadow, a hundred yards off. What was it?

Closer and closer. He was no more than two hundred feet up when he realized that the barn was flattened. Down here on the surface of this tiny earth, the barn had collapsed, just like in real life. But how did the Laithe know? And that blob in the meadow—he shifted over to it easily, drawing nearer. He had to get down to a hundred feet, the rabbit nearly back to the top of the meridian now, before he recognized what he was seeing.

A golem. Or what used to be a golem, anyway. A great lifeless pile of stones that looked like it had been dumped there. Was it dead? And how would he know?

Movement caught his eye. Not the golem. Was it a raindrop? *No, no . . . not here, not now.*

But it wasn't a raindrop. It was smudge of pure black, sliding slowly. He went in closer. Fifty feet now. The smudge was like a caterpillar made of shadow, inching across the surface of the Laithe. Or maybe more like the trail of a ghost—a thick black dot at the forward end, growing fainter at the tail.

Now another one, over by the barn, like a dripping streak of grease on the Laithe's surface. Something was wrong. Joshua hadn't seen anything move in the Laithe before except water, clouds, and trees. No people, no cars, no animals, nothing. Something wasn't working right. Maybe he was hoping too hard, asking the Laithe to do too much. After all this, after bringing back sand from Africa, maybe he still didn't know what he was doing.

He could only think one thing: he couldn't let the black smudges get bigger, or spread. If they did, he might not be able to see the meadow at all. And if he couldn't see, he'd never be able to open a portal to save the others. If they were even there. If they even could be saved. Maybe he was a Lostling after all.

He realized he was breathing hard. He was panicking. He pulled back on the Laithe, rising swiftly into the sky, leaving the meadow far behind. The black smudges disappeared.

He shoved the Laithe away. It slid a few feet through the air and hung there. He turned away, taking his eyes off the Laithe for almost the first time that morning. It hurt to do it. The Laithe seemed . . . disappointed in him, somehow. And he couldn't blame it. He was not good enough. Maybe if it weren't for him, if it weren't for Isabel, the Laithe would have found a better Keeper. One who could see everything, everywhere, without fear of raindrops or smudges.

He got to his feet. He left the office, feeling sorry for himself and feeling angry for feeling sorry. The Laithe followed him silently. Out in the Great Burrow, he saw no one. He wandered up toward Vithra's Eye. Earlier he'd come across that water, experiencing the Nevren as a Keeper for the first time. It had been as terrible as everyone said it was—cold and lonely and lifeless. Frustrated or not, he couldn't bear to be without the Laithe. Did the Laithe feel the same way about him?

He passed Mrs. Hapsteade's doba. Light peeked out from under the curtain of her door, and voices, too. It sounded like Horace's mom was in there. Meanwhile, Mr. Meister was probably with Ingrid somewhere, and Brian was finally napping. Joshua couldn't bear to face any of them.

Down the hall stood Neptune's doba, tall and thin. Her door was open. As he passed, he spotted her inside, hovering cross-legged over her bed. She was talking to someone. But who? Joshua came closer, right to the door.

Arthur stood on the bed. Neptune, hanging in midair, spread her arms for the bird and flapped them. "Like this," she said. "Nice and slow. Very quiet."

Suddenly she whipped her head around, spotting Joshua. Her expression didn't change. "Greetings," she said.

"What are you doing?"

She looked down at Arthur. She flapped her arms again, going nowhere. The raven cocked his head at her. "Just showing him how it's done. You know."

Arthur plucked at the sheets and snapped his bill at Neptune. He was probably missing April. Neptune was fine—as far as he knew—but she was no April. Did Neptune know to give him dog food, or beef jerky? Not knowing the answer made Joshua feel like he might cry.

"Um, hello?" Neptune said. "Is the plan to stand there? Because let's not."

Joshua went in shyly, the Laithe drifting in after him. Arthur croaked at him in a friendly way, fluffing his feathers.

"To what do I owe this . . . visit?" said Neptune.

"I don't know."

"You just randomly wandered over here."

"Well, I was randomly wandering, and then I guess it stopped being random when I heard you talking to Arthur."

"I see. You weren't really going toward anything, then. You must have been going *away* from something."

"I guess."

Neptune eyed the Laithe. "Is it your new little friend here?"

Joshua bowed his head, ashamed.

"It is, isn't it?" Neptune teased.

"Well, I thought I wanted to be alone with the Laithe, but then when I was alone with it, I . . ." He shrugged.

"Oh, I see. Shotgun wedding. Buyer's remorse."

"I don't know what those things are."

"Lots of doubt and awkwardness between the two of you. Long silences over dinner, that sort of thing. It's tragic, really."

Joshua frowned at her. Her eyes were wide open and there was no expression on her face at all. "I think you're making a joke," he said.

"I think I am too. I appreciate you noticing."

"Are you mad at me?"

Now her face did change. She sighed. She produced a piece of dog food from somewhere and slipped it to Arthur.

411

He gulped it down. "Not at you," she said. "Not really. I'm mad at Isabel. I'm a little mad at Brian. I'm worried about Gabriel—and the others, of course."

Joshua burst into a flood of tears.

"Oh, god," said Neptune, waving her hands. "Oh, no. Let's not do that."

But Joshua couldn't stop. She was worried. Everyone was worried, and Joshua was supposed to fix it.

"Hey, come on." Neptune floated over to him and patted him awkwardly on the back. "Honestly, if you start crying, then I'm gonna start leaving, and soon I'll be complaining about you behind your back, and that's how I get my reputation for being heartless."

Joshua laughed. Snot came out his nose. "You're not heartless," he said as he wiped it away. "You love Gabriel."

"Wow. Still working on your filters, I see." She scratched her forehead, maybe to hide her reddening cheeks, and then she gave up and shrugged. "I was the same way when I was a kid."

He sniffled and looked up at her. "You used to be a kid?"

She narrowed her eyes. "I think you're making a joke."

"I think I am too."

She smiled. "I am not going to ask you why you started crying just now, because I'm afraid you'll start crying again."

Joshua understood that this was her way of asking. And it was maybe the only way she could have asked that didn't make him want to cry. He went over to the bed and flopped down on it without asking, which maybe was rude. The Laithe came with him. Arthur flapped his big wings and rose into the air briefly as it came near, but then settled again.

"The others are trapped," Joshua said into the sheets. "April and Gabriel and Horace and Chloe. And I'm supposed to save them. With the Laithe."

He expected Neptune to feel bad for him, but instead she just said, "That's the general idea, yeah."

"But when I try, I just . . ." He rolled over. He didn't know how to describe the smudges he'd seen. "It's just not working right."

Neptune leaned back, reclining in midair, her long hair and her cloak dangling to the ground. She looked like a magic trick. "I don't know what you're talking about," she said. "You can open portals already. Just open a portal and bring them back."

Joshua was getting angry. "Okay, well, what's the big deal for you? Just fly to the moon already. I can open a portal fine, but if I can't find the others it doesn't matter."

"Does Mr. Meister seem to think you can find them?"

"Yes."

"Then you can. He's the Chief Taxonomer. He's sees things we don't."

"Maybe he wants to do it for me, then."

"You know he doesn't. And can't." Neptune just hung there awhile, then rolled over to look at him. "This is all pretty new for you, I guess. This Keeper business."

"Yes."

"But I see you've officially been made a member." She pointed to Joshua's chest. He looked down at the jithandra that hung there, a long, azure blue crystal in mounted in a metal flower. He'd nearly forgotten. Brian, unable to sleep after their return from the meadow, had busied himself all morning making jithandras for Joshua and April. All the Wardens had one of the strange crystals, in their own particular colors according to their talents—red for Chloe, purple for Neptune, silver for Gabriel. April's, fittingly, was a beautiful forest green. Tears started to well up again as Joshua wondered if she'd ever see it.

"What do your parents think about all this?" Neptune asked.

Joshua froze, all thoughts of April swept aside. It was the first time anyone had asked him about his parents, besides Isabel. "They don't know. I mean, I don't even have a dad."

"Everyone *has* a dad, technically." Neptune paused and frowned. "Don't they?"

"I mean I don't *know* my dad. And my mom has . . . problems. I lived with a foster family."

Neptune just looked at him warily.

"They didn't pay very much attention to me," Joshua went on. "I spent a lot of time at the library."

"Here in Chicago?"

"Minneapolis."

"And you ran away?"

"Some Mordin came to the house. A bunch of times. They talked to me. They wanted me to come with them. They did something to my foster parents, I think. Made them sick or something." The memories were hazy, memories he didn't really want to have. Neptune mumbled something—"Malkund," she said. Joshua didn't ask what she meant.

"Anyway, I didn't really know them very well. But then one day Isabel was there. She told me what I was." He glanced at the Laithe. "Or I guess she told me what I would be someday. A Keeper. She took me away."

Neptune was staring at him so hard he thought her big eyes would pop out. "Have you told Mr. Meister this story?" she demanded.

"No."

"I've never heard of that happening before. I think you must have been putting off pretty big sparks. It means you were really ripe for the Find. Overripe, probably."

"Okay."

"That's good. That's good for you and the Laithe." She dug around in her mouth with her tongue thoughtfully for a minute, and then stretched a long leg to the floor. She pushed herself toward the bed. She drifted closer, digging around in her pocket as she came. "Let me show you something."

She reached the bed and dropped down onto it. Arthur rasped and lifted off, fluttering heavily over to the table. He began to strut back and forth, clucking softly to himself.

Neptune held out her palm, revealing a shiny black stone about the size of her thumb. It looked sort of like a dinosaur tooth, but it was chiseled smooth on all sides. Somehow Joshua knew, just by looking at it, that it was Tan'ji. "This is the Devlin tourminda," Neptune said. "That's my last name. Devlin, not tourminda."

"Why is it named after you?"

"I'm a legacy. That means it's been in my family for a long time. My great-grandfather was its last Keeper. I took over after he died. I was younger than you."

A legacy. Joshua didn't even know that was possible. "So, they just gave it to you?"

"No, I had to have a proper Find. Mr. Meister arranged it. I was six, and I had only seen glimpses of the tourminda. He put out a bunch of similar-looking stones, but I went right to the real thing." She held her Tan'ji up like a prize.

"And so . . . you already knew what it did. You didn't have to figure it out."

"That's the point of my story. I knew what it did, yes, but I didn't know how to make it *do* what it did. I was leaping around the yard, jumping off little things. I hurt myself a lot. Months later, I still couldn't do it. Not a hover, not even a slow fall, nothing."

"Did someone finally teach you?"

"Of course not. If someone teaches you too much, you get stuck. And things are never quite right."

"How did you learn, then?"

"My dad is pretty old-fashioned. He took me to the Aon Center—that's a skyscraper, used to be the old Standard Oil building."

"Big Stan," said Joshua. "I know what it is."

"Of course you do. You know what it looks like, then—a thousand feet high, straight up and down. Well, my dad had a friend who could get us out on the roof of Big Stan. We went up there with the tourminda one night, and . . ." With a thrust of one leg, she launched herself high into the air, then began to drift slowly back down. "My dad threw me off."

Joshua's mouth fell open. "He threw you . . . But you could have died!"

"Could've. Didn't. Instead I learned the one thing I hadn't been able to figure out on my own. I can't *wish* for the tourminda to work. I have to *know* it will work."

"But what if you hadn't figured it out?"

"Then splat. Neptune sauce. But I actually only fell about a hundred feet. I wasn't even afraid. I still remember what my dad said to me right before he threw me off. He said, 'There won't be any regrets, and no apologies either. I'll see you in a minute.' And as I was falling, I knew. I just knew. And then I floated."

Joshua couldn't even begin to imagine it. "That's not a good story."

"Yes it is. But anyway, it's not the story that matters. It's the moral."

"What's the moral?"

She pointed at the Laithe. "You have to *need* it to work. You have to *know* it will work. And then it *will* work."

"But there are these smudges, and—"

"I don't want the details. I'm giving you general advice about being a Keeper, not about the Laithe. But if something seems wrong, you need to ask yourself: is it a bug or a feature?"

"I don't understand those words."

"What I'm saying is, believe that your Tan'ji works for you, even when it seems like it's not. For example?" She closed her eyes. She pointed at him. "Get up. Move around the room."

"Why?"

"For example, I said. Move. Quietly."

Joshua slid off the bed. He moved quietly away. Neptune's finger followed him as he went several steps left, and then back right.

"How are you doing that?"

She opened her eyes. "My secondary power, unique to the Devlin tourminda. I can sense the gravity of objects around me. It even works in the humour. But when I first started becoming aware of this power, I thought I was going to puke."

"Why?"

She patted her belly. "Because I feel it here. It's like car sickness. But back in the day, I just told myself to believe it was something working, not something going wrong. And it was."

The Laithe floated patiently. Joshua could feel it waiting for him, slow and blue and breathing. Somewhere on that tiny earth, April and the others were waiting too.

"If I believe it will work, it will work," he said. "You promise?"

"I mean, I wouldn't throw you off a building, but how wrong could I be?"

"I'm going to try, then."

"So try. Do you want privacy?"

"No," said Joshua. Neptune was comforting. She was honest. He liked honest. "But don't talk to me."

"No promises there either. I'm a talker. I'll try not to be judgy."

Joshua nodded, and bent over the Laithe. He wasn't surprised at all to discover that it was already centered where he needed it to go—where he needed to be himself, right over northern Illinois. That was what the Laithe did. He zoomed in quickly, zeroing in on April's town. Over on the table, Arthur let out a series of sweet trills. They sounded like encouragement.

In no time at all, the meadow loomed, and April's house, too. Joshua almost cried out. The smudges were everywhere—little black worms crawling over his view, a dozen of them. He almost pulled away, but stopped himself. He told himself the Laithe was working. He was its Keeper, and he was doing it right.

Still the worms didn't disappear.

He went in closer. Not away from the smudges, but toward them. There were more of them over April's house. As he zoomed in, the collapsed barn a half mile away slid over the horizon, out of sight. The question he'd asked Mr. Meister earlier came back to him.

"How does the Laithe know?" he whispered again now.

"How does it know what?" Neptune asked.

"Everything," said Joshua.

She scoffed. "Nobody knows everything."

"It knows things that happened in the meadow. The barn collapsed in real life, and it's collapsed on the Laithe too."

"Whoa. Can it see cars moving? What about people?"

"No, no people. Maybe the Laithe can't—"

"The Laithe is alive," Mr. Meister had said. *"As we know it, as we walk it, as we breathe it."*

Joshua was right above April's house now, looking down. The black trails were everywhere, maybe eight or ten altogether. Some were shorter, moving slow. Some longer, faster. A few, he saw now, were simply dots—barely moving at all. He sucked in a deep breath. The Laithe was working. He *knew* it worked. He understood these smoking black spots.

The Riven.

He came in closer. They had surrounded the house. There was only one reason to do a thing like that.

And then he saw them. Two little dots like water stains on paper, inside the house.

One silver.

One green.

"People," he said to Neptune, coming in closer still with the Laithe. "But not just any people."

"What are you saying? What people?"

Joshua went all the way to the ground, to the driveway at the front of the house. He would open a portal. He would see what he could see. And maybe it would be enough. He looked up at Neptune, fear and thrill filling him. The silver dot and the green.

"Keepers," he said.

CHAPTER TWENTY—SEVEN

Sharks Circling

IT WAS NOON, AND THE HOUSE WAS UNDER SIEGE. THE STRANG-est siege imaginable. April stood at her bedroom window with Gabriel, peering out into the woods. She could have seen— and smelled and heard—much more by using the vine, but she didn't dare do that now.

The Riven were here.

Or almost here, anyway.

It was Isabel who'd spotted the first one, just before dawn, a Mordin striding through the woods on the south side of the house, twenty yards back from the property line. It had been searching, sniffing the air. April had run quietly out onto the back porch, startling Baron out of a nap and shooing him inside. They couldn't afford to have the dog barking now. Not with the leestone's powers hanging by a thread.

Because the leestone *was* working, but not as well as they

had hoped. As Gabriel had immediately pointed out, the Mordin in the woods this morning had seemed unaware that the house was less than a hundred feet away. Something had drawn it near, but it couldn't quite find the place. The Mordin had wandered off blindly. April hoped that would be the end of it.

But it wasn't.

Twenty minutes later, another Mordin, on the north side. And ten minutes after that, a pair of them, pausing in the corner of the backyard, looking right past the house with no recognition at all. They'd wandered off, and not long after that, she and Gabriel and Isabel had heard the rumble of the golem, somewhere up along April's long driveway, moving briefly closer before sliding away. All morning it had gone on like this, giving them no chance to slip away.

"Explain to me again how a leestone works?" April whispered to Gabriel now. "Is the house invisible?"

"No, not invisible. A leestone absorbs unwanted attention. The Mordin may see the house, but the house won't have any meaning. It won't register, won't seem any more important than a tree or a rock."

"So we're safe, then," said April.

Gabriel shrugged. "A leestone is not a guarantee. Certain things can break the bubble, draw unwanted attention. Using our Tan'ji, for example, or indicating to the Mordin that we've seen them."

"But why aren't they wandering away?"

"I don't know. The Riven won't normally hunt like this, especially during the day."

"It *is* a bubble," Isabel said suddenly.

April looked over at her. Isabel was gazing out the other window, nose against the glass. "What do you mean?" April asked.

"You didn't give the Riven enough time to forget this place. Bad things happened to them here. They have memories of this house, memories connected to the both of you. They can't help but come looking. But your leestone, under your pillow there—it's very strong."

April blushed. She wasn't surprised that Isabel knew where the leestone was, but she was embarrassed she'd bothered trying to hide it, much less in such a childish place.

Isabel craned her neck, turning her eyes to the sky. "The leestone is pushing out blankness, insisting on it just as hard as the Riven are insisting there's something to be found here. The two forces are pressing against each other. I can feel it. Like the skin of a bubble. It's quivering. And the Riven are circling."

Like sharks, April thought. *Blood in the water.* This was how her entire adventure had begun. "Did we make a mistake coming here?" she said.

Isabel turned from the window. She looked April in the eye. "Not if your plan was to keep me silent," she said softly.

Gabriel stepped toward her, gripping the Staff of Obro.

"What do you mean?" said April, alarmed. "Silent how?"

"You know how," Isabel said. She hefted her little white harp. "You brought me here—under the leestone—to prevent me from doing exactly what I would have done. And it's working. The leestone is too powerful, and the harp is weak."

"Wait, so you *were* going to call the Riven down on us?"

Isabel leaned against the window again. "Once I got the hang of this harp, yes. But not for the reasons you think."

"What possible good reasons could you have for summoning the Riven?" April asked.

"It's not the whole horde I wanted." Isabel exhaled angrily through gritted teeth, fogging the glass briefly. "Just him."

Now April understood. "Dr. Jericho," she said.

"He destroyed Miradel. He took what was mine. He savaged her right in front of me, as cruelly as he could."

"And if Dr. Jericho was standing here right now, what would you do to him, exactly?" April asked, exasperated. "Throw rocks at him? You said it yourself—your new harp is weak."

"I don't have to sever him for long. I might manage it, even with this toy."

"How long is long enough?"

Isabel looked sharply over. "Two or three seconds, I think."

"Two or three seconds." Gabriel laughed. "You'd leave him with a headache, at best. I've seen Riven endure severing for nearly ten seconds, and still recover. The Nevren in Vithra's Eye takes at least twenty seconds to cross. That's the

425

only way to be sure that no Riven can survive the severing."

"Severed a lot of Riven, have you?" Isabel said, but April thought she heard doubt in her voice. "Anyway, it doesn't matter. I can't lure Dr. Jericho closer now. Anything I try just gets swallowed up by your leestone."

So she had already tried. April squeezed her eyes closed, pulsing with rage. She'd had enough of this woman, if woman was even the right word. Isabel was a child—certainly more of a child than her own daughter, who was as steady and faithful and brave as Isabel was reckless, and selfish, and cowardly.

"If it's the leestone that's stopping you, then leave," April said. "Leave now."

"You'd trust me to do that, I'm sure," Isabel scoffed. "You probably think I'd lead the Riven right back here."

"Actually, I don't think they'd listen to you again. What do they call you? Forsworn? You said it was because they pitied you, but that's not it. The truth is, you disgust them." April realized she was nearly shouting, something she tried to never do. She didn't care. She felt Gabriel's hand on her arm and shook it off. "You're a parasite. A greedy leech. Whatever respect the Riven gave you before, it was only because they feared you." She pointed out the window. "Go on out there and see how much they respect you now. They'll chew you up just like they did Miradel."

Isabel screamed, her face red with rage. She shoved April hard, knocking her to the floor, and lunged toward the bed, yanking the leestone out from under the pillow. She spun, her red hair flailing wildly, and hurled the heavy stone at the bedroom window, still shrieking. Glass shattered, and the lee-stone sailed out into the afternoon sun.

April scrambled to her feet. Pushing Isabel aside, she rushed to the window. The leestone had landed in a patch of dirt at the edge of the lawn, lying there in plain sight. Downstairs in the house, Baron began to bark. *Noise. Danger. Protect.*

"What happened?" Gabriel said. He clearly wanted to let the humour loose, but wasn't sure he should.

"The leestone," April said, fuming. "She threw it out the window."

Gabriel bared his teeth. "Where is it now?"

"Way out in the yard. At the edge of the trees." April rounded on Isabel. She let all her anger surge into her fists, but kept them clenched at her sides. She made her voice stay calm, even as Baron's angry barking threatened to tear her throat in two. "Go," she said, her jaw trembling with rage. "You're not welcome here. Not anymore, and not ever again."

Isabel glared at her with red-rimmed eyes. A few specks of blood dotted her cheeks, blowback from the shattered glass. Through the gaping window, the victorious cry of a Mordin rang through the woods. And then another.

"We're past that now," Gabriel said. "Brace yourselves."

The humour swallowed them all.

Almost by instinct, April opened herself to the vine. Downstairs, Baron was still free, barking and listening and smelling. Gabriel was keeping the humour small, letting April reach out.

Gabriel took April's hand in the void now, his grip gentle but strong. "Reach for Isabel," he said. "She must come with us."

It was clear Gabriel was speaking only to her, not letting Isabel hear. "No way," said April. "Are you kidding?"

"We cannot leave her."

April shook her head in disbelief. "I'm pretty sure we can."

"The spitestone has been destroyed, April. Isabel knows the location of the Warren."

April's skin went cold. Of course. And suddenly she understood—that was why Mr. Meister had brought her the harp. It was a bribe, a tease. Enough, hopefully, to keep Isabel on the Warden's side.

"We cannot let the Riven take her," Gabriel prompted.

Reluctantly, April reached out for Isabel. She found her frizzy hair—Isabel had slumped to the ground, apparently.

"Isabel," Gabriel said, his voice deep and commanding, but thick with an almost fatherly kindness. "Fear not. Come with us. Come with us, and we will try to put right what has gone wrong."

"There's way too much wrong to put right," Isabel said bleakly.

"If that could ever be true for us, I would have surrendered my staff years ago." Gabriel's words were so soothing, so right, that April felt a sudden sympathy for Isabel rising in her chest. She tamped it down angrily—was this a power of Gabriel's that no one ever openly acknowledged? This compelling voice, this magnetic presence ringing out through the abyss of the humour?

But Gabriel's wasn't the only voice in April's head now. Downstairs, Baron was still barking, and she could hear more Riven calling to each other, closing in on the house.

"I know why you won't leave me," Isabel murmured. "The Warren. You don't trust me."

We don't, April wanted to say, but she kept her mouth shut.

"You haven't earned our trust," Gabriel said. Not an accusation, but a gentle and inexorable truth. "Earn it now."

"I can't. And if you won't leave me—kill me. Kill me and then go."

The words chilled April's blood. Gabriel's casual response froze it solid.

"I would prefer not to," he said.

"Because you need me."

"I do not. But you have a husband. Daughters."

"My daughters don't need me, either. They don't love me."

"Perhaps not, but that is not for you to say."

Downstairs, the back door shook beneath a thunderous blow, and then was kicked off its hinges with a crash. Brimstone flooded April's nose. At the front of the house, Baron cowered into a corner, tail tight between his legs. *Stinging. Hate. Fear.*

"They're here, Gabriel," she said. "They're inside."

"Get up, Isabel," Gabriel pleaded forcefully. "If you have regrets, make the only decision now that might truly erase them."

Isabel groaned, her voice rolling through the humour like a dirge.

"Get up," said Gabriel. Power and warmth. April squeezed his hand.

And then suddenly, another hand, reaching for her in the gray. April grabbed it, pulling Isabel to her feet. At the same instant, at the bottom of the stairs, a Mordin strode into the front hall. The front door slammed open, and two more entered the house.

Baron yelped at them desperately, flooded with fear, backing into a corner. He piddled on the floor. Warmth flooded through April. *Terror. Shame.*

And then the same nothingness that now buried April abruptly blanketed the dog, sight and sound. His senses were swallowed as Gabriel let the humour open wide. He had said he could bury the whole house, and apparently he was doing it.

"We're trapped," Gabriel said, obviously sensing the Mordin at the bottom of the stairs.

"Out the window," April said. "Onto the porch roof. We can—"

Suddenly, below, April felt Baron on the move. He scampered out of the corner, blind and frightened, trying to get

430

away. *Fear. Hurt. Bite.* He brushed against a Mordin's leg, growling, but somehow he managed to get out on the front porch—she could feel the peeling paint of the porch boards under his paws. Out of sheer habit the dog kept going, launching off the porch with the muscle memory of years, and within a second he was free of the humour.

April clung to him. An Auditor was in the driveway. Dr. Jericho stood beside her, huge and bristling. Baron paused, barking uneasily at the Riven.

"Dr. Jericho is out front," she said, her heart hammering. "And an Auditor too. We need to get out of here."

Dr. Jericho lunged at Baron, cocking back one huge arm. April flinched. Baron scampered away. He barreled down the driveway, not looking back, kicking up stones with every loping step. They dug into April's hands, her feet, but didn't hurt. Baron kept going until he was nearly at the end of the vine's reach, and she was about to let him go, and then—

The dog stumped to a halt, perplexed.

Shimmer. Strangeness. Curiosity.

"April," said Gabriel. "We must—"

"Wait. Wait."

A golden ring, barely a foot across, hung in the air over the driveway. It made no noise and had no smell, but for a moment it had all of Baron's attention. *Danger. Listen. Smell.* And then suddenly the ring widened, opening like the iris of an eye, growing as tall as a Mordin. Baron skittered back a few steps.

April had seen this ring once before, in the meadow. "A portal!" she said, hope leaping up in her heart. "Right out front."

Baron eyed the portal warily, watching it grow, but then swift clawing footsteps from behind made him turn. Dr. Jericho was galloping straight toward him—or more likely, straight toward the portal, kicking up driveway stones as he ran.

"Joshua's looking for us," Isabel crowed. "We need to get to him."

But no sooner had Isabel spoken than the hanging ring began to shrink. "No, no, no," April murmured. The portal dwindled rapidly to the size of a plate, and then vanished altogether.

Dr. Jericho slowed to a halt, glaring. Baron took off again, down the driveway away from the house and away from danger. In seconds, he sprinted beyond the range of the vine. She lost him, lost his eyes and his nose and his ears. She came back to her own dull human senses, flattened by the humour. But at least Baron was gone. She shut the Ravenvine down, panting as if she'd been the one doing the running.

"It's gone," she said. "The portal. Joshua closed it. Dr. Jericho was charging at it and . . ." Isabel's hand went slack in hers.

"Joshua did what he had to," Gabriel said. "Now out the window. Let me clear the glass."

A few long seconds passed, some of the longest of April's life. Baron was safe. Away. But his terror, and her rage, along

432

with the sudden spike of hope the portal briefly brought, left her feeling exhausted. And now, beneath her own feet, she thought she felt faint steady vibrations. She immediately recalled all the nights she'd felt Uncle Harrison climbing the stairs to his bedroom, vibrations like this. Heavy bodies, creeping on the stairs. In the humour, April had lost all sense of where her own bedroom door was. How long before a Mordin stumbled through it?

"Okay," said Gabriel at last. "Hurry."

He pulled them forward. April had climbed out this window a hundred times, and she managed it easily now, even in the humour. She hadn't forgotten the last time she went this way, either—pulled outside by Baron's barking, as Dr. Jericho lurked in the woods behind her house. Despite all her fears that night, she could never have imagined a moment like this one.

She climbed onto the porch roof. This, at least, felt familiar. There was no sun in the humour, of course. It could have been day or night. But the feel of the warm sloping roof beneath her feet gave her confidence. Isabel, coming out behind her, seemed much less confident, though she was usually sure-footed. She said nothing—nothing that Gabriel was letting April hear, anyway—but she squeezed April's hand so hard she thought her fingers might break.

"Stay close to the wall, and you'll be fine," April said. Isabel said nothing, but clung to her hand harder than ever. April let her, resisting the urge to pull her hand away. It occurred to her, briefly, that a blind fall from this height might break Isabel's legs, but wouldn't be enough to kill her. April was ashamed to wonder if that was the only reason she didn't let Isabel go.

"Can we get higher?" asked Gabriel. "Up onto the highest roof?"

"Yes, the next window down. We can climb up on the air conditioner. It's not easy."

"I found it," Gabriel said. "I'll go first."

April was afraid to ask, but had to. "How many Riven are with us?"

"Seven Mordin in the humour," said Gabriel. "But it's a big house, and I'm filling it. I'm in the attic, in the basement, halfway across the yard. I won't let them find us easily."

Gabriel released April's hand. "Here's the air conditioner. I'll climb up and reach for you. Isabel, you come first."

April pulled Isabel forward, letting her inch past. They brushed against each other in the gloom, and April could feel her breathing hard. "You'll be okay," April said.

"I can feel them, you know," Isabel said. "When they get close enough, I can feel their Tan'ji. There's one inside your bedroom right now."

Of course—Isabel could feel the Medium. But April wasn't sure she wanted to know that a Mordin was in her bedroom. "Maybe we should jump," April said. A crazy idea, when she'd been thinking of broken legs just a moment ago, but getting trapped on the roof didn't seem a whole lot better.

And the porch roof wasn't *that* high. She'd seen a stupid friend of Derek's jump off it one time. He'd gotten away with a sprained ankle.

But Gabriel was already pulling Isabel up. "Not an option," he said darkly.

"Will I regret asking why?" April said.

"The golem is here. It's below you now."

April pressed closer yet against the house. And was the house trembling, or was she? She imagined the golem just beneath her, creeping along the side of the house like a hungry black flood.

A hand touched her shoulder. "Here." She took Gabriel's hand and found the air conditioner with her foot. As she stepped up onto it, it gave just a little, threatening to tip out of the window and dump her onto the lawn. But Gabriel's grip tightened, and he practically hoisted her airborne onto the topmost roof of the house.

The roof was much steeper here. April got onto all fours and scrambled to the very peak. She straddled it. She longed to reach out with the vine, to see what was happening beyond the border of the humour, but resisted. She told herself that all the most important action was happening inside the gray fog anyway. It wasn't a very comforting thought.

"Now what?" she said.

No one responded, and for just a second the starkest jolt of terror she'd felt yet shot through her—were they gone? Was she alone here in the gray? But then Isabel spoke, and April realized Gabriel hadn't answered because he had no answer to give.

"We wait for Joshua," said Isabel.

"Wait for him how?" April said. "Wait for what? We missed our chance."

"He'll find us again. He'll open a portal and save us," Isabel insisted.

"Up here on the roof? Are you crazy? He'll never find us."

Gabriel rumbled in agreement. "He is a neophyte at best, and a Lostling at worst. He is less than half a day into a poisoned Find. What skills do you imagine he has?"

"Neither of you know the Laithe," said Isabel. "And maybe you don't know Joshua either, any better than you know me. It can be done."

"There is another way, if it comes to it," Gabriel said. "Something I can do."

"What way?" said April.

"Fusion."

Isabel scoffed angrily. "Don't be a fool."

"None of the Riven will survive it," Gabriel insisted. "Not even Dr. Jericho."

Isabel seemed to hesitate for a moment, but then said, "And neither will you."

"That is a matter of opinion," said Gabriel. "And in the meantime, you can get April out and safely away."

April pawed at the humour, as if she could part it to somehow comprehend what was being said. "Fusion? What's fusion?"

"It's a way out," said Gabriel. "But I will wait. I'll do nothing until there's nothing—"

A sudden crumpling roar took April's breath away. She threw up her hand as the blinding sun poured down on her from a blue sky. The nasty bite of brimstone stung her nose.

The humour was gone.

CHAPTER TWENTY—EIGHT

Above and Beyond

JOSHUA SPUN THE PORTAL CLOSED, FAST AS HE COULD. HE FELT like a coward doing it—there was no way Dr. Jericho could get through. Dr. Jericho couldn't even *see* him, much less get to him.

But Joshua had seen plenty. Enough to make his belly squirm, with some messy mix of hope and worry. Dr. Jericho, yes—charging down the driveway, straight at the portal like a bull—but also, beyond him, April's house, wrapped in a smoky cloud. He'd seen that cloud before, back in the meadow.

The humour.

And in the humour, there were Mordin. All those black smudging trails he'd seen on the Laithe were Mordin on the move, swarming around and into the house. And an Auditor too, with her long pale braid.

Gabriel and April were inside the house, he knew now. The silver dot and the green. He had no idea whether they'd seen his portal or not, but Baron had. And maybe—just maybe, if April had been in the dog's head—she had seen it too.

Joshua plucked the closed portal out of the air and swung it around the Laithe again. Arthur rocked nervously from foot to foot on the table. Neptune looked like she wanted to swallow Joshua whole.

"Why did you close it? You said there were Keepers."

"Dr. Jericho is there. Gabriel and April are inside April's house, but the Riven are all around."

"Get them, then! Save them!"

"It's not like that. I can see them from above, but I can't get inside the house."

"Get close. Get to the door."

"You don't understand. I can't just be close. I have to be *right there*."

Neptune gritted her teeth, but then nodded. He nodded back at her, grateful. He was the Keeper of the Laithe, not her.

He was already going back down to the house, falling through the sky like a rock. The ghostly trails of the Riven were coming together now, collapsing around the property. An inky black blot jittered along the north side, different from the others, bigger. An object, not a being. A golem.

He came in close, just over the top of the house, looking

straight down at the roof. Inside, April and Gabriel were moving now, slowly. He could see the dots that represented them, right through the roof. They were at the edge of the house, close to where the golem was. What were they doing?

It occurred to him suddenly that he'd never really been to April's house. It was strange to think it. Maybe with all the practicing he'd done today, he was learning to forget the difference between a place he'd been on his own two feet and a place he'd only seen through the Laithe. Was that a good thing? Either way, he wished he knew more about this place, this house. He had to understand.

"I need to get in the house, but I don't know how. And I don't know where to be to get them out."

"Can't you just . . . dive in? You know. Zoom in?" She stabbed the air with her hand. Arthur, startled, flew up from the table and flapped loudly over near Joshua.

"It doesn't work that way," Joshua said. "I go down to things, not through."

"So you're an expert now?"

He frowned, hurt. "I'm not, I just . . . you told me I was supposed to know. I think I know this."

"Okay. You're right. Sorry."

In the Laithe, Gabriel and April had stopped moving. Now they seemed to separate a little bit, Gabriel moving away. "You fight the Riven all the time," Joshua said. "If you were there, what would you do?"

"With their powers? God, I don't know. How many Riven?"

"I think nine. There's an Auditor. And a golem."

Neptune looked away. "Nine. Okay. And probably blocking the exits too. Well, Gabriel is brave, and he'll be most worried about protecting April. . . ."

Joshua suddenly realized that Neptune was terrified. She'd said she was worried about Gabriel, but she was more than worried. But somehow, her being afraid made him *less* afraid, like they were standing on opposite ends of a scale. "I'm going to get them," he told her. "I am."

She smiled at him. Not an easy smile. "Okay. All right. So, in a small place like that, Gabriel can't hide forever. He'll try to get somewhere where they can get out, and sneak away."

Joshua studied the house. Neptune was right—the Mordin were guarding what had to be the doors, one front and one back. "They could go out a window, maybe."

"Maybe."

But even as he said it, it seemed wrong. The green and silver dots—short streaks now, moving faster—were moving toward the middle of the house. In fact, they moved to dead center, and came to a stop.

"But wait," he said. "They're—"

"They're what?"

He studied the dots. The black trails of the Mordin were closing in from both sides, north and south. The golem was creeping over the north wall. They were close now, so close. Get outside—of course. It was the only way.

"Does April's house have a porch?" he asked quickly. "With a roof?"

"Yes. Front and back."

"I can get them. I'm going to get them." He looked down at Arthur. "I'm going to get her."

The raven bobbed his head eagerly, eyeing him. *"Getter,"* he squawked hoarsely. *"Getter."*

Neptune stood up, standing gingerly on her injured ankle. She didn't ask how he knew, or if he was sure, and he sort of loved her for that. "I'm coming with," she said.

"Of course you are," said Joshua, and he took the Laithe all the way down to where he needed to go.

IN THE NEW, blinding light of the sun, the humour torn away, April searched for Gabriel. He stood on the peak of the roof like the captain of a ship in a storm. He clenched the Staff of Obro with both fists, his face twisted with anger and effort. He grimaced and grunted. "Get . . . out!"

The Auditor. From somewhere unseen, the filthy parasite had entered the staff. She was wrestling Gabriel for control of the humour, and he couldn't keep them covered. They were exposed to the world now.

Without the least bit of effort or intent, April opened her mind wide to every possibility of the Ravenvine. In an instant, countless animal minds tumbled into her own, from every direction. Patient spiders in the attic and under the eaves, teeming ants in the woodwork, peaceful carpenter bees on the back porch. Earthworms and beetles and roly-polys, down in the dirt. And in the trees all around, brighter minds, less

442

oblivious minds. Squirrels and sparrows. A cardinal pair. And keenest of all, three crows, watching from the north. All of this came to her in an instant, flooding her. The sharp sight of one of the crows lay over her own, easy and familiar and keen. She saw herself, saw all of them, perched insanely on this roof, as helpless as stranded nestlings, while chaos roiled around them.

Because there were shouts now, from down below, from everywhere. They'd been seen by more than crows. On one side of the house, two Mordin on the lawn. One of them reached casually up to the porch roof, fourteen feet up, and began to climb, watching April greedily. And on the other side, an even worse sight—Dr. Jericho. He began to climb too, but as he climbed, the golem rose out of the grass all around him, helping to lift him, bearing him up like some horrible serpent riding the waves of a black sea.

Isabel saw them coming too. She plucked desperately at her harp, first this way and then that. The Mordin on the south cried out and crumpled, falling to the ground. Isabel had severed him. April heard his rasping shout through a dozen ears, watched him fall through her own eyes and the distant crow's. But the Mordin struggled to find his feet again the moment he hit the ground. His companion hoisted him, and together they began to climb once again.

On the other side, Dr. Jericho folded over for just a moment in obvious pain—Isabel had gotten to him, too—but it was far too brief, and he did not fall. The golem held him fast, and after a vigorous shake of his evil head, he grinned at them.

"The power you wielded was never truly yours, Forsworn," he sang. "And neither is this quarrel. Step aside."

Isabel cursed at him. She severed him again, but still it no more than staggered him. Now two more Mordin appeared below him, climbing up the golem's growing face. And through the crow, through the entire teeming mass of life all around the house, April knew even more were coming. The hated Auditor was on the front porch, fists clenched as she fought her silent mental battle with Gabriel. Gaunt shadows moved behind the windows of the house. The Mordin were everywhere. They couldn't be stopped.

"The Altari have taken your friends," Dr. Jericho said, and smiled cruelly again at Isabel. "Or daughter, as the case may be. But they won't come back for you."

Isabel shrieked with rage. She threw the little white harp at Dr. Jericho.

"No!" April cried as the Mordin swatted the harp away. It splintered into shrapnel.

The humour swallowed them briefly again. Light and sound ceased to be.

"Sit tight," said Gabriel, his voice curling with effort. "I'm going to set this right."

"Don't do it," said Isabel. "We can—" The humour vanished again, leaving her last word to spill out into the open air. "—surrender."

Dr. Jericho was even closer now. Just ten feet below her,

his outstretched hand clawed at the shingles, tearing them like cloth.

The crow in the tree cawed. April saw herself, her hair shining in the sun. She saw Gabriel, neck bent, the handle of the staff pressed against his forehead. Isabel, on her hands and knees. She saw the Mordin climbing toward them like monsters out of the deep. And then one more thing, hardly an arm's length behind her at the top of it all—an astonishing, wonderful thing, a shimmer in the air.

A circling glint of floating gold.

THE RABBIT RAN. The portal began to open wide. The first thing Joshua saw was April, straddling the peak of the roof. She was looking away, but then she swung her head back toward him, right at the portal. Her eyes were cloudy and faraway, the way they were when she used the Ravenvine. But he knew she couldn't see him, not while he stood on this side of the one-way door, holding the Laithe.

Twenty feet past April, Gabriel stood holding his staff. He looked like he was in pain. There was no sign of the humour. But there was someone else, lying on her belly between them, clinging to the roof. Isabel.

The rabbit slammed to a stop. The portal was wide and clear.

"Ready," he said to Neptune, and she was through it in a flash, launching herself into the air. Joshua staggered a bit as she did it—something pulsed in his head, a flicker of a shadow across his mind, like a bird across the sun. That was new. Had he actually felt her going through the portal?

No time to wonder. On the other side, Neptune hovered high above the others. Heads turned up to her, listening. But no one could get back through the portal to safety without Joshua, without the Laithe.

He stepped through right behind her, carrying the glowing golden sphere. He barely felt the portal as he passed. But as he stepped into sunshine, and into the foul stink of brimstone, he forgot he was going from flat ground onto a steep roof. Stupidly, he fell.

For a second he slid. The shingles tore at his knees and hands. But April, kind April, reached out and caught his wrist, stopping him. Her mouth flashed a smile of relief at him. Her eyes were wide with fright.

"Go," he said, jerking his head toward the portal. And then something grabbed his leg, tearing him away, hauling him upside down into the air. Joshua hugged the Laithe to his chest.

"Patience is a virtue after all," sang Dr. Jericho, grinning victoriously into Joshua's face. "Have you come to reconsider?" The Mordin was half wrapped in the golem. It slithered around his legs, holding him aloft on the rooftop. Two other Mordin climbed up it from lower down, and two more were coming from the other side of the roof. Then Dr. Jericho glanced over through the portal, where Neptune's room in the Warren was plain to see. "Oh my," said Dr. Jericho. "Oh my, oh my."

Joshua thought he might faint. He'd been so stupid. He saw it now and couldn't imagine how he hadn't before.

He'd opened a door to the Warren right in the middle of a pack of Riven.

Before he could even pretend to imagine some way to fix the problem, to take back his terrible mistake, something fell from the sky. It crashed into Dr. Jericho's wrist. Joshua heard the crisp snap of a bone breaking in his arm, and the Mordin dropped him with a painful growl, toppling backward. Joshua fell belly first onto the roof and started clawing his way up the slope. Neptune crouched there—she'd dropped in from high above, saving him. She clutched her ankle briefly, wincing, but then sprang back into the air.

A shadowy pulse swept across Joshua's mind, his vision. He looked up to see Isabel crawling through the portal, back into the Warren.

And then he saw nothing.

The humour was back. Gabriel's voice roared through it. "Now!" he cried. "April, go!"

Apparently Gabriel was guiding her through the humour somehow, because Joshua felt her pass. She was safe. She was safe, and the Riven were blind for the moment.

"Neptune, go!" said Gabriel. "We're right behind you."

"One more," Neptune said. "Got to clear a path." Joshua felt the roof shake beneath him as she dropped onto another Mordin.

Suddenly a thousand crawling fingers slithered up onto

Joshua's legs. The golem, cold and strong. But then a firm hand—a human hand—scooped him up from under his armpit, and yanked him free. "We'll go together," said Gabriel, dragging him.

"I have to go through last," Joshua told him.

"I'll make sure you do."

Joshua felt Neptune slip through the portal. Just he and Gabriel were left now. Joshua could feel the meridian looming, very close, the portal pulsing with power. He could feel the globe tucked under his arm, greeting it.

"We're going," said Gabriel, and then something terrible happened.

Joshua wasn't alone with the Laithe. Someone else was there, some . . . thing. Another mind, reaching for the Laithe and the Meridian too, willing the rabbit to run. This new mind was trying to shut the portal. Joshua fought back before he even understood, as fiercely as he could, forcing the portal to stay open. It was an Auditor, all through him, all through the Laithe—across its surface and through the ring, into the blue eyes of the rabbit.

It happened fast. Hardly more than a second. But this was far worse than the Nevren. This was a kidnapping, an invasion, a theft. He threw every bit of anger he had at the Auditor, but she wouldn't budge. She knew everything about the portal that he did, understood everything it could do. A fury blazed up inside him, a hate he'd never known he could summon.

He was falling backward now, into the portal. He felt Gabriel go first, and the humour winked out. Sunshine blinded Joshua. And then he went too, still clutching at the Laithe's power. He thought he saw the Auditor, a pale figure snarling at him beautifully from the other end of the roof, staring with bright blue eyes that seemed to see . . . everything. And then the golem rose up over all.

Joshua fell into the Warren. The Auditor's terrible presence vanished at once. The Laithe was his again. Completely his.

He lay in Neptune's room atop Gabriel, heaving. "Well done, Keeper," Gabriel said. "Well done."

Other voices murmured at him, worrying over him, congratulating him. He could barely hear them, barely see their faces. On the other side of the portal, the golem was rearing up over the meridian, blanketing it.

Joshua squirmed to his feet. He asked the rabbit to run. It listened to him. Only to him. The portal closed swiftly, the rooftop and the golem vanishing from sight. When the rabbit stopped, Joshua plucked the meridian from the air, hands trembling. He didn't say anything to anyone.

He'd brought them back to the Warren. Out of the thick of danger, away from Dr. Jericho, and away from that awful Auditor. He'd opened that window—Joshua had, and Joshua alone—into the one safe place they had.

The one safe place.

CHAPTER TWENTY–NINE

Veritas

WHATEVER ELSE COULD BE SAID ABOUT KA'HOKA, IT WAS CERtainly more comfortable than the Warren.

Horace lay on a stuffed mattress bigger than any bed he'd ever seen before—ten feet long and nearly as wide. The room he rested in now had its own peculiar light, too, whiter than the amber lights that lit the Great Burrow. They shone from behind round openings high in the stone walls, like little windows. If he got tired enough, and let his eyes droop enough, he could almost forget that he was hundreds of feet underground.

But he wasn't very tired, despite coasting on only three hours of sleep, and despite the undeniable comfort of the huge mattress on this bed. He was too antsy, too eager for whatever was going to happen next. It didn't help that he knew *when* that next thing would happen. The box had told him. It was

5:35 in the afternoon, and at 5:44 Dailen would come and get him and take him away. He didn't know where, exactly, but he had a guess. He and Chloe would be taken to meet the Wardens' Council.

Brula, the scarred Altari who'd greeted them that morning—was "greeted" the right word?—was one of the Council members. The leader, if Horace was reading the situation correctly. Once Horace had revealed the Fel'Daera, Brula had acted quickly. Several of the Altari had hustled forward to take Horace away, separating him and Chloe. Horace suspected that only Dailen's intervention had prevented them from actually locking him up. Not that he wasn't a kind of prisoner now anyway—the room's wooden door, ordinary in every respect except for being twelve feet tall, was definitely locked. But behind that locked door, the accommodations were very nice. He'd been given clear, cool water, and a truly gigantic loaf of some weighty, spicy bread.

Best of all, they hadn't separated him and Chloe, which was just as well, because they couldn't have held her even if they wanted to. She would have come looking for him, and all sorts of trouble might have ensued. He looked over at her now, curled up into her usual sleeping ball on the room's other huge bed, looking extra tiny. She'd been asleep for hours. He envied her.

They'd been promised a meeting with the Council sometime today. Dailen seemed to think there was nothing to worry about, and was sure that Brula would do as he'd promised. But unable to leave something knowable unknown, Horace had used the box that morning to fast-forward through the day, to see when things would begin. And now the time was nearly here.

Idly, he fussed with the box. He played with the breach, filling and emptying the silver sun. He was working on nice round numbers—twelve hours, four hours, ten minutes, thirty seconds. He thought of his mom, and where she must be now, what she must be worrying. As far as he knew, no word had gotten back to Mr. Meister and the others at all.

There was a Mothergate here. His mom had practically said so, and Horace could feel it in his bones. Besides, surely all these Altari were here for a reason. In addition to the tall Altari with the blue-bladed sword, he'd seen a handful of others with weapons as well—a hammer, and two spears, and a particularly nasty-looking pair of daggers carried by the only ugly Altari he'd seen, a short, crooked-faced male. Weapons, for sure, but also Tan'ji. And why weren't those Keepers out there fighting with Horace and the others? He could think of a few reasons, maybe, but only one really made sense. They were here to defend a Mothergate. Defend it? Heal it? Save it?

Could it be saved?

There were answers ahead, he knew. Answers that frightened him. Not least of all because he wondered how many of those answers would come from Sil'falo Teneves herself. The thought of meeting the Maker of the Fel'Daera in the flesh had filled him with a kind of terrifying anticipation. Truth be told, he'd been fussing with the box most of the day in the hopes that Falo might suddenly burst into the room, glorious and terrible and wise, and then . . .

Well, he didn't know what then. But something. Something was better than nothing. And the last nine and a half hours had been a whole lot of nothing.

He looked over at Chloe. "Hey," he said softly. No response. "Hey," he said more loudly, kind of crooning the word.

Chloe stirred. "Hey, schoolgirl," she sang back sleepily, nuzzling her face into the mattress.

He laughed. "I'm not a schoolgirl. You're a schoolgirl."

"Second row," she mumbled. "Way down low." Suddenly she rolled over, her black hair plastered across her face. Her wild, confused eyes found him. "You wake me up a lot," she said after a few seconds. "What was I talking about?"

"Honestly, I have no idea," Horace said.

"Is it time?"

"Almost."

She sat up, tucking her hair behind her ears. Too short to stay, it flopped back down around her chin again. She stretched extravagantly and then reached out for the giant loaf of bread. She scooped a soft handful out of the middle of it and began to pluck it apart, munching unapologetically. "Geesh, I'm hungry. You think they got any fruit here? I could use a banana."

"I don't know. It's weird there's any food at all. Or I guess it's weird there's never any food in the Warren."

"The Wardens usually eat upstairs in the Mazzoleni Academy. I think the students think they're teachers, or something. Mrs. Hapsteade keeps crackers in her doba, though."

"Really?"

"Like five kinds. They were all sort of gross. As was the school food." She tore off a big hunk of bread and popped it into her mouth. "But this stuff is delicious. I could eat it all day. What even is it?" She pointed a warning finger at Horace. "If you find out it has owl milk or some weird . . . cave moss in it or something, don't tell me. I don't want to ruin it."

"I will definitely not tell you about any owl's milk." Horace turned to the door. "Come in, Dailen."

There was a pause, and Dailen entered, looking elegantly confused. "How did you know I was here?" he asked.

"It's five forty-four," Horace said. He held the Fel'Daera aloft, wiggling it, then slipped it into its pouch.

Dailen frowned. "That's the kind of thing Brula is going to frown at, I think."

"Let him frown," said Chloe. "We're not here for him anyway."

"I know you're not," said Dailen. "But it'll go easier for you if you stay in his graces. And you're about to meet with him. The Council has called for you. I'm here to take you to the Proving Room."

"That doesn't sound sketchy at all," said Chloe. "What are we trying to prove?"

"That you are worthy of being here," Dailen said.

"And if we're not, we'll be asked to leave?" said Horace.

Dailen shook his head. "You will not be asked. And you will not be allowed to return."

"Ah, hospitality," Chloe sighed. She stood, stuffing the rest of the bread into her mouth. "Let's go prove some things, then."

Dailen led them out, and through the corridors of Ka'hoka. The architecture of the place continued to impress—no low passageways here, but plenty of high ceilings held up by pointed archways. And lots of light, everywhere, from mysterious sources hidden cleverly in the walls. The very fabric of the place seemed to glow, one of the brightest places Horace had ever been.

They passed a dozen or so Altari. Some of them murmured greetings to Dailen in their own tongue, nodding politely but warily at Horace and Chloe. They saw two humans, too, a middle-aged man and a plump woman in her twenties. Most of the residents bore visible Tan'ji.

After a few minutes, they passed through a wide archway into the darkest room they had yet encountered in Ka'hoka. This chamber was lit by the familiar amber lights, bulbous crystals that gave off rising swirls of golden light. No one was here. At one end of the room stood a crescent-shaped table, with four huge chairs. Within its arc, a wide round patch of dirt floor filled the center of the room. And on the opposite side of the circle, another table, this one heaped with food—fruit, and meat, and more loaves of the spicy bread.

"The Proving Room," said Dailen. "The Council will be here shortly."

Chloe marched on in. "Well, while we're waiting, I'm about to prove some of this food."

Horace followed her, suddenly hungry for the first time that day. He found a huge leg of some kind of meat on the table. After verifying to his satisfaction that it was turkey, he began to eat. Chloe, meanwhile, pulled a banana from an enormous bowl of fruit. "I love this place," she said.

They ate greedily, using only their fingers. Dailen nibbled on some of the spicy bread, but Horace got the impression he was only doing it to be sociable.

"Where do you get the food?" Horace asked him.

"The same place you do, mostly. Our human residents do our shopping for us."

Horace heard footsteps. He turned around just as a small group of Altari entered the room. Brula came first, followed by two females and the towering male Altari with the huge blue-bladed weapon. It was strapped to his back now. And the taller of the two females carried a weapon, too—a massive black bow, six feet long, slung over her shoulders. It, like the blue-bladed sword, was Tan'ji.

The four Altari said nothing but proceeded to the crescent-shaped table at the head of the room, taking seats around it. Plates of food stood ready for them there, and huge stone pitchers, but they showed no interest. Instead they gazed intently at Horace and Chloe, obviously waiting.

Dailen bent to whisper to Horace and Chloe. "I brought you here, so I must introduce you. But after that, it's all you."

Horace swallowed the chunk of turkey he was devouring. "You're leaving?"

"I'll stay to observe. But this is between you and the Council." He glanced at the others. "Remember, Brula's the one to worry about."

Dailen turned and approached the council's table. Chloe shoved half a banana into her mouth and waggled her eyebrows at Horace, and together the two of them followed Dailen into the wide ring of dirt in front of the Council's table.

Brula spoke first, his words like a song. "Who comes before the Council? Who comes beneath the Veil?"

Dailen cleared his throat. "Chloe Oliver, Keeper of the Alvalaithen. Horace Andrews, Keeper of the Fel'Daera. Here under my auspices."

Horace glanced at Chloe. She made a face. Apparently, the Wardens here were quite a bit more formal than Mr. Meister's little crew. But then one of the female Altari spoke, the one with the bow. Her face was leaner than the others, more severe. Her voice was strong but reedy, like a clarinet.

"It seems every visitor comes under your auspices these days, Dwen'dailen Longo," she said. "Are we not enough company for you? Or do you hope to start a zoo?"

"Sorry," Chloe sniped, "I thought *you* were the zoo. We're the visitors."

The Altari seemed to consider Chloe for a moment, and then said, "My name is Ravana."

"O'ravana Omri, Keeper of Pinaka," Dailen explained.

"Like I'll ever remember that," said Chloe.

Ravana leaned forward. "You will call me Ravana," she said icily. "Remember it before you leave."

"Moving on," said Dailen hastily. He turned to the Altari sitting next to Ravana. "This is Sol'teokas Notiana, Keeper of the Thailadun—the Moondoor."

Another female, this one so beautiful that Horace almost wanted to look away. Almost. Smaller than the others, she had wide hazel eyes, and the ring around her irises was golden. When she blinked, her double eyelids seemed to curtsy. She stood gracefully, smiling a gorgeously radiant smile. "Call me Teokas, please," she said, her voice low and sweet. "Welcome to Ka'hoka." A band encircled one of her wrists, a round bauble the size of a chestnut dangling from it. Horace had no idea what it was, but it was definitely Tan'ji—the Moondoor.

"Hi," Horace said, waving at her. "Thanks." Chloe snorted. Teokas waved back with a long, silken hand.

Dailen gestured to the Altari with the blue blade. "And this tall drink of water is Grul'go'nesh Tulva," he said. "Keeper of the Guan'dao, the Fairfrost Blade."

The hulking Altari said nothing, not introducing himself, but Horace was getting the hang of Altari names by now. This must be Go'nesh. Horace got the feeling he let the Fairfrost Blade do most of his talking for him.

"And finally," said Dailen, "you've met Brula. Mal'brula

Kintares, Keeper of Veritas. Head of the Wardens' Council."

Brula nodded once, his face stern. "Enough," he said, waving a curt hand of dismissal. "Formalities used to mean something, but apparently times have changed."

Dailen bowed again and stepped nimbly aside, drifting into the shadows along the far wall.

Brula reached into his robe and pulled out a small, flat bowl. It was simple, made of plain gray stone, but clearly Tan'ji. "It is time we spoke," he said, laying the bowl on the table. "We will begin with Veritas."

"Truth," Chloe said. When Horace gave her a puzzled look, she shrugged. "Veritas means truth."

"Indeed," said Brula. "Perhaps you'd like to tell me what my Tan'ji does, then?"

"Your little bowl there . . . tells the truth," Chloe said dubiously. "It's not one of those lying bowls."

Brula frowned. "Veritas brooks no lies," he said. Horace still didn't understand. Brula picked up a stone pitcher and poured a small amount of water into the bowl. He spread his arms. "Come. Take the bowl. Don't be shy. I have just a few questions for each of you."

So Brula wanted them to actually touch his Tan'ji. Apparently Veritas was like Mrs. Hapsteade's quill, the Vora—it only worked in the hands of others. And somehow it would be able to know the truth?

"What if we don't want to answer your questions?" said Chloe.

"Then we will have no more to discuss," Brula replied.

"Your visit here will come to an end. You will be returned to the surface."

Horace didn't want that. There were answers here, to a thousand questions. He stepped up to the huge table and stood on his tiptoes, cautiously taking the bowl. He didn't allow himself to hesitate at all, but he also didn't want to spill any of the water. Though it had looked small in Brula's hand, it was several inches wide. Through the clear water, Horace saw that the bottom of the bowl was engraved with a crude, plump sun. But as he watched, the water began to cloud over, developing a faint greenish tint. Soon the sun was totally obscured. Horace's own face gazed back at him.

"Good," said Brula, closing his eyes. "Now observe yourself in the water and tell me a lie."

Horace looked down at his own reflection again, at his shaggy brown hair. He really needed a haircut. "Okay, then," he said. "My hair is . . . blue." The lie came out easily, and he felt nothing—at first. But when he uttered the word "blue," the lips of his reflection refused to move. They remained sealed. The illusion was profoundly disorienting, as if Horace's reflection had betrayed him, revealing itself to be someone that wasn't Horace. He recoiled a bit, nearly sloshing water onto the floor.

"What happened?" Chloe asked.

"In Veritas, your reflection will refuse to lie," Brula said. "And I will know it."

Horace pondered the bowl, thinking it through. "But

Veritas can't actually *know* the truth," he said.

Teokas leaned forward, unbearably beautiful. She raised her exquisite eyebrows at Horace. "Can't it?" she asked, her voice like the sweetest choir.

"Well, that . . . that would be impossible," Horace stammered. "The bowl would have to contain all the knowledge in the universe. I'm guessing the bowl can only know that *I* know I'm not telling the truth. It's just a lie detector."

Now it was Brula's turn to frown. "Three questions, Keeper—assuming you do not lie. Keep your answers simple and straightforward."

"Fair enough." Horace ignored Chloe's exaggerated eye roll. He had nothing to hide.

"First question," said Brula. "How long have you been Keeper of the Fel'Daera?"

That was easy, even if the true answer still seemed absurdly inadequate. As he spoke, Horace watched his reflection's lips move in perfect unison with his own. "Only about two months." He thought he heard a soft murmur of surprise from one of the Altari, but no one said anything.

"Second," said Brula. "How did you acquire your instrument?"

Even easier. "In Chicago, in a warehouse of the Wardens. The House of Answers, it was called."

"Last question. Have you ever knowingly given aid to the Riven?"

Horace hesitated. The easy answer was no, but the true

answer wasn't exactly easy. Only three days ago, he had saved Dr. Jericho's life. Had he done that knowingly? He watched himself in the green water and said firmly, "No." And inside the bowl, to his relief, his reflected self said the same.

Brula opened his eyes. "Good," he said flatly, sounding neither pleased nor disappointed. He turned to Chloe. "And now you, Keeper."

Chloe took the bowl from Horace. "I'm gonna rock this, don't worry," she said to the room. Brula then asked her the same three questions he'd asked of Horace, but instead of telling the truth, Chloe answered with three outrageous lies:

"Since the time of the dinosaurs. Rest in peace, you noble beasts."

"Got it for Hanukkah one year."

"I helped a Mordin build a sand castle last summer. Does that count as giving aid?"

In the corner, Dailen had his face buried in his hand. The other Council members looked lost somewhere between confused and amused—except for Brula, who had managed to find a frown so deep it became a snarl.

"Very amusing," he said. "One last question for you, I think. Has the Keeper of the Fel'Daera, after claiming to witness the future, ever put your life at risk?"

Chloe didn't hesitate. "I put my own life at risk. Horace just sees it."

Teokas nodded, smiling. Chloe reached up to set Veritas back on the table, sloshing a bit of water. She wiped her hands on her thighs. Although Horace was sure she was pleased with herself, her face looked anything but happy.

"I'll tell you what," she said. "Last night, I helped destroy a golem. Dailen saw me do it. A few hours before that, I killed an Auditor. A month ago, the Riven set fire to my house, and I sat inside it while it burned down around me. I've also impaled a Mordin with a crowbar, wrestled a malkund away from my father, and extinguished a crucible with my own flesh." She held up her arm, displaying the broad, dark scars that stretched from wrist to elbow. "So here's a little bit of truth for you, and you can either accept it, or suck it: I don't need your freaking *bowl*."

There was a moment of quivering silence, and then Teokas began to giggle merrily, looking around at the others. "Veil blind me," she laughed. "I don't even care if she lies to us. I don't even care what her powers are. I want her on our side."

Brula, still scowling, reached for his Tan'ji and tossed the water out impatiently. It splashed darkly onto the dirt floor.

"I'd like to agree," said Ravana, the one with the bow. "But I want demonstrations." She leaned forward to peer down at Chloe. "You were inside your home while it burned down, you say. That's a power I'd like to see. And if the Fel'Daera truly has returned, we must witness its Keeper in action, too. I call for a Ro'ha."

"Seconded," said Teokas at once. "Ro'ha."

The tall Altari, Go'nesh, simply nodded slowly, his heavy eyes fixed on Chloe.

Brula sighed. "Very well," he said. He stood up and began to recite. "Because we cannot trust what we have not witnessed, demonstrations are in order. Prepare your Tan'ji. It is time for the showing of hands. *Do regalo chith'net Ro'ha*."

Chloe leaned into Horace. "Oh, man, these guys are serious," she muttered.

Horace looked over at Dailen, pressed inconspicuously against the far wall, half in shadow. The young Altari gave him an encouraging nod. "What if we don't impress them?" Horace asked Chloe.

She mustered up a look of fake outrage. "When have I ever not impressed?"

CHAPTER THIRTY

The Ro'ha

"Keeper of the Alvalaithen," Brula intoned. "Will you go first? Will you share with us your power?"

Horace backed away, giving Chloe room for whatever she was about to do now.

"Since you asked nicely," said Chloe. "What do you want to see?"

"Whatever you can manage to achieve."

Chloe spun around to face Horace. She crossed her eyes and mouthed Brula's last words silently, mimicking him. Then she grinned mischievously, and the dragonfly's wings flickered to life. "Hold still," she said.

She marched straight at him. Horace just stood there as it became clear she meant to walk right through him. And when she did, his knees threatened to buckle. As always, the experience was breathtaking, monumental—an exquisite tangle of nerves and flesh and blood and bone. He held his breath. His fingers went rigid. He thought he felt her pounding heart pass just below his own. He felt the magnificent, quivering song of the Alvalaithen itself, sliding through him from sternum to spine.

And then she was through, leaving him empty. The Altari watched keenly, Teokas holding her hand over her pretty mouth, her double-lidded eyes twinkling. Horace turned away, blushing, trying not to clasp his chest where Chloe had entered him.

Chloe, meanwhile, didn't look back. She kept walking to the back of the room to the table full of food. She scanned it, picked up a green apple, and only then turned to face them. She held the apple high, sitting on her flat palm. Without warning, the apple fell clean through her hand. She caught it nimbly with the other. She repeated the trick, and then, slowly, began to sink into the dirt floor. Feet, ankles, knees. At the Council's table, Go'nesh grunted brutally in surprise. He sounded like a bull.

Chloe kept sinking, and as she sank, she lifted the apple higher and higher. Her torso went under. Her face. Now only her arm was visible, still holding the apple. She kept sinking until only her hand remained. At last that too disappeared, but as it did, she left the apple sitting on the ground, rocking slightly.

"Impressive," said Ravana.

"She couldn't take the apple," Brula pointed out. "She has limits."

As if she'd heard him, Chloe's hand suddenly sprang out of the ground again, grabbed the apple, and pulled it beneath the earth. Teokas laughed and clapped her hands.

Barely a second later, Chloe popped out of the floor right next to Horace. She shot three feet into the air and landed nimbly beside him, still holding the apple. He was astonished—it was a distance of forty feet, at least, and she'd traveled it faster than a sprinter. Across the room, he heard Dailen murmur, "The Earthwing."

"How am I doing?" Chloe whispered to Horace.

Horace tried to think of something clever to say. "It's a little bit embarrassing, to be honest. Nobody likes a show-off."

She elbowed him in the ribs—actually *in* the ribs, under the skin, bone against bone. He grunted.

At the Council's table, Teokas was still grinning. The other Altari looked stoic. Ravana stood and came around the front of the table.

"You're not the first stonewalker I've met," she said to Chloe. "How long can you stay ghosted?"

"Three or four minutes."

Ravana looked surprised. "I've never seen anyone travel as you just did. How fast can you fly, underground?"

"Fast enough."

Ravana pulled the great bow from her back with a smile. "As fast as an arrow from Pinaka?"

Chloe shifted uneasily. "I doubt it, actually."

"So do I," said Ravana. And then swiftly—although it was empty—she drew back her bow, pointing it at Chloe. The

467

great wooden crescent bent with a musical creak, and as it did a glowing red arrow appeared, nocked to the string. Or not an arrow, exactly—it had no point, no feathers. It looked most of all like a finger-thin rod of molten metal. "Toss the apple," she said.

Chloe glanced at Horace, and then she hefted the apple straight up into the air. Ravana loosed her bow. The sound of Pinaka's plucked string reverberated through the room with a jarring *thunk*, like an ax hitting a tree. But the arrow didn't fly. It simply disappeared. In the same instant—the same exact instant, Horace was sure—the molten rod rematerialized inside the apple. Bizarrely, it carried no momentum. It was simply *there*. The apple fell straight down again, and Chloe caught it. She and Horace both stared at the red arrow. Where it pierced the apple, the green skin was beginning to blacken.

"Careful," Dailen called out.

"Let them learn," Brula said sternly.

A moment later, the apple burst into flames. Horace leapt back, but Chloe simply stood there, gritting her teeth slightly, holding the roaring ball of fire in her hand. While she was thin, the flames couldn't burn her, he knew. But she would still feel the pain.

Calmly, Chloe knelt down. She shoved the apple down into the dirt floor—through it, into the ground. The fire went out at once with a violent *whuff!* She buried the apple elbow deep, melding it in the earth, and came up empty-handed. Teokas clapped again, bouncing in her seat.

But Ravana hardly smiled. She came closer, knelt down in front of Chloe, and drew Pinaka once more. Another molten arrow appeared, pointed directly at Chloe's face. "Let's try this," she said.

Chloe actually stepped back, though the dragonfly's wings were still whirring. "Wait, are you sure—"

Ravana fired the bow. The twang of it seemed to shake the room. Chloe stood frozen, hands in the air. Horace panicked—had she somehow been struck? But in an instant, something on the banquet table at the back of the room caught savage fire—some large piece of meat. Horace could see Ravana's molten arrow glowing in the depths of the angry flames. However it was that Ravana's arrows found their targets instantaneously, they couldn't find Chloe while she was thin.

Chloe watched the meat blaze for a moment, then turned to Ravana. "How sure were you that that wouldn't kill me?"

Ravana shrugged, and now she did smile. "A Keeper knows her instrument. And now you know yours that much better." She swung the bow back across her shoulders and bowed deep. "*Ro'ha nahro*," she said.

At the front of the room, the other council members did the same, bending their necks and intoning the words. "*Ro'ha nahro.*" Ravana spun away and returned to her seat.

Chloe turned to Horace. His heart pounded wildly, but her eyes were shining with delight. "I like them," she said.

"You would," he said.

Now Go'nesh, the tallest Altari, stood up from his seat. He towered over the others. He strode toward Chloe, hefting his weapon as he came, swinging the blue blade slowly through the air. Horace backed away, alarmed at this new threat. But Chloe just watched the huge Altari approach, looking thoroughly unconcerned.

The wings of the dragonfly went still for a moment. Just enough for Chloe to catch her breath, Horace knew. As they flickered back to life, she nodded at the approaching Altari and said, "Next."

Just as Go'nesh reached her, he spun, lifting his hands and pointing his weapon down at the ground. The blade whistled through the air, blurring and crackling. Go'nesh danced powerfully past Chloe, looking every bit Dr. Jericho's equal. His blade didn't strike Chloe, but instead swirled completely around her, leaving in its wake a glistening blue curtain. Horace blinked. The curtain hung there like a frozen sapphire ribbon, like a painter's brushstroke brought to life. It surrounded Chloe from thigh to neck, just as thick and as long as Go'nesh's blade.

She studied it, clearly surprised, but then her surprise turned to alarm as she tried to move through the curling blue swath. It seemed she couldn't do it. She cried out, cursing. "God, that's cold!" she said. "What is this stuff?"

No one answered her. Go'nesh leaned on his bladed staff and watched impassively. Chloe bared her teeth and pushed against the blue curtain. Slowly but surely her hands began to

470

edge through it. Her fingertips emerged. They looked purple with strain. Go'nesh let out another deep grunt of surprise. Horace's heart hammered—what if she got stuck halfway through? But then, with a sudden gasp, Chloe withdrew her hands. She scowled angrily at the encircling curtain, and then, shockingly, let herself sink out of sight into the ground. She popped up again right beside Horace, glaring back at the ribbon. Horace could hardly believe it—he'd never before seen a substance Chloe couldn't pass through. He heard Brula let loose a long, thoughtful hum.

If Chloe heard it, she didn't react. She rubbed her hands together and blew on them. Her palms were red. She threw a nasty glance up at Go'nesh, and then turned to Horace.

"It's barely vibrating," she said. "Everything vibrates. But that thing is almost totally still inside. And so cold it's burning hot."

Horace thought he understood her. He knew that all matter *did* vibrate, at the tiniest levels—the molecules that made up matter were in constant crazy motion. And the faster the vibration, the higher the temperature. But the *slower* the vibration . . .

"Maybe it's absolute zero," he said, hardly believing the words. Absolute zero was as cold as anything in the universe could possibly be. "Or close to it, anyway. The molecules would barely be moving." Go'nesh watched him as he spoke, his thick, angular face giving nothing away.

"Molecules again," Chloe muttered. She'd never shown

any interest in knowing exactly how her powers worked, but Horace had hypothesized long ago that her ability to pass through solid objects might be happening at the level of molecules, of atoms. Matter, after all, was mostly empty space—in a manner of speaking—and it was mostly electrons refusing to come near each other that prevented normal objects from doing what Chloe could do. Somehow, he reasoned, the Alvalaithen allowed her to overcome those forces of repulsion.

"Maybe the molecules of the curtain aren't cooperating with the molecules of your body," he said. "It must have something to do with the lack of vibration."

"Why should the vibration make a difference? I've never had trouble with cold things before."

"This is beyond cold," Horace said. "Four hundred and sixty degrees below zero."

Chloe jerked her head back, startled. "Whoa," she said. "So what you're saying is, don't put my tongue on it." No sooner had she spoken than the hanging sapphire ribbon dissolved with a sharp hiss, vaporizing instantly into a blue haze.

Teokas spoke up, her voice merry and light. "Is this how you usually operate?" she asked. "You freely discuss these technical matters?"

"Sometimes," Horace said, unsure whether the Altari would consider that a good thing or a bad thing. "When we have to."

"Horace operates that way all the time," said Chloe. "It's in his job description. My job is a little different." She stepped away from Horace, turning to Go'nesh. "Do it again."

Go'nesh gripped his blade. He looked to Brula, almost as if asking permission. When Brula nodded, Go'nesh reared back, eyeing Chloe, and spoke for the first time. "Don't move," he said. His voice was so deep that Horace felt it in his heart. Literally. The words reverberated in his chest, seeming to jostle his pulse out of whack for a moment.

The huge Altari straightened his arm, gripping his staff halfway down, and swung the blade in a wide circle. It hissed through the air just inches from Chloe's face, leaving an arc of glistening ribbon hanging in front of her.

Chloe squinted at the ribbon, then pressed a hand against it. She grimaced but didn't pull away. "If it's moving slow inside, maybe I should too," she said, almost to herself. Gingerly, she reached out and touched the frozen curve of blue. She closed her eyes and let her shoulders fall, relaxing. "I just have to take it slow." Then she began to move forward steadily. Her hand slid through the ribbon. When her belly met it, she shivered violently, just once, but took another deep breath. She kept on moving, sliding slowly but surely through the glistening swath of blue. "I got it," she said. She opened her eyes and looked up at Go'nesh. "I got it."

Two more steps, and she was through. She released the Alvalaithen and smiled up at the towering Altari. "Are you impressed?"

To Horace's great surprise, Go'nesh smiled back down at her. "I am," he rumbled.

"It hurt," she said. "I didn't like it. I think that banana I ate might be a frozen banana now." She pointed at the Fairfrost Blade. "I saw a picture of a weapon like that once. From a story. But it was called something different. The Green Dragon something."

Go'nesh rubbed his chin thoughtfully. "The Green Dragon Crescent Blade," he said. "Just a name. Just a story."

"Many of the old Tan'ji have given rise to stories," said Ravana. "To legends, to myth. It's only natural."

"One of the Wardens here carries Excalibur," Dailen said.

Horace thought his eyes would pop out of his head. "*The* Excalibur?" he said. "The sword? Like, King Arthur?"

"The sword's not even Tan'ji," Ravana said, faintly scolding. "Just the scabbard."

Chloe hardly seemed to be listening, still eyeing the Fairfrost Blade. "How old is it?" she asked Go'nesh.

"The Guan'dao is in its third millennium," Go'nesh replied. "I was lucky to earn its trust."

Horace let loose a ragged whistle. The blue blade was over two thousand years old.

Suddenly the Alvalaithen flickered back to life. Chloe thrust her arm out, exposing her palm. "Cut me," she said to Go'nesh. "Try to."

But Go'nesh shook his head, pulling the Fairfrost Blade to his chest. "No," he rumbled.

"I want to see if you can. Don't you want to see if you can?"

474

"I have seen enough." And then he bowed to her deeply, murmuring sonorously in his own tongue: *"Ro'ha nahro."* The other Altari echoed the strange words once again. Go'nesh straightened, looking down at Chloe expectantly.

"Okay, what is he saying?" she asked, clearly as bewildered as Horace. "What does that mean?"

Dailen spoke from the shadows. "Say the words back to him. *Ro'ha nahro*—'the open hand is held.' You've shown him your power, and he accepts it. He wants the same from you now."

"Oh. Sure." Chloe bobbed forward awkwardly. *"Ro'ha . . . nahro."* She pointed at Go'nesh. "And on a personal note, your power is badass."

Go'nesh looked confused but broke into a warm smile anyway. "Thank you, Keeper," he said, and then he returned to his seat at the table.

Brula gazed at Chloe for several long moments. "We have seen all we need to see of the Alvalaithen," he said at last, his tone heavy with finality. He flicked his fingers at Chloe dismissively. "Now it is your turn, Horace Andrews. A most unexpected Keeper, bearing a most unexpected instrument."

The other three Altari leaned forward, even Go'nesh, their faces full of curious doubt.

"I can't walk through walls," Horace told them. "I can't dodge arrows. I'm not sure what you're expecting to see."

"The true Keeper of the Fel'Daera should know when the arrows are coming," said Ravana.

"You say true Keeper like there's some other kind," Horace objected. "Besides, that's not how the box works. Anyone who tells you different doesn't know any better."

"And how did you come to know better?" Teokas sang. "You must be barely out of the Find yourself."

"I've been lucky. I like to think I've been smart. I've been through a lot already. I've mastered the breach, and I—"

"But have you surrendered to the Fel'Daera?" Brula asked impatiently.

"Yes," said Ravana, nodding eagerly. "Have you?"

"That's . . . not a thing," said Horace. "I don't surrender to the box, but I don't fight it either."

"When it suits you," Brula said. His voice curled with condescension.

Horace chewed his lip, thinking. They were afraid. Especially Brula. And Horace understood that, he really did. Even he was frightened by the Fel'Daera's power sometimes. Maybe the best way to convince them that he was a worthy Keeper was to share their fears.

"Look . . . I know you're scared. I get it. I have my own fears. I'm claustrophobic—do you know what that means?"

Dailen piped up. "Fear of small spaces."

"Right. A bad fear to have when you're a Warden. And one time, when we were inside a Riven's nest—"

"The same nest where Chloe destroyed the crucible?" said Teokas.

"Yes. We were there to rescue Chloe's father. While we

were searching for him, I looked into the future and the Fel'Daera showed me that Dr. Jericho—do you know him?"

Go'nesh rumbled deeply. "I know him," he said.

Horace had to shiver, imagining that encounter. "Right. Well, the box revealed that Dr. Jericho was going to lock me in an old boiler—like a metal coffin, buried in the wall. No light, hardly any air, no room to even roll over." He closed his eyes for a moment, the memories coming on too strong. He took a deep breath. "I knew that I would be trapped in there for a long time. An entire day, in fact. But I also knew—*thought* I knew—that it was the only way to destroy the crucible, and to save Chloe's dad. So I let it happen. I let Dr. Jericho catch me. I let him lock me up." He looked at Chloe, standing beside him. She had her fists pressed against her mouth. "I knew Chloe would save me."

"Because the box showed you she would," Teokas prompted gently.

Horace shook his head, still watching Chloe. "No. Because it was the only logical conclusion. It was the willed path. And at the end of it, she did save me. She destroyed the crucible. We saved her dad."

Silence dropped over the room. Teokas's lovely eyes looked wet. Ravana was gazing down at her own hands.

But Brula stood up. "The willed path," he sneered. "Logical conclusions. These things only matter if you are able to see truly in the first place. How clear are your visions?"

"It depends," said Horace, feeling emboldened by the

respectful silence of the others. "You can test me if you like."

"I intend to." Brula picked up the huge pitcher in front of him, and then stretched to grab another. He brought both of them around front and walked toward Horace. "Nothing dangerous. No boilers, no burning houses. A simple test of accuracy. If you are quite ready?"

After what Chloe had just been through, Horace had no idea if he was ready, but he pulled the Fel'Daera from its pouch. Teokas rose halfway out of her seat, craning her delicate neck to get a look at it. Ravana and Go'nesh, however, both wore worried frowns. One of Ravana's hands lay lightly on her bow.

Chloe pressed her foot against Horace's. "You got this," she said softly, and then slipped away to Dailen's side.

Brula stopped in front of Horace, hoisting the stone pitchers. "Each of these pitchers contains water. In a few moments' time, I will pour out the contents of one of them."

"And you want me to tell you which one," said Horace, relieved that the test could be so simple.

But Brula said, "Hardly. This is Ka'hoka, not a child's magic show." He reached out with a single great foot and smoothed a wide patch of dirt on the floor in front of him. "Look into the future, Keeper. Watch me pour the water. And then outline for us all the shape of whatever spill the water will make on this floor."

"You've got to be kidding," Chloe said.

Brula raised his eyebrows at Horace. "Is it beyond you, Keeper?"

Horace's mind raced, trying to picture it. A puddle of spilled water. Simple on the surface, but actually a nightmare. The Altari was asking for an insane level of precision regarding a very imprecise and unpredictable event. Messy processes that involved complicated physics—fire, running water, even clouds—were never completely precise when viewed through the box. Too much uncertainty, too little . . . humanity.

"Spilling water is a very random event," Horace said. "The Fel'Daera doesn't do random very well."

Brula nodded. "I am aware."

Horace didn't like hearing that. The problem of randomness was one of the first lessons Horace had learned with the box, when he had attempted to watch the lottery results a day in advance. It seemed like years ago. He'd watched the next day's little white balls on TV, bouncing around inside the lottery machine, but when the balls were chosen, the numbers on them had been unreadable, black digits flickering madly from one to the next. Too many variables, too many tiny influences, with very little willful contribution from anyone living. Just the smiling, lipsticked woman who opened the little plastic door to let a random ball shoot out.

But then again, that was before he'd learned to control the breach. He'd been watching the lottery drawing a full day in advance. Now, though, he was only being asked to look a few seconds ahead, and viewings in the near future were of course more accurate. He glanced at Chloe. She knitted her brow and nodded at him encouragingly. Or more like insistently, to be honest.

"Is there a problem, Keeper?" Brula said, his deep voice sickly sweet.

"Using the Fel'Daera requires thought," Chloe said snarkily. "You should try it sometime."

"There's no problem," Horace told Brula. "I think you know you've given me a difficult challenge."

"I'm familiar with the Fel'Daera's many limitations," Brula said.

Suddenly Horace wondered whether the Altari wanted him to fail. The Council was searching for evidence that the box could mislead, could see falsely, could fail to witness whatever might occur. He reasoned it through as quickly as he could—Brula's hopes, his motivations, his possible paths.

"Let Chloe pour the water," Horace said, knowing the Altari would refuse.

Sure enough, Brula shook his head. "Your closest allies will act in a manner most agreeable to whatever future you witness. The Riven, however, will not—and therefore I won't either. I will pour the water. As I see fit."

One offer refused. But that was fine, because it was the next one Horace really needed. "Then you at least have to close your eyes," he said. "It's only fair. If I sketch out the spill ahead of time, and you see it, you might change what you do."

Brula's eyes narrowed as he considered it.

"Besides," Horace pressed, "keeping my prediction secret won't compromise your test. I don't share my predictions with the Riven, either." This last bit, of course, wasn't strictly true—he'd shared his visions, for various reasons, with Dr. Jericho more than once. But Brula didn't need to know that. "In fact," Horace said, feeling braver and looking around the room, "I want everyone here to close their eyes. Like it or not, I am the Keeper of the Fel'Daera. What the box reveals is for me alone."

At last Brula nodded. "As you wish, Keeper." He closed his magnificent eyes. Everyone else did the same, Chloe last of all. "Tell me when you have witnessed what I ask," said Brula. "Trace the spill you see in the dirt. Then I will pour the water, and afterward we will learn how true a witness the Fel'Daera can be."

Horace bent his head, clearing his mind, gathering the necessary threads—this place, this test, this reluctant ally standing before him. And Brula *was* an ally, Horace felt sure of it. An ally who needed convincing. It wasn't a matter of guessing what Brula would do. Guessing meant having expectations, and expectations could steer the box astray. Still, Horace had to wonder: why would an ally give him an all but impossible test?

At last, his thoughts settled. With the ease of long practice, he shed himself of all hopes, all guesses, all theories. Anything was possible. But only one thing would happen.

When he was ready, Horace opened the box. The breach lay at thirty seconds. And there in that future—*Brula, still standing with eyes closed, pitchers by his side; almost immediately*

481

the left arm moving, lifting the pitcher.

Horace watched as Brula started to pour the water. And as he watched, he nearly laughed. He could do this; he *would* do this, no matter what Brula's intentions were. When he had seen all he needed to see, Horace bent to the ground, leaving the box open. With his fingertip, he traced lines in the dirt, revealing the future of the water that Brula—for the present moment, anyway—still held in his hand.

When he was done, twenty-one seconds after he'd seen Brula begin to lift the pitcher, Horace stood up. He closed the box. "It's done," he said. "I've seen it. Keep your eyes closed and do what you're going to do."

For a moment Brula didn't move. A sudden fear gripped Horace that the Altari would fail to act at all. But then, at thirty seconds on the dot, Brula raised the pitcher in his left hand, just as Horace had foreseen. Instead of pouring it onto the ground, however, as he'd suggested he would, the Altari tipped back his head, spread his lips wide, and poured the water into his waiting mouth. Horace watched stoically as Brula drank it all. When he was done, Brula tossed the empty pitcher aside and wiped his wide, smiling mouth.

"And now we see," he sang happily.

Brula opened his eyes. He dropped his chin and gazed down at the ground at his feet. His smile faded. He said nothing. Around the room, other pairs of eyes began to cautiously open. When Chloe opened hers, she stormed forward angrily.

"What gives?" she said. "There's no water. You said you

were going to pour it—" And then she got close enough to see what Horace had scratched into the dry dirt at Brula's feet. Not an outline of a spill at all. There was no spill. There was never going to be a spill. Instead, Horace had written two simple words:

THIRSTY MUCH?

Chloe stared. She started to laugh. "He *drank* it? Oh, man. Oh my god." She turned to Horace, her face wrinkled with glee. Then she actually poked Brula in the leg. "And you thought you were being so *sneaky*!"

"You can't lie to me," Horace said to Brula. "Not about any future I can see. I'm better than that." Horace stretched out his foot and kicked away the words he'd written. It seemed only polite. "And I don't know what happened to the last Keeper of the Fel'Daera, or why that got you so spooked, but I'm better than him too. Or her. Or whoever. The point is, I—"

"You're a Paragon," said a new voice, rippling across the room like a rain of tiny crystals, like a distant chorus of bells carried on the wind. Horace whirled around.

There in the doorway stood an Altari, tall and thin and seemingly made of alabaster. She was wrapped in gauzy white fabric, her long arms folded at her belly, the slender fingers of her strong, delicate hands intertwined like the strings of some imagined instrument. Her face was ancient and smooth and almost too beautiful to behold, the shining rings of her dark eyes as bright as halos. A long braided chain hung around her neck, from which dangled a large oval pendant, black as night. She smiled at Horace, and his knees went weak. Light seemed to spill from the Altari's face.

"Welcome, Keeper," she said. "Well met at last. I am Sil'falo Teneves."

CHAPTER THIRTY—ONE

Thus Are We Protected

"IT'S NOT MUCH," MRS. HAPSTEADE SAID, "BUT IT'LL HELP GET the stink of the Riven off you."

April bent over the bowl of golden, steaming soup. It smelled like a forest. "What is it?"

"Ginkgo-leaf soup. A special dish of mine." Mrs. Hapsteade shrugged. "My *only* dish."

"There's no spoon," Joshua said, frowning at his bowl. The Laithe of Teneves hung in the air just beside him here in Mrs. Hapsteade's doba, astonishing and lovely. When they'd first arrived back at the Warren after the escape on the rooftop, April hadn't been able to take her eyes off the Laithe. In the few hours since, she'd gotten used to it. Sort of. The little globe had a magnetic presence that was—to April's mind, anyway—almost animal-like. Joshua himself, meanwhile, had been moody and sulky, despite the fact that he'd saved them all. When congratulated or thanked, he just looked darkly at the ground.

"Spoons," Mrs. Hapsteade scoffed genially. "Why bother with what you don't need?" She didn't explain, but April understood. She picked up her bowl and sipped at it cautiously. The soup, surprisingly, tasted nothing like it smelled. It was sweet and delicate. Delicious. April made herself sip slowly, trying not to slurp. She could feel Arthur, sitting on her shoulder on the leather perch Brian had made her, watching her with polite, intelligent interest. Joshua, meanwhile, just sat staring at his bowl.

Without turning around, Mrs. Hapsteade spoke, raising her voice slightly. "Would you like a bowl of soup, Ingrid?" she asked.

April went on sipping as if she weren't perturbed, but she watched intently through Arthur's eyes as Ingrid, sitting alone in a chair against the shadowy wall of Mrs. Hapsteade's doba, sat forward into the light. The girl smirked scornfully. "I've lost my taste for it, thanks."

"You never cared for it much, as I recall," said Mrs. Hapsteade briskly.

"You might also recall I never cared much for *any* of this." Ingrid spread her arms, seeming to indicate the entire Warren and everything in it.

Mrs. Hapsteade sighed. "Except for Gabriel, of course. We are all fond of Gabriel, aren't we?"

Ingrid glowered and leaned back into the shadows.

April had been startled to discover, when she first walked in, that Ingrid was simply sitting here in Mrs. Hapsteade's living room. Or whatever room it was. She'd heard Ingrid had been captured, of course—it was all Neptune had talked about since April and Gabriel's return. Neptune seemed to have a particular hatred for the former Warden turned traitor.

At first sight, April had wondered why Ingrid wasn't chained up, or locked in a room somewhere. But she'd come to realize that she *was* chained. A scarlet belt, seemingly made of light, encircled her waist tightly. It held her in place, scarcely budging more than a few inches in any direction. A matching band was looped around Mrs. Hapsteade's wrist.

"I might enjoy it more if you'd take this bola off me," Ingrid said now, squirming but trying not to let it show. "It pinches, you know."

"I do know," Mrs. Hapsteade replied lightly. "And *I* might enjoy it more if the bola were around your neck instead of your waist." She leaned over to Joshua and laid a kind hand on his arm. "Joshua, it seems like you and this soup can't agree. Would you like some crackers?"

"I'm not hungry," Joshua mumbled.

"I'm sorry I don't have more to offer. We haven't had this many souls in the Warren since before you all were born. It's getting a bit crowded."

April did some mental counting. Joshua and herself, the five other Wardens, Isabel and Ingrid, plus Horace's mom—ten people in a massive place like the Warren didn't seem like much of a crowd to April, but she supposed Mrs. Hapsteade had gotten used to far less.

"With any luck," Ingrid said, "you'll have an even bigger crowd to deal with soon. Much bigger."

Joshua jerked his head up to look at her. "What does that mean?" he said, obviously alarmed.

"She's just trying to scare you," said April. "Don't listen to her."

"All the portals you've opened in this place today," Ingrid went on, shaking her head. "You might as well have put up a—"

Mrs. Hapsteade whirled to face her. "I know you're frightened, dear. Worried about your Tan'ji. It must be truly terrifying to know that you might never see it again. Do you think you'll receive any warning before they send it to the ether?"

Ingrid flinched. "Mr. Meister would never do that to me."

"It won't be up to him. Two of our Wardens went to speak to the Council hours ago. I wonder if your fate has already been decided?"

Ingrid lapsed into silence. April kept a straight face, trying to pretend that she knew what Mrs. Hapsteade was talking about. The ether? The Council? And the two Wardens—did she mean Horace and Chloe? Gabriel and Mr. Meister seemed to think they'd been taken to some mysterious haven of the Altari, some tremendously secret place. But no one had mentioned any Council.

Right at April's ear, Arthur made his soft chuckling noise, a kind of friendly concern. He was looking at Joshua, and Joshua, in turn, was still staring at Ingrid.

"Hey," April said softly to the boy. "Don't worry about it."

"But people saw my portals," he said. "The Riven, I mean. Dr. Jericho, and—"

Mrs. Hapsteade interrupted him. "Even Dr. Jericho can't discover the location of the Warren just by looking through a portal. No more than I could discover the location of a house by looking at a photograph of a bedroom."

"But . . ." Joshua's voice and face twisted painfully, and a sudden surge of silent tears poured from his eyes.

"What is it?" April said. "What's wrong?"

Joshua pushed his chair away from the table, nearly falling over, and ran out of the doba. April moved to follow, but Mrs. Hapsteade stopped her, rising.

"Stay here," she said. "He needs reassurance you can't give him." She swept out of the room after him.

April sat down. She felt Ingrid's eyes on her. She reached back to scratch at Arthur, for comfort, but the bird squawked and flapped away, cracking her hard on the head with his wing. She felt the impact through the vine, too, in her wrist—a strange reminder of the shared anatomy between herself and the raven, their homologous bones.

"Nice bird," said Ingrid, watching the raven strut across the floor.

"He is nice. But I didn't make him."

"You're new, aren't you?" Ingrid said. "A neophyte."

April didn't reply. Arthur walked out the front door, following Joshua and Mrs. Hapsteade. They had wandered deeper into the Great Burrow, too far for Arthur to hear them, but she could see them clearly.

"I wonder how long it will take you to figure it out?" said Ingrid. "It took me years."

"Everybody learns at different speeds," April said, only half listening.

"You'll have to learn fast. The end is coming soon unless we stop it."

Now April looked at her. "The end of what?"

Ingrid pointed to the Ravenvine. "That." She nodded at the Vora, standing prominently on a bookcase several feet away. "That." She tugged at the bola around her waist. "Even this."

"Sounds very apocalyptic," April said. Outside, Joshua was still crying. April saw him mouth the words "I'm sorry."

"Oh, I'm not the one preaching the apocalypse," Ingrid said. "That'd be your new friends. They believe in their ridiculous omens so much they're willing to let the true end come. They're scaring themselves to death—literally."

April was so confused, so angry. "I don't know what you think—"

Mrs. Hapsteade exploded into the room. Her face was thick with concern. She ignored both of them, however, instead bustling over to the Vora. She tucked the quill and ink into a large pocket of her black dress. Only then did she turn to April.

"I need you," she said, and left as quickly as she'd come.

"In a hurry to get to nowhere, as usual," said Ingrid.

April started after Mrs. Hapsteade, but stopped at the door and looked back at Ingrid. "By the way, you don't smell so great," April said, and then she left her there.

Outside, Mrs. Hapsteade spoke quietly, urgently. "Go to Vithra's Eye. See what only you can see."

"Is something wrong?"

"I don't know. I need to speak with Mr. Meister."

"Is it the Riven? The portals? You said Dr. Jericho wouldn't be able to find the Warren."

"He can't."

Up ahead, Joshua watched them talk with his fists pressed against his mouth. All at once he threw his arms down to his sides.

"I didn't mean to!" he cried. "She was in my head!"

April frowned, confused, but then she froze. The escape on the rooftop. The portal, open back into the Warren. The Riven everywhere, Mordin and the golem and—

"The Auditor," she whispered. She looked at Mrs. Hapsteade. "But that's crazy. Even if she was in Joshua's head, in the Laithe, that doesn't mean—"

"Maybe not. Neither of us are the experts here. Go to the Eye. Meet us back in Mr. Meister's office." She turned to go.

"But what I am I even looking for?"

"The owls," she called back. "You'll know if something's wrong."

The weird little owls of Vithra's Eye. April had felt them before. She ran up the passageway to the lake now, reaching out with the vine. Before she was even twenty feet from the shore, she felt one, cruising silently above the water. And now another. The owls here were like none she'd ever encountered. They lived somewhere high above the water, she knew, in the crown of the huge chamber. They lived in holes in the rock, almost like swallows. She had absolutely no idea what they ate.

Whereas most owls were sort of catlike—sleepy one moment, alert and predatory the next—the owls of Vithra's Eye reminded her more of turtles, their minds slow and unconcerned. She stood on the lakeshore, listening to them. They seemed as calm as ever. Bored, even. She assumed the eyes of one of them, its night vision lighting up the massive chamber—she saw herself, and the mysterious unwalkable walkway that ran across the water. There was a large, dark pit in the middle of it, she saw now, covered with a heavy, ornate grate. The owl circled closer to the opposite shore. She stared, holding her breath.

Nothing. No one.

"She said I'd know if something's wrong," April muttered to herself. "But I *don't* know, so I guess nothing is?"

Could it be true? Could the Riven have learned the location of the Warren because of the Auditor, and Joshua's open portal? She stayed by the water for another minute. The owls went on circling silently, untroubled.

April left them. She jogged back into the Great Burrow, between the towering trees of stone. Arthur joined her, gliding overhead. More than ever, the place felt like a forest to her, an elven forest lit with golden light and crowned with a canopy of stone. She was relieved she had felt no sign of danger from the owls. She'd had plenty of danger lately. This was just a scare, all Ingrid's doing, getting Joshua worked up over nothing.

She kept repeating that to herself, again and again, all the way to Mr. Meister's office.

Inside, Mrs. Hapsteade and Mr. Meister were waiting for her. Isabel stood next to Jessica, Horace's mom. Joshua curled on the couch with the Laithe, his head buried in his arms.

"You've been to the lake," Mr. Meister said. "And?"

"I didn't see or see or hear anything," said April. "The owls seem fine. Same as they always are."

Mr. Meister didn't exactly look relieved. More like he *wanted* to feel relieved. He pressed a finger to his upper lip, his bushy brow furrowing. "The Auditor was occupying the Laithe when Joshua returned here through the portal. He believes she was able to determine the location of the Warren." He turned to Jessica and Isabel. "Tuners? Tell me what you think."

The women looked at each other, surprised. April had a sudden, sadly sweet vision of them as girls, her own age or even younger, here in this very room, taking instruction from this very man. The image made April feel older. Or if not older, closer to who she might one day become. Still, she couldn't imagine why Mr. Meister would care what Isabel had to say. April wouldn't trust Isabel with a goldfish. Judging by the fiery look on Mrs. Hapsteade's face, she seemed to feel the same way.

Isabel opened her mouth, but Jessica cut her off. "I'm sure I don't know as much about the Laithe as Isabel. But *none* of us know as much about it as Joshua."

Joshua sat up. "I felt what I felt," he said sullenly.

"Henry," Jessica said, "I know it's hard to imagine that the Warren could ever be found—"

"It has been found before," said Mr. Meister. Everyone except Mrs. Hapsteade looked shocked. "The Riven did discover our whereabouts once, long ago, in an act of treachery. The Warren's final defenses weren't breached. The attack was driven back, and secrecy restored."

"And those defenses are the same ones we have today, right?" asked April.

Mr. Meister said nothing. He pinched at a little pile of sand on his desk, picking up grains and letting them fall again, watching intently as if he were counting a pile of gold.

"Right?" she said again, louder.

When he still didn't answer, Jessica said softly, "Henry?"

Mr. Meister stood up. He swept the sand away and plucked the red-needled compass from his desk. He held it out to Mrs. Hapsteade. "Dorothy, you and Joshua stay with

494

Isabel and Ingrid. I'll send the others up to you, just as a precaution."

Mrs. Hapsteade hesitated before taking the compass. "Should I be worried?" she asked him calmly.

"You should be strong, as always." He bowed to April, and then to Jessica. "If you two would come with me, please? I need your insights."

"Let me come," Isabel pleaded, the first words she'd spoken. "Give me a harp. I can help. I helped at the meadow."

Mrs. Hapsteade shot to her feet. "You will never hold another harp again. You throw a shovelful of dirt into a grave you dug us all, and call it help. No more."

Joshua began to cry. Mr. Meister left the room without looking back. Frightened and fighting to stay steady, April followed him, with Horace's mom in tow, the satchel holding her harp slung over her shoulder. Behind them, Mrs. Hapsteade began to murmur soothingly to Joshua.

Mr. Meister led them down the Perilous Stairs without a word. Arthur, watching April closely, flew out into the Maw and circled on the rising breeze. At the bottom of the stairs, Mr. Meister told them to wait, and he hustled down the hall to Brian's workshop. April stood on the ledge with Jessica, wondering how much more the woman knew—if anything— about what they were doing.

"Penny for your thoughts," said April.

"That'd be a bad bargain at the moment, I'm afraid."

"Because you don't know what your thoughts are, or because your thoughts are unpleasant?"

Jessica smiled. "I do so love Horace's friends." Then her smile faltered and she said, "My thoughts were: change swallows everything."

April was almost sorry she asked. "Mr. Meister wants our insights. He's taking us somewhere."

"He's worried. There's a chink in the armor of this place. He wants to reassure himself."

Before April had a chance to ask more, Mr. Meister returned with all three of the other Wardens. April gaped at Brian. He looked like a prisoner, hauling Tunraden between his knees, his hands buried to the wrists in it.

"Now you see my true form," he declared glumly to April, nodding at Tunraden.

Of all the people she might have blamed for everything that had gone wrong tonight, Brian was the one she truly couldn't hold a grudge against. Not with what he'd done for her. "I've already seen your true form," April said. She turned her head and tucked back her hair, showing him the Ravenvine, and the little black flower he'd repaired.

He nodded gratefully, then stuck out his chest. "You must have read my shirt." The shirt said:

WRONG TREE.
PLEASE DO NOT BARK.

"Gabriel, take Brian and his shirt upstairs," said Mr. Meister. "Wait there with the others. Neptune, you'll be with us.

And April, can you bring the bird?"

Arthur was still circling high overhead, enjoying himself.

"He generally does what he wants," she said.

"I hope he will want to come with us, then."

April had never traveled in the direction Mr. Meister led them now. The bridge across the Maw was first, a precarious journey through a buffeting wind that blasted up from below, growing stronger as they went. Neptune had it easiest, going high into the air and leaping across, her cloak fluttering magnificently. She dropped back down on the far side ahead of them, where the wind faded abruptly to nothing. To April's surprise, Arthur followed her, thrilled to have an airborne companion. And when April reached the sheltered balcony opposite Brian's workshop, the raven settled in neatly on her shoulder again. Mr. Meister grunted with satisfaction.

They entered a long dark hallway. Neptune went first, lighting the way with her purple jithandra. Twice a door appeared along the walls, materializing out of nowhere as her light fell across them. April glanced behind at Mr. Meister bringing up the rear, his white jithandra shining. To her shock, door after door sprouted out of nothing as he passed, doors that couldn't be seen by Neptune's light alone.

"The Gallery," he said to her, apparently not intending to explain any further. "One of the wonders of the Warren."

They went on for another hundred feet, until Mr. Meister called for them to stop. He slid past April and Jessica, and as his jithandra illuminated the wall in front of them, a thick wooden door suddenly appeared. They went through it and found themselves at the bottom of a tall, wide shaft. Arthur took flight. He circled up the shaft, and through his eyes April noticed that an intimidating series of iron rungs were embedded in the rock face, leading up to a ledge high above. Arthur landed there, strutting proudly, feeling wild. He let loose three triumphant squawks that echoed down around them.

Mr. Meister craned his neck. "If only we all had it so easy. Neptune, perhaps you can take April?"

April stepped back. "I can climb."

Mr. Meister put a hand on her shoulder. "Let us not waste energy where we don't need to. Go with Neptune. Jessica, you've made this climb before, I believe."

"Only a hundred times," Jessica said, gazing up at the metal rungs. "I never thought I'd be here for number one oh one."

"Nor I," said Mr. Meister, and then he started to climb, with astonishing speed. Jessica followed him, not nearly as fast, but faster than April could have managed.

"Whoa," said April.

"We'll get there first," said Neptune. She looked April up and down, examining her, considering it. "Do you know how much you weigh?"

"I don't believe in weighing myself."

"I won't tell you then," said Neptune. "You're just under my limit, so we're good. Here, put your arms around my neck."

Awkwardly, April wrapped her arms around Neptune's

neck. The older girl scooped her up beneath her knees and her shoulders, lifting her easily. As easily as a pillow. And now April felt the power of the tourminda in her own body—a blissful kind of peace, the earth's gravity gone from every cell in her body. Her hair began to lift.

"Oh, wow," said April. "How are you not doing this constantly?"

"Sometimes I am," said Neptune. "But I've got to keep my legs strong. Now hold on tight—if you fall, fixing you won't be easy."

Neptune squatted low, and with a powerful thrust of her long legs, launched them both into the air. It was a bizarre sensation, a jump that seemed to have no end. They rocketed quickly past Jessica and Mr. Meister, headed for Arthur high above. April hugged Neptune tight. Up and up they went.

Gradually, air resistance slowed them. They drifted to a stop just a few feet below the ledge. Neptune stretched for a fingerhold on the wall of the shaft and pulled them up the last little bit. Arthur danced back and forth, chuckling, delighted. April stepped cautiously onto the ledge beside him. Her knees nearly gave way as she released Neptune and her weight returned to her.

"Kind of a bummer getting it all back, isn't it?" said Neptune, still hovering.

April didn't ordinarily believe in escaping from the realities of the world, but it was hard not to deny the thrill of being weightless.

Soon Mr. Meister joined them on the ledge, much more quickly than April would have believed possible. Jessica followed soon after. Incredibly, neither of them seemed short of breath.

April glanced down at the rungs stretching out far below them. "That's not an ordinary ladder, is it?"

"This is the Warren," Mr. Meister said simply. "Now make way, make way." He squeezed past them along the rock wall. Arthur flapped out into the shaft and swung back, landing on April's shoulder once more. Mr. Meister stopped in front of a small section of bricks in the natural stone wall. He pulled a glass Tan'kindi from a vest pocket, a kind of crystal key with a bristling end. He touched the tip against the brick wall, pushing. It slid in easily. He gave it three swift twists, and then turned to them all.

"We are about to enter Sanguine Hall. Jessica, you'll be fine, but April and Neptune—do not wander. Stay close to the wall."

"And what, exactly, is Sanguine Hall?" April asked, not happy about the implication that if she wandered, she might not be fine. "Is this where you took Horace last night?"

Jessica grunted, but didn't say anything.

"Yes," replied Mr. Meister. "This is the Warren's back exit. A second way out . . . and in."

"You're worried the Riven might come in this way," April said. "But isn't there a Nevren?"

Mr. Meister didn't answer that, seeming to avoid Jessica's

500

steady gaze. April's heart got suddenly heavy, as if all the weight Neptune had taken from her before had found its way there.

Mr. Meister's big gray eyes shifted to Arthur. "Bring the bird," he said, and he stepped through the wall, vanishing. Neptune went after him.

"Why does he want me to bring Arthur so bad?" April asked Jessica.

"Birds get keyed up around the Riven. They hate them. And being in a protected place—being around leestones—exaggerates the effect. That's why they keep the owls in Vithra's Eye."

"So Arthur's supposed to be the canary in the coal mine, then. Or I guess . . . the raven in the Riven pit."

"Yes, though I'm not sure I see the point."

"But aren't you worried?"

"Yes."

"So, you do think it's true. You think the Riven really might have figured out where the Warren is."

Jessica opened her mouth, closed it, then opened it again. "I think Joshua knows what he knows. I think we should have left already." Seeing April's frightened face, she smiled ruefully. "Do you want your penny back?"

"No. I want to find out what's going on."

"Then let's go. Let's see."

Unsure how to get Arthur through the wall, April did the only thing she could think of. She grabbed his head gently, covering his eyes, and immediately plunged through the bricks.

He squawked and struggled, but it only took a second, and on the far side of the cold wall she let him go. He flapped away, offended, and landed twenty feet off.

Beyond him, the mysterious Sanguine Hall stretched into the distance. The walls were high, the ceiling a dark cloud. The place seemed totally empty.

Neptune and Mr. Meister stood just there, beside her. Jessica came through last, and sighed at the sight of the gloomy hall. She must have been here before, traveling in and out of the Warren, doing the Wardens' work. April tried to picture it.

"He seems fine," said Neptune, watching Arthur.

"Yes," April reported. "He's annoyed with me a little, but he's fine."

"Can we make him go farther?" Mr. Meister asked.

Neptune reached into her pocket, pulling out a little handful of dog food. "We could see if he'll fetch," she said.

Arthur was already watching Neptune with his sharp eyes. "Do it," said April.

Neptune heaved the kibble far down the hall. It sailed over Arthur's head. He was airborne before it landed, tracking each individual piece. The kibble skittered across the stone floor far beyond him, halfway down the hall.

Arthur dropped to the ground and began collecting it all, one piece at a time. April was so intent on him she didn't even bother masking his sense of taste. Dry spicy powder seemed to flood her mouth, scratch down her throat.

"All seems well," said Mr. Meister.

"He's good," said April. Arthur went farther, chasing down the last couple of pieces. Through him, she could see the far end of the hall now, a jumble of collapsed stone. "He's happy. He's not—"

And then rage flooded her.

At first she didn't even know where it was coming from. But the raven skittered away from the last piece of kibble, flapping his wings and croaking shrilly, his eyes trained down the hall. *Bad. Hate. Claw.* She'd never felt such intensity of emotion from him.

"What's happening?" Neptune asked. "That's just a happy food cry, right?"

Mr. Meister laid a hand on April's shoulder. "Tell us, Keeper."

"He's mad. He wants to attack. He—"

Far in the distance, a shadow moved. April could never have seen it in a thousand years, but it filled Arthur's sight, his mind. A stealthy dark form emerged from the rubble at the opposite end of the hall, materializing out of the stone just the way she and the others had come through the bricks behind her.

A Mordin.

Arthur went on fuming, his calls echoing down the hall as a second Mordin appeared. And then a third.

"They found us," April whispered.

Neptune inhaled sharply. Jessica pulled her harp from her bag. Mr. Meister stood utterly still for a moment, as if in shock, and then bustled the group into the corner, thick into the shadows.

"How many?" he asked.

"A hunting pack of Mordin," April said. "They're coming."

The three Mordin crept stealthily closer. They seemed nervous, unsure of their surroundings. They'd seen and heard Arthur, of course; she could see their eyes. The raven threw one more loud challenge their way, and then took wing. He flew halfway back to April before alighting again, strutting furiously.

"We need to get him out of here," April said. "We all need to get out."

"Wait," said Mr. Meister. "Let us see."

The Mordin were close enough to be seen now, and heard, nearly halfway down the long corridor. One of them was laughing, a hissing crackle that slid across the stone floor of the hall.

"They'll see us," April hissed.

And then, out in the hall, it began to snow. No, not snow—a blizzard. A slow but blinding cloud, pouring down from the darkness high over the Mordin's heads. The Mordin stopped, looking up, shouting in their own language.

"What is that?" April whispered, terrified for reasons she couldn't begin to guess.

"Sa'halvasa," Mr. Meister replied quietly, gazing. "It has come to feed."

April took Arthur's eyes, trying to make sense of it. These weren't snowflakes at all. They were tiny shining blades, a countless multitude on the wing. They swarmed down and started to land on the Mordin, gathering on their shoulders and backs. The Mordin bellowed, dancing and swatting at the cloud, and the drifting horde immediately flared into a frenzy. The swarm thickened, seeming to roar and buzz. The little blades kept coming, swirling around the struggling Mordin like an unstoppable tide around stranded swimmers.

And now the Mordin began to cry out in pain. With every swing at the deluge of blades, they took a hundred cuts, fine and piercing. Their clothes tore open, and the flesh beneath, blood pouring from a thousand little wounds—hands, arms, faces. The silver cloud of blades began to turn red. April squeezed her eyes shut, but she could still see. Arthur was watching the slow slaughter, dancing on the ground and croaking raucously. She pushed his sight out of her mind.

It went on forever. April realized she had her hands slapped over her ears. Slowly . . . slowly . . . the cries of the Mordin began to fade. Soon there was only a single voice, gurgling, and then it too went quiet. The only sound left beyond the coursing pulse of her own heart was the glassy rattle of the sa'halvasa.

She opened her eyes. The three Mordin lay motionless under the hanging, swirling hive of blades, their bodies strewn across the stained floor.

No one spoke. Neptune stared, expressionless. Jessica grasped April's hand and pulled her into a hug. April let her.

"Thus is the Warren protected," Mr. Meister said softly.

Arthur, calmed now, began to walk toward the fallen Mordin. April turned to watch him. The sa'halvasa still hovered, and she almost called out to him. She knew he was in no danger, but . . . she just didn't want him anywhere near any of this. For one horrible moment, she thought he might be wondering if he could find food out there in the carnage. Ravens would eat anything, she knew, and Arthur certainly wasn't above a bit of carrion—far from it. But to her relief, she felt no such interest rolling around in his mind. He was only curious, and satisfied.

And then suddenly he stopped. His satisfaction vanished. He cocked his head. Then he spread his wings and let out a series of furious cries.

Rrawwwk! Rawk! Rrawk!

Hurt. Chase. Stab.

"What's happening?" Neptune shouted.

An explosion like a train collision rocked the very walls. The far end of the hall burst into a cloud of dust and debris. Before it even settled, a golem writhed in like the striking neck of a dragon. Dark shapes poured in around it, a dozen Mordin or more.

They were coming.

CHAPTER THIRTY-TWO

Sil'falo Teneves

HORACE COULDN'T MOVE. NO ONE SPOKE.

Sil'falo Teneves, Keeper of the Starlit Loom itself, came into the Proving Room as if carried by the wind. "Council," she said with a nod.

Brula stood up. "Sil'falo Teneves. We are glad you here. We called for you some time ago."

"So I heard," Falo said, glancing at Dailen. "My apologies. No doubt you simply wanted me to greet our new guests. I trust they have passed your little tests? Surely they are free to roam Ka'hoka now—with your kind permission, of course."

"Lies have been told, Sil'falo Teneves," said Brula. "The Council is displeased."

"As it should be," said Falo, her voice growing sharp. "Lies should not have been necessary."

Horace tried to think of words. Any words. They were

talking about him. The Fel'Daera. And here was the Maker herself, defending the very act that had allowed Horace to become a Keeper in the first place. He felt he should say something, stake his claim, but he had no idea where to begin.

Ravana leaned in. "We were told that the Fel'Daera had been destroyed."

"So I recall," Falo said. "It was I who told you."

"Why did you tell us that lie?" asked Ravana.

"Why should I not have? Had the Council learned that the Fel'Daera still existed, you would have insisted that it be brought here, for safekeeping. To languish in the belly of Ka'hoka."

"It would have been the Fel'Daera's rightful end," Brula said.

Falo turned to Horace, gesturing with a graceful sweep of her long arms. "This is its rightful end. Do you deny it?"

Horace all but quivered at the words, bursting with a pride and a fear that couldn't possibly be named. *Rightful end.*

"You left the Fel'Daera with the Taxonomer, to seek a new Keeper," Brula accused. "After what happened to the last?"

"I did. And that new Keeper has been found. A Paragon—the first the Fel'Daera has ever known."

"Paragon or no Paragon, you endanger us all. Your abomination—"

Falo held up a hand, her spidery fingers curling elegantly, silencing Brula. She glided toward Horace, her haloed eyes brimming with light. "My abomination, yes," she said, almost fondly. "My greatest mistake." She walked right up to Horace and bent down before him, gazing first at the Fel'Daera and then into his face. The Fel'Daera seemed to hum, trembling with a power as pure as falling snow. "I believed you would be Found," she said to Horace. Her breath smelled like freshly split wood, like honey, like every clean and honest thing. "And so you have. Are you frightened?"

"I . . . yes," Horace said. "But I don't know why."

"All this talk of abominations. Lies and destruction and mistakes. It's been over a hundred years since I forged the Fel'Daera. A long time, one might imagine, to live with regret."

"And have you?" said Horace, wanting to hide the box away, but finding himself unable to do so. "Have you lived with regret?"

She smiled, radiant. She took his wrist, and guided the hand holding the Fel'Daera toward its pouch. He slipped the box inside, grateful for reasons he couldn't begin to explain.

"I have not spent a single day wishing my creation back," said Falo. "Least of all this day." At the Council's table, Brula cleared his throat unhappily.

Chloe leaned into Horace. She couldn't take her eyes off Falo either. "I think she likes you," she whispered hoarsely.

Falo laughed. "We Makers are not supposed to *like*, or even approve. No more than parents are supposed to have a favorite child. But even the most impartial minds are anchored to the heart." She gripped Horace by the shoulders warmly, her hands so large that it felt like a hug. "I knew you from the moment you first laid eyes on the Fel'Daera, Keeper. But I do not know your name."

"Horace. Horace Andrews."

"Well met, Horace Andrews. The honor belongs to me."

Horace's eyes fell to the large oval pendant that hung from Falo's neck. Not much bigger than a bar of soap, it was so black it was almost unseeable. The Starlit Loom was about this size, he knew, smaller even than the Fel'Daera. But this couldn't possibly be it. This was not Tan'ji.

"Falo, please," Brula said impatiently.

Falo ignored him. "All will be revealed in time," she said to Horace kindly, as if reading his thoughts. She turned to Chloe. "And you, Keeper. I have never seen your Tan'ji before, but I can recognize a scion of the Starlit Loom when I see it. Will you introduce yourselves?"

"Chloe Oliver. This is the Alvalaithen."

"Well met, indeed. Never in my memory have two Paragons come into our halls on the same day. These are rich times." She stood up straight, turning to the Council. "If we are finished here, I would very much like to walk and talk with our visitors. There is much I would discuss with them."

"There is much we would discuss with *you*, Sil'falo Teneves," said Brula, lowering his brow.

"What is there to discuss, Mal'brula? Do you wish to debate what cannot be undone?" Falo gestured back toward

Horace. "Or do you seek to undo it?"

Teokas and Ravana leaned back from the table, gasping and murmuring softly. Go'nesh swung his heavy head toward Brula.

Brula looked pained, surly. "We do not unmake the bond, Keeper," he said. "You know that as well as anyone."

"Better than you, I sometimes think." Falo turned back to Horace and Chloe. "Will you walk with me, Keepers? May I speak with you more?"

Horace nodded. Chloe said, "You absolutely may."

Brula rose, his fists planted on the table. "At the very least, we would hear what you have to say to our visitors, Falo," he said.

"Come to my chambers, then. All are welcome, as always." Brula didn't move. His expression suggested that going to Falo's chambers was not very appealing. After a moment, Teokas stood up and left the table.

"I'll come, Falo, if I may."

Falo smiled. She bowed to the others and said, "Thank you, Council," then glanced back at Horace and Chloe, seeming to suggest they do the same. They did so, awkwardly. Ravana bowed. Go'nesh nodded. Brula twitched.

They left the Proving Room then—Falo in front, Horace and Teokas behind, and Chloe and Dailen bringing up the rear. It was a relief to be out of there, even if Horace wasn't sure exactly how much they had proved, especially to Brula.

As they moved through vaulted, light-filled halls, Horace

was embarrassed to discover that he was embarrassed to be walking beside the beautiful Teokas. It was hard not to let his eyes drift to her. He decided she moved like a mermaid, which made no sense. Just as he was beginning to desperately hope she wouldn't talk to him, she did.

"Tell me, Keeper," she crooned, somehow making the word "Keeper" sound like the dearest pet name. "What did you think of Brula?"

"Brula? Oh, uh . . . he seemed a little . . . tightly wound."

Ahead of them, Falo laughed. Teokas glittered down at Horace. "Brula does much for us here," she said. "His intentions are good."

"I'm sure that's true."

"But also, he is a complete turnip, and I prefer not to be around him."

Now it was Dailen's turn to laugh.

"Turnip," Chloe said dryly. "Good one. . . . Hey, not to make this about me, but what's a Paragon, and why am I one?"

Dailen said, "A Paragon is the ideal Keeper. The perfect match, if you like. Someone so supremely suited to their Tan'ji that only they can realize the full potential of his or her Tan'ji."

"Stop, I'm blushing," Chloe teased.

But Horace didn't know about any that. *Perfect. Ideal. Supreme.* Is that what he was supposed to be? He reached out for the Fel'Daera at his side. It didn't seem to have much to say on the matter.

"Are you a Paragon?" Chloe asked Dailen. She sounded almost hopeful.

"If he were," said Teokas merrily, winking back at him, "he'd still have all sixteen of his lives left."

Dailen frowned and sighed. "They're not lives, Teokas. Please don't call them that."

Teokas whispered loudly down to Horace. "He's afraid if he loses another, he'll forget how to dance."

Horace tried to imagine what Altari dancing looked like. Not a lot of dancing happened at the Warren. He wondered if Teokas and Dailen danced together, and to what strange music.

"Paragons are rare," Falo said. "I've only met five, before today."

"Including yourself?" Dailen asked.

Falo bobbed her head, as if conceding the point. "Six, then. But I have always known myself."

They walked on. The place was enormous, many times the size of the Warren, it seemed, and much grander. He felt a stab of guilt, thinking it. What was happening at the Warren now? Had the others gotten away, and were they safe in the Great Burrow? Something about Ka'hoka, he thought, was making that place and even those people—his friends, his allies—seem faraway and foggy.

As they walked, Horace noticed even more open stares now, often for Falo. Some looked at her with awe, others with something that looked more like anger. They passed a few more humans, too, including a girl who looked to be about Joshua's age. A transparent sphere the size of a beach ball rolled along the floor ahead of her, obviously Tan'ji.

Falo stopped at a rough-hewn opening in the wall, speaking inaudibly to a thick-limbed Altari who stood there, as if on guard. A huge green ax Tan'ji hung at his side. The guard nodded, and Falo led them into a natural cave, the first one they'd seen since the cavern above the Well of Giving.

"Looks like we're headed to the boonies," Chloe said, but in no time at all she was proved wrong.

At the far end, the natural cave opened into a magnificent sculpted vault, no wider than a house but as tall as a skyscraper, chiseled from the bedrock and lined with what seemed like black marble. The chamber rose hundreds of feet overhead, the walls curving away gradually until they were lost out of sight, away and above, buried in a soft ocean of white light that poured down from the heights. Horace tipped his head back, his mouth open, full of wonder.

At his side, Chloe was doing much the same. "What is this place?" she breathed.

"We do not name it," Falo said. She led them across the smooth stone floor, to a towering set of double doors, twenty feet high at least. Gleaming white, they'd been polished so smooth that Horace could see a faint reflection of their little group. The upper edge of the doorway was shaped almost like a crown, an inverted arch, dropping low in the middle and rising into high narrow points at the sides. There were no handles or knobs.

"You're not a queen, are you?" said Chloe, looking up at the doors.

"Oh, goodness no," said Falo. "Far from it. These doors aren't for me. I only keep my chambers here to be near the Veil. No one else wants them."

"The Veil of Lura," Horace said, remembering the name.

"Yes, that's right."

"It's through these doors?"

"The Veil is everywhere," said Falo. "It surrounds you even now. But here behind these doors, the Veil is made manifest. It can be seen, touched. Parted."

"And what does the Veil do again?" Chloe asked.

Horace knew. "It hides the Mothergates," he murmured. "There *is* a Mothergate here."

Falo looked down at him sharply. For a second, he was sure she would ask how he knew such a thing. He didn't know whether Falo knew who his mother was—or Chloe's, for that matter—but he found himself utterly unready to talk about it. To learn who his mother had been then, maybe. Or to explain who his mother was now. And judging by the look on Chloe's face, she was even less ready to get into that than he was.

To his relief, though, Falo only said, "There is a Mothergate here, yes. Have you not wondered at all the strength and might you've seen here in Ka'hoka? Instruments in the form of weapons. True warriors. And none of it coming to your aid as you've fought the Riven out in the world above."

"They're protecting the Mothergate," said Horace.

"Guarding it, yes. Others stay for different reasons. But

515

do not judge too harshly." She glanced at Chloe, who looked ready to unleash a fiery complaint about warriors shutting themselves in underground. "These are difficult times. Even those who know the right path to take struggle to stay on it."

Falo stepped up to the towering white doors. On the instant, a huge section of the doors began to glow before her, a perfect white oval standing on end, twelve feet tall. A black seam split it down the middle, growing wider, and the doors swung slowly open, revealing a smooth corridor exactly the same shape and size as the doors.

"We will not approach the Mothergate today," Falo said, "but we will be near enough. You may find it takes some getting used to." She stepped through the doorway.

Horace followed Falo over the threshold and immediately understood her. Here beyond these doors, the Medium was . . . thick. Busy. Insistent. He couldn't feel it directly, but the presence of the Fel'Daera in his mind suddenly ballooned, threatening to take over his thoughts. It reminded him of being in the Find, but without the confusion and doubt. It wasn't unpleasant at all—in fact, it was *very* pleasant. But his hands itched to take the Fel'Daera out and use it—use the hell out of it, actually—and he wasn't sure that was allowed.

Chloe, however, had no such reservations. "Ohhh, *man*," she said delightedly. Her face was lit with joy, her mouth as round as her eyes. The dragonfly shone brighter than ever, gleaming, and its wings fluttered so madly Horace thought they might actually lift Chloe into the air. "Are you feeling this?" she said.

He smiled at her. "I feel it."

Chloe let her feet sink halfway into the floor, just the soles of her shoes, really. She began to glide around him in circles, not even moving her legs, just propelling herself somehow via that little union with the floor. "I am like . . . one hundred percent Tan'ji now. One hundred and *ten* percent."

Dailen jogged past them down the corridor. And then another Dailen. And another. Chasing one another. Chloe skated after him, shrieking with glee.

Apparently, using your Tan'ji was welcome here. But Horace still had no idea what he would even do with the Fel'Daera, with all this extra juice. Instead he just basked in the coursing, comforting presence of the box, content to feel its power.

Teokas came up beside him, a vision. She elbowed him gently in the shoulder.

"Some Tan'ji are more fun in the penumbra of the Veil than others," she said, watching Chloe and the Dailens race past Falo. "I am more like you." She held out her hand, indicating the round ball hanging from her wrist. Her Tan'ji—Thailadun, it was called. The Moondoor. There was a slit in the ball, Horace realized now. A trickle of light spilled out. He longed to look inside.

"What does it do?" he asked.

"Not here. I have trouble controlling it here. Another time,

I promise. But perhaps now you'll understand why Brula the bore didn't want to come to this place. Could you imagine it? Him and his little bowl?" She laughed merrily, a silver song.

He couldn't help himself. "Teokas, how old are you?"

She laughed again. "Far too old for you, Horace Andrews. By a hundred years, I think. Our stars didn't align this time, sweet one."

Horace thought he would die from embarrassment. He was glad Chloe wasn't hearing this. "Sweet one." He'd never hear the end of it.

Sweet one.

They caught up to the others in a round room with a high dome. It was dim here, but apparently this was where Falo lived. It was sparsely furnished with enormous chairs—some big and some small. Dailen sat on two of them. There was a table, and a few sets of shelves neatly decorated with strange little objects. Doorways to the left and the right led to other dark chambers.

Directly ahead, though, lay a third path. An opening as tall as an Altari, but scarcely three feet wide, cut into the stone. It stretched on far ahead, straight as an arrow and clean as glass. At the distant end, white light seemed to swim, pulsing irregularly, like ripples on water. Chloe stared down the narrow corridor—if it could even be called that—and Horace did too. He had no doubt that the Mothergate lay this way.

When Horace pulled himself away from the sight, he found Falo standing right in front of him. She squatted down.

She came in so close to Horace he thought their noses might bump. He felt no urge to pull away. He wondered if she could sense the power of the Fel'Daera, coursing through his veins. She studied him intensely, reminding him of nothing so much as some tranquil woodland creature, fascinated by some unknown thing of man.

Finally she drew back.

"It is a strange thing, Horace Andrews, to encounter the Keeper who so fully brings all one's hope to fruition. I plan and I design and I craft and I toil, but to see the fulfillment of all that effort, here in the flesh . . . it is one of the great pleasures of my life."

Horace had no idea whether to say "Thank you," or "You're welcome." Instead he just said, "That's very nice." He hoped she understood how much he meant it.

Falo sat in one of the giant chairs and gestured for Horace and Chloe to take two of the human-sized ones. "And yet," she continued, "you are not the guests I expected to receive, when I sent Dailen out to find the Laithe."

The Laithe, Horace thought as he sat. *Joshua*. Again, it all seemed so far away. "You knew something was wrong with the Laithe," Horace said. "Because you made it. What can you feel, exactly?"

"I feel it when any of my creations are Tan'layn—unspoken. They are like . . . holes that need filling. Mouths that need feeding. Once they are Found, and as they become part of the Keeper who claimed them, my claim is gradually pushed aside. As it should be. Eventually, when the bond of Tan'ji is in harmony, I feel nothing."

"What about Auditors?" Chloe said suddenly. "Can you feel them? They're pretty unharmonious."

All three Altari reacted to the name. Dailen growled. Teokas shivered. Falo made a childish face of disgust. "The Quaasa," she spat. "Disgusting creatures. But no, I cannot feel them—no more than I can tell the difference between a face and its perfect reflection."

"But it seems like you can feel more," Horace said. "You knew where the Laithe was."

"A peculiarity of the Laithe, because of its powers. And I only knew it because the first few portals made by its new Keeper were clumsy, creaking things. I felt them quite strongly."

"Wait, so . . . can you feel it when I open the box, too?"

"At first I did, yes. But not anymore. The Fel'Daera belongs to you now." She laid a giant hand on his knee, suddenly seeming very grandmotherly. "Your mastery of the box was very swift, very gratifying." Her face got bright, eager. "Do you like the trick with the silver sun? The way the rays dim and brighten as you move the breach? I sometimes think it was an unnecessary flourish."

To Horace's surprise, she seemed genuinely interested in the answer. "No, I like it. It's cool." And somehow the purity of the question, the almost girlish excitement in her face as he replied, made this entire improbable encounter feel suddenly,

520

comfortably *real*. Like . . . kitchen table real. These hands and this mind and these eyes, right before him, they had actually *made* the Fel'Daera. Real inspiration, real planning, real toil. The deed had happened, just like any deed, and this person— well, not person, but close enough—had been the doer.

"You are having the moment," Falo said, watching him.

"What moment?" Chloe asked.

"The moment when he thinks of me as real." Falo reached out and stroked Horace's hair. It honestly wasn't weird at all. "I encourage this kind of thinking. My life is filled with pedestals that couldn't hold me."

"And some that do," said Dailen.

"I prefer the ground," Falo said with a smile. "But back to the Laithe. Regarding the instruments I've created, you might say I only truly hear the act of . . . becoming. As the Find progresses, and if it progresses harmoniously, I become less and less aware. If it does not progress smoothly, however . . ." She grimaced. "Last night, I felt that the Laithe had been found. But I knew at once that this Finding was not harmonious. The Laithe did not willingly take a Keeper. It was simply taken."

"Don't blame Joshua," said Horace. "It wasn't his fault."

"Joshua, that is his name? He is young, I think."

"Yes, only eight or nine. But he's very serious for his age."

"Serious like a rock," Chloe murmured.

"I would be foolish to blame young Joshua," Falo said. "When these things happen, it can never be the Keeper's fault. Someone else must interfere."

She paused, and Horace realized she was letting the implied question hang there. Chloe's eyes briefly touched Horace's, then slid away. She wasn't going to say it.

"I mean, it wasn't *us*," said Horace lamely.

"The thought had not occurred to me," Falo said, sounding amused. She seemed to know Horace and Chloe were holding something back. "But however it came to pass, Joshua is improving. Impressively well, and on his own. Each portal he makes is quieter than the last. Earlier today, he opened a portal from the Warren back to the area Dailen found you last night. It was very swift, quite clean. Harmonious. I barely felt it, but I rather gathered it might have been a rescue."

"A rescue!" said Horace. "So he got the others away?"

"I can't say that for sure. But he came out of the Warren by portal and went back again quickly, as if he was gathering passengers. And I haven't felt him use the Laithe since."

Horace slumped back in his seat. He was surprised how much the news relieved him. He'd been the one that put them all in danger, leading them to the meadow without revealing their fates, and he'd remained committed to that path. But now his friends were safe, and he felt a huge hitch in his chest unexpectedly unravel. He'd been clinging to his worries harder than he thought.

Chloe pressed her foot against his without looking at him. She seemed to know it too. He heard a small, tinkling chuckle of pleasure and looked up. Teokas was wiggling her mesmerizing eyebrows at him. Horace pulled his foot away.

"These are strange times," said Dailen. "A Lostling becomes the rightful Keeper of the Laithe of Teneves, in less than a day's time."

"And the Fel'Daera lives," Teokas added. "Despite the rumors."

"I am sorry I lied to you, Teokas," Falo said. "I told no one but the Taxonomer. But I hope you will agree that the end has justified the means."

"The end," Horace repeated. "Back in the Proving Room, you said that I was the Fel'Daera's rightful end. Why did you say that? Why am I the end?"

Falo let loose a long, woeful sigh. "All things are coming to an end, Horace," she said. "The Mothergates are dying, as I think you know by now."

Chloe glanced down the narrow corridor, filled with flickering light. "They don't *feel* like they're dying."

"Mothergates are not fires. They will not wane and gradually sputter out. They are more like . . . me or you, or any living thing. When they die—if they die—it will be sudden, and absolute." She smiled sadly at them. "I do not relish telling you this. But there can be no doubt—the Mothergates are dying."

For Horace—in this place, of all places, with power and certainty and promise raging through the Fel'Daera—what Falo was telling them seemed both preposterous and horrifying. It sounded like she was saying the Mothergates could die at any second.

"And then what?" said Chloe. Falo didn't answer her.

Chloe looked around the room, frantic. "And then what?" she said again. Dailen only looked down at the floor. Teokas sat there shimmering with silence, watching Chloe. And Chloe, of course, already knew the answer. All Tanu—every Tan'ji, every Tan'kindi—got its power from the Mothergates. And if the Mothergates ceased to exist . . .

"How long?" Horace made himself ask.

"I cannot count the days. I do not know. In all likelihood, you will be the last Keeper of the Box of Promises." She slid her celestial gaze to Chloe. "You, the last Keeper of the Alva-laithen. Me, the last Keeper of the Starlit Loom."

Chloe shook her head, her fingers worrying the Alva-laithen. "You say that like there's nothing we can do. Like it can't be stopped."

In the corner, Dailen shifted uneasily from one foot to the other, arms folded across his chest.

"I do not say that, precisely," Falo said.

"Then what do you say?"

Falo hesitated. Teokas got up from her seat and slid in next to her. She took the older Altari's hand in hers. Their long fingers intertwined. Falo smiled at Teokas gratefully.

"The words are not easy to find," said Falo. "You are so young, and I—"

She cut herself short. She dropped Teokas's hand and shot to her feet, cocking her head and squinting her deep eyes, as if she were listening to a distant sound.

"What is it?" said Dailen.

"Something is amiss." She looked straight up into the air. "A new portal has been made, from the Warren to our grounds above."

A great bell began to ring, shaking the very ground beneath them. It came from everywhere. Dailen sprinted out of the room, back the way they'd first come in.

"What's happening?" Chloe demanded.

"Someone is sounding the alarm," said Teokas. "We have unexpected visitors, somewhere aboveground."

"What kind of visitors? Wardens? Is it the others?"

Falo spun in a circle, still gazing up. "I cannot say who comes," she said. "But someone does."

CHAPTER THIRTY–THREE

This Fragile Hold

"Run!" Mr. Meister cried. He hauled April to her feet as the Mordin poured into the far end of Sanguine Hall, beneath the billowing golem. And now April saw that the Mordin weren't alone—there were much smaller Riven with them too, not much bigger than herself. They scampered swiftly on all fours.

Arthur took flight, fleeing. The sa'halvasa swirled angrily and flocked toward the coming Riven, but the golem met it first. The two swarms collided head-on in a blistering shower of stone and steel. The cloud of the sa'halvasa was larger, but the golem denser and heavier by far, and it drove through the brittle blades like a plow through snow.

Some of the blades still found the Riven below, and wherever they did, the Mordin fought back angrily, and were cut. Other Mordin made it through untouched, galloping toward

April and the rest. But somehow most frightening of all were the smaller Riven, fast and hard to follow. April watched as one vanished into thin air with a hiss, rematerializing in a soft burst ten feet on.

"Ravids!" Mr. Meister shouted. "We must flee!"

He lifted his hand and fired his tiny black weapon. The air split with a *crack!* One of the creepy little Ravids was thrown back like a rag doll. Mr. Meister fired again, and a Mordin was blown off its feet. At his side, Jessica had her harp out. She plucked wildly at the stings, and another Mordin tumbled to the ground, keening. But it wasn't enough. Not nearly enough.

Arthur was flying straight at April. Someone grabbed April and tried to shove her through the brick wall. She fought free, calling for the raven. Miraculously, he alit on her shoulder, digging his talons into the leather perch there. He was terrified, flapping his great wings. She stumbled backward through the bricks, taking him with her.

On the far side of the wall, still staggering—the roars of battle suddenly muted and distant—April abruptly found herself in midair. She'd staggered clean off the ledge at the top of the laddered shaft. She shrieked as she fell. Almost immediately someone caught her weight, slowing her, and for a second she thought what an impossible thing it was for Arthur to have done. But then she realized she had no weight, and Arthur had leapt free. Above her, Neptune had her by one hand, clutching the tail of her cloak with the other, slowing their fall.

"I've got you," Neptune said. "We're going to go down fast, but we'll land soft, okay?" Her voice was calm, but her eyes were wide with terror.

"Where are the others?"

"Jessica is here. Mr. Meister won't be far behind."

"Those Ravids . . . what are they?"

"Trouble."

April spotted Arthur, fluttering heavily down the shaft. And now she saw Jessica, scrambling down the iron rungs of the ladder. Soon she and Neptune had left them both behind.

They hit the ground—soft for Neptune, maybe, but not for April. Her breath left her as her knees buckled jarringly. She forced herself to her feet and looked up.

Jessica was still coming, practically falling from rung to rung. At the top of the shaft, a tiny white light shone like a star. Mr. Meister. Neptune launched herself up after him. The hammering of the golem in Sanguine Hall made the earth tremble. She couldn't see Arthur, but felt him overhead, saw herself in his eyes, tiny and frightened. She took in his fear, letting it soothe her. Everyone was afraid. It was okay to be afraid. The Warren was falling.

From ten feet up, Jessica leapt to the ground. She staggered and then wrapped a hand around the back of April's neck.

"Are you hurt?" she asked, her eyes wild. "Are you all right?"

"I'm fine. I . . . I'm fine."

Arthur landed noisily beside them. Jessica yanked open the sturdy wooden door that led to the Gallery, and the raven skipped madly through it.

"Go on," Jessica said. "Warn the others. I'll stay here and help."

"Not alone, you won't."

"You can't help with this. Go and—"

Another explosion, this time directly above. A deadly cascade of rock and brick began to tumble down the shaft. Jessica yanked April into the doorway as the debris showered down around them, as gritty dust rose into their faces. The golem had broken through the wall above. A moment later, Neptune and Mr. Meister landed brutally hard—apparently the old man was a shade too heavy for the tourminda. The pair crumpled awkwardly onto the ground even as little rocks continued to rain down on them. Mr. Meister cried out, grabbing his leg.

Neptune tried to haul him up, but he fought her off. "It's broken," he said, still clutching his leg. "Leave me. Get them out." He ripped his glowing jithandra free and smashed it against the ground. It shattered and went out.

"No," Neptune said. "I'll carry you."

"There's no time," Mr. Meister said. Suddenly one of the awful Ravids popped up right next to him, out of nowhere. Neptune roared, heaving a rock the size of a cardboard box at it, but the creature simply skipped aside, flickering from one spot to the next. It was a Riven, for sure, with beady black eyes and long pale limbs, but it moved like no Riven could. It spun and reached for Mr. Meister, hissing. And then it fell, blank eyed and writhing, as Jessica plucked the strings of her harp.

Mr. Meister reached up and shoved Neptune, hard. She stumbled back and fell into the hallway. "Take the light away, Neptune. Take the door away, and buy them some time."

Now a roar from above, not falling rocks this time but the golem itself, pouring down the shaft like black water down a pipe. Neptune scrambled to her feet and tried to go back to Mr. Meister, but Jessica grabbed her. The old man reached into a vest pocket and pulled a small silver star out of his vest—the backjack. He threw it into his mouth and swallowed it, wincing. From another pocket he pulled out a small disc, and tossed it at Jessica. Jessica snatched it nimbly out of the air, and April almost gasped. It was the compass, its red needle pointing directly at Mr. Meister. "Fear is the stone," he said, his eyes clinging to Jessica's. "Tell Dorothy to look for me."

And then the black avalanche of the golem thundered down and swallowed him up.

Jessica yanked April into the hall as the golem landed, then spun and heaved her body against the wooden door, slamming it shut. "Put the light out!" Jessica shouted at Neptune. "Lose the door!"

Dazed, Neptune just stared at her. April tore the purple jithandra from around the girl's neck and threw it to the ground, crushing it under her heel. As the light flickered out, the door disappeared, and they plunged into darkness. The golem pounded against the stone wall like a battering ram, deafening.

"Go!" Jessica yelled. Faint light flickered in her hand, the shimmering strings of her harp. "We don't have much time."

They ran through the Gallery blindly, stumbling in the dark. Neptune wept. Behind them, the golem went on raging, tearing at the stone.

JOSHUA SAT IN the Great Burrow at the edge of the Maw, the Laithe floating by his side. He knew, even if the others didn't yet. He knew.

The Riven were coming. The Riven were already here.

He watched the balcony on other side of the Maw, waiting for April to return. For Neptune and Horace's mom and Mr. Meister. For Arthur. It was all his fault. Coming here in the first place, helping Isabel steal Brian away, using the Laithe and—stupid, bad—coming back through the rooftop portal with the terrible Auditor still his head. And he hadn't told. He hadn't said. Not soon enough, anyway—if there even was a soon enough. He'd been too scared and too ashamed.

All his fault.

And then he heard it. A dull and distant impact, stone on stone. It came again, louder, drifting out of the tunnel across the Maw and rising on the breeze. Joshua wasn't even scared. Or he was so scared that there was nothing but fear. It didn't matter.

He heard footsteps. He turned and saw the others running toward him, drawn by the sound—Gabriel and Mrs. Hapsteade and Brian, and even Isabel. Isabel who was no good, Isabel who'd started all of this. He should have known better. He should never have let her take him away.

They stopped when they reached him. "What is that?" said Gabriel, cocking his head and listening.

"I told you," said Joshua. "I felt what I felt. They found us."

Another distant, deep thud shuddered through the air. Mrs. Hapsteade turned to Gabriel. "Stay here. Keep Joshua and Brian hidden." She knelt in front of Joshua. "Keeper, if it comes to it, you must be ready to take us out of here."

She wanted him to make a portal. But it was his portal—his terrible, careless portal—that had brought the Riven here in the first place. It was the sort of thing a Lostling would have done, Joshua knew that. A real Keeper would never have been so stupid.

"No more portals," he said numbly.

A rumble of falling rock sounded in the distance. Mrs. Hapsteade stood. "Talk to him," she said to the others—to Gabriel or Brian, it didn't matter. *No more portals. Not ever.* Joshua reached out and shoved the Laithe away. It drifted a few feet out over the Maw and then circled gently back beside him.

Mrs. Hapsteade was already running down the Perilous Stairs, her skirts hoisted. Isabel followed. Nobody stopped her.

"This isn't happening," Brian said. "It isn't happening, right?"

Something moved down below. A tiny black shape darted out of the tunnel on the other side and rose into the air. Arthur. Joshua got to his feet. The raven was croaking wildly, hoarse sounds of alarm. And now the pounding started again, closer and louder, pulsing out of the tunnel.

"Brian, go get Tunraden," said Gabriel. "Be prepared."

Brian hesitated, then turned and ran back into the Great Burrow.

"No one could have known," Gabriel said, as the hammer blows went on and on.

"The real Keeper of the Laithe would have known," Joshua said, watching Arthur.

"The Riven may be waiting for us on the far side of Vithra's Eye," Gabriel said. "A portal is our only safe way out."

Safe, Joshua thought bitterly. "You'll find a better way," he said. "You were better off without me, better—" He sucked in his breath. Far below, April burst from the tunnel at a run, with Horace's mom right behind her.

"What is it?" said Gabriel. "What do you see?"

Now Neptune emerged, leaping easily over the heads of the others. They ran and flew across the bridge. Joshua waited, his heart a heavy, tumbling stone. Where was Mr. Meister?

"What's happening, Joshua?" Gabriel asked insistently.

Joshua couldn't answer him. The hammer blows went on,

like war drums. His friends spilled from the tunnel opening.

But Mr. Meister did not.

APRIL DASHED OUT of the tunnel and onto the narrow bridge, the golem's enraged pounding chasing her. The heavy wind rising through the Maw threatened to upend her and drop her into the deeps. She sprinted on nonetheless, not sure if she didn't care or just couldn't stop. She kept her eyes locked on her feet, but through Arthur, circling above, she could see everything. Jessica, running right behind her. Mrs. Hapsteade, hurrying down the Perilous Stairs to meet them, with Isabel prancing past her like a cat. Higher up, Gabriel and Joshua standing at the edge of the cliff. Gabriel looked either angry or afraid, but Joshua's eyes were dull and sad. The Laithe hung at his side.

Neptune soared over April's head, clinging to her cloak and letting it fill with air, the wind briefly lifting her. She crossed the span easily and dropped onto the far ledge at the bottom of the stairs just as Isabel and Mrs. Hapsteade arrived.

Miraculously, April made it across too. "Riven," Neptune was panting. "They're coming. They brought Ravids."

Mrs. Hapsteade scarcely seemed surprised, her face like stone. And the hammering of the golem was plain enough to hear for all. "Where is Henry?" she asked.

Neptune turned away, her eyes red. April tried to imagine how to explain what had happened, but then Jessica joined them safely on the ledge and walked right up to Mrs.

Hapsteade. She took the older woman's hands.

Mrs. Hapsteade nodded at the unspoken message. "Was he alive when you left him, Jess?" she asked steadily.

Jessica nodded. "Alive. And kicking." She handed over the little silver compass. "He said . . . he said to tell you to go looking for him."

For a frozen moment, Mrs. Hapsteade gazed at the red needle, pointing solidly across the Maw and into the Gallery. She squeezed her eyes shut, opened them again, and tucked the compass into the pocket of her dress. "And so I will. But first we have to escape. Get upstairs, April. See if you can convince Joshua to open a portal for us. He's refusing."

"Refusing?" April said. But after a spurt of confusion and anger, she understood. Joshua thought all of this was his fault. He was checking out, not wanting to do any more harm. But without him, they had little hope.

As if to punctuate the point, a thundering rumble rolled out of the tunnel across the bridge. The golem had broken through the last wall and into the Gallery. There was nothing to stop it now. The greedy shrieks of the Riven pealed out into the Maw.

Mrs. Hapsteade stepped up to the edge of the bridge. "I'll hold them off while I can," she said. "Don't wait for me." She reached into her pocket and pulled out a bony white wand. A phalanx. She caught April's surprised look. "It's quite fresh. We put Brian to work today. Now go."

April turned to head up the stairs, but then Jessica spoke,

freezing her in her tracks. "You can't do it alone, Dorothy," Horace's mom said, and she began to unfold her harp.

April could hardly believe it. Jessica was planning to stay here and fight, to do what she could with her harp. But there was no chance—she wasn't Isabel, and although April had the sense Jessica's harp was more powerful than the little white one Isabel used in the meadow, it was certainly no substitute for Miradel. What would Horace say if he were here?

And then Isabel spoke, as soft and meek as April had ever heard her. Her eyes were locked on Jessica's harp. "No," Isabel said. "Not you—not either of you. It has to be me."

Mrs. Hapsteade growled, but Jessica just gazed at Isabel thoughtfully.

"Give me the harp, Jess," Isabel said. "I can do better than you both. I can help."

Jessica hesitated only for a second. She held out her harp. The strings shimmered and danced. Isabel put her hand on it but didn't take it away. "This is the end of it," Isabel said.

"I've always been ready to let it go, this fragile hold it has on me," Jessica said. "I'm sorry it wasn't the same for you." She released the harp and stepped back, her lip between her teeth.

Isabel tipped her chin into the air, blinking. "That's not what I meant."

Jessica put her hand on Isabel's cheek. "I know."

The golem burst out of the tunnel on the far side of the Maw. It reared up, as if searching, and then began to spread

itself out over the far end of the bridge, creating a wide platform. On the instant, Mordin sprinted out of the hole, and
the nasty Ravids too. The Mordin began stalking across the
golem, straight for April and the others. The Ravids, meanwhile, began to climb the far wall of the Maw, spreading and
skittering upward like a horde of insects, hissing and popping
forward like spattering grease as they flickered in and out of
sight.

"Go," Isabel said. "Tell Chloe I . . ." Her eyes clouded
over and her face seemed to crumple. But then she shook her
head and turned away. "Go." She sat down cross-legged at the
foot of the bridge, the harp in her lap, and began to play.

A Mordin fell. And then another. A third actually toppled
over the edge of the golem and into the Maw. But there were
too many, far too many, and the Ravids—

Mrs. Hapsteade fired the phalanx, jolting one of the of
Mordin to a painful halt midstride. "Up to the Great Burrow,"
she said. "Now." She turned and began running up the stairs,
Jessica on her heels.

Neptune grabbed April around the waist. April felt all
her weight leave her, and they launched into the air. Beneath
her, Isabel grew smaller and smaller as they rose, leaving her
there. The Mordin kept coming, and falling, but whenever
one fell two more came roaring from behind. And the golem
was moving too, rippling across the narrow bridge like a flat-
backed dragon, coming ever closer to where Isabel sat, still
playing Jessica's harp. There was no hope for her, but April

understood—Isabel was giving whatever hope she could to the rest of them.

April shut her eyes. And when that wasn't good enough, when Arthur's keen eyes overhead could still see the flood of Riven bearing mercilessly down on Isabel, April pushed the bird out of her mind. She could still hear, of course—the furious cries of the Mordin, the deadly grind of the golem, the hiss and crackle of the Ravids.

But April believed that there were some things that should not be seen.

JOSHUA WATCHED FROM above as the charging Mordin began to fall. He leaned over the edge of the Maw and saw Isabel, far below, facing the onslaught alone. She was bent over something in her lap—*a harp, it must be.* The Riven continued to fall. But the golem underfoot made the crossing easy for them, and the Mordin kept coming fast. April and the others were still down there too, and they had to hurry. They had to get away.

Somehow.

Gabriel, meanwhile, had his head held high. A swarm of little Riven, a kind Joshua had never seen before, were scrambling up the far wall of the Maw. Every now and again, each one would disappear with a hiss and then reappear with a pop many feet farther on. It was clear they meant to avoid the bridge, and Isabel, entirely—they were going to climb up and over the Maw and right into the Great Burrow. Gabriel could obviously hear their approach. "Ravids," he said. "We need to get back." He grabbed Joshua by the shirt and hauled him back from the edge, but not before Joshua glimpsed a terrible sight below, the one sight he dreaded most in a day full of dreadful sights.

An Auditor, streaking out of the tunnel and onto the golem bridge.

Suddenly Neptune rose up over the edge of the cliff, carrying April.

"Gabriel!" Neptune cried. April stepped onto the ledge and pulled Neptune after her. Rather than alighting, though, Neptune simply drifted forward and wrapped her arms around Gabriel, pressing her face against his chest.

"Where are the others?" Gabriel said into her hair.

"Mrs. Hapsteade is coming," Neptune murmured. "And Jessica too. But Mr. Meister—"

April grabbed Joshua's hand. She led him away, out of earshot, and crouched down in front of him. "Joshua, we need you to make a portal."

He pretended not to hear her. He could not make a portal while an Auditor was near. There was no point. There would be no escape, not really. "What happened to Mr. Meister?" he asked.

"He was captured," April said. "And the rest of us will be too, if we don't get away."

"And what about Isabel?"

April just shook her head.

Arthur sailed in then, his huge wings hissing through the air. He landed at April's feet and turned back in the direction of the Maw, where the Ravids had reached the top of the opposite wall and were beginning to swarm across the ceiling of the chasm. Arthur squawked his angriest squawks at them, his harsh voice echoing through the Great Burrow. "You've got to make a portal, Joshua," April said. "For Arthur and me and everyone else. It's our only hope."

"No," Joshua said. She didn't understand. "A portal is how this all happened."

"Yes, and a portal can fix it."

Mrs. Hapsteade and Horace's mom emerged from the top of the Perilous Stairs at a run. Mrs. Hapsteade paused and fired the phalanx out across the Maw. Far off, a Ravid squealed, pinned against the stone. But there were dozens more, still coming.

"Get to the Keystone," Gabriel called. "I'll try to slow them, but you don't want to be anywhere near the Ravids— not even in the humour. They are as unpredictable as sparks from a fire."

Neptune rose into the air above him. "I'll stay with you. I'll help."

"May yours be light, then," said Mrs. Hapsteade. "Slow them as much as you can, and meet us at the lake. We'll need you." After a nod from Neptune, Mrs. Hapsteade bustled toward April and Joshua, Jessica at her side. The Warden's dark eyes were ablaze.

"Gabriel told us to get to the Keystone," April said as she

approached. "What's the Keystone?"

"A desperate measure," Mrs. Hapsteade said briskly. "One that will buy us only a few extra moments." Then she looked sternly at Joshua. "I asked April to talk to you, but I don't see a portal."

"There's nothing to talk about," said Joshua.

Mrs. Hapsteade squared herself in front of him, planting her hands on her hips. "Should we talk about who has already fallen tonight?" she said. "About who might be next? About who is to blame?"

Jessica laid her hand on Mrs. Hapsteade's arm. At the edge of the Maw, where Gabriel stood beneath a hovering Neptune, a Ravid suddenly popped into existence at Gabriel's side. The Warden swung his staff and knocked it over the precipice, then planted the tip of the staff in the ground. With a crackle and a roar, the entire cliff edge and the yawning Maw vanished, as the humour burst to life. The Great Burrow now ended in a massive wrinkle that couldn't be seen, the swarming Ravids buried inside with Gabriel and Neptune. Joshua turned away, queasy and full of dread.

"Those are your friends back there," Mrs. Hapsteade said, pointing at the unseeable sight. "Risking their lives to save you. And you'll do nothing for them?"

Joshua felt tears welling up, desperate and angry. He couldn't give them any help—only harm.

"Let's get away," Jessica said, soft but urgent. "Let's give everyone a moment to think."

Mrs. Hapsteade glowered, but nodded. "Get Brian. Get to

Vithra's Eye. I need to take care of something." She stepped away, heading for Mr. Meister's doba.

"What are you doing?" Joshua said.

"Whatever stays behind here tonight belongs to the Riven," she called back. "I'm saving what I can, and destroying the rest."

Joshua's misery deepened. All the Tanu in Mr. Meister's office, all those little wonders—soon to be lost, thanks to him. Mrs. Hapsteade ducked through Mr. Meister's doorway, and a moment later, a flurry of the little birds that lived there burst out the door and scattered, chattering wildly.

"Let's go," Jessica said, taking Joshua's hand. "Let's find Brian."

They hurried up the Great Burrow, through the dobas towering silently in the golden light. The humour loomed unseen behind them, silent. Arthur flew on ahead. Joshua let himself be dragged, the Laithe following him stubbornly. Was he being stupid? Piling one dumb decision on top of another? He had no idea. But better a bad nothing than a disastrous something—right? He reminded himself that Horace and Chloe were safe. There was that, at least. But no sooner had he thought it than the tears that had been threatening him broke loose, silent and wet.

They found Brian halfway up, shackled by Tunraden, waiting for them. His face was whiter than ever as he stared past them, back toward the Maw. "It's not happening," he said. "It's not happening, right?"

Joshua glanced back, blinking through his tears. Because of Gabriel, he couldn't see the far end of the Great Burrow, but he could certainly see that the massive chamber was shrinking. The patch of unsight that was the humour was slowly creeping closer. Joshua understood that the Riven were advancing, and Gabriel was moving with them, trying desperately to keep them from finding their way through the humour. Mr. Meister's doba had been swallowed, and whatever Mrs. Hapsteade had done in there, it was over now. She darted to and fro now, just outside the humour, firing the phalanx whenever one of the Ravids managed to slip past Gabriel and Neptune.

Suddenly a Mordin materialized out of the nothingness. Mrs. Hapsteade pinned it immediately, but Joshua knew what it meant. The Mordin had made it across the bridge and into the Great Burrow. Whatever time Isabel had bought them, that time had run out.

"How many are there?" Brian asked, breathless.

"Too many," April said. "We're supposed to get to Vithra's Eye. Gabriel said something about the Keystone."

Brian's eyes widened. "This is the day," he whispered.

They hurried on, moving as fast as they could, April filling Brian in on what had happened. Joshua couldn't bear to listen. They passed the doba where Ingrid was still held prisoner, and Joshua waited for someone to mention her, but nobody did. Nobody wanted a Lostling.

They were nearly to Vithra's Eye now. Suddenly April

stopped cold, her eyes hazy and distant, which meant she was using the vine.

"What it is?" Jessica asked.

"The owls," April breathed.

And now Joshua heard them, ghostly cries up ahead, whistling and low. April sprinted toward them, and Joshua and the rest followed to the water's edge, where the owls were swooping in and out of the darkness. Their worried cries filled the big chamber, echoing.

"The Riven are there," said April, staring across the black lake. "They can't cross, but they're waiting for us. There's no way out."

Joshua could smell the brimstone, and thought he could hear movement across the water. Meanwhile behind them, the humour continued to retreat, coming closer. It was only a hundred yards off now. Neptune was outside it, fighting alongside Mrs. Hapsteade, as more and more of the Riven found their way through Gabriel's void.

No way out. Joshua gazed at the Laithe, the perfect little earth orbiting him like the sun. "I don't deserve this," he said, and he thought no one would understand him, that they would think he meant he didn't deserve what was happening right now.

But April—smart, sweet April—understood. She shook her head sadly and said, "Never say that again, Joshua. You are the Keeper of the Laithe of Teneves. You don't deserve what happened to you, but you *do* deserve your power." She put a hand on his head. "And I think you know it's the only power that can help us now. Only you can make right what went wrong."

Joshua held his breath. The Laithe shone at his side. *Make right what went wrong.* Here, at last, were words that made sense to him. All the sense in the world. He felt his muscles go slack, the sadness and pity that had numbed him sinking into his bones. An owl swooped past him, whistling frantically. So many wrongs, and most of them could not be undone. But there was one thing Joshua could do. One thing for these people who'd tried to be good to him.

"Okay," he said softly. "Okay."

Joshua reached for the Laithe. He found North America with ease, hardly knowing if he was even using his hands. He slid the rabbit around the meridian, and down he went, toward Illinois. He came in swiftly, toward the clawed hand of Horseshoe Lake.

Suddenly Mrs. Hapsteade was beside him, breathing hard. "Where are you taking us?" she asked, watching. The humour loomed so close now that Joshua felt as though he and the others were standing on the edge of existence, a hopeless black sea on one side and a sightless nothing on the other. But there was a way out.

"Someplace safe," Joshua said. "Someplace you'll find friends."

He slid the rabbit onward, zooming in. The Mississippi River slid over the horizon. The strange mounds of Cahokia bloomed into sight.

Neptune shouted. A Ravid had materialized out of the

humour and gotten past her. Mrs. Hapsteade fired the phalanx at it, but the creature hissed out of sight and instantly
reappeared with a pop, not ten feet away. Its beady eyes
darted across their little group, and then it sprang at April,
teeth bared, long fingers reaching.

The soft *whump* of the phalanx sounded again. The Ravid
lurched and jolted to a halt, immobilized. It snarled and spat
at April and Joshua like a trapped animal. Mrs. Hapsteade
spun away as two more Mordin appeared out of the humour.

Joshua stepped calmly clear from the Ravid and went
back to the Laithe. It wasn't Ravids he was worried about. He
steered the Laithe's view swiftly down onto a field between
two thick arms of forest, closer and closer. At last the rabbit
came full circle, back to the top of the meridian. He was close
enough to see blades of grass now, and a scrubby thistle. He
was there.

He gripped the meridian and looked over at Mrs. Hapsteade. "I'm ready," he said. "But when I tear the meridian
loose and open the portal, Dr. Jericho will come. He'll feel it."

Mrs. Hapsteade gave him a curt nod. "Neptune!" she
called out. "Get Gabriel out and get to the Keystone. The
time has—"

Before she could finish, a huge ripping sound tore through
the cave. The Great Burrow suddenly reappeared, the humour
gone. Something flew through the air and clattered to the
ground at Joshua's feet, gray and silver and long.

The Staff of Obro.

In the newly revealed swath where the humour had been, a small army of Riven howled and roared. Dr. Jericho stood in the middle of it, the golem rearing up behind him. Gabriel lay on the ground several feet in front of the Mordin, as if thrown there. He struggled to get to his feet, baring his teeth. Joshua saw blood.

"Ah," sang Dr. Jericho. "Here they are, the little bunnies in their burrow."

Terrifying as the Mordin was, Joshua hardly had eyes for him. Instead he scanned the horde frantically, looking for the Auditor he'd seen. An Auditor could wreck it all, maybe even stop Joshua from opening the portal in the first place. But he saw only Mordin and the twitchy Ravids, and the golem behind. Slowly he understood—Isabel must have stopped the Auditor, as only Isabel could.

And then he saw Neptune, high over the heads of the Riven. She was upside down, her feet planted on the ceiling at the very top of the arched passageway. She was tugging at a large, square knob of rock that stuck out conspicuously from the rest. The size of a chest, and chiseled smooth, the stone began to slide free. Neptune looked up—or down, rather—at Gabriel far below her. "Run," she said clearly.

At Joshua's side, April whispered softly to herself, staring at the huge rock slipping loose beneath Neptune's hands. "The Keystone," she said.

Gabriel found his feet and lurched into a staggering run. Dr. Jericho looked up just as Neptune gave a great tug and the

Keystone came loose like a tooth from a mouth.

The stone fell, tumbling. With a roar like a thousand golems, the mouth of the Great Burrow began to collapse with it, down into the horde of Riven below. Neptune shot free as the passageway crumbled in a shower of stone and grit and dust. The Riven cried and shouted and fell back. Mighty stones, some as big as cars, fell among them. Gabriel narrowly escaped being struck by one as he ran toward the Wardens. Some of the Riven weren't so lucky.

The avalanche went on and on. Arthur, who'd launched himself into the air as the tunnel began to crumble, squawked raucously overhead. Stones bounced and skittered all the way to Joshua's feet. Angry, piercing howls of dismay echoed from across Vithra's Eye. Neptune landed beside April just as Gabriel reached them, and they turned back to look.

The earth stopped quaking. Dust hung in the air, but as it settled, Joshua could see that a monstrous pile of freshly jagged boulders and rocky debris had completely sealed off the Great Burrow. The entrance to the Warren was in ruin.

"Did we kill them?" Brian asked, his voice high and hopeful. "Did we do it?"

Mrs. Hapsteade shook her head. "We've only delayed the inevitable," she said. As if to prove her point, Dr. Jericho's raging voice crept through the towering heap of rubble. And then the sound of boulders shifting, rocks being tossed aside by a mighty hand—the golem was already at work, coming after them still.

Mrs. Hapsteade turned to Joshua, but he didn't need to hear or see any more. He tore the meridian free from the Laithe and hung it in the air. The Laithe became a golden moon, smooth and glowing. Atop the meridian, the blue-eyed rabbit sat up and began to run. The portal swiftly opened. Everyone gathered around, watching and waiting. The tunnel of shapes tumbled briefly, and then—

Blue, early evening skies. A curving stretch of summer trees. And in the distance, a square-sided grassy mound, rising high into the sky.

"Ka'hoka," Mrs. Hapsteade breathed.

The rabbit stopped running. The portal was wide open.

"Go," said Joshua. "Everyone out."

No one moved. No one wanted to leave him, he could see that on their faces. But they would all have to leave him. That's how the portal worked, yes, but also—this was what had to happen. For the good of everyone.

Joshua bent over and picked up the Staff of Obro lying at his feet. Gabriel's head snapped around, and Neptune gasped. The staff was much heavier than Joshua could ever have imagined, heavy as iron. It threatened to slip from his grasp. "Go," he said again, and with all his might he heaved the staff through the open portal. It slid through and bounced onto the grass, two hundred and fifty miles away.

Gabriel grunted as if punched. "Joshua!" April cried.

More grinding thumps from the other side of the cave-in, more muted voices, slashing and furious. "You have to leave me, you know you do," Joshua said.

Neptune took Gabriel's hand. She walked him over to the portal, frowning worriedly at Joshua. "We'll wait for you, of course," she said, and together the two of them stepped through the portal and into the sunshine. Gabriel bent and picked up his Tan'ji at once.

Brian went next, and then Jessica, both without a word. On the other side, they turned and looked back, but there was nothing for them to see. The portal was only open for the Laithe, and the Laithe was here.

The mound of collapsed stone shifted, and a rock the size of a watermelon bounced down the slope as the golem's powerful digging continued. Mrs. Hapsteade stepped up to Joshua and laid a hand on his shoulder.

"You've done well, Keeper," she said gently. Joshua looked away. "When we are safely underground together in Ka'hoka," she went on, "we will speak more."

"When we're safe," he said.

She frowned at him faintly, and then stepped out of the Warren and into the shimmering green field.

And now just April. April and Arthur. The raven drifted down and landed on her shoulder. Two pairs of eyes gazed intently at Joshua, one hazel, one jet black.

"You're not coming," April said quietly.

It was pointless to pretend. "No," said Joshua.

"The Riven will take you. They'll have the Laithe."

Whatever stays behind here tonight belongs to the Riven. That's what Mrs. Hapsteade had said. But not everything had to stay behind. "I may be a Lostling, but that doesn't mean I'm going to join them."

"No one ever said that," April insisted. "No one ever thought that."

"Yes they did. But it doesn't matter."

"Why doesn't it matter? Why are you doing this? Because you made a mistake?" April bit her lip, as if she wished she could take the words back.

The pile of rubble groaned and began to collapse under the grinding pressure of the golem. The voices of the Riven reached them clearly now. Dr. Jericho was barking orders. They were almost through.

"I *am* a mistake," Joshua said. And it wasn't even sad. It was just the truth. "You have to go. I'll make it so they can't find you."

April squinted her eyes, confused and suspicious. "What are you planning?"

"Just go, please. Tell everyone I'm sorry." He stepped back, suddenly wary of the look on April's face. "Don't try to force me, April. If you do, I'll close the portal down before you can drag me through."

"I wasn't thinking that," April said sadly. She stepped up to the portal. Arthur, eyeing the open fields beyond, flapped his great wings and took flight, flying through the portal and out over the heads of the worried Wardens gathered in the grass. "I was wondering," said April, "if I could make you stop believing that you aren't who you are. But only you can do that."

Joshua closed his eyes. A moment later, he felt her go. A ripple, a pulse, and she was safely through into the green grass of Cahokia.

It was all for the best.

The ground trembled beneath him as the golem dug at the caved-in passage. He had to act now—had April known? Had she guessed what he was planning?

He opened his eyes, looking down at the golden sphere of the Laithe in his hand. The portal was only open for the Keeper of the Laithe, Isabel had told him. But he didn't believe that was really true. He believed it was open for the Laithe itself—and no matter what April thought, he was not a true Keeper. Just a pretender. He had the talent, but not the right. And so yes, he would fix it so that the Riven couldn't find the others. But he wouldn't let the Riven get the Laithe, either.

Instead, he would send the shining globe through the portal. Alone.

He would send the Laithe to Cahokia while he himself remained behind. The one-way door would flip-flop, so that the Riven couldn't get through. And then he would close the portal from here—he was sure he could do it, making the rabbit run. He would toss the meridian into the deeps of the lake.

After that, it would be over. The Riven could do what they wanted with him.

He stepped up to the portal. On the far side, April was standing silently apart from the others, not saying a word, but they had obviously figured out he wasn't coming with them. Mrs. Hapsteade faced the gateway—just a giant hollow ring on her side—and shouted pointless words he couldn't hear.

In just a few moments, she would understand.

Joshua heaved back with the Laithe. He swung his arm hard as he could and threw the little globe into the portal, his gut clenching as he let it go.

The Laithe bounced off the portal with a hollow, resonant *thung*, like a rock striking off a sheet of metal. It rebounded and drifted right back to him. Startled, he snatched it from the air and tried again.

Thung!

It wouldn't go.

Joshua heard a pop and a screech behind him. A Ravid had made it through the collapsed rubble and was coming for him. And now another. Panicking, he tried to shove the shining globe through the portal, but it wouldn't budge. It wouldn't go through, no more than a rock could go through metal.

It wouldn't go without him.

One of the Ravids grabbed him ferociously by the ankle, yanking his feet out from under him and dropping him to the ground. The other popped into existence right in front of the portal. In the same instant, the caved-in pile of rock burst open with a boom and a crunch, and the golem poured out. A flood of Riven came behind it, Dr. Jericho out in front.

In shock, hardly able to let himself think, Joshua focused on the blue-eyed rabbit atop the meridian. He asked it to run—as swift as a real rabbit in full flight. The meridian spun madly, closing all the way down in barely two blinks of an eye. The Wardens on the other side scarcely had time to flinch before they were gone. Joshua kicked at the Ravid that held him, making it squeal, and he scrambled to his knees just long enough to wrench the meridian from the air. He dropped it back onto the Laithe.

The little globe dimmed into soft blue and whites. The portal was gone, the destination erased.

A cold, stony grip wrapped around his legs from foot to belly, lifting him, hauling the breath out of him. The golem hoisted him into the air as Dr. Jericho stalked forward. The Mordin was holding one forearm stiffly against his belly, and dimly Joshua remembered the crack of bone, back on the roof of April's house when Neptune had crashed down onto him. Joshua clung to the Laithe, his plan in ruins. His thoughts were scrambled and mad and useless, flickering across every possibility at once. His friends were safe, his friends were stranded and in danger, his friends were not his friends. He was the Keeper of the Laithe because the Laithe wouldn't leave him, he was a Lostling because he hadn't known what the Laithe wouldn't do.

He was a Warden, he was a faker, he was just a boy. He had been brave, cowardly, lucky, doomed.

He would survive whatever came next.

He would not.

Dr. Jericho came up close, his face inches from Joshua's

own. The golem squeezed Joshua so tight he wondered whether his legs might break.

"Well now," Dr. Jericho sang. "I can't tell you how often I discover what the Wardens have lost. Tell me, Tinker, *are* you lost?" He leaned in closer, his mad grin widening, the Laithe reflected in his glassy black eyes. A bitter cloud of brimstone rolled off him. "Or are you *found*?"

CHAPTER THIRTY-FOUR

∞

If Not Ourselves

THE PROVING ROOM AGAIN. BUT THIS TIME NO PROOF WAS ASKED for, or offered.

Instead, a shocking and terrible tale.

Horace listened, aghast, as the words crept from the mouths of the six new arrivals. April and Brian. Gabriel and Neptune. Mrs. Hapsteade, and Horace's own mother. They were here in Ka'hoka, facing the grim and silent Council, pouring out their impossible story like an apology, like a dirge.

The Warren had fallen.

Horace ached to hear the dreadful story again, a thousand times more. He longed to hear something that would confirm the guilty burn that curled in his chest, something that would help him understand once and for all just where he had gone wrong. He hadn't set these events in motion, no, but he had steered them wildly, blindly, trusting in the Fel'Daera. He had traveled alone to the meadow to face Dr. Jericho and the golem, choosing not to tell the Wardens who followed him that they would not escape. He hadn't bothered to consider the rescue that would of course come after. He hadn't thought to wonder whether that rescue could have led to the unmasking of the Warren's location. He hadn't seen far enough, considered all the players, imagined all the consequences.

He and Chloe sat in the shadows along the wall of the Proving Room, like forgotten spectators. Out in the center of the room, Neptune did most of the talking, her voice dull and flat, as Brula and the other Council members listened. Sometimes April clarified or agreed—many hunting packs of Mordin, dozens of the frightful-sounding Ravids—but her eyes were as hazy and wounded as Neptune's voice.

Mr. Meister, injured and captured. Isabel, taking a fearless last stand and never seen again. The Keystone and the cave-in at the mouth of the Great Burrow. Joshua, staying behind when he could have easily escaped.

It was April who told this last bit, and Horace wasn't sure he understood her. Had Joshua thought he was being brave? Had he thought he wasn't wanted? Had he turned? April herself seemed broken and sad and strangely, achingly pretty as she spoke, obviously distracted by knowledge and memories no one else in the room possessed. Or so it seemed to Horace. Arthur the raven plucked at her shoelaces and cooed up at her, but she didn't react.

Mal'brula Kintares asked question after question.

About Isabel, about the sa'halvasa, about Joshua. About the Fel'Daera, and whatever role it might have played, or failed to play, in the disaster that had just unfolded. Why Brula was asking these six about the box, and not Horace himself, he couldn't understand. Mrs. Hapsteade—somewhat to Horace's surprise, since she'd always been wary of the box—swatted the questions aside impatiently. It was clear that she and the Altari knew each other, and that there was no love lost between them.

At last Sil'falo Teneves swept forward from her silent stance at the back of the room, interrupting Brula. "That is enough for now," she said. "These are friends and allies, come to us in an hour of great need. They owe us no explanation."

"A vital sanctuary is lost," Brula growled. "A great trove of Tanu has fallen into the hands of the Kesh'kiri." He spat out the Altari word for the Riven with a venom that caught Horace by surprise. The heat of his hatred was palpable.

"I destroyed some of what the Warren held, Brula," Mrs. Hapsteade said briskly. "And some of it is buried safe, where it's unlikely to be found."

"Some," Brula grunted. "But not all. And we have reason to believe that you and the Taxonomer have been hoarding more than we ever suspected."

Falo rounded on Brula, lifting her graceful eyebrows. "Have you a solution for us, Brula? Have you the means to go back and undo what has been done this day? If so, I am sure the Council—and the brave survivors that stand before

558

you—would be most grateful to hear it."

At Horace's side, Chloe grunted in angry approval, startling him. He'd been so intent on hearing the story, he'd almost forgotten her. But now a cold and ragged realization flooded over him. Isabel. No one had even implied that Chloe's mother might still be alive. Far from it.

"Hey," he began softly, nudging her.

"No," she whispered sharply, her voice like a falling blade. Horace looked away.

Brula, meanwhile, had no answer for Sil'falo Teneves. Falo turned her back on him and spread her graceful arms to the refugees from the Warren. "Come with me, all of you. Join me in my chambers. This is a time for companionship, not confrontation."

She turned to leave. The Wardens and Horace's mom fell in behind her, and Horace and Chloe got to their feet.

Brula stood too. "I would remind you that our secrets are still sacred, Sil'falo Teneves," he said.

Without so much as a glance back, Falo replied, "Yes, and I regret ever sharing them with you."

They left. Horace found himself wishing Dailen was here, with his sureness and his steady good humor. But the Altari were on high alert after Joshua's portal, and apparently Dailen was still needed above. Meanwhile, here below, the Wardens' dismal little procession moved mostly in silence. Horace snuck worried glances at his mom—they'd barely spoken since she arrived, just a long hug and calm reassurances that they were both okay—but he was worried just the same. She'd given up her harp. That had to mean something. A pain, maybe, that she'd keep for herself.

Falo led them back to the guard with the green ax, back through the narrow, rough-hewn cave, and into the grand vaulted chamber beyond. Arthur rose high into the air above them. April gasped.

"What do you see?" asked Brian. He stood with his hands buried in the surface of Tunraden, looking like a prisoner.

April shook her head, her eyes still cloudy.

"You are an empath," Falo said, not really asking. "Do you feel it?"

April looked up sharply, searching Falo's face. "Yes," she said simply. "I felt it the moment I stepped through the portal."

Falo seemed impressed but unsurprised. "You are terribly strong. It may be hard for you, then, when we get closer."

Horace could only assume Falo meant the intense thickness of the Medium as they got closer to the Mothergate. Maybe April, being a powerful empath, was especially sensitive to it. Not that he could imagine why, or how.

On the far side of the chamber, the great white doors split open for Falo. The Medium surged richly around Horace, through him, into the box and Horace's flesh, his bones.

"Oh, there it is," said Neptune, lifting lightly off the floor. Gabriel twisted his hands around the Staff of Obro, making them squeak. April cocked her head down and to the side, as if she were walking into a powerful wind.

They reached Falo's chambers. Gabriel and Mrs. Hapsteade took seats on two of the human-sized chairs. Brian set Tunraden on the floor, freeing his hands, while Neptune hovered over one of the giant Altari seats. Mrs. Hapsteade pulled out the little silver compass, and the four of them began discussing Mr. Meister's whereabouts—whether he was still in the Warren or not. Across the room, Falo was crouched down in front of Horace's mom, and they murmured to each other like old friends.

Chloe was looking at Mrs. Hapsteade, clearly still uninterested in talking. Horace glanced over at April. She stood alone at the entrance to the tall, narrow passageway that lay straight ahead, staring down it, gazing at the rippling white light that swam in the distance. The Mothergate lay that way. And it was clear April could feel it.

Chloe, still watching Mrs. Hapsteade and the others as they fussed over the compass, suddenly spoke. "I don't know why you care," she said to them.

Neptune's head snapped around. Mrs. Hapsteade sat up straight.

"Chloe, what are you talking about?" Horace asked.

"I don't know why anyone really cares about the Warren," she said. "About the Tanu that were lost. About any of it. You heard what Falo said, Horace, and I'm sure we're the last to know—the Mothergates really are dying. Soon there won't be any more Tan'ji, not even us. So why should we care about what happened today? Or any of the days we've been with the Wardens?" The dragonfly's wings were fluttering wildly, but Horace wasn't sure she even noticed. She went on, getting louder. "Why should I even care about the people we lost tonight? Why shouldn't I just go home to my dad and my sister and my aunt and be with them—be with my family?"

Horace wanted desperately to argue with her. And maybe she was just lashing out, talking about her family because there was little reason to believe her mother was even alive. Everything that had happened tonight mattered. Of course it did.

And yet.

She wasn't wrong. Logically speaking, wasn't this a pointless fight? Horace felt the heavy flows of the Medium coursing through the Fel'Daera, thick and alive. He watched April in the doorway, her eyes still locked on the light that quivered in the distance. The Mothergate down there was fading. When it and the other two Mothergates went out, the power of the Fel'Daera—and all the rightness and wholeness it brought to Horace—would forever cease. What would he be then? *Would* he even be?

He realized his mother was watching him. Her eyes were agonizing pools of sadness, still and deep. She knew, of course. She'd always known. He could barely scratch the surface of the idea.

"Your thoughts are misguided, Keeper," Mrs. Hapsteade said to Chloe. "You don't yet know everything you should."

"Well, I wonder whose fault that is," Chloe snapped. "All I know is, I've been asked to battle the Riven to save my Tan'ji, and now I find out my Tan'ji is doomed anyway. How does that make sense?"

Falo stood, towering over them. She spread her long, elegant hands, her fingers like rays of light. "These are fair questions," she said. "Because of the Mothergates' impending death, our struggle with the Riven may seem pointless. Why should a setting sun bother to battle a passing cloud?"

"Exactly," said Chloe doubtfully, obviously confused by Falo's agreement.

"However," Falo continued, "the fall of the Warren, and the capture of the Chief Taxonomer, and above all the loss of the Laithe—these are not mere clouds. With the Laithe, and with the power and knowledge held within the Warren, the Riven may be able to find the Mothergates at last. That cannot happen."

Chloe scoffed. "What do you think the Riven are going to do?" she said. "Make the Mothergates die *faster*?"

"Enough of this talk," April said suddenly, softly, still fixed on the distant, swimming light. "Enough of this listening. I need to see." And then she left the room, stepping into the passageway.

"She is right," said Falo. "It is time to see. It is time to understand." She looked around the room. "If you have never stood before the Veil, come with me now."

Horace stood up, his knees threatening to buckle. Chloe

rose beside him. No one else moved. "Seriously?" said Chloe, looking around.

"I went when I was younger," Neptune said. "After I was solidly through the Find. It was required of me." Gabriel nodded.

"Even me," said Brian sheepishly.

"Go and see," Mrs. Hapsteade told them. "Go and learn."

Falo entered the hallway after April, walking slowly. She nearly filled its narrow heights. Horace and Chloe went after. Horace's heart was a racehorse, his belly a pit.

The Medium grew ever thicker as they walked. The slowly flickering lights grew thicker, too, heavy washes of brilliance between bands of utter black. Horace's hand felt warm, and he realized Chloe had taken it. She'd released the dragonfly, and together they walked this way, into the deepening light and power.

At last they emerged into a place with no walls, no ceiling. The size of the place seemed to crush him, make him small. A vast curtain of light—the Veil of Lura—arched high over them like a crashing wave that never fell, rippling with a brilliance so complete Horace was sure it could be touched, felt. It blinded him but caused no pain. He stared wide-eyed into it, at April standing tiny at its foot, seeming to glow.

But there was something beyond that curtain. Something Horace couldn't see or even imagine, a presence that seemed to know him, that seemed to somehow *be* him in some small and flickering way, him and the Fel'Daera both. It was expecting them, had been waiting for them all along.

April turned. "I need to see what it is," she said. "It's hurting. I need get through—how do we get through?"

Sil'falo Teneves approached the arching Veil. Even she looked small beneath it. "You could learn to find your own way," she said to April, "but I will lead you this time. And the others will certainly need my help." She took April's hand in one of her own, and turned to Horace and Chloe, holding out the other.

Chloe moved forward, pulling Horace toward the Veil. They came up beside April and Falo, and Chloe took the Altari's hand. The light swam across April's clouded, worried eyes.

"I'm afraid," April said. "I'm afraid of what's on the other side. The Mothergate, it . . ."

"The Wardens like to say that fear is a stone, and to wish that that stone will be light," Falo said. "But I cannot pretend that the stone that lies ahead of you now will be not be heavy. The heaviest stone you have yet encountered."

"Is it dangerous to be near the Mothergate?" Horace asked.

"No," Falo said. "That's not the danger I mean. Those who come to the Veil come to learn the truth, and that truth will be your stone today." And then as one of the roving pillars of light swept past her, she stepped inside, pulling them with her.

Inside the Veil, an ocean of moving light, coming from

and going to nowhere, everywhere. Their footsteps fell upon a floor their eyes wouldn't see, featureless and white.

They kept walking. Deeper into the presence that pressed against them like the heat of an unseen sun, the push of a motionless wind. Then a darkness ahead, slowly coalescing until it became a bulging black mass. Slowly the darkness grew, rippling and swaying, suspended like a great slab of dark water that gravity couldn't touch.

The Mothergate. It burned with intensity, a furnace that gave off no heat. Meanwhile the Fel'Daera was its own magnificent fire, a newborn thing, straining with a power that coursed through Horace's veins.

Chloe dropped Horace's hand, and Falo's too. At her throat, the Alvalaithen bled a blinding light as bright as the Veil itself.

Falo approached the pulsing, suspended Mothergate. It towered over her, twice her size, though Horace wasn't sure what size meant in this place. "Come closer," Falo told them. "Come and witness."

They went. As they drew nearer, Horace began to see specks of light within the Mothergate, streaking outward toward the surface. It was impossibly deep, a thing that could be seen into forever—into, but never through. Its blackness was total, threatening to erase itself. And yet it was the most . . . *present* thing Horace had ever seen. A miracle of sheer being.

April crept up close. "It's alive," she whispered.

Falo reached out a hand to the teeming mass, and it

billowed toward her, sparkling and black, caressing her palm, seeming to greet her.

"All the universe is alive, Keepers," Falo said, her voice like a storyteller's song. "But it is only alive because living things witness it. Me. You. The tiger. The tree. Our thoughtful gaze—our consciousness—is the spark that stitches the fabric of the earth and all the heavens together, and turns the very wheels of time. And here in this place, in the presence of the Mothergate, that gaze is returned. This is a gateway, a gift, an opening into the mind of the universe. Here, the universe spills its consciousness into us, just as we spill ours into it. Here, Keepers, we are *seen*. We are *known*."

And although Horace could barely wrap his head around it—certainly not in the way the old Horace would have needed to, the Horace who had not yet been through the Veil—still, here and now, he felt the truth of Falo's words in every atom of his body.

"And that consciousness spilling through the Mothergate—that's the Medium," he said.

"Yes," Falo replied. "It brings life to our instruments, connects us to the universe. It is the reason for the depth of our bonds."

"It's the reason for everything," April murmured.

"What lies *within* the gateway is the reason for everything," Falo corrected. "Not the gateway itself." She watched April closely and then murmured, "What do you see, Keeper? What do you feel?"

April squeezed her eyes shut. She swayed in place, her

arms rigid at her side. The Ravenvine gleamed in her hair. "I see life," she said, trembling.

"A manifestation of life, yes," Falo said. "A messenger without a message. A visitor without a destination."

"And it's dying." April's cheeks shone beneath her faraway eyes.

"But it's the universe," Chloe said. "It's everything. If it's dying—"

"As I said, the Mothergate is not everything," said Falo. "Merely a window . . . *between* everything. The universe is not dying, any more than it ever was. Only these gateways are fading, these windows. They are collapsing, as they were always destined to."

"And when they do collapse, our instruments will die too," Chloe said.

"Yes."

"And what about us?" said Chloe. "What about the Keepers?" This wasn't a question that needed to be asked. Not here, not now. But somehow it seemed right that an answer should be uttered.

"Some may survive," Falo said simply.

No one spoke. Horace wanted desperately to touch the Mothergate, as Falo had, hoping somehow to give it comfort, or strength. To help heal it somehow. But he was afraid. The Mothergate might scald him, freeze him, erase him, replace him. This was a window into the mind of matter itself, a messenger of space and time, a doorway into everything that ever was or ever could be. He was only Horace Andrews, a boy. He stood still and let the Mothergate's power spill through him.

"There's one last secret, though," he said. "Something we still don't know."

Falo nodded. She cast her marvelous eyes at the ground, in a gesture—Horace would realize later—of apologetic shame. It reminded him of his mother. "As I said, the words are not easy," Falo said. "And even the best words I could find would not be easy to hear."

"We don't need the best words," said Chloe, clutching the Alvalaithen. "We just need the words."

The Veil's light washed over Falo, rippling slow, like moonbeams sweeping through a deep black sea. The Mothergate glittered and roiled. Falo lifted her gaze to Horace and the others in turn, her bottomless eyes soft with sadness, but unflinching. Quietly she said, "We could prevent the Mothergates from dying if we wished to."

Horace's mouth went dry as Falo's words found him. He had to play the sentence over again in his head—twice, three times. "You could . . . ," he said at last, but got no farther. "I don't understand."

"I could heal the Mothergates myself, in fact," Falo went on, gesturing at the sparkling black well beside her. "Here and now. It would be far from the hardest thing I have ever done. But I refuse."

"Why?" Chloe demanded. "Because of the Riven? Are you so afraid of the Riven taking your Tan'ji that you're willing to let it all come to an end?"

Falo shook her head. "Our refusal to interfere with the fate of the Mothergates has nothing to do with the Riven. But our war with the Riven has everything to do with the Mothergates."

"The Riven *want* to interfere," April said calmly.

Horace's head swam as the truth began to grasp him. "No," he said. "No, no." Dr. Jericho's sneering voice rose in his mind, full of dark promises Horace had refused to believe.

"It is true," said Falo. "The Riven would save the Mothergates if they could. We stand watch to prevent that from happening. Indeed, that is our entire purpose—to ensure that a rescue does not occur. We are not warriors. Rather, we are sentinels, custodians, guards." She took a deep breath, straightening to her fullest height. "We are Wardens."

Horace could scarcely let himself hear it. With every word Falo spoke, the world seemed to roll under his feet, capsizing everything he thought he'd known.

Chloe threw her arms open wide. "This is crazy. You're telling us you're prison guards. The Mothergates are your prisoners? And when they die, we'll all die too—do you have a death wish, or something?"

"We have no death wish," Falo said. "Far from it. We wish for life, for all." She lifted her gaze to the Mothergate and sighed, clutching the black oval pendant at her throat. "The truth, Keepers—the stone I lay upon you now—is that our power comes at a price. To witness the heartbeat of

570

the universe is to invite unchartable chaos into the ordered existence that defines us. To unravel the knotted rules upon which life depends. As long as the Mothergates remain open, our world is in peril."

"But how?" Horace asked, fighting off her words even as they clung to him. "What chaos? What peril?"

"I will explain, but for now I ask only that you imagine I speak the truth. There is a price for our power." Falo looked suddenly old, as old as she must truly be, as fragile and wrinkled as the petal of a wilted flower. When she spoke again, her musical voice seeped into Horace's flesh like a chanted dirge—into his chest, into his bones, into the Fel'Daera blazing with life. Horace's life. "For the sake of this world, if not ourselves, the Mothergates cannot be rescued," Falo said. "For the sake of this world—if not ourselves—the Mothergates must die."

GLOSSARY

Altari (all-TAR-ee)	the Makers of the Tanu, and the ancestors of the Riven
Alvalaithen (al-vuh-LAYTH-en)	Chloe's Tan'ji, the dragonfly, the Earthwing; with it, she can become incorporeal
Auditor	a type of Riven; though not Tan'ji, Auditors can imitate the powers of nearby instruments
backjack	a small silver Tan'kindi whose location can be tracked with a paired, compass-like device
breach	the gap in time across which the Fel'Daera sees the future
cleave	to forcibly and permanently rip apart the bond between a Keeper and his or her Tan'ji

cloister	one of the small safe havens of the Wardens, usually a walled garden containing a leestone and a falkrete circle
dispossessed	term for a Keeper who is permanently cut off from his or her instrument, usually by cleaving or being severed for too long
doba	the little huts in the Great Burrow
falkretes	strangely shaped stones found in cloisters; Keepers can teleport between them
Fel'Daera (fel-DARE-ah)	Horace's Tan'ji, the Box of Promises; with it, he can see a short distance into the future
Find, the	the solitary period during which a new Keeper discovers and then masters his or her instrument
fusion	when a Keeper and his or her Tan'ji draw in too much of the Medium at once, binding together permanently in a suspended state
Gallery, the	a corridor deep in the Warren whose doorways will only appear by the light of certain jithandras

golem	a massive swarm of moving stones; a powerful Tan'kindi controlled by the Riven
Great Burrow	the uppermost chamber of the Warren
harps	instruments used by Tuners; only Tuners can operate them, but they are not Tan'ji
humour, the	the blinding, invisible cloud of gray Gabriel releases from the Staff of Obro
jithandra (jih-THAHN-drah)	small Tan'kindi used for light, identification, and entry into the Wardens' sanctuaries
Ka'hoka (kah-HO-kah)	a major sanctuary of the Altari
Keeper	one who has bonded with an instrument, thus becoming Tan'ji
Kesh'kiri (kesh-KEER-ee)	the name the Riven use for themselves (*see* Riven)
Laithe of Teneves (TEN-eevs)	Joshua's Tan'ji, a miniature globe that grants the power to open portals anywhere on earth
leestone	a Tan'kindi that provides some protection against the Riven
Loomdaughters	the first Tan'ji made with the Starlit Loom; there were nine in total
Lostling	one who possesses an

instrument, but did not go
through a proper Find

mal'gama (mahl-GAH-ma) similar to the golem, a Tan'kindi
comprised of thousands of green
stones, capable of flight

Medium, the   the energy that powers all Tanu

Miradel   Isabel's harp, a wicker sphere

Mordin   tall, ferocious Riven who are
particularly skilled at hunting
down Tan'ji

Mothergates   the three enigmatic structures
through which the Medium flows
before reaching out to power all
Tanu in the world

Nevren   a field of influence that
temporarily severs the bond
between a Keeper and his Tan'ji;
Nevrens protect the Wardens'
strongholds

oraculum   a Tan'ji belonging to Mr. Meister,
a lens that allows him to see the
Medium

passkey   a Tan'kindi that allows passage
through certain walls

phalanx   a small Tan'kindi, made from the
fingerbone of a Mordin; it fires a
blast of energy that pins Tan'ji in
place

polymath's ring	a Tan'kindi that allows its wearer to bond with more than one Tanji; shaped like a Möbius strip
raven's eye	a weak and portable kind of leestone, a Tan'kindi
Ravenvine	April's Tan'ji, a silver vine she wears around her left ear; it grants her the power to empathically absorb the thoughts of nearby animals
Ravids	small, quick Riven with the ability to teleport short distances
Riven	a hidden race of beings who hunger to reclaim all the Tanu for their own; they call themselves the Kesh'kiri
Ro'ha, the (RO-ha)	an Altari ceremony in which Keepers formally demonstrate their abilities; literally "open hand"
sa'halvasa (sah-hahl-VAH-sah)	related to the golem, a swarm of tiny insectlike Tanu with razor-sharp wings
Sanguine Hall	the back entrance to the Warren, home to the sa'halvasa
sever	to temporarily cut a Keeper off from his or her Tan'ji
Staff of Obro	Gabriel's Tan'ji, a wooden staff with a silver tip; it releases the

	humour, which blinds others but gives him an acute awareness of his surroundings
Starlit Loom	the very first Tanu, a Tan'ji that gives its Keeper the power to make new Tanu; Sil'falo Teneves, called Falo (FAY-lo), is its Keeper
Tanu (TAH-noo)	the universal term for all of the mysterious devices created by the Makers; the function of these instruments is all but unknown to most (two main kinds of Tanu are Tan'ji and Tan'kindi)
Tan'ji (tahn-JEE)	a special class of Tanu that will work only when bonded with a Keeper who has a specific talent; *Tan'ji* also describes the Keeper himself or herself as well as the state of that bond—a kind of belonging or being
Tan'kindi (tahn-KIN-dee)	a simpler category of Tanu that will work for anyone, without requiring a special talent or a bond (raven's eyes, passkeys, etc.)
Tan'layn (tahn-LAIN)	Tan'ji that do not currently have a Keeper; the unclaimed
tourminda (tour-MIN-dah)	a fairly common kind of Tan'ji

	that allows its Keeper to defy gravity; Neptune is the Keeper of the Devlin tourminda
Tuner	though not Tan'ji, Tuners can use instruments called harps to cleanse and tune other Tanu
Tunraden (toon-RAH-den)	Brian's Tan'ji, a Loomdaughter; with it, he can create and repair Tanu
Veil of Lura (LOOR-ah)	a shimmering curtain of light that hides and protects the Mothergates
Vithra's Eye	the Nevren that guards the Warren
Vora	Mrs. Hapsteade's Tan'ji, the quill and ink; it is used to determine the abilitites of potential new Keepers
Wardens	the secret group of Keepers devoted to protecting the Tanu from the Riven
Warren	the Wardens' headquarters beneath the city, deep underground
Well of Giving	the massively powerful Nevren at Ka'hoka

Acknowledgments

My tremendous gratitude goes out to everyone at HarperCollins for all they've done to continue to make this series happen. First and foremost to Toni Markiet, whose insights and perseverance have been invaluable, and sometimes forgotten. Thank you, Toni, for every little thing I know you've done for me and this book, and for every big thing I don't. There's been so much, and I'm grateful for it all.

An enormous thank-you to Kate Morgan Jackson and to Suzanne Murphy for their continued support of The Keepers, support that means everything, both to the books and to me. Thank you to Tessa Meischeid, Amy Ryan, Gina Rizzo, and everyone else who had a helping hand in every aspect of this project. And a special thanks to Laaren Brown for checking my maps and knowing her Paul Simon.

Thank you to my agent, Miriam Altshuler, for somehow

being a rock, a hard place, a friend, and a mother. I'd be lost without you. And thanks to Reiko Davis for all the nitty-gritty.

Thank you to my dad for his ongoing belief and love, and to all my loud and wonderful cousins—Jim, Olivia, Madeline, Jody, Zach, Teena, and the rest. And of course to Matt Mulholland, for all the help with the science—with everything from time travel viewings in a moving car to the terminal velocity of falling children.

Much love and gratitude to Matt Minicucci, Laura Koritz, Russell Evatt, Kathy Skwarczek, Jeff & Rosita Durbin, and Michele Whisenhunt. Your support buoys me even during all those stretches when I'm too busy to remind you just how much it means to me.

Thank you, too, to my students at the University of Illinois. Everything I try to teach you is a lesson for myself, and I've learned so much from all the work that you do. I'm a better writer, and person, because of you.

Thank you to Rowan and Bridget, for continuing to become the fascinating humans that you are and letting me watch. I love you.

And thank you beyond everything to Jodee, who managed this last year of writing and fretting, of late nights and long conversations, during the first year of our son Milo's life. I owe no one more than you, for everything that continues to happen, and every future that awaits us. I love you.

Turn the page for a peek at what's in store for
the Keepers in book four, *The Starlit Loom*

CHAPTER ONE

The War Party

Traveling by mal'gama at night was almost enough to make Chloe forget everything.

Not that she wanted to forget. In fact, she was annoyed that so much of her anger had slipped away—anger about the Warren, her home and sanctuary for these past few months, now invaded and conquered by the Riven. Anger at Joshua, whose fault it sort of was and who was maybe a traitor. Anger at Isabel—that was a given. Anger at Mr. Meister and Brian and Sil'falo Teneves and the rest of the Wardens, who had hidden the wretched truth about the Mothergates all this time.

It had only been a day since the Warren had fallen.

A day since she had learned she was going to die.

But up here, Chloe found it hard to cling to that anger. It was well past midnight. The mal'gama sped through the darkness, a thousand feet above the open farmland of Illinois, carrying its small crew of Wardens. All around them, the night sky was a black dome of unbroken cloud. Somehow it seemed right that there were no stars, since Horace wasn't here to name them. Chloe was glad he'd stayed behind. It was safer for him back at Ka'hoka, a sanctuary deeper and better protected than the Warren had ever been. The thought made her almost sleepy, him being safe.

And it didn't hurt that the mal'gama itself, a massive carpet of small soft stones, cradled Chloe as it flew, undulating like water. The front edge of the mal'gama had formed into a kind of a prow, so that the wind barely licked at her short black hair. The overall sensation, she realized, as she fiddled with the Alvalaithen hanging from her neck, felt a little bit like going thin and diving into the dark earth, soaring through solid ground, as only she could. Except that here she was not in control. And although she hated to admit it, not being in control right now was . . . nice.

She supposed Dwen'dailen Longo, the Altari warrior, was in control. That was nice, too. The mal'gama wasn't Tan'ji, and so it didn't have a Keeper, but Dailen wore the ring that controlled the huge Tanu. Did that make him the pilot? The dog walker? Flying carpet wrangler? She'd been watching the young Altari, to see what he did, but he didn't do much. Maybe the mal'gama had a bit of a mind of its own. All Chloe knew was, they were going fast. Fast was good. The faster the better.

This was a rescue mission. Allegedly. And Chloe had to

2

admit that the rescue team she was a part of was definitely badass, even if the word "team" made her gag a little. Besides herself and Dailen, five other Keepers rode the mal'gama now, all of them Wardens. They were headed back to Chicago to try and save those who had been captured by the Riven in the raid on the Warren. They were going to find Mr. Meister, for sure. And possibly Joshua too, whether he wanted to be saved or not. And maybe Isabel—her mother.

Even if the word made Chloe gag a little.

If her mother was even alive.

Most of the Altari Council was here, with their towering bodies and their powerful Tan'ji. The hulking Go'nesh carried his blue-bladed staff, the Fairfrost Blade, whose every swing left a swath of impenetrable ice hanging in the air. Okay, not quite ice and not *quite* impenetrable. But bitterly cold and brutally dense, as Chloe knew all too well. Beside him, dark and surly, Ravana wore her faultless wooden bow over her shoulders. Named Pinaka, it was as thick as a man's arm and three times as long. And off to Chloe's side, exasperatingly beautiful Teokas had her . . . whatever it was. Some kind of bracelet. Thailadun, she called it: the Moondoor. She'd shown it to Horace, but Chloe had no idea what it did, and it was nagging at her. Whenever Chloe glanced over at Teokas now—a painfully graceful silhouette, a magnet for anyone's eyes, her long legs dangling over the edge of the mal'gama—it seemed Teokas was looking back at her.

Gabriel was here too, the tallest of the humans, though

still dwarfed by the Altari. He sat with Dailen, well back from the edge, the Staff of Obro across his lap. The staff was the only cure for Gabriel's blindness, and a temporary one at that, but he would never use it here. Not when calling forth the humour that gave him sight meant blinding everyone else.

Gabriel and Dailen were talking animatedly in low voices, even laughing now and again. Other than Chloe, Gabriel was the youngest here, five or six years older than she was. And as far as she understood it, Dailen was not much older than Gabriel, in Altari years—he was a kind of teenager himself. Barely an adult, anyway. But because the Altari lived much longer, Dailen was closer to eighty than eighteen.

The final member of the party sat with Gabriel and Dailen, mostly silent. Mrs. Hapsteade bent over her own lap, tiny and dark, her prim black dress piled around her. Every now and again she muttered something quietly to Dailen. Unlike the others, Mrs. Hapsteade hadn't come to fight. Her Tan'ji was no kind of weapon; it was useful only in identifying the powers of new Keepers. But she had insisted on carrying the Tanu that told them where to go, a compass whose red needle pointed straight at Mr. Meister.

Before being captured, he'd swallowed a small Tan'kindi called a backjack, and as long as it was inside him—no matter where the Riven might take him—this compass would track him down. The others assumed the old man must still be in the Warren, deep under the streets of downtown Chicago. But Chloe wasn't so sure. If she were the Riven, she would have

4

gotten Mr. Meister out of there quick. The Warren might have fallen, but she suspected it was still full of traps, and Mr. Meister certainly knew them all.

But whatever. Wherever the compass took them, that's where they would go. Chloe was ready. She was ready because she had no idea what else to do.

And she had to do *something*.

The mal'gama rippled beneath her, pulsing. Teokas walked along its very edge, coming toward her, the green stones shifting under her graceful steps. She was small for an Altari, only seven feet tall or so. Watching her move, it occurred to Chloe that Teokas wasn't as old as Chloe had thought—again, for an Altari. Older than Dailen, but younger than her splendor and confidence made her seem. Maybe a hundred years old? It was hard to guess, to say the least.

Teokas stopped beside her, gazing down over the edge of the mal'gama, looking like the sculpture of some untouchable goddess atop a windswept cliff. Or something equally daunting and majestic. Her Tan'ji, the Moondoor, hung from a strap around her wrist, a shadowed sphere as big as a plum.

Chloe frowned up at her, opening her mouth for the first time since they'd left Ka'hoka. "Will the Moondoor save you if you fall?" Chloe asked. "You seem pretty carpe diem about the whole falling-to-your-death thing."

Teokas laughed, a thick, enchanting chorus of oboes and low bells. All of the Altari had rich, musical voices, but Teokas's voice was especially full of slinky woodwinds and soft

5

percussion. As Brian had put it, she sounded like the sultry part of the orchestra.

"It won't save me, no," Teokas crooned. "But it is hard to fall off the mal'gama." Abruptly, she took a step forward, as if she planned to walk right off the edge. With a leathery rustle, the mal'gama shifted in an instant, stretching out to catch her foot just as it alighted.

"Teokas, please," Dailen said, looking over.

"*Ji tolvë tanduvra?*" Teokas said lightly, stepping back. Chloe only understood a few words of Altari, and none of these, but Teokas was obviously teasing. Flirting, maybe.

"When do you never?" Dailen replied, and Teokas and the other Altari all laughed.

Teokas sank to the floor beside Chloe, stretching out her long form as the mal'gama rose to meet her. "What I've always wondered," she said quietly to Chloe, as if in confidence, "is whether he could *stop* it from saving me."

Chloe shrugged. "He couldn't stop it from saving me, if I didn't want him to." She blushed as the words left her. It seemed like one of the stupider things she'd ever said.

"No, I suppose not," said Teokas. "Even Go'nesh couldn't stop you." She gazed at the Alvalaithen, openly fascinated. Even in the feeble light, Chloe could see the golden rings around Teokas's dark irises, like halos. When Teokas blinked, her crisscrossed double eyelids seemed to flicker. Suddenly the Altari frowned at Chloe's Tan'ji. "Why a dragonfly, do you suppose?" she asked.

6

"What do you mean?"

"I'm not complaining. Our Tan'ji are what they are. But why do you suppose your Maker chose a dragonfly?"

Chloe looked down at the Alvalaithen. She didn't much like the question. Perfectly white, with intricate mazy wings, the dragonfly was precisely what it needed to be. Chloe tapped briefly into its sweet song, letting its power fill her. How many more times would she get to do this before the Mothergates died? The dragonfly's wings fluttered buzz-ily, blurring. She felt her body go thin, become a ghost. She kept herself afloat atop the mal'gama's rippling stones with no effort whatsoever, though she could've just as easily fallen straight through them, with nothing to stop her. Not even Dailen. After a moment, making sure everything was clear of her flesh, she released the Alvalaithen. Its song left her, and the dragonfly's wings went still.

"Wings," Chloe said. "I can fly underground."

"I know. I witnessed as much, in the Proving Room."

"Oh, but you didn't know that Alvalaithen means 'Earth-wing'?" Chloe said, letting her voice bend with irony. "I could have sworn I just heard you speaking your own language."

"You did," said Teokas earnestly, as if sarcasm were so far beneath her it couldn't touch her. "But why a dragonfly, and not a bird? We are fond of birds, we Altari."

Mrs. Hapsteade's voice rang out in the dark. "A dragonfly is always a predator," she said.

"Ah," said Teokas, as if that answered everything. She

pointed at Chloe's forearm, where two dagger-shaped patches of dark skin ran from palm to elbow, front and back. "These are the scars of a predator, then?"

"You could say that," Chloe replied. She still remembered the awful burn of the crucible the day she'd gotten these scars. Certainly not her only scars, or even the worst. Still, it had been one of the two or three most excruciating things she'd ever done, extinguishing the Riven's mind-consuming flame with her own flesh and bone. Were they heading to another Riven nest even now? Would there be another crucible dog there, with its beckoning green fire?

"I know how you got the scars," said Teokas. "But you won't tell me the full story, will you? You're not a bragger."

Now Gabriel stirred. "Chloe brags *before* she does things," he said. "Not after."

Chloe found herself fighting a sudden grin of pleasure. This was maybe the nicest thing Gabriel had ever said about her.

"Confidence," Teokas sang, smiling at her. "I respect that."

"Yeah, well," said Chloe, "it's easy to be confident when you know you're going to die. Consequences schmonsequences, am I right?"

Teokas blinked at her thoughtfully, and then clearly chose to pretend she hadn't understood what Chloe meant. "I wonder if your friend Horace feels the same way. The Keeper of the Fel'Daera deals purely in consequences, after all." She

8

shook her head as if in wonder. "My talents have to do with time too, but Horace is on another level altogether, far beyond my own."

Across the mal'gama, Ravana raised her head, watching them. Go'nesh stood beside her like a boulder. It was no secret that Horace hadn't come with them tonight because his Tan'ji, the Fel'Daera, made some of the Altari uneasy. Most of the Altari were still adjusting to the fact that the Fel'Daera still existed, since it was supposed to have been destroyed long ago. Chloe blamed them for their discomfort, but only a little—partly because Horace was better off where he was and partly because, well . . . it wasn't exactly easy, having a companion who could see the future.

Horace could only see one day into the future, sure. One day at most. And only in his immediate surroundings, looking through the rippled blue glass of the Fel'Daera, the Box of Promises. But to be honest, when Horace looked through the box and then told you your future, told you—just for example—that you were going to let yourself be captured by the Riven, or that you were going to surrender your Tan'ji, or that you were almost definitely going to figure out a way to survive some deadly dangerous thing you hadn't even imagined yet . . .

No pressure. No biggie.

Just your fate.

On a plate.

No, it wasn't always easy being Horace's friend, even for

Chloe, even though she trusted Horace with her life. In fact, she had done precisely that, more than once, and wouldn't hesitate to do it again. She trusted Horace more than she trusted herself.

Chloe looked Teokas in the eye. "Horace is on a whole other level, yes," she said.

She meant it as a dig. But Teokas gave her a warm, eager smile in return, not at all condescending. Not the knowing smirk of a grown-up, but a childish smile of enthusiasm. Chloe realized abruptly that Teokas didn't fear Horace; she admired him.

"I'm glad you have such a friend, truly," Teokas said. "We'll all have need of good friends in the days to come."

Chloe decided to stop trying not to like her.

They sailed on, she and Teokas sitting silently side by side. After a while, the glow of Chicago became plain in the northeastern sky, lighting the clouds above. Eventually the city itself came into view, a golden spiderweb of light. Or half a spiderweb, anyway. On the far side, the spray of light ended abruptly, the dark unbroken expanse of Lake Michigan stretching out to the far horizon beyond.

"About the Mothergates," Chloe said, and she had no idea why she was saying it. She had no idea what she expected Teokas to tell her.

"What do you want me to say?" Teokas said, when it became clear Chloe wasn't going to finish. "That we will survive?"

"I want you to tell me that the Mothergates have to die. Tell me that the Riven are wrong to want to keep the Mothergates open."

Teokas shrugged. "They are not wrong to want. But they are wrong to try and make it happen. If the Mothergates remain open, the entire world will come to an end."

"And you're staking your life on that."

"My life is not the issue." Teokas pointed at the sprawling city lights below. "You have family down there, I think. Will you stake their lives that the Riven are correct? That the Mothergates should be forced to remain open, and our powers allowed to live on, regardless of the consequences?" She spread her great arms wide, encompassing the city as whole. "Will you stake *all* these lives?"

Chloe glared down at the city, practically beneath them now. Her father was down there somewhere, and her sister, too. She said, "I asked Falo what would happen to us Keepers when the Mothergates die. When the source of our power is cut off, and we lose our bonds with our Tan'ji."

Teokas nodded. "Vital bonds," she murmured, holding Thailadun aloft. "Bonds that cannot be safely broken."

"Falo said—and I'm quoting here—'*Some may survive.*'"

"Maybe," said Teokas. "But if the Mothergates remain open, no one will survive."

"Define 'no one.'"

Teokas fixed Chloe with her golden-green gaze. "No one you have ever known, or ever will, or ever could."

A shiver jittered down Chloe's arms, nothing to do with the sky's night air. "That's . . . very thorough," she said. "Thanks."

"The Mothergates cannot remain," Gabriel said suddenly. "The Riven cannot be allowed to save them. Mr. Meister is the Chief Taxonomer, and he knows more about the Tanu and the Mothergates than any living Keeper, except perhaps Sil'falo Teneves herself. He would never betray us, but we cannot risk the Riven learning what he knows."

"We'll save him, then," said Chloe. "So that he can die when we win this war." She meant for the words to sound bitter, but they spilled into the air like a resolution. Like a fate that had already been sealed and delivered.

"Spoken like a true Altari," Teokas said, and she laughed. "We'll rescue him to death."

They sailed into the heart of the city. Downtown Chicago rose around them like an electric forest. The tops of the tallest towers stood hundreds of feet above them, even as high as they already were. A few cars, tiny as toys, roamed the nighttime streets below.

Mrs. Hapsteade was on her feet now, peering down at the compass that would lead them to Mr. Meister. Maps were not especially Chloe's strong suit, but from what she could tell, they were headed straight for the Warren. The Willis Tower loomed just ahead, off to the left, a chunky stack of dominoes. She'd never liked the looks of it. Its two huge white antennas rose like bleached bones, towering high overhead as they passed, just a block away.

"He's still in the Warren, after all," Chloe said.

But Mrs. Hapsteade shook her head. She laid a hand on Dailen's arm. "Circle east. Take us to the lakeshore."

Dailen nodded, and the mal'gama gently swerved. They sailed toward Grant Park, passing directly above the Art Institute's glass roof and then out over the harbor. Rows of pale boats bobbed in the dark water like sleeping birds. With a gesture, Mrs. Hapsteade directed them north, toward Navy Pier, where the Ferris wheel glowed, motionless, shut down for the night.

But they weren't headed there, either. Instead, with Mrs. Hapsteade guiding him, Dailen steered back toward shore, cruising over Streeterville between Michigan Avenue and the lakeshore. Everyone was on their feet now, gathered around Mrs. Hapsteade. The mal'gama circled tighter and tighter, the needle of the compass swinging. At last Mrs. Hapsteade raised her hand.

"Stop," she said, and she pointed straight down. "He is here."

The mal'gama eased to a stop, hovering. "Watch your step," said Dailen.

The stones beneath their feet rustled and began to part, like water circling a drain. A wide hole opened in the mal'gama, revealing the city below. Chloe peered through it cautiously, Teokas at her side. Far beneath them, a rectangle of dark, undeveloped land jutted out into the water, just where the

Chicago River emptied into Lake Michigan. Lakeshore Drive was a pale golden band crossing high above it, sprinkled with drifting cars, and in its shadow—directly below them on the dark spit of land—a great round hole yawned. A perfect circle a hundred feet across, black as pitch.

"There," Mrs. Hapsteade said, pointing.

Chloe stared, hardly able to believe it. "The hell pit?" she said.

The hell pit was a notorious eyesore in the city. Years ago, there had been plans to build an enormous skyscraper here, one of the tallest in the world. But no sooner had the hole been dug for its foundations than the project was abandoned. The hole was never filled. It had been here for as long as Chloe could remember, plainly visible from above on Lakeshore Drive. The city had made an effort to disguise the hole—small hills had been built beside it, and trees now grew in the surrounding empty lot. But the pit was still there, barred by only a stout chain fence around the edge. Inside the pit, Chloe knew, the walls of the hole were lined with rusted steel girders. She had no idea how deep it went.

"You know this place?" Teokas asked.

"I mean, everyone knows this place," said Chloe. "Kids tell stories about it. But no one actually goes there. It's off-limits."

"In other words," said Dailen, "just the sort of place the Riven would love."

The mal'gama swirled, becoming whole again. Smoothly

Dailen steered them back out over the harbor, dropping low once they were in darkness. Then they came back ashore, skimming the water. They passed beneath the Outer Drive Bridge, a hulking rusty skeleton, out of sight of the traffic that crossed above. The mal'gama slid stealthily over a metal retaining wall at the shoreline and a white concrete fence beyond, settling into a shadowy patch of scrubby green between Lakeshore Drive and some apartment buildings to the west. The hell pit lay just a few hundred feet ahead in the darkness. Chloe's heart began to pound. What would they find below?

Dailen removed the ring that controlled the mal'gama and handed it to Mrs. Hapsteade. She gave him the compass in return. *"Du'gara jentro,"* she said, shocking Chloe a bit. She had no idea the woman could speak Altari.

Dailen bowed low. *"Ji mogra jentro duvra."* He reached down to clasp her hand. *"Dak'fol ka laithen,"* he added solemnly. *"Tel tu'vra fal raethen."*

"Tel tu'vra fal raethen," Mrs. Hapsteade repeated.

And though Chloe didn't know the words, she recognized the ritual at once, and knew what they were saying.

Dak'fol ka laithen. Fear is the stone. *Tel tu'vra fal raethen.*

"May yours be light," Chloe whispered.

Teokas nodded, her eyes shining. "May yours be light," she said.

"They won't be expecting us," said Gabriel, thumping the ground with the tip of his staff. "Not so soon, and not here."

Go'nesh stepped off the mal'gama. He hefted the Fair-frost Blade, big as a stop sign. "They certainly won't be expecting *me*," he growled, his voice rumbling like a platoon of bass drums. He looked down at Ravana. "It feels good to be out. Good not to hide."

Ravana unlimbered her mighty bow, nodding. She pulled back on its thick string, testing it. For a moment a bloodred bolt of fire appeared, fuming in the dark. She eased up on the string and let it fade. "Good indeed," she said.

"It's time, then," said Dailen, and suddenly there were two of him. Then four, and then eight, their little band effectively tripling. "Let's go get our friend," all the Dailens said together.

Chloe grinned, drinking deeply from the Alvalaithen's song, letting herself go thin. Nothing could stop her, nothing could touch her. She looked around at the band of warriors with her now, mighty and magical.

"Now this is what I'm *talking* about," she said.